First Dim Shores Original Edition, October 2022
DS-030TP / DS-030HC

Illustrations © 2022 Yves Tourigny
Edited by Justin Steele and Sam Cowan
Proofreading by Lewis Housley
Layout by Sam Cowan

Dim Shores
Carmichael, CA
DimShores.com

Printed in the United States of America

Being an Anthology of Original Weird Fiction

LOOMING LOW

LOW

VOLUME II

Edited by Justin Steele and Sam Cowan

This edition is limited to
150 paperback copies and 100 hardcover copies.

This is copy __WFA__ of _____.

DIM
SHORES

CONTENTS

INTRODUCTION

JUSTIN STEELE

Five years have passed since Dim Shores published *Looming Low Volume I* — five long, troubled, and… weird years.

A global pandemic has the entire world in its grasp. America is more divided than it has been in a long time and is ready to tear itself apart. People are still fighting for civil rights, or having longstanding rights stripped away. People are fighting over shutdowns and mask mandates. People are fighting over facts, over what media can be trusted. The Capitol building was stormed by people angry that they lost an election. Mass shootings are a weekly occurrence. On the other side of the globe, Russia is openly invading Ukraine and people fear that the wrong move can mean WWIII.

It has been a weird time, a time where I often find myself wondering where all the madness stems from. And it's not just me. The stories in this volume, many of them bear scars. The scars of people who have been living through these maddening times.

Throughout my life, fiction has meant many things to me. It has been an escape, a way to temporarily step away from this life and into the shoes of other characters, other worlds. It has been a lens to see through the eyes and into the mind of an author, or a lens into the period of time the story was written. It has been an inspiration, a shining light of creativity, art, and meaning.

I really hope you enjoy the stories contained within these pages. I hope this fiction can bring you escape, joy, inspiration, or anything else you hope to take from it. I know, for myself and Sam, these stories have been all of these things and more.

Justin Steele
Delaware
7/11/22

RADIUS UNKNOWN

KURT FAWVER

Ten Mile Radius

As far as we can tell, the stench originated from the sewer ducts along Murdoch Street, in our city's well-to-do neighborhood of Redland Park. That's where it kicked at our nostrils the worst. If the residents of Murdoch Street noticed the stench, though, they didn't seem particularly bothered by it, which was odd.

Everyone in the city knows what Redland Park stands for: wealth, status, and power. It's a neighborhood where the lawns are manicured thrice-weekly by teams of underpaid migrant laborers, where every multi-million dollar house that dots the street has gated access and state-of-the-art security systems, where plumbers and electricians and carpenters and service workers of all trades attend to renovations and remodels practically every day.

If the wind blows the wrong way, the residents of Redland Park throw money at the sky and demand it gust in a different direction. Sometimes it does.

That's the kind of neighborhood Redland Park is.

Yet its residents didn't seem concerned about the putrid melange of urine, bile, sulfur, and rotted meat that hung over them. Maybe they didn't notice that something in their neighborhood had begun belching the most noxious of fumes. Maybe they didn't care. Either way, we found it difficult to believe.

For months, we smelled the stench in Redland Park and, as far as we know, its residents said nothing about it. They issued not one complaint to the city's wastewater department, made not a single call to their many friends in positions of government authority. They didn't talk about it or acknowledge it existed in any visible way.

If anything, they went outside their houses more often and seemed happier than usual.

When we drove through their neighborhood (we only ever drove *through* Redland Park—we never dared stop unless we were among the workers called to its denizens' service), we saw them on their sidewalks, strolling aimlessly, their heads held high. From the oldest to the youngest, they grinned at one another like sharks thrilled by the promise of blood.

For our part, we didn't mention the stench to anyone, either. As long as it stayed in Redland Park and out of our noses, it was none of our business. It became just another aspect of the neighborhood that disgusted us, but which we had neither the means nor the motivation to prevent.

So we worked. We slept. We tried to enjoy those precious slivers of happiness that slip between sleep and work. And nothing changed. The air in our neighborhoods remained pleasantly neutral, so we had no reason to complain.

But the stench didn't stay bound to Redland Park for long. Gradually, it seeped into the less prosperous communities that abutted Redland Park—communities where many of us lived and worked full time.

It started as just a hint, a memory of the most terrible odor we'd ever experienced. We shrugged it off as a trick of our senses and tried to push it from our minds. We refused to imagine that the stench might be right outside our doors.

It grew stronger, though. Every day, it gained more body, more tang, more power, and every day we forced ourselves to live in a more complicated delusion where the stench wasn't in our neighborhoods, where it couldn't be extending its grasp beyond Redland Park.

We stepped outside to walk our dogs, to play with our kids, to take a stroll to the convenience store, and the stench rolled over us.

Our eyes grew red and swollen from the vomitous tsunami; our throats and lungs tightened and burned. Some of us were sent into fits of uncontrollable coughing. Some of us developed headaches that beat at our skulls like barbarian clubs.

We tried to fend off the stench by wrapping bandanas and scarves around our noses and mouths, but it tore through all fabrics. Even medical grade face masks couldn't filter it out. Only a retreat to indoor spaces and several hours spent with air purifiers, deodorizers, and essential oils alleviated our symptoms.

We sheltered in place, forbidding our children from leaving our homes and taking our pets outside only for the briefest bathroom breaks.

Finally, we conceded that the stench was a problem. We had no other option. The world beyond our tightly sealed windows had become poison, and we had become prisoners to it. Whatever the stench was, whatever the source of its emanation, it needed to be cleared, so we lodged inquiries with our city officials over the phone and online. We asked them to look into the issue, to help us breathe again. Heresy of heresies, we asked them to investigate Redland Park.

We were told that our concerns would be addressed by the proper authorities in a timely manner. We were told that our concerns were important. We trusted that we were told the truth.

So we waited, and while we waited the stench grew ever thicker and more pungent. We smelled it at the windows in our houses. It followed us to work on our clothes and weaved itself tight with the upholstery of our cars. And it spread further.

No longer confined to the neighborhoods directly adjacent to Redland Park, it assaulted us from one end of the city to the other. Even in industrial zones, with their billowing smoke stacks and chemical halos, the stench reigned supreme.

Those of us who worked for the sewage department and the local gas companies took matters into our own hands. Without official directive, we checked the pipes and lines that ran beneath Redland Park. What we found disturbed us: there was absolutely nothing wrong with the utilities—no leaks, no blockages, and no backups. If anything, the underground of the city smelled better than the topside. Our discovery meant that the source of the stench had to be at ground level or above.

What could be so massive and so foul that its reach enshrouded an entire city? The problem seemed beyond our comprehension. We speculated that, perhaps, a very large animal had died somewhere in Redland Park or maybe a factory had secretly dumped noxious waste somewhere in the neighborhood, but neither suggestion made sense. Really, no answer made sense. It was as if the atmosphere within the city had turned on us and was trying to drive us out.

But that didn't explain why the people in Redland Park weren't affected by the stench. And it definitely didn't explain how such a change could happen in the first place.

We needed our government officials to do their jobs. We needed more information, more voices of reason and optimism. We needed someone to say, "You're not crazy. There's something in the air in this burg."

What we received was silence.

Fifty Mile Radius

After nearly three months of waiting for an official response, the stench had gained substance. The sunlight throughout the city seemed to have taken on a sepia tone and we swore that we saw rippling disturbances in the air outdoors. It felt as though we were living in an antiquated photograph without a frame.

Worse, we could no longer see when we were outside. We set foot beyond the thresholds of our homes and our eyes watered like broken dams, blurring our vision. We wiped and rubbed and wiped and rubbed, but the tears kept streaming, reducing the world to nothing more than a miasma of color and shape. Outdoor work and exercise was nearly impossible without goggles. Travel was hazardous at best. We had been transformed into a procession of eternal mourners, weeping at all times and in all places.

Our lungs weren't faring much better. Those of us with asthma or chronic pulmonary conditions inhaled medications with every other breath. Some of us invested in military surplus gas masks, which took a bit of the caustic edge off the stench but still left us coughing like fifty-year smokers. Our doctors couldn't explain the cause of our distress, even as they prescribed more and more expensive tests and treatments.

In short, everyone suffered.

Everyone except the residents of Redland Park, that is.

They still strolled about the sidewalks in bubbles of laughter and played in their yards as though the stench provided a metabolic boost. While we gagged, they did cartwheels. While we choked, they danced. They lit their homes like amusement parks and threw lavish parties on their patios. We harbored suspicions that they knew the origins and nature of the stench, but we had neither the money nor the influence to pry secrets from them.

Without answers or aid, we sought escape. When we had time off from work, we drove out of the city or rode public transport to the most distant end of its lines. We fled past the suburbs, into the semi-rural forests and fields we hoped might still lay fresh and unspoiled by the stench. We wanted to catch a whiff of wildflowers or a puff of pine—something, anything, that might prove to us that clean air, that *normalcy*, was more than a comforting memory.

Escape, however, was impossible.

Even thirty or forty miles from Redland Park, the stench clung to the breeze. In wooded thickets and grassy meadows alike, it overpowered the scent of nature. It swept across farmlands and drifted along the main streets of small towns.

People who lived in these outer orbits of the city seemed divided on its effect. Some, like us, shielded their eyes and lungs from its harm with glasses and masks. Their faces set hard in the many stations of desperation, it was obvious that they continued working outdoors only from necessity.

Others—the majority, really—seemed to feed off the stench the same as the residents of Redland Park. Though they boasted none of Redland Park's wealth or influence, they too strode about outside with manic, vaguely predatory enthusiasm and obscene smiles that offered no welcome. Their eyes watered like ours and their coughing fits were just as ferocious, but they gave every appearance of enjoying the suffering.

Finding no immediate limit to the stench's influence, we made u-turns, stepped back on buses, and retreated to our homes. We feared how far the stench had spread. Did it stretch to the next city? The next state? The next country? Was any place free from its misery?

We messaged friends and family in distant locales to try to determine the extent of the disaster.

Some shrugged us off, assuring us that nothing was different, that, if anything, the air where they lived was cleaner, crisper, and clearer than ever before.

"Just go to work and have fun like normal," they said. "It's probably nothing. And trust your leaders to solve the problem, if there even is a problem at all."

Others, however, confirmed that we were not delusional, admitting they'd taken measures to stay indoors as much as possible.

"Yeah," they said. "Air's been weird here for a while. Doesn't smell right. And it kinda burns. It's getting worse every day. We've asked around, but no one knows what's happening. Not everyone seems to care about it, either."

Our conversations revealed that the problem we faced wasn't exclusive to our city. Whatever it was that seeped out from Redland Park had begun to suffocate the world.

We needed to take more drastic measures. We needed to prod officialdom into action. We needed to take to the streets and demand solutions.

What we did, instead, was trudge to work as usual, buy more air fresheners, and post our worries to social media.

Surprisingly, the stench did not abate.

One-hundred Mile Radius

Weeks flew by without any change in our situation. Then, without any advance notice, city officials released a statement concerning our stench-related queries. It read, in its entirety: "Regarding a possible air quality concern, we have determined, after a comprehensive study, that no unusual pollutants or unexpected substances have been found in air samples taken within city limits. There is little to no danger presented by the current air quality and we see no reason to recommend extra precautions or perform further unscheduled investigation."

We contacted our mayor's office and the city council offices to ask for copies of the air study's results, but were informed that the study had been outsourced to a private company that kept all its research records sealed. We doubted an investigation had ever been launched, and, if it had, the true results were being suppressed.

The whisper of conspiracy theory haunted our every move. Still, we needed allies with knowledge and resources if we were to turn back the stench tide. So we enlisted academe as a potential ally.

We emailed local colleges and universities in an effort to obtain scientific verification that our air had putrefied, but the faculty members who responded said that their institutions' administrators had recently issued strict instructions that forbid the use of university funds and equipment for the study of air quality.

We didn't know where to turn next. We burned through official channels and proper protocols in vain. We needed aid and we needed it as soon as possible, because the stench had taken on a new and terrifying quality: it made us bleed.

When we ventured outdoors, we strapped on goggles and masks and breathing apparatuses of all sorts, but these no longer held the stench at bay. Like a cloud of needles, it slipped under and through our protections, pricking our softest tissues and drawing blood. Crimson tears stained our cheeks. Our noses ran red, as though broken. Tiny open sores erupted from our heads to our toes, hemorrhaging freely until we retreated from the outside world to rinse and bandage them.

With all the bloodstains crusted into our hair and our clothes, we might as well have been characters straight out of a slasher movie— whether the hapless victims or the savvy heroes, though, we couldn't say.

The stench's increased strength and danger forced us to seek out medical advice. Doctors could doubt our olfactory powers all day long, but they couldn't deny our blood when it was dripping onto their shoes.

We visited clinics and family practices and hospitals, and the nurses and physicians there poked and prodded us, but with only minimal gain. They said our tissues were extremely abraded, which resulted in the bleeding. They said we should use over-the-counter skin lotions, eye drops, and nasal sprays to prevent future irritation. A few told us, in quiet confidence, that the air was definitely to blame, but they couldn't explain how or why. They advised us, off the record, to move far, far away.

We trusted the doctors and their intentions, but most of us lacked the means to pick up and start a new life elsewhere, so, without alternatives, we followed their more traditional treatment plans. We bathed in ointments and gels and nourishing liquids. We swabbed our nostrils with hydrating balms. We drowned our eyes in oceans of protective drops. We oozed medicine.

And still we bled.

There was simply no remedy for the scouring atmosphere that surrounded us. Unless help arrived from outside the stench's domain to help us clear the air, it seemed we were doomed.

Three-hundred Mile Radius

As the stench spread further into the world, the handful of us who worked in the media thought that we could send up a signal flare for aid.

We pitched the stench and its expansion as a story of interest at the newspapers, television stations, and internet news sites where we worked, but the owners of these outlets didn't agree. They said there was no story because there was no such thing as "the stench," and even if the air was a "little different," it "wasn't hurting anyone." They said we needed to focus on real problems and real issues or get out of the business. Any stories about the stench got shelved. Our casual suffering clearly wasn't going to lift ratings or generate clicks, so it was best ignored.

Without the possibility of publicity from media coverage, our only hope for salvation lay in finding the source of the stench ourselves. We had to infiltrate Redland Park.

Those of us called to the neighborhood to perform services for its residents began to investigate every structure and every inch of land as thoroughly as we could. If we mowed a lawn, we made sure to look in every window of the house it surrounded. If we fixed a business's internet line, we fabricated reasons to look in every room of its building. We spent countless hours as delivery drivers and mail carriers just wandering Redland Park's streets and alleyways, scanning for something, anything, out of place.

We discovered nothing but the unerring fact that the stench seemed worse *inside* residences. The select few of us who worked inside the homes of the Redland Park elite were forced to quit our jobs, the stench so powerful in those inner confines that every inch of our skin blistered, burst, and bled so severely that some of us required emergency medical attention and blood transfusions. Most disturbing of all, many of us were convinced that the stench was at its caustic peak in the proximity of the residents of Redland Park, which suggested that it was from those affluent denizens of our fair city that the stench originated.

We had no way to substantiate this claim, however. The people of Redland Park never allowed us to get near them. They never opened their doors to strangers and they never made more than the most casual acquaintance with their revolving staff of service workers. Their social circles were small, tight, and impossible to enter without the right heritage and net worth. Having been raised in lower classes, we possessed neither of these tickets to their good graces. Unless fortune suddenly blessed us with a rain of gold coins, we were locked out of any meaningful direct contact with the Redlanders.

Without the ability to interrogate the people of Redland Park, we turned our attention to our neighbors and the citizens of our city outside Redland. From our jaunts to the lands beyond the city, we already knew that the stench had a polarizing effect on the poor rural dwellers we'd seen and met, with most seemingly invigorated by its presence even as it killed them and a small but significant minority of others wary of its lightest brush. A similar binary existed in our own communities, only in reverse.

While most of our friends and family in the city suffered stench ailments and tried to protect against them, a tiny portion of people we knew—almost always random coworkers or obnoxious neighbors—strutted through the outdoors as though proud that the breeze had turned to slaughterhouse runoff. This minority still bled from their pores. They still coughed up pink phlegm and rubbed at cracked eyes. But they seemed to derive pleasure from their destruction.

It was these people we questioned.

We struck up conversations with them over lunch breaks and when we saw them in their driveways.

"Crazy weather," we said. And they responded, always with exactly the same bombastic tone and volume, "Beautiful weather!"

"Have you been to Redland Park recently?" we asked. "It's even crazier over there."

"Redland Park" they repeated. "What I wouldn't give to live there. Bet it's beautiful every day. Those people have it made."

"Yeah, in a way," we said. "But there's something a little obscene about those homes, don't you think?"

They shook their heads and blood flew from their brows. "Naw. They're just amazing. Just beautiful. If you can get in one of those houses, you deserve it. Maybe one day. Maybe one day."

"What you have to do to make that kind of money, though. Lying and stealing and cheating? Is it worth it?"

They laughed. More blood gushed from their noses. "Well, I bet it was mostly just hard work that got them where they are. But when you have the money, you *do* make the rules, I guess!"

In our brief conversations, here was the common theme: our neighbors and coworkers who didn't care about the stench venerated the people of Redland Park, their homes, and their lifestyles.

They saw in Redland their own blind and impotent ambition somehow reflected like a funhouse mirror, and so they loved its residents. They wanted to *be* the people of Redland, even as they knew next to nothing *about* them. They held no special bond with the Redlanders but the full-blown delusion that they held a special bond. And yet that was enough for them to ignore the stench and their own inevitable deterioration.

Seven-hundred Mile Radius

As the stench crossed borders and boundaries, people well beyond our city's reach began to take note of its presence and effects. They posted their concerns to social media and discussion websites, explaining how the stench flooded their outdoor spaces and ate at their flesh. They, too, found certain neighborhoods in their own cities and towns where the stench was more pronounced, more stultifying, and those neighborhoods were, like Redland Park, always centers of wealth and privilege. They wrote of a nameless conspiracy, of a wild, massive, festering infection beneath the surface of the world. They knew something was terribly wrong, just as we did.

We sent messages and emails to these distant allies. *We might have traced the stench to its source*, we said. *If you join us in investigating, maybe we can stomp it out. We understand your pain. We're suffering too.*

They responded with skepticism and self-interest.

The epicenter of the stench is here, we're sure of it, they wrote back. *Once we clear it out of our city, we'll be in touch about your city. Things are bad here.*

In fairness, we couldn't be certain that the stench in their home-towns and the stench in ours didn't have different points of origin. It was possible that whatever catalyst had set the stench in motion in Redland Park had caused simultaneous outbreaks elsewhere, and maybe those outbreaks were every bit as severe as ours, if not worse.

We couldn't fault anyone for dealing with their immediate prob-lems, but the lack of solidarity still stung.

We were, as from the beginning, as always, on our own.

And the stench's effects were growing more dire.

Plants and trees throughout the city began to die, their leaves turned white as bleached bone. Wild animals—from the rare deer to the ubiquitous squirrel—utterly disappeared from our sight. We hoped they'd run away, to cleaner, more hospitable environs. We had to be-lieve something could escape.

The homeless in our city suffered the worst. They hung about in any public indoor space they could find, but local ordinances forbid them from staying at any one place for more than a few hours. We tried to give them money to find shelter, but, having little ourselves, couldn't even provide enough for them to rent cheap motel rooms.

Instead, we began to see them in motionless, bloodstained heaps on park benches and in alleyways.

Not long after, we didn't see them at all.

As for ourselves, we worked from home as much as we could and left our houses only for essentials, but, even in our confinement, the stench found us. Our doors and windows and cheaply insulated walls reached the limit of their strength, and an attenuated stench seeped through.

We couldn't sleep with it pricking our nostrils; we couldn't eat with it rushing into our mouths. It drained the color from our hair and the heat from our bodies. We stumbled through life, half-awake, starving, and angry. Domestic disputes happened with disturbing regularity. Some of us lost our jobs. Some of us lost our minds.

Our homes, our last sanctums, had been breached. With nowhere left to hide, no security to be had, a few of us packed up our belongings and drove away, never to be heard from again.

Most of us stayed. We taped over our windows and stuffed blankets around our doors and spent most of our time huddled in the centers of our homes, furthest from the stench's winding tendrils. We dabbed at our wounds and prayed to gods that couldn't hear us over the clink of Mammon's coins.

Those of us with strength and resolve still left in our bones wrapped ourselves in as many protective layers as possible and marched off to Redland Park. We had had enough. We demanded answers.

We showed up at a Redland borough council meeting to confront its members about the stench and push for a real investigation, but the city hall where the meeting was held was barricaded by police in gas masks and full riot gear. These police stopped us at the entrance and told us that all official Redland business was closed to non-residents.

We asked why. They waved rifles in our faces.

We asked how they knew we weren't residents. They ordered us to disperse.

We asked how this whole arrangement was legal. They advanced.

We weren't remotely prepared for an armed conflict, so we retreated.

How did they know we were coming, we wondered. *And what are they trying to hide by not letting us in?*

As we left Redland Park city hall and drove back to our homes, dozens of Redland's residents appeared at the ends of their driveways. They stood rigid as department store mannequins, watching us with amusement, wide, unfaltering grins stretched across their faces. Though the strength of the stench was suddenly at its most overwhelming, we passed the Redlanders slowly, trying to show we weren't afraid, that we could hold some sort of ground in this battle. We even waved in mock friendliness.

Their response dissolved all the courage we'd tried to summon, as well as a fair amount of our remaining sanity.

As we drove by, playing tough, the Redlanders' grins grew wider and wider, stretching beyond reason, swallowing up their noses, their cheeks, their chins and eyes. Their heads disappeared into upturned lines of pure malice. At first we thought it must have been a trick of light or a hallucination brought on by the thick stench, but no. They really stood there, at the edges of the streets, faceless smiles set atop well-attired bodies.

They waved back at us, slower than we'd waved, finger by finger, as if they knew they had all the time in the world and we were wasting what precious few minutes we had left.

We shuddered and hurried home. We worried that they were right.

Thousand Mile Radius

We texted and emailed and called everyone we knew.

There's something wrong with them, we said. *The Redlanders. Horribly wrong. The stench has to be coming from them. There's no doubt anymore.*

We detailed what we'd seen, from the ever-widening grins to the jackbooted police barrier, but we were met with derision.

People who hadn't joined us in our voyage of protest suggested that we were under too much stress, that we must have imagined the demonic grins, that there was probably a logical reason for the police presence. They said we should just stay out of Redland Park and keep hanging on as best we could. They didn't want to acknowledge the threat of a greater malignancy at work in their lives because they knew they had neither the resources nor the energy to combat it.

We implored them to believe us. We said that our only chance to clear the air was to remain united.

They scoffed. They said we should keep searching for the stench's source, just in case it wasn't the residents of Redland Park. They said we should spend our efforts in better insulating our homes and stocking up on non-perishable goods. They said many things and gave many suggestions for our actions, but never once did they tell us, "We're in this together."

Without support from our own scourged ranks, we could do little more. There would be no mass protests, no campaign for truth and change, no forest of pitchforks or torches leveled at the Redlanders. Those things required time and effort and the organization of too many able and willing bodies.

We had to feed and shelter ourselves and our families. We had to concentrate on surviving. We couldn't fight the stench unless we took the battle in shifts, and if no one was willing to cover half those shifts, then there could be no meaningful fight at all.

So we kept working. We kept sending our children to school. We hid away in our homes as much as we could and bled rivers all the time.

We were living through a creeping apocalypse that ravaged everything just slowly enough to let us acclimate to its destructions and find complacency in its lulls.

The byways of the internet continued to buzz with reports of the stench's expansion, even as major media outlets remained silent on the matter. If the reports could be trusted, it had spread across our entire nation, maybe our entire continent, and showed no sign of weakening. Our situation played out the same in distant towns and cities, with confusion reigning supreme and fragmented peoples stumbling about, uncertain how to defy the very air they breathed.

In Redland Park, life went on as usual—or as usual as it could, under the shroud of the stench. Construction crews and yard workers and service employees of all sorts still maintained the neighborhood in its most pristine condition. Now, though, this labor force was solely composed of the people from outside Redland who desperately wanted to be Redlanders. They ignored that their employers were monsters; in fact, they wished they were better monsters themselves.

On the rare occasion that we were forced to pass through Redland Park, we saw these Redland aspirants toiling outside the neighborhood's homes. Bathed in their own blood, they staggered about like zombies in an opulent graveyard. Some lay on the ground in dark, spreading puddles, twitching and covered with thick tarps.

They were dying for Redland Park and Redland Park didn't care.

We shook our heads. We didn't understand.

If this wasn't the end of the world, it was certainly a convincing rehearsal for the real thing.

Radius Unknown

A small fraction of us decided that any action against the stench was better than no action at all. This minority made signs that read TRUTH

NOW, REDLAND STINKS, and CLEAR THE AIR, then picketed the Redland Park borough council meetings.

One by one, week after week, these protestors met with the police barricades and were arrested on fabricated charges. We didn't see any of them again after their arrests; Redland Park PD claimed they were detained in a state facility just outside city limits, but, as far as we know, they've vanished from the earth.

No one pickets the meetings anymore. No one even bothers to find out when the meetings are held.

A few others among us—the very brave and the very foolish—decided to directly confront the residents of Redland Park. They walked straight up to the gates and the doors of Redland's lavish manors and knocked. Most often, the gates did not part and the doors did not open, but, every once in a while, someone—or something—answered.

We have no idea what exchanges took place or what words were spoken by either party, but we do know that our comrades all eventually stepped inside the Redlanders' homes. Were they invited? Were they ordered? Were they compelled by desires they'd never felt before?

Whatever the reason, they entered those mansions of misery and ornate doors slammed shut behind them. And that was that. We never saw them again, either. They never exited the houses, never called or texted friends, family, or loved ones. They simply vanished into Redland Park's coffers.

We filed missing persons reports with local police and contacted the FBI, but we were laughed at.

"The people in *that* neighborhood?" the law chuckled. "Kidnapping visitors? Sure. Okay. We'll get on it."

No one "got on it." Our reports were, in various instances, lost, filed away as low urgency cases, and prematurely closed.

Those of us who remained in the city became despondent. Some of us drifted to the bottom of vodka bottles. Some of us found solace in pharmaceuticals. Some of us simply overate and refused to leave our couches.

We didn't venture into Redland Park for any reason. We would find excuses to avoid it, ways to travel around it. "Here be monsters," we scribbled across our mental maps of the neighborhood.

We lived fearful half-lives.

And so it continued, for a while.

Then, one day, a day that seemed like any other but clearly wasn't, we woke up and realized we could no longer leave our homes for even a brief time. The stench had become too powerful. Every tree and bush and blade of grass in sight had shriveled and turned bone-white. Vehicles rusted over in their driveways, their tires misshapen and partially dissolved. We hadn't seen a single squirrel or bird or even a housefly wandering wild in months.

We took a few tentative steps out our doors and our flesh immediately blistered and seeped blood. Our noses bled, our ears and eyes bled, and our chests felt like we'd snorted sawblades. A few minutes of full exposure melted skin, fat, and muscle from our bones; it drowned us in our eroded lungs.

We screamed and retreated to our houses.

We've stayed there since.

Schools closed weeks ago. Most of the stores and businesses in our city have closed, too; even if their employees somehow find a way to reach the workplace without dying, there are no customers or clients to serve. Most of us are out of work, with tiny savings accounts quickly drying up.

We subsist on cheap canned food bought online and delivered to us by drivers clad in smoking hazmat suits. We watch tv and browse the internet, but tv tells us everything is well and the internet offers nothing but cheap speculation.

We wait and we wait and we wait because we are trapped. We suspect the stench has wrapped itself around the entire globe, that there is nowhere the skies remain clear and clean and free. We suspect we will eventually starve or be liquidated. We have no other options. That's our future. That's *the* future.

And in that world of the future, a world of people turned to slush, we assume the things in Redland Park will still throw massive parties and take long vacations and try to expand their already-overblown houses. We assume they will strut about their sidewalks, with their all-consuming grins wider than ever, and revel in the stench and the dead universe it has created because they will own it all.

That's the future. Our future. Everyone's future.
It's already in the air.
Try not to breathe.

UNDO

ALVARO ZINOS-AMARO

Late one night Krystyna hits "undo" on her spreadsheet program.

Ms. Dugal's taxes are boring as fuck, but Krystyna has to grind through this one last form before crashing. Since Jacob moved out four hundred and eight days ago, Krystyna's gig as a grocery clerk hasn't been enough to cover rent. Enter her inglorious side hustle—tax prep. Combing through the income of her economic betters generates just enough extra dough to survive; the resentment is free.

Krystyna's eyes water. The table is stained from her favorite cup, which she dropped and shattered two weeks ago. Jacob took the coasters and she hasn't been able to make herself buy new ones; likewise, she can't make herself clean the stain. The ring of dried grit is like an eclipse. First brown, now black. She imagines space bending. Sometimes she stares into it, hoping her vision will curve into another planetary system, another galaxy. Next to the stain lives the cup she's been using since the demise of its predecessor. Because she fills it up each morning without first washing it out, residue has built up inside. An inner stain to twin the outer. You can only see both stains when you look down from above. Krystyna doesn't spend time wondering if someone feels that way about her life, because she knows no one is looking.

She's itemizing bullshit when her cell phone rings and she accidentally copies a figure into the wrong cell. The phone goes quiet. Thumb-scrolling shows no missed calls. Jacob? she wonders. What if the call dropped? I've missed you, he says. Maybe he utters these words in a drunken slur, but she wouldn't care. She remembers what his breath tastes like, sweet with an undercurrent of bitter. Her eyes water again, this time for a different reason. She sets the phone down. Returning to the laptop screen, she catches her error and selects "undo," but her finger is trigger-happy, or maybe bored, and that's when she clicks it twice.

The coffee cup before her incandesces. She blinks and thinks about a quasar millions of light-years away. The cup's ceramic turns to golden goo. Handle goes last, like a donut waving goodbye. The whole sorry mess pools on the table, burying the older cup's stain. Submits to gravity.

Drip drip drip.

After her shift the next day Krystyna sits in front of the small table in the corner of her studio apartment and opens her laptop.

The hum of the ageing machine as the tiny ventilators wheeze to life during the boot-up makes her think of emphysema. She remembers being six years old and catching her dad smoking a cigarette in the courtyard of their apartment complex in Warsaw. Don't tell your mom, he said, and decades later when he died of lung cancer, Krystyna still upheld her promise, though the odds were pretty good that by then her mom had figured it out.

Beating its own odds, the OS proceeds to load. Krystyna examines the coffee mug area like a dentist looking for cavities.

Flakes of yellow detritus from the cup-melting incident dandruff the laminate surface. She touches them.

Pliant.

A suggestion of warmth, like sunlight colandered through memory.

She accesses the tax program and creates a new spreadsheet. What sublimely arrogant words, she thinks, "creates" and "new." All blank spreadsheets are precise duplicates of those that preceded them. There has only ever been one spreadsheet in the whole world, she thinks, endlessly populated by the illusion of change.

The background color is set to white but it looks off-white to her. She ups the brightness on the screen. Keeps going until it nicks her eyes. The laptop flashes an energy usage warning. "Fuck you," she says.

Top ribbon. Edit selections. Pristine workbook, undefiled by her. The "undo" and "redo" buttons should both be greyed out. The "redo" is nicely compliant with this logic. But the "undo" is all brattitude. She drags her index finger on the trackpad until the mouse cursor hovers right above it. She rests there as long as it would have taken Jacob to feed their pet fish, Suds, in the tank that he took with him when he moved out four hundred and nine days ago, which is to say that she rests there unnecessarily long.

Then she clicks it.

Diffracted light behind her, in the nowhere-everywhere of peripheral awareness.

Kitchen?

Abdominal pain. You know you have an unusually short torso, Jacob once told her. She hadn't been sure if he was kidding. She imagines what he might have thought about that torso harboring a small being. Will our baby be squat too? he might have joked. No, don't do that, she tells herself, contorting in her chair, trying to pretzel away from the discomfort. Don't turn him into a caricature. You have to recall him as he was. As he is. Pain is the limo, accuracy the driver. Jacob wouldn't have quipped about our baby, she thinks. He would have cried. Our baby, she realizes, startled. She remembers the quasar from the previous night. How much energy does a quasar pour out? Is she crying? The laptop screen stabs at her eyes. She dims it to ash.

Lurches to the kitchen. Surveys counters and shelves, looking for anything gloppy.

Side twists again. Pill grope. Her pain meds are expired but she keeps them in the dairy compartment of her fridge. She imagines the tide of cold pushing against the reservoir of rot. Maybe one day the refrigeration will break through that barrier and the pills will become younger. If that happened she could cut down to five or six a day.

One, two, three, down with milk. Mealy aftertaste. More milk. Something curdles inside her abdomen.

You need to eat, survival mechanisms say. They are often displeased with her. Unrelenting. How about an omelet, she thinks back at them, will that appease you tyrants?

The pan, sitting on the right front burner, which is her favorite burner because it's the only one that ignites without farting out a pungent smell, is still greasy from the last time she used it. Back to the fridge for eggs. Carton says they expired two weeks ago. She fills a glass with water to see if the eggs will float or sink. But the glass has some kind of film on it. Or is the water muddy? She scrubs the glass clean with an old towel. Gulps down more milk. Can you use milk instead of water for the egg test? It seems indecent, an obscene buoyancy contest between animal products.

Grease runs on the frying pan.

She cracks open the first egg.

A golden, half-formed chicken fetus drops out.

Krystyna found out two months after Jacob left. She hadn't had sex for longer than that and her boobs had gotten bigger. One of her fellow cashiers at work had said, You look bloated. Take the test? Krystyna's periods had been irregular ever since she'd stopped using the implant so she'd never considered the possibility. The evening after her co-worker made that comment she found out in a Walmart bathroom. She peed on the strip and when it turned the wrong color, she imagined that it said to her, Do you realize what you've done? That night she didn't sleep and every few minutes every hour of every day during the next week she had thoughts about the small being inside her and about the pee strip. The two images became so interconnected in her mind that they broke cause and effect, so that at times she came to believe that the pee strip was the father.

Her manager at the grocery store asked her about her health because by this time people were talking. She tried to stay calm and lie but instead she told the truth and cried. Her boss looked like he remembered he had to pick up dry cleaning across town. "Will you be needing time off?" he asked.

She wanted to say, Yes, the next eighteen years, BECAUSE IT'S A FUCKING HUMAN BEING I'LL BE RESPONSIBLE FOR RAISING, but she realized the absurdity of that before the words came out because one, there were plenty of working moms, and two, she needed to have this small being vacuumed out of her right away, what was she thinking? Of course she wasn't prepared to be a mom. This was not the life she wanted to provide a baby—a baby! the seed of an adult—it wasn't even the life she wanted to provide for herself, but they hadn't yet invented the technology where you could vacuum yourself out of your own life in a way that others would approve of.

She thought about telling Jacob, or her mom back home, but remembering her manager's facial expression discouraged that.

The process was quick, almost too fast. She felt like she kept leaving parts of herself behind at each stage. One piece of her was still out there, in the past, clinging to the emergency appointment with the doctor, another clasping onto the consultation to which the doctor referred her, another stuck in the abortion clinic. The ultrasound determined that she was too far along for the pill, so they decreed surgical removal. They told her not to go alone but she did anyway. It wasn't really a choice.

During the first moments of the procedure she was surprised. A full small-scale operating theater, bright lights, a wide table, imposing stirrups. They've done all this for me, she thought. A dream of self-importance realized in all the wrong ways.

It didn't last. Her nerves smothered everything. The surgeon, a man, tried to reassure her, but she couldn't stop trembling. The anesthesiologist, another man, fixed her into position and knocked her out.

When she woke up in an armchair in a room with other women in armchairs she wondered how she would have felt going through all this back in Warsaw. The perverse tendency to recall her native city always flared up at the worst times, an anti-nostalgia that fueled fantasies of hypothetical pains rather than a longing for recalled pleasures.

Everyone around her looked sad and she felt incredible pain. She knew she was broken. The hurt was so intense it verged on enlightening. She called out for relief and they dosed her up with something but she was too spaced to remember the name. She knew from her discharge papers that during her procedure she'd been given mifepristone and misoprostol, which sounded like substances harvested on faraway worlds.

She continued to experience debilitating pain for several weeks. More bleeding. She burned through her sick time at work. Cried a lot. Knew one hundred percent that it had been the right decision. Still cried. Eventually the physical symptoms passed and only the deep shame remained.

· · ·

The morning after the failed omelet, queasiness stirs Krystyna to a facsimile of consciousness. She rushes to the toilet and vomits into the bowl. She's never had her face this close to the bowl, she realizes. Pretty. Smooth white curvature, like the outside of a space helmet.

As the day passes a prickling erupts on her skin.

By the time she finishes work that evening she knows what this sensation is.

· · ·

She saved all of her documents from the first abortion. At the time, she thought she might die, and consoled herself with the whimsical notion that preserving her paperwork could assist posthumous investigators. One of these imagined investigators, sporting a five-o-clock shadow, would say, Look at this, and wave around the stash of papers. I'll be damned, he'd declare. She died from sluttery. Did you realize that was a medical condition? His amiable companion, a younger investigator in training, would chuckle.

She makes an emergency appointment with the same doctor as the last time.

She apprehends immediately when he greets her in the small office that he doesn't remember her, but he still expresses surprise, as though he does. This soon after the last time, he muses.

She's not sure how to respond. She wants to ask, Will I be okay, but there's no reason to set him up for failure.

Do you know who the father is, he asks. Maybe he doesn't say anything, but she is asking herself that question in the doctor's voice, so he may as well have said it.

It's been months since the last time Krystyna dated, and the lucky fella came inside her mouth. You have amazing lips, the guy said. Now they feel dry, she thinks. She touches them as though they belong to someone else. She remembers thinking that Mr. Lips was fishing for a compliment. Really luscious, he added, forcing the issue. Before they met he had said, I'm a good kisser. So after he put his clothes back on, when he leaned down to kiss her, she told him, Have you considered Tic Tacs? She saw his expression change and she knew they wouldn't meet again.

"I'm not sure," she says. The doctor frowns.

How can you not know, he doesn't probe after a question he never asked, but she's onto his game, can read the disapproving tilt of the head, the flicker of judgment in the way he reviews her case history.

I don't know because I don't fucking know, she thinks. In the now four hundred and fourteen days since Jacob bailed, she's been out with exactly three guys, and the guy before Mr. Lips never even made it to second base. She remembers these long nostril hairs that kept scratching at her face when they made out. She wanted to tell him that he should clip those nose hairs, but in the end she asked herself, who am I to interfere with this grown man's grooming regimen, and she let him go. Staring at the only plant that thrived under her care after Jacob left, she deleted Mr. Hairy Nose's messages. Being ghosted brings you closer to the person you were always supposed to be with, a friend at work said. Yourself, Krystyna thought.

"I don't know," she repeats.

<hr />

Operating theater.

I'm cold, she thinks.

Bright lights.

No, no, no, please don't touch me.

Stirrups.

There, just settle into it, a man says.

IV.

No, you don't understand, I've made a mistake, I have to get back home, I'm sure Jacob is worried, I didn't tell anyone, I—

Anesthesia.

Please, please. Make it so I never wake up.

Armchair.

I'm awake, she thinks. Everything was a lie.

Prescription.

They broke me. I asked them to, and they did it. It's the only time my wishes come true, when I ask to be broken.

Crying.

I'm made to be broken, she thinks.

Shame.

———◦———

Her recovery is worse the second time. Her cervix and ribcage feel at risk of imminent collapse nineteen hours out of the day. A steel clamp pressing upon her and simultaneously a seismic pressure pushing at her from within, her body mangled in the middle. The sky and the earth meet in me, Krystyna thinks. Is the phone ringing? Maybe Jacob found out somehow. Maybe he's full of love and compassion in the end. She reaches forward to push aside the shower curtain so that she can get to the phone and her knees buckle. Turns out to be a robo-spam call for a fake free cruise to a real destination that ironically Jacob and her had once discussed visiting.

She thinks again about calling her mom, but they've never talked about sex, and pretending none of this has happened would be worse than speaking her truth into the phone and receiving no answer. Her mom would sense that things were off and that would be irksome to her. Why can't you just be happy, she would chide. You left this country to be happy. So be happy. Jacob was a nice boy, she would say. Maybe he'll come back one day, Krystyna would reply. When he gets bored of the girl with whom he cheated on me.

After he moved out Krystyna blocked his number and deactivated her social media accounts and kept things like that for four months. She suffered from nausea and depression. She became fascinated with astronomy textbooks. She preferred the out-of-date ones, because she understood obsolescence. The older pictures were better too, their black-and-white grain and lack of clarity a more honest representation of the great cosmic unknowns than today's flashy high-res artist composites. One morning she woke up at four a.m. with her heart beating so hard that she almost passed out, sure that Jacob had been in an accident. We had our chance and we blew it, she thought. We were so foolish, and now he's gone. But if he's somehow still alive, we can make things right. Oh my God we can fix everything. She unblocked him and when the sun came up she sent him a text. Are you okay, she asked. What's up, he said. I thought, I dunno, she replied. I'm not ready to be friends, he wrote back. That day a customer at work pointed out to Krystyna that she'd given him the wrong change and she started sobbing.

Up to ten pills a day, she feels a river open up inside her. She can ride these currents for a long time, she decides. She remembers doing rapids with Jacob once. His wet auburn hair and beard shone in the sun. She had never thought someone so handsome in her whole life. That night back at their hotel room he said he was too tired for sex and she didn't care. He fell asleep while she watched him and stroked his hair. When she woke up the next morning she discovered bruises from the rapids all along her legs and her ankles hurt. She examined her body while he took a shower and she thought, Look at me, I'm a disappointment, I'm disgusting, of course he doesn't want me.

The doorbell rings. She makes herself believe that it's Jacob. I'm so, so sorry, he says to her, and an understanding passes between them that reverses disorder and heals all pain. The dead plants come back to life and the coffee stain disappears. When Krystyna opens the door she finds Ms. Dugal holding her small Bichon Frise dog in her arms. Krystyna tries to remember the dog's name.

"I was expecting that we'd claim a bigger return," Ms. Dugal says. "But I assume it's the best you could do. Do you know Ms. Quliyev? Widow. My floor. How about you give me a referral discount, how about that?"

"What time is it?" Krystyna asks. It's overcast outside and she's not sure if she's had dinner yet. The dog stares at her with sadness.

"Apartment 322," Ms. Dugal says. "She moved here from Azerbaijan thirty years ago. She's estranged from her son. He won't talk to her. Only when he needs money. Tragic story. You can visit her after eight p.m." She walks away. Her dog looks back at Krystyna, who still can't remember its name.

"Okay," Krystyna says, when the old woman is out of earshot. She wanted to reach out and feel the dog's soft coat, but it's too late now.

The inside of her apartment chills her. Do I have a fever? she wonders. How fast does a pulsar rotate?

On the couch she nods off and sweats under her favorite blanket. Her squat midsection wakes her up and sends her to the bathroom with diarrhea. If I was encased in a spacesuit, she thinks, would I wear a diaper, or would I just shit all over myself?

An email comes through from Ms. Quliyev. Like an automaton Krystyna opens up a new document on her laptop.

No, she thinks. I'm on my way somewhere else. With our fastest spaceship today, how long would it take to reach Alpha Centauri? She deletes Ms. Quliyev's message. Gazes into the eclipse that swims in place on her table.

The blank file stares at her.

The "redo" command is once more unavailable, but the "undo" button is ready to tango.

Like a toddler jabbing a cat with a jutting thumb, she clicks it.

The diary where the grief counselor told her to write down her darkest thoughts after her first abortion shines with a peachy hue, turns to honey.

Oh not that, Krystyna implores. I swear--

Too late. The liquid gold laps on the table for a moment, then oozes down its front legs.

Who needs that bullshit anyway, Krystyna thinks.

Her wrist is quick; before she's consciously aware of the movement, she's deployed the "undo" weapon again.

She watches a plate with leftover almond biscotti go, and though she'll miss the plate, a rare gift from her mom after she moved away, she's glad for one less dish to clean up.

The third time she isn't so lucky.

This could be light from another universe, she thinks, as she watches her wallet, with her driver's license and her maxed out credit cards, turn to a radiant persimmon sludge that seeps on to the carpet.

"I'm trying to be as clear on this point as I know how to," the doctor says.

"But I felt it... I know what this is... inside..."

This morning, the four hundred and twenty-seventh since Jacob moved out, Krystyna still considered asking him for a ride. Without her license and no friends nearby he seemed like a viable alternative to public transportation. Ever since seeing a rat in the subway once, she dreads it. She imagined texting Jacob casually, Hey babe, I need a lift, and he'd reply with mirror-perfect nonchalance, Np, what time? and she'd write back, Why did you leave me? That's when she started crying and counted the cash in the reserve box under her bed. I can afford a taxi one way, she thought, and that drive was the freest she's felt since the anesthesia. Her body relaxed so much in the back seat that she felt she might levitate away, and the cabbie had to call to her when they arrived. All of the weight returned, twice as exacting. Don't celebrate, she thought, the vermin are patient, they'll wait you out.

"You may be experiencing side effects from your current pain relief medication. Are you by any chance taking antidepressants at this time?"

Not 'by any chance,' Krystyna wants to say, you don't do something like that accidentally, but her tongue waggles in her mouth, producing an incoherent sound. She clears her throat. "No," she says. "Can I get some from you?"

The doctor shakes his head. "I'm afraid that's not how it works," he says. "You'll need to apply for those through your regular MD, who'll refer you to a psychiatrist if he deems it necessary. Here's the result of your sonogram. See, all clear." He pauses. She imagines him in front of a classroom, explaining Hawking radiation. Everything he says now sounds more interesting. "You're lucky. A third pregnancy so soon after your two... events... could have been problematic. You should be thankful you were wrong. It's best to give the body time to heal before subjecting it to further dramatic changes. Pregnancy can be an extraordinary stressor."

I treated the extraordinary as ordinary, Krystyna thinks, and this is where I am. She smiles at the doctor, disconsolate, on the edge of collapse. Jacob was extraordinary, she thinks, and by taking him for granted I terminated him. Everything that made him special, I vacuumed out of him. She remembers a distant life, glimpsed through a dusk that spreads in tendrils, in which they both strived to become better, to build a common future. Long nights as she studied for her CPA exam, which she never ended up taking, while he worked out the logistics of starting a floral business, which he successfully did months before the end. She remembers, with stunning precision, the Thursday evening after a Chinese dinner in which he suggested that they capture the moment in a photo booth. What moment, she had asked.

"What moment?" she asks the doctor.

He glances at his phone. "It's a little after three. Did you have any further questions for me?"

You'll see, Jacob said, and there was something about his grin that devastated her. Here it comes, she thought, before even being aware of what it was. Inside that photo booth, on a street she has been unable to walk since that day, in between candids, his hand scurried into his pocket and out it came with a small black box, and she couldn't breathe, and he opened the box in one jittery movement--this was it, this was happening, this would be the instant that irrevocably changed everything--and he took out the ring and he said to her, I love you. Krystyna, how I love you. Will you be my wife until the end of time? And she had looked away, and turned, her head had *turned with violence away from Jacob*, and her field of vision collapsed into a constellation of unresolvable daggers of light, and she had gasped and bolted from that crepuscular, confining, treacherously intimate place. He came running out after her and eventually caught up, and they talked, and they cried, and they made up, but in her bosom she had fostered the thought, I can run faster and farther than you'll ever be able to understand, Jacob, no one can catch me because I elude myself. And that's exactly what she had done. Scampered on and on through the emptiness, into the austere wasteland that was her heart, and eventually he had tired of chasing her, because of course he would, and that was when she had made the catastrophic mistake of thinking, if he's giving up his pursuit, he doesn't deserve me. How surprising was it, really, that he would find his fire somewhere else?

I am an aborter, she thinks.

"No questions," she says. "Unless you have thoughts on the cosmological constant and the energy density of the vacuum?"

The doctor looks displeased. "Here's your paperwork," he remarks, giving her her test results and also returning to her the social security card and birth certificate she brought in lieu of her now obliterated drivers license. The birth certificate glances back at her, a confusing symbol of a branch that, offshoot-less, twists back on itself.

On her trip back home, she gets off at her station and makes it a point to slow her gait and look, really look, in the dark corners, but there are no rats to be seen.

I didn't mean to push you away please forgive me, she thinks in a dream, or maybe as she's brushing her teeth, remembering what it felt like when Jacob would wait so that he could brush his at the same time, and he'd walk in and give her a warm hug from behind and she'd melt. He was a good flosser, she thinks, and his mouth always smelled good, unlike Dad's.

Ruminating is a word her counselor used, not the affable grief therapist she'd seen after the abortion, but the compact, hyper-precise, unyielding woman she'd talked to several times after the break-up. Step by step, you have to learn to let go of the past, the counselor would repeat, herself seemingly stuck in a looping present, and her recurring entreaty would only drive Krystyna deeper into the past, where she'd marinate, cooking up an elaborate personal mythology that no professional would ever be able to digest. Ruminating is one of your mechanisms, the counselor told her one day when the AC was turned on too high, and catastrophizing is another. Refusing to accept it's over. In time we'll identify some of your grief patterns so that we can work on them together, she had said. Maladaptive thoughts. Believing you are unworthy of love. Losing your sense of self. Giving in to codependent impulses. The identifying went on and on, but the work never seemed to start. Eventually Krystyna demonstrated she could rise above maladaptive and codependent tendencies by breaking up with the counselor.

But the prissy doctor's words and phrases visit Krystyna sometimes, when she's working on taxes or going to the bathroom or reaching into her fridge for some of that pain relief manna. She finds that she's listened to that inner voice so many times that she can no longer hear it. The words mingle with other terms, dearer to her, like radiative instability, and perturbative expansion, and renormalization. That is her world, one of leaking energy, one swelling with anxiety, one in which normalcy and containment are always one more transformation away. Her apartment is so quiet tonight. Nothing is happening and none of the neighbors exist. Inactivity, stasis, this is the catastrophe she's living through. Surely, she thinks, it can't be more catastrophic to think of a future in which something, *anything*, happens?

She slouches in front of her laptop. The "undo" button tempts her like a totem. A gamma ray burst, she thinks. Maybe that's what feeds it. Or perhaps its source is more primal, an ancient galactic nucleus. The "undo" siphons off the light of other days and channels that torrent to things around her, a blaze so intense that it regresses whatever it touches into a molten honey elixir of proto-matter. For her. It is doing this for me, Krystyna thinks. The thought reminds her of her perverse feeling of grandiosity the first time in the operating theater. Her midriff palpitates. No, no, please. I can't go back there. I'll do anything to stay away from that place.

She closes the laptop.

Not tonight.

Breathing heavy, she staggers to the couch.

When she goes horizontal, Jacob's words ring in her head, the way they have done innumerable times since he left. Dying on the vine, he said. When, wracked by spasms of disbelief, convulsions stemming from a true understanding of the magnitude of her impending loss, when shaken by these paroxysms of prescient desperation and grief she had gotten on her knees and asked why things between them had to end, why did it have to be this way? He simply said, Our relationship has been dying on the vine for some time. And he stopped there, as though that were enough.

She feels that vine whenever she lies down, wonders if anything grows on it these days.

Krystyna falls into sleep quickly and dreams of Jacob.

This brings her great joy. She always craves dreams of him, the only chance she has to really be with him. She glides into the operating room of her own mind, where she is both the physician and the patient, the mother-not-to-be and the small unborn being inside it. She nestles inside this cocoon of non-being, loses herself in a swirling vortex of neutrinos that will never be felt by anyone except her. She is brushing her teeth again, or never stopped, and she is saying, I didn't mean for any of this to happen, you have to believe me, please, please, I'm begging you. In the dreams she always worries that Jacob won't speak back to her, that he'll merely be a stand-in for her emotional muteness while their relationship fell apart, but after a few seconds he beams at her and says, Of course, Krystyna. How I love you, until the end of time. And she feels safe and protected, and tonight even the sound of her cell phone can't disturb her peace.

The next few days of Krystyna's life are screened for her by a despondent projectionist. Lip-syncing errors, film roll stutters, sequences played out of order plague her small interstitial interactions, and the not-so-small ones, as when her boss at the grocery store issues a warning about her performance and expresses his disappointment at what he keeps referring to as her "recent lapses."

That describes the sum total of my life, Krystyna thinks. For the first time, and for the last time, she observes, I have fully lapsed into myself, and I can't lapse any farther than that. It's almost enough to make her laugh.

"I'll do a better job," she says, careful not to specify with what.

"And another thing," her boss continues. "Your co-workers say you're always checking your phone. Like it's a tic or something. Corrina said you left a customer in the middle of check-out because you had a call."

"It wasn't a call, I thought that maybe--"

"I want your phone on silent, and in your pocket. You can check it on your assigned breaks."

She says nothing. Looks down. Towards her belly.

Her manager pauses. There's perspicacious caution in the way he regards her in the following second, as she holds her chin down. He takes half a step back, runs his hand through his beard, squints at potential ramifications. "Well," he says, "if it's an emergency I suppose that's fine. But you understand what I'm saying."

She nods, with great determination bringing her gaze back up to eye level.

<hr />

That night Krystyna takes a cold shower. She skips her pills. Refuses to eat dinner. Pukes a little. Fine veins thread the surface of her cheeks and her forehead like ruddy filaments. Rosaceous, she thinks. Dying on the vine.

Ms. Dugal has left her a note saying that she forgot to include something in her filing, can Krystyna work on an amendment? She's in no mood for that bullshit. Taking the night off, she thinks. Which should bring relief. Instead, within minutes, she starts to fret, pacing in her tiny living room. Out of habit, she's opened up a spreadsheet and the "undo" button awaits her pleasure.

No, she thinks.

I'm not yet ready to give anything else up.

She re-arranges the knick-knacks on her kitchen counter. She thinks about calling her mom. Considers fishing out an old paperback called *While Still We Live*, which she sometimes rereads for sentimental reasons. Her mom shoved it into her hands when she was twelve and said, "This will teach you about how our country was violated." In no mood for any history longer than last Tuesday's dinner, she does dishes, but can't bring herself to quite finish the load. With the hot, spumy water running through her blistered fingers, she gives up on the pretense of cleaning the remaining plates in the sink and leans forward. Eyes closed, she thinks about the hottest thing she's ever heard of. Quark-gluon plasma. More than seven trillion degrees. Over three hundred thousand times hotter than the center of the Sun. Before the Universe was a microsecond old, quarks and gluons danced freely inside an unimaginable nuclear furnace. Her mind peels back ancestral time and wanders into that purifying inferno, and at that perfect moment of blazing surrender her phone rings.

Leave me alone, she thinks, and returns to the conflagration.

But the ringing persists.

She opens her eyes, relinquishing that marvelous holocaust of the infant cosmos, and turns the water off.

Her ringtone is erupting in petals, blooming in a cascade of limpid notes that shimmer and ripple with each repeating cycle.

She holds up the screen and studies the display as though it's a Geiger counter. Caller ID shows a word that she thinks she recognizes. Yes, it is familiar, somehow, but she can't bring herself to articulate it, to sound it out inside her head. The word is—

Jacob.

Jacob is calling her.

Fast—don't think—don't think about not thinking—hit it—hit it; accept.

"He-hello?" she says, her voice unrecognizable to herself.

A loud background hum snakes into her ears, mirror to the roar inside her head, audible silence a fellow participant on the call, outer stain to match the inner.

"Hello?" she says again. "Jacob, are you there?"

A rattling sound, something being thrown or knocked over.

She sounds urgent to herself now. "Jacob," she repeats, "are you okay?"

Voices, very faint at first, wafting in like the miasma of food that's gone bad at the back of the fridge.

Two voices.

Jacob.

And another player.

Woman's voice.

Girly.

What's moving, Krystyna realizes, are their bodies, as they change positions.

The voices are loud enough now to distinguish utterances, to parse words. And moans. And gasps.

"Oh yes," she is saying. "Oh God, yes. Yes. Just like that. Don't stop. Exactly like that. Keep going! Yes! Oh fuck!"

Krystyna feels the lower lip of her mouth tremble and the blood drain from her hands as she says "Jacob?" As though in response the female voice says, "I love how you fuck me open Jacob! You're opening me so wide! Yes, yes, yes, I'm so close! Don't stop! Fuck me open!"

Follows a shuddering release, lengthy exhalations, a circus of panting followed by a procession of words of adoration, reciprocal approbation and giggles and a kind of disbelief on the part of these immaterial voices about what they have accomplished in their invisible realm of delight.

Krystyna says the only thing that she can, what she should have said so long ago but was unable to. "I love you," she says. "I have never loved you as now."

She disconnects the call.

Deposits the phone in her trash bin, right atop the oily pan with the half-formed chicken fetus still lying there akimbo, as though in supplication.

She walks towards the laptop and sits down.

Easy steps. Body feels limber.

I love you.

The universe is a swill of intermeshed forces and fields. A churn of monstrous proportions and elemental configurations. Everything teetering on an endless vacuum that might collapse in on itself without a moment's warning. Surrender forever imminent. No paddles provided.

And yet she has been gifted with an oar.

"Undo" glows anticipatorily, like oven coils on pre-heat.

To dissolve something into the flaxen soup from whence it arose. This is a rare opportunity.

I love you.

A twitch in her torso.

I can't go back there, she thinks.

Why do some things mature and others decay? When two mouths kiss, when her lips melded with Jacob's, were they merely vehicles in a transfer of entropy?

I love you.

Pain skewers her core.

I won't go back, she thinks.

Impaled now, she can barely flex her wrist enough to push her finger on the trackpad.

Has she been thinking about this all wrong? What if the golden light doesn't revert things to their earliest selves but instead smashes them into terminal degeneration? When you remove nothing from emptiness, what remains?

I love you.

Krystyna hits the undo button over and over and over and over and over, until the world starts to recede, and at last, in an untroubled place where an ageing red supergiant is about to go supernova, she feels herself overcome by the familiar slippage of the birth canal.

VIGIL IN THE INNER ROOM

BRIAN EVENSON

I.

By midday Father had sickened again, and by night he was dead. Gauri was assigned by Mother to sit in vigil beside the corpse. Gylvi, meanwhile, was told to seal the inner door and station himself on guard before it.

Gylvi made a disgusted noise. "Gauri always does vigil!"

"Yes, she does," said Mother absently.

She wasn't, Gauri felt, really listening. "I don't mind," offered Gauri quietly. "We can switch if you want."

But now Mother was listening. "It doesn't matter what either of you want," she said. "What matters is how it is. And this is the way it is."

And so, as usual, Gauri found herself in the inner room sitting in vigil, imagining Gyvli waiting just outside the inner door. Once she was inside, she heard him lock the door, then the clatter of him setting up the campstove right outside. She imagined him lighting it, heating the dark wax until it melted. He would spread it carefully until it filled and sealed the gap between door and frame. He would cover the lock with a piece of cut black paper and then smear hot wax over it until it stuck. Then he would press an ear against the door and listen.

He wouldn't hear anything. How could he? Inside, Gauri was being still, silent. And as for Father, he didn't even breathe.

Inside the inner room, holding her own breath, Gauri imagined Gylvi with his face pressed against the door, whispering her name. Did she hear something? Was he really whispering?

"Gauri," he whispered. But his sister did not respond. Perhaps she could not hear him through the wood of the door. Perhaps she simply did not want to respond. Perhaps he was not whispering at all.

———

Meanwhile, Gauri knew, Mother would be standing at the window with a lit taper made of tallow, as was required. It was not possible to stand perfectly still, but she was to stand as still as possible and not move her hand as the melted tallow spattered down upon it. She was not to cry out or weep for the pain. She was to stand imperfectly still, a statue but not a statue, staring out into the darkness, and wait.

One of her hands, the one holding the candle, had become crippled. Father was to blame for this, thought Gauri. She was certain, or nearly so, that mother thought this as well—though this was nothing Mother would ever have admitted to. Sometimes as she lay in bed at night Gauri would imagine Mother still awake and staring at her crippled hand, at the places where the burnt tissue had incompletely recovered. She imagined Mother opening and closing the hand, the burnt skin cracking and weeping a nearly clear fluid as she did so. She imagined Mother cursing Father for having so little consideration—though in truth Gauri did not know if Mother thought any of this. She only knew that, had it been her, this was how she would have felt.

———

Gauri had never been the one stationed just outside the inner door, the one assigned to seal the door with wax. That was her brother's task. Her brother had always been the one to seal the door: even when their mother had shown him the first time how to do it (how to heat the wax, how to apply it in an even, smooth coat, how to make certain there were no gaps left unfilled) Mother had not done it herself, had only mimed doing it. Similarly, when she had first shown Gauri how to sit in vigil she had not sat in vigil herself, not even for an instant, almost as if she felt it to be dangerous for her to do so. *What am I to learn from that?* wondered Gauri, and then thought: *That each must be in their rightful place.* The mother at the window, the brother at the door, the sister by the bed, and the father dead, dead, dead.

Or perhaps she was meant to learn something else. Or nothing at all.

⋯⋯⋯◆⋯⋯⋯

II.

Every time now that she was in the inner room like this, Gauri would think of the first time. The first time Father had died, Gauri had not known what to think. Wheezing, Father had stood stock still, in deep distress, and then had collapsed. He was dead by the time he struck the floor.

Gylvi had started crying and Gauri had followed, but both had quickly stopped when they saw their mother's face.

"Swiftly, children," Mother had said, and under her guidance together they had dragged Father's body into the inner room and heaved it up and onto the dais. They folded his arms over his chest and pushed closed the lids of his eyes.

"Gauri," Mother said evenly. "I need you to listen to me. Do you see that chair? Move it so that it stands near the head of the bed, above and to the side of your father's head." And once Gauri had done so: "Now sit, in a reverential posture... Good. Do not be afraid, no matter what you see, and do not leave the chair." Mother, she saw, had taken her brother by the hand, was drawing him toward the door. "There's nothing to be afraid of. Your brother will be just outside the door, keeping watch."

"You're leaving me alone?" said Gauri. She hardly recognized the high, strained voice as her own.

Her mother shook her head. "Not alone," she said. "You're with Father."

And then she shut the door and Gauri was left in darkness.

She was tempted to leave the chair, to rise, to beat on the door and beg to be let out. But Gauri was an obedient child—doubtless this was among the reasons Mother had chosen her rather than her brother to sit in vigil. For a few moments, just after her eyes adjusted, she could see the vaguest lines of light around the edges of the door and a fingertip of it at the keyhole. And then, as her brother filled the gap with dark wax, the line slowly vanished. Soon only the keyhole remained, then that too was gone and she found herself alone in the dark.

Or, rather, not alone. She could sense the presence of her dead father looming there, just below her on the dais. She struggled to see him in the dark, failed. She lifted her hand in front of her face and wiggled her fingers, and though she could feel the fingers move, could feel her mind moving them, she could see nothing of them, not a thing. But then, as she kept staring into the darkness, kept straining her eyes, she began to hallucinate little flashes of light, her mind struggling to save her from the darkness.

She began to feel that there was nothing but herself and the chair, that nothing else in the world existed. She reached down and touched the edge of the dais and felt in her mind that portion of the world begin to form again. She moved her hand a little and touched something soft as mossy grass and realized it was her father's hair. She slid her hand along, felt out the cold whelk of his ear. She was traveling up his face when she heard a rustling sound and an instant later felt something clamp around her wrist. It was all she could do not to cry out. She tried to pry it off with the other hand and felt fingers, and knew they were Father's.

Settle, said a voice that both was and wasn't his. There was very little air to it, and it was so soft that she felt perhaps that she was imagining it rather than actually hearing it. But was she imagining his touch as well? Could you hallucinate touch?

Not again, her father breathed, as if in despair, and she felt his grip softening on her wrist and then releasing it altogether. She carefully withdrew her hand and settled it into her lap. For a moment she could begin to imagine that she had imagined all of it. She looked toward the door, toward where in the darkness she thought a door might be, and considered standing and rushing toward it, banging on it until they let her out.

Do not be afraid, no matter what you see, and do not leave the chair. What a strange thing for Mother to say, *what you see:* she could not see anything at all. And you could not make someone not afraid simply by commanding them not to be afraid. She *was* afraid, that was certain. She wanted to leave, and yet she still felt like it would be a bad idea, perhaps even a fatal one, to leave the chair.

———

She was not sure how long she waited, seeing nothing, hearing nothing but the beating of her own heart, her brain misfiring as it continued to try to receive from her visual organs a stimulus that wasn't there. Or, at least she didn't *think* it was there. Her hands were in her lap now, lightly touching, each comforting the other, two separate creatures. She breathed slowly in and out, as silently as possible. It was not possible to be perfectly silent, but she sat in vigil as silently as possible, trying not to think, trying not to panic, trying not to be afraid.

And then everything changed.

———

Her dead father took a huge juddering breath, coming back to life. *Hold still, hold still,* she told herself, *do not leave the chair.* He began to breathe very quickly, emitting a panicky whine at the termination of each breath, and then all at once he settled and was silent. Or not silent exactly: she could still hear the sound of him breathing, but now almost normal.

"Who is in here with me?" he asked. "Is anyone in here with me?" His voice was his normal voice, or nearly so. Not the airless voice she had heard before.

"I am," she said.

"Gauri?" Father was silent for a moment—thoughtful, she thought later—then said, "I suppose that's all right. You're old enough, or nearly so... Who is at the door?"

"Gylvi," she said.

"Yes, of course. Which means Mother must be at the window."

She didn't know, not then, nor did she know about the candle. But yes, as it turned out, she had later determined that Father was correct.

"I'll be my old self in a little bit," his voice said from the darkness. "Once morning comes. At least I believe so. If it doesn't turn out to be the case, I'll have to ask something of you."

"What?"

He became evasive. "Better not to go into it unless it's needed. Until it's needed. Probably won't be this time."

"This time?"

"This death. The flesh is still in decent condition. We probably won't have to take a drastic step."

She did not know what he was talking about. Though, in a way, she worried she did.

Her father took a deep breath, released it as a sigh. "No, not this time, I think."

For a long time they were both silent. Gauri listened to the sound of Father breathing. She did not know what Father listened to, or if he listened to anything at all.

"There is no afterlife," he said absently, as if to himself. "At least none I could find. I buzzed around like a fly and then came back. There was nowhere for me to go."

III.

That was several dozen deaths ago. Now, Gauri had sat vigil next to Father in the dark enough times that she was no longer frightened. She just sat and waited until Father gave that deep gasp and came back to life again. The deaths were coming more quickly. There had been months between them at first, but now they came every few days. It was selfish of father to die so often, she felt. It was killing them.

Once I die will I come back too? she wondered as she waited in the darkness. She didn't know. She had tried to ask Father about this but he had avoided the question. She tried to ask Mother but she avoided it too. She would, she was told, just have to wait and see. *Good things come,* she was told, *to those who wait.* But she was not sure she believed this.

What if she did not do as she was meant to do? What then? She had been wondering this more and more frequently.

What if she left the chair? Would anything change?

Three deaths ago, she had brought a chestnut knife in with her, a knife with a small flared blade, and as she had sat vigil beside her father she had kept one hand in her pocket, wrapped around the wooden handle of the knife. *What if,* she kept thinking, *I left my chair and pierced a hole in the wax seal of the door? Would that allow my father's soul to finally escape? Let him find the afterlife?*

But she had not left the chair. She had kept to the chair long enough that it was hard for her to bring herself to leave it.

Still, she was sure she would do so eventually. She just had to build up the courage. And so in all the subsequent deaths she had brought the small knife, and had clung to it like a buoy. But each time when her father finally juddered back to life, she always forgot about it, focusing instead on him and his voice, waiting to see if he would tell her what he had always kept from her, the thing he said he might one day have to ask of her.

He had not asked it yet. She had had hints of it, though. Father had said he could not go on like *this* forever, but would, he said, still go on nonetheless. She imagined his eyes staring at her in the dark, appraising her. But of course it was dark, and she had no way of knowing where he was staring, if anywhere. And indeed, when she reached cautiously forward and touched his face, she found his eyes to be closed. Still, she could not help but feel that whatever way he chose to go on would be the end of her.

Waiting, she was waiting. In the inner room. Attending the latest death. Thinking all these things through again and turning them around in her mind, the chestnut knife in her pocket and gripped tight, the wood of the handle softened by the sweat of her palm. She would stand and cross the floor and gouge a hole in the wax, and then Father's fly-like soul would get out and wouldn't come back, and Father would be dead for good.

But what if instead, another part of her thought, it was a question of not letting someone or something else in? What if it wasn't merely Father not staying dead, but keeping out whatever would desire to occupy his body?

Her brother was guarding the door, but it hardly seemed the purpose of him guarding it was to keep Father from getting out. No, rather, it seemed he was trying to keep something from getting in.

But what?

She didn't know. Nobody had told her enough. She was being made to do her part without knowing exactly what her part entailed, waiting to find out what it was that, eventually, her father would demand of her.

She rubbed the handle of the knife. Why was it called a chestnut knife? There were no "chestnuts" in this place. She did not even know exactly what a "chestnut" was. But Father used the word and so they all used the word, and perhaps that was exactly the problem.

Her eyes, open and staring into the dark, were once again beginning to see flashes of things that weren't there. Nothing distinct, which made it somehow worse.

She could stand and leave the chair and feel her way across the floor and gouge a hole in the seal. She could. But what if she did that and as a result this time when he came back to life he was no longer Father but someone else?

Would that be worse?

Or better?

Sitting there, alone in the dark—or not alone exactly, sitting there with mostly dead Father in the dark—she remembered that first time, that first death. She remembered the sound of Father standing and the movement of his bare feet as he crossed the floor, and then a sound that she couldn't recognize, a clanking of sorts, which later, once they were out, she realized must have been him turning a key in the lock. For though the keyhole had been papered over and covered in wax on the outside, it was open on the inside. He had yanked on the door and yanked again, and suddenly the wax seal had given way and the door had opened and she was blinded by the light pouring in, which, to be honest, was not all that much light, but infinitely more than the none they had had in the inner room. She came stumbling out of the inner room, blinking, head pulsing. There was her brother, lying stiff and motionless beside the door. What had happened to him she didn't know, something to do with standing guard. And there, in the other room, beside the window, was Mother with the candle burned out and melted tallow crusted all over her hand, the smell of burnt flesh an undertone in the air.

Mother blinked once. "Hello, Father," she said, and then looked at Gauri. "You didn't have to use her?" she asked.

Father shook his head. "No, not yet."

How bad could it be? Gauri wondered now, in this, the most recent moment of being with dead Father in the inner room. *If Mother and Father would allude to it in front of me—"you didn't have to use her?"—it couldn't be that bad.* But she was not sure this was true. *Use me how?*

She sat, stared into the dark. *If I pierce the wax seal,* she thought, *I am not sure what will happen. But at least there will be a change.*

That was enough to decide her. She took the chestnut knife out of her pocket and grasped it firmly in one hand. She scooted forward and left the chair and placed her feet on the floor, and made her way to the door.

Or would have anyway, if on the way a hand had not grabbed her.

At first she thought it was Father's hand. Why should she think otherwise? What other hand was there here, beside her own?

And yet, she felt, she had traveled too far across the floor for it to be Father's.

Very quickly, though, she found herself wishing it was. If it had been, perhaps she would have had a chance. There in the dark, she could not be sure whose hand it was, only that it wasn't father's and wasn't hers. She struck it once, then twice, with the chestnut knife, but this just made the fingers close tighter. She felt the bones in her wrist break. And though her father had, by his own admission, buzzed around like a fly and then come back, she found she couldn't speak, couldn't resist, couldn't do anything but be dragged out of this world and into another.

What awaited her there, beyond the inner room? Who can say? Certainly not her. At least not anymore.

DEAD BUT DREAMING STILL

MICHAEL KELLY

Will you talk to me? Please?

In the still of each obsidian night, in her restless half-sleep, her torment, she doesn't know what is dream and what is memory. Even her waking hours are cloudy and blurry, often distorted, like she's viewing the world through a rain-streaked, ash-strewn window.

She stirs. Sits. Rubs her eyes. Blinks. Early morning. Quiet. No wind. No birdsong. It's been a while since she's even seen a bird, or another living creature.

She's alone. She hasn't always been alone. She's almost certain of that. But she is alone now. Once, she thinks, there were others. A family, even. A child. Small and happy as only children can be. A few years, she thinks, that's all we get. A few years of unfettered freedom and happiness before life begins its inexorable toll.

But the child in her splintered memories is happy. Smiling. Laughing. And their laughter is a summer laughter, bright and gentle and musical and soothing. Nourishing. And all too brief.

These dream memories are fragmentary and fleeting, like the grainy static transmissions that winked on then off again on her comm-plate when it was out of comms range. Now, she knows, everything is out of comms range. The towers are toppled. The lines are cut. Invisible wavelengths and frequencies aborted. The comms, like a lot of things, are long dead. Still, every morning she pulls the comm-plate out and presses her fingertip to the blank black screen. Sometimes she even speaks to it. Holds it up to her face and stares at her fuzzy reflection in the dull screen. Always the same one-sided conversation, as if recited from dream memory: "There you are," she says. "Look at you. What will you do today? Will you talk to me? Please?" She's no-one else to speak to, after all.

Hunger twists in her gut like a living thing, coursing like a river or a disease. She imagines it as both of those things; flowing, spreading, changing. Mutable. A river never retreats. Nor does disease. What's streaming through her body, she wonders? What's in her head?

She rises slowly from her bed of thin thread-bare blankets, crawls to the tent entrance, unzips it and peers out. Even through her mask she smells ash and a peculiar tangy acidity. The world gone sour.

Blinks again. Hazy. Still as death. The air cool with sorrow. The copse of birch trees are limned in silver-grey light. The ground is dew-spackled. Mist-shrouded. A still and static world daubed in thick grey splotches like a renaissance oil painting. A world that somehow, like her, beyond all expectations, still exists.

She zips the tent flap closed and moves to her depleted backpack, opens it and pulls out a small dented tin. She pulls the ring tab, unsealing the sardines. Pulling her mask free she eats the sardines, licking the oily juices greedily from her fingers. For now, she's a brief respite from her hunger pains.

She dreamt — or remembered — that she forwent meat once, when beans and grains were plentiful. Dreamt she was at a large party with abundant drink and food; a large pig on a spit turning, its skin darkening and crackling, grease spilling from open seams, the char of burnt meat like a heat haze above her. It's snout curling into a sardonic smile. And later, at the table, the swine's hollow and sightless eyes scrutinizing her as someone walks up, snaps off one of the pig's fire-crisped ears and eats it.

Breakfast finished, she packs the blanket and small tent and folds them expertly into her backpack to join her cutlery, bowl, small pot and fry pan. Then she heads out. To where, she doesn't know. Uncertainty is one of the only certain things left to her.

Moving cautiously, she keeps to the broken tree line, straddling the pitted fields and the desiccated forest. She wears grey pants, and a grey hoodie, carries a large grey backpack that grows lighter each day as her provisions diminish. She's wrapped her cutlery, pan, pot, and bowl in cloth so as to make as little noise as possible. Her boots are a scuffed charcoal. A mask of grey cloth completes the ensemble. She is a grey shape in a grey world. Blending in. Indistinct and ephemeral. Like a ghost. Perhaps she always was.

Briefly there's a sharp, bright pain in her head, like a darning needle stuck into the meat of her brain, and her vision blurs. It's like looking through glassine. She weaves unsteadily then orients herself. Her vision clears and the momentary sting in her head subsides. They're coming more frequently now, she knows. She wonders if these episodes are nothing more than the onset of some buried memories trying to be unearthed. Some memories are painful, after all.

She looks up. Through the haze, she sees patches of chalk-white sky. Weeks ago she saw a lone crow flying in a wedge of dust-blurred atmosphere, but nothing since. The crow disappeared into the grey mist with a feeble cry, a tiny black speck like a final, forlorn punctuation.

Once, she woke in the night to the crunch of footfalls and a sudden silence, like a breath held. In the night-dark she packed and hurried away. She did not wait around to see what it was. Anything large enough to disturb the ground-brush was a danger, man or animal.

Straddling the divide between field and forest is best, she thinks. The field is open and wide and if she sees anyone out there she can take cover in the forest. Conversely she should be able to hear if anyone approaches from the forest and, depending on the sounds, decide on a course of action. Though she's had no survivalist training, this is what she reasons. Forest and field. Shelter or escape. Until she runs out of one or both. Until she runs out of reason. Or hope.

Despite a lack of training, she's alert to any food sources; mice or mushrooms or wildflowers. Hunger simmers always at the edges, consuming her thoughts. If she has any protein sources, she eats them at breakfast to help carry her through the day. Lately though she hasn't seen any mice in the fields or squirrels in the forest. No fish in the black streams. No birds in the darkening sky. Aside from some plants and a few crops, it's as if all living things are dead or dying or hiding. Like her.

So, it's a shock when she finds the baby.

It's around midday and her stomach is a twisting anguish of complaint, and she's scavenging the edge of the parched and browning field of heather — poking a stick into the grass, into the dry scrub, looking for any food source so that she might still save some of her final provisions — when she hears a faint rustle. Vole or mouse, she hopes, or (even better) a rabbit.

She eases the hunting knife from the sheath at her hip, whisper-soft, and steps toward the rustling noise. Here, the tall and dying grass forms a slight depression and she peers down to see a small brown bundle of sackcloth juddering on the hard-packed dirt among the dead leaves and wilted heather. Like an offering. A sudden gust and grassy tendrils fan across the bundle and there is a jerky twitch, then the unmistakable cry of a baby – shrill, keening, and persistent – and her heart, already hard and fast in her chest, does double-time. Her skin prickles. It's as if she can feel the blood coursing through her faster and faster. *Trap,* she thinks. She crouches, does a 180 degree scan, turns and scans behind her. The cries continue, a hard wailing followed by a short gasping for breath then more shrieking. She moves away, slowly, still crouching, knife tight in her hand, heart hammering, and inches toward the trees. In the forest she finds a suitable spot behind a stand of pines and sits low. Breathes. Breathes. Calming. Calming. Heart rate slowing, slowing, like an engine idling but ready to go.

She waits. In the still of the forest, beneath the proud pines, among the stately birch, she waits. She's unclear what she expects to happen. She should just keep going, through the dim forest like a passing wraith, quiet and unseen. Surely, she thinks, someone will come for the child. It isn't her problem.

The child cries, insistent, and in the cries she hears the child's fear, aware somehow of its abandonment, its precarious situation. Alone and defenseless, all it can do is cry for help. Her eyes blur. She wipes moisture from her cheek, tries not to think of the infant.

Her stomach clenches in agony. She pulls a canteen from the backpack, unscrews it, takes two long gulps of the stale, tepid water — sharp and alkaline. She finds a crusty heel of stale bread at the bottom of the pack, and chews at the hard exterior. She'd found it the day before at the edge of a road. A gift. She eats half the bread and then puts it away.

Not much left in the pack — a tin of peas; a couple small dried apples, and the half-eaten heel of bread. She'll have to chance a town soon.

The meager daylight is failing now. The world is a greyer grey, curdling to dusk. Twilight used to enchant her, a time when magic seemed possible in that silent and beguiling liminal space between day and night, light and dark. Now this edge of darkness heralds just more darkness. Dark thoughts for a darker world.

She pulls the comm-plate from the side pocket of her pack, stares at the dull, blank screen. In the dim light she angles the screen toward the forest-top, tries to catch some light, tries to catch her reflection on the matte black surface. How does she look? Bad, she thinks. And would she even recognize herself? This isn't my face. She can barely remember what she looks like anyway. And it doesn't matter. It never did.

Another dream memory tugs at her, makes her wince, another painful little shard in her head — she's outside, huddling with someone, a child, she thinks, both their faces wrapped in wet gauze as a hot wind blows and blows. Then they are running, running....

She looks at the comm-plate. "There you are. Look at you." She hugs the comm-plate to her chest. "Will you talk to me? Please?"

There's a sudden blue silence and she realizes the child has gone silent. She was supposed to be on alert, but she'd drifted off. Stupid, stupid, stupid. That's how you die, she thinks. Looking back. Don't look back. Never look back. None of that matters. Move forward. Keep moving.

Steadying her breathing, she stands. The night is coming, suffocating the last vestiges of pearly twilight. Quietly she moves out from the trees to the field. The dying light and the coming night form a grey penumbra on the horizon, an arc, like a protective shield. She grins behind her mask. There's nothing to protect us, she thinks. Nothing.

She creeps toward the child. It's still there, in the slight depression in the grasses that form a sort of natural cradle. Bending, she reaches down and touches the still bundle. There's a sudden wail and she snatches the child up, pulls it to her chest to silence it and races back into the darkening woods. She runs and she runs, and in her head she pictures herself from another time, running with another child, as a hot wind sweeps the land, and she doesn't know if it's memory or dream or nightmare. All she can do is run. Run.

The child is fussing, and she's rocking it in her lap, trying to calm it, making "sshhhing" noises at it. The night is oil-dark, but with the child she doesn't want to risk a fire, risk bringing attention to herself from those that abandoned the child. So she rocks the child in the thick night, under a black and pitiable sky; a bed of dry pine needles hastily kicked together as a sort of rug for some small comfort.

Food, she thinks. The child needs food. And so does she. She can feel the knotting beginning in her belly that will soon wrack her in agony. And for the briefest of seconds she catches herself staring at the child, at the baby fat puffing their smooth cheeks, and… *no!* She doubles over, retches, dry heaves. Then straightens, and still clutching the child holds it up and says softly, "There you are." Squints in the dark. "Look at you." She holds the child close and sobs.

They are deep in the woods, in a cradle of ancient pines. She found a small hollow that she filled with pine needles and leaves, affording a view from all sides, and camped there. She didn't set up her tent. She wanted to be out in the open, not caught unawares. Though country dark, she figured she'd hear anyone or anything approaching.

But the child is squirming and she needs to feed them both. She'd done this before, cared for a child, she was sure of it.

She puts the squawking child down and wipes the wetness from her eyes. "Shush. Shush now," she says. She tries a smile but doesn't know if the child sees, and then remembers she still has her mask on, anyway. She pulls her hoodie up and off, lifts her shirt, and brings the child up to her breast. The child's mouth latches onto her and it suckles. It releases and cries but she pulls the complaining child back to her and it quiets and continues to try to nurse. There's no milk to draw from her breast, but it's a familiar feeling to her. And to the child as well, suckling softly and looking up at her calmly now with bright eyes. There is a dampness to the child's rags. It's soiled them, of course. She'll have to deal with that, she knows, but for now, in the dark, in this quiet moment, the child is seemingly content.

Light begins to filter into the forest. Above the tree line she sees a plum dawn spread across the sky, a bruise. She can't remember the last time she's seen the sun. It could have been months or days. Life has been a grim parade of grey days. She looks down at the child, now sleeping.

There you are, she thinks. *Look at you.*

Carefully, she places the child down on a nest of leaves. Like every morning, she pulls the comm-plate from her pack and presses a finger to the dead plate. She barely glances at the screen and is placing the comm-plate back when it suddenly hums, startling her into dropping it. She snatches it from the ground and looks at it, expectant. Blank. She shakes it. Nothing. She presses her finger to the plate again. Still nothing. She continues to shake it and press the screen over and over, but it remains black and dead. Defeated, she places it back in the pack and weeps quietly to herself.

Did she break it? Was it coming to life, and dropping it somehow broke it? She knows things can break when you drop them — gadgets and tools. People, too. She glances at the child. People can break.

If the comm-plate was coming back on, what does that mean? Are the comms back? If so, that's good, right? Surely that is a good sign. If the comms are back, there must be people. Good people. Only good people would want to set the world right.

The child is sleeping soundly, wrapped in brown rags. She should try and rest, as well, but she's a tight jumble of nerves. And hunger. Always hunger. A constant, often painful need. A gnawing. And she's the child to feed, too. And wash. And keep from harm. She recalls these things, half-forgotten, or buried somewhere deep. It's what we do, she thinks. Women. Mostly women. Mothers. Provide. Care. Heal.

Above, the sky is greying over with cloud and fog and dust, choking out the meager dawn. She tightens her mask. She'll have to try and rig one for the child.

The child.

She has a *child.* A surge of conflicting emotions sweep through her, threaten to overwhelm her.

A child.

She had one once before, she thinks. Another memory or fragment half-buried, half-forgotten, only conjured recently. Because of the comms, she wonders? When the comms come back will all my memories come back? Will my child?

The clouds thin, and a faint orange glow lights the sky. She smiles, stands. And a sharp bright pain pierces her head, hot and stinging. She wobbles and her vision blurs. The sky and trees smear like ribbons of wet paint. Then the sensation of falling in slow motion. Then darkness.

The cry startles her to consciousness. The child!

She's up and over to the child — crying and squirming and still on the ground, still in its sodden brown rags.

"Hush, sweet child," she says. "Shh."

By the quality of the dim light and the faint shadows cast from the tall trees, she guesses it's mid-afternoon. The child has been alone for several hours. The realization shakes her, and something brittle inside her tugs loose as a dull ache pulses through her. She's tired. So very tired.

"Look at you," she says, bending and kissing the child's forehead.

She retrieves her pack, pulls out the thin blankets, and her canteen. Using her knife she cuts a blanket up into manageable square-like pieces. She unwraps the dirty brown rags from the child and sets them aside. A girl, she sees. The child is a girl. Her breath hitches and inside herself she feels more pieces sliding free, falling.

The child is wet, but there's no excrement, and she wonders when the child last ate, last drank, had any nourishment.

Child. She can't just keep thinking of her as *the child*. She'll name her. And once you name something, she knows, you own it.

Eve.

She'll call her Eve. It was near evening when she found her, and she liked the name, liked the way it felt on her tongue, all short and elegant and full of promise.

She unscrews the canteen and pours water on one of the smaller squares and scrubs and swabs at Eve's exposed skin. She works quickly, drying her with a clean piece of the fabric. Finished, she ties one of the rough-cut blanket squares into a passable diaper, and uses a whole blanket to fashion a make-shift combination covering and carry-all, Eve nestled tightly inside. She can pull the fabric close to Eve's face, providing a makeshift mask without obstructing her breathing.

Inside her pack she finds a can of peas, the last of the tinned goods. She opens the top part way, pours some peas into a bowl and mushes them thoroughly with the flat of her spoon. Lifting the carry-all, she pulls Eve close, pokes a finger into Eve's mouth, runs the tip along her gums. One tiny tooth, and another about to come free. She spoons some peas into Eve's mouth and grins as Eve accepts the food, eats it, her tiny body shaking, arms spasming, then opens her small mouth wide again, expectant, hopeful.

Eve finishes the peas. She debates preparing more, but Eve seems satisfied. Her own hunger sweeps through her. She tips a few peas into her mouth and chases it with a swallow from her canteen. She folds the slightly open tin closed as best she can, saving the rest of the peas, places them in the pack and pulls free the comm-plate.

Will you talk to me?

With the same finger that she poked into Eve's mouth, she presses the screen of the comm-plate, holds it there. There's a small buzz, and the comm-plate vibrates. Hums quietly. The screen brightens from black to grey to white. Her heart thuds. Icons populate the screen. She reaches out, tentative, touches one, the smiling face. A voice, static-filled, garbled…

… *There you are… talk… today's news…*

… *August twenty-eight two-thousand thirty-eight* — Then muddled, the voice weakening — *press to check your vitals…* Distortion now as the screen flickers. … *have assumed control … checkpoints … medications…* The screen flashes, and the voice winks in and out. …*vaccinated against…* The comm-plate shuts down, the display black and dead. She presses the screen over and over, but it's now lifeless.

Eve is silent. Too silent. She scoops her up, pulls the fabric from her face, and Eve cries out, annoyed, and she's overjoyed at the angry wail from Eve, and she feels another tugging inside herself, a different wrenching from another part of her — a deep, plaintive and powerful joy — and she wonders how much of herself is left. The world just tugs and pulls and she's given so much and she's so very tired.

A stinging pain in her head, and she winces. If she succumbs, what becomes of Eve? She has a momentary image of another child, in another time and place, and then the image is lost to her, like so many things.

She packs away her things, cradles Eve, stands. With the pack on her back and Eve in front, it's a burdensome load. But she'll manage. She'll have to. Women are used to burdens.

Another grey and still day. Afternoon already. She'd lost so many hours to her 'headache'. She starts out, threading her way through the tall trees, and steps out of the forest into a dry and dying field. Rain, she thinks. When did it last rain? She'll need water. And something else for Eve.

She glances down at Eve. Calm. "There you are." Smiles. "Look at you."

She walks west, the world silent and still, following the dim light. That sour tang hanging in the air, curdling everything. Briefly there is another bright jab of hot pain in her head, and her vision smears and darkens, but it soon dissipates.

She's crying now, clutching Eve close. "I'm sorry, sweet child." Kisses Eve's forehead. "I just need some time. That's all I need. All I want."

Walks in the ghost world. Carrying her load. Through field after field. Stops to tighten her mask and adjust Eve's coverings. Stops to feed herself and Eve the last of the peas, the last of her water. Walks. Walks. West, following the failing light.

Eve cries. She stops, sets down her load, lifts her shirt to let Eve nurse from her dry breasts. Eve settles, and she lets her nurse until she falls asleep. She imagines breast-milk seeping from her nipples. Thinks and dreams and imagines a healthy Eve, a different Eve, a different world. For a while she just sits, holding Eve close. Sits and rocks and coos and cries.

Standing, with Eve asleep in front and pack secure behind, she moves west again in the twilight haze. The wind rises, moving and singing like a living thing, blows across them, and she can feel the air chilling. The field opens to a small valley and below her she can see a glint of dark water, can hear it rippling.

She eases down the slope to the bank of the stream. The water is dark. She places Eve down gently, bends over the water and sniffs. It smells good. She dips the canteen into the water, lifts it out, takes a tentative sip. In the stagnant grey light, she's never tasted anything so good. She drinks long, emptying the container. Bending again to fill the canteen, she sees something floating past a couple feet away, caught in the current, twisting in the eddies. A small creature. A puppy, she sees, its eyes closed, as if asleep, peaceful. It's underbelly pale and bloated as it rolls over and past her in the black churn. She watches it float away along the black creek in the darkening valley, dead but dreaming still. *You can't save everything,* she thinks.

A cold breeze brushes past. She hugs herself, looks up at the blackening sky. Nightfall soon. She'll have to find a place to camp. Cradling Eve and balancing the pack, she moves up the slope and edges westward. She keeps the creek in view below her, not wanting to stray too far from a water source. It's not quite full dark when she finds a small stand of thin dying trees forming a small glade just over the slope-edge of the valley. It isn't much, but it'll have to do.

She unloads her pack, places Eve down on a grassy patch, then sits. Cold. The season must be changing. Even though they are more exposed here, she'll have to make a fire to keep them warm. There are plenty of dead branches scattered nearby, like the discarded bones from a great feast. And briefly her mind flashes to that roast pig on the table, plump and pink and char, staring from its eyeless sockets.

Gathering the driest branches, she heaps them into a small pyramid-shape, and with a small piece of cloth and her lighter manages to start a fire. Her stomach tightens painfully, and Eve is now fussing. From the pack she pulls out a bowl, the heel of bread, and one hard dry apple. She devours the rough, tasteless fruit. With some water she makes a passable gruel from the bread, and feeds it to Eve, who takes it gratefully.

After, as she sits by the fire, she lets Eve suckle. She rocks her gently, cooing "Look at you. There you are." Smiles. Then, from somewhere deep, a sliver of song, "Hush little baby, don't say a word. Mama's going to…" *What? Mama's going to what?*

The fragment eludes her. And Eve is sleeping. For a time, as the fire crackles low, and the stars pierce the night sky, she just sits with Eve attached to her, rocking slow, slow, content in the warmth and glow of the flames. She yawns. Wonders when she last slept.

She builds a little cradle of blankets and dead leaves near the fire and places Eve down. She pulls her knife and small whet-stone free and sharpens the knife until the edge glints in the firelight, then sheathes it by her side. From her pack she retrieves the comm-plate, squints at the black screen. Thinks, *Are you dead or just dreaming?* Maybe *she's* dead but dreaming still.

Her finger touches the screen and it brightens and sparks to life just as her head explodes in a fountain of pain and everything goes dark…

…and something pulls her from the dark; something urgent and primal and her eyes snap open to see a figure bending toward Eve, reaching.

Suddenly the knife is in her hand and she's up and diving and slashing and rolling and stabbing. The figure lurches away, and collapses a few feet from Eve, clutching at her. Her heart thudding wildly, she moves to Eve. Sheathing the knife she picks Eve up and checks her over. Satisfied, Eve cradled in one arm, she steps over to the prone dark figure. She stops shy of the reaching arm. A man, she sees. Black blood gurgling from the side of his neck, under his ear, like a small geyser. One hand is trying to staunch the wound while the other still spasms at the ground, fingers digging into the night soil.

He's speaking, all muffled and gargled. "Shmine." Points at them. "Mine," he says.

She pulls Eve close, takes a step back. Her breath is coming hard. Eyes darting. Frantic.

The man coughs, glares. "Mine." His eyes dark and hungry. She's seen that hunger in many men.

Eve cries out, a keening screech piercing the icy darkness.

She retreats from the fire, from the dying figure. Her breathing has calmed, but she's a taut spring of anxiety and alert to every little pop and crack from the fire, every feeble little movement from the man. Clenching Eve tight, she fishes in her pack and pulls out the canteen, the withered apple, her spoon, and her bowl; wrenches the knife free again and cleans the blood from it with a bit of their water and the hem of her hoodie. She cuts the apple into tiny pieces and mashes them with some more water and the spoon.

A loud, wet and phlegmy coughing from the man. She can see him shudder, arm in the air reaching to the sky. Reaching for what, she wonders. Salvation? Then silence, a stillness, as the night presses down.

She spoons the apple sauce into Eve's expectant mouth. Her own stomach heaves tightly. There's a static buzzing in her head and the corners of her vision darken.

Eve finishes the apple sauce, squirms in her arms, uptight, her little face flushed even in the dark. She lifts Eve over her shoulder, rocks her, bounces her gently, strokes her back until a burp escapes her and she settles. Then another sort of belching and Eve squirts out some runny shit.

And she laughs, though she knows she shouldn't, as someone may hear her, but she can't help herself. Laughs madly, deeply, joyously.

She moves Eve to the ground, stares down at her, smiling. "There you are. Look at you."

From the pack she tugs out the last blanket, cuts half of it away. Picks up the half-empty canteen, pulls her mask down and takes a small sip of water. With the rest of the water she cleans off Eve and fashions her a new diaper, then cleans herself. Eve is attentive so she nurses her, lets her drift off to sleep. Do babies dream? What do they dream?

After some time she places Eve down, swaddled in cloth so that only her eyes are visible. Eyes closed to the terrible night.

Sitting on the cold bare ground, she peers into the fire then up into the shadow-black sky, scrutinizing the silent stars, searching for answers to questions best left unasked, as if the sky or stars or fire could answer. As if they would. They just exist eternally, unjudging.

Where will we go?

What will we eat?

What will happen to me, when…?

What will happen to Eve?

Her stomach is cramping, and her head still tingles with an icy static, blackness edging her vision. Her breasts are changing, too, Eve's suckling hardening them, making them sore to the touch. Glancing at the sleeping Eve, she stands, pulls the knife from her sheath and walks over to the motionless man, nudges him once, twice, three times with her boot. Nothing. Dead. Looks at his inscrutable face. Does he dream, still?

She crouches, pushes his head to one side and examines the wound in his neck, below his ear. Black and ragged and wet. His pitiless dark eyes regard her with a cold indifference. She shivers. Even the long-ago swine, butchered and cooked, hollow-eyed and sightless, observed her with less enmity.

She decides. Places the knife-edge behind one ear — bracing his head with a knee and tugging on the meaty flap of flesh — and starts cutting with a sawing motion. The springy meat soon pulls free with a snap and rests in her palm, like some sort of shabby pastry, a sticky breakfast Danish. She flips his head to the other side and extracts the other ear.

The fire is dying. Ears in hand, she walks to the dwindling flames, pats and tamps them down with her boot so that there is just a small bank of glowing coals and embers. She fetches her small fry pan, places the ears in them, and positions the pan on the coals. And waits. Checks on Eve, sleeping still. Quiet, calm, content. Checks on the ears, crisping slowly in the pan. Her stomach roils in distress, as does her head.

The stars stare down like icy eyes, glinting shards of secret knowledge. To the east a band of indigo is rising up to purple the sky like a fresh plum.

Fragments crowd her thoughts, of times past and recent; hazy and hot, a child clenching to her then slipping free in the chaos; a dead dog dreaming; a smiling swine; and Eve. She'd lost a child once, she now knows. She won't lose another.

She looks at her hands, turns them front to back, seeing the wear, the small scars and nicks, the chipped and worn fingernails. She clenches them, and sees their strength, too. A lifetime of use. And sometimes that lifetime isn't long. She brings her hands to her face and sobs into them, deep and wracking. And freeing. She will lay her anguish bare.

A sudden shock of pain in her head makes her flinch. She blinks, stares at the fire. Wrapping the handle in cloth, she pulls the pan from the fading coals and waits as it cools. The ache in her stomach is constant and obstinate, unending. Like grief. Thinking of Eve, and looking up at the shrewd stars, she plucks the blackened flesh from the pan, shoves it in her mouth, chews, and forces it down. Then she rolls over on her side, clutching her abdomen, weeping, letting all her sorrow leak out.

A squawking noise brings her quickly back up to her feet. She moves over to Eve, but Eve is sleeping still, little chest rising and falling with each little breath. Another squawk from behind her and she turns to see the comm-plate where she'd dropped it, forgotten, its screen glowing now amid the darkness. She picks up the device, squints at the sudden brightness. There are words emanating from the comm-plate, over and over, a repeating loop, faint but discernible.

There you are. Look at you. There you are. Look at you. There you are look at you. There you are look at you. There you are look at you. There-youarelookatyou. Thereyouarelookatyou. Thereyouarethereyouarethereyouare.

"Hello," she utters. "Hello. Will you speak to me? Hello. Are you there? Will you speak to me, please?"

But the comm-plate continues its monotonous drone, repeating the same phrase again and again and again. She presses the screen, and it powers down. She packs it away with the fry pan, scoops up Eve, and though still mostly dark, with dawn just cresting, she walks toward the river. Briefly, she thinks of the man lying dead behind her. But only briefly.

When she reaches the river, morning has broken orange and bright like an egg. She's momentarily dazzled by the sun. Eve is awake, squirming, making blubbing sounds. She puts Eve and her pack down, fills her canteen and drinks deeply, greedily. She wets her fingers and dribbles water onto Eve's lips, watches her mouth respond. She fills the canteen again, caps it and puts it away.

By the riverbank she sits and pulls Eve to her chest to suckle. The river flows languid, unhurried and unceasing. She feels its pull. Eve nurses, insistent, and she can feel Eve's mouth on her hard breast pulling sustenance from her. She can feel her own stomach, queasy and unsettled.

Satisfied, Eve pulls free, stares at her unblinking, eyes bright like marbles.

With her last half blanket and some river water she manages to clean and change Eve. Her head is prickling inside, as if tiny electric stingers are poking the meat of her brain. She looks around at the glinting river, the blooming sun, the distant forsaken fields and trees. The air smells of grass and earth. Then, as if in a dream, a bird soars silently past above her and disappears into the horizon.

She takes the comm-plate from her pack, presses the screen. It illuminates immediately.

"There you are. Look at you."

She laughs.

A pain behind her eyes and everything darkens. She presses the medical symbol on the screen.

"What assistance may we offer you today, Hamida?"

Hamida? Is that her name? She'd never considered her name, herself. Perhaps this isn't even *her* comm-plate. No matter, she liked it. *Hamida.* Liked the sound of it. It felt good. She smiles. "Hamida," she says.

"What assistance may we offer you today, Hamida?"

"Food," she says. "We need food." And everything, she thinks, peering at Eve. "Medicine, too."

"There is a temporary reintegration center 3.4 kilometers south from your present location. Follow the map on your screen."

Reintegration. Into what, she thinks. What's left?

South. The river runs south, and the map now on her screen shows the way. They can follow the river.

She drinks from the canteen again, refills it, and packs it away. Affixes her ragged mask to her face. Gathering Eve and her pack, she heads south, along the riverbank. She enjoys the sound of the water, almost musical, drowning out the buzz in her head. She likes the scent of dirt and earth in the air. There's a sudden sharp recollection of a rainy day and the smell of worms in the air. And she wonders if it's her own memory as a child, or that other child. Wonders if her memories will return. The air has that earthy quality to it now. But it's sunny and bright, not a rain cloud in sight. She misses the rain. Misses a lot of things.

That other child.

Powerless to stop it, a surge of melancholy overtakes her, forcing her to stop and catch her breath. She turns around, looking back to the north. She pulls Eve up, kisses her forehead, says "I love you. No matter what. I love you," then turns and walks south again.

Time has no reference point to her anymore, but she figures it's been about an hour of walking when they crest a small rise and see the large domed shelter in the distance. Here, the river angles away slightly to the east. There's a vast open meadow of tall grass in front of them. They'll have to cross it to get close to the shelter. She consults the comm-plate. That has to be the reintegration center.

Briefly she sits. The sky is beginning to cloud over. The river continues to sing to her. Eve smiles. She bounces Eve up and down on her lap.

"Hush little baby, don't say a word. Mama's going to … Mama's going to…" She looks to the south, to the dome. "Mama's going to…"

Standing, she pulls on her pack, cradles Eve, and begins to cross the meadow. The long grass is dry but still alive. Bent but not broken.

As they near the dome she sees activity, people moving around the perimeter. She crouches low in the grass. Men, women, children. Lined up at tables. Some of the children are playing, chasing each other. Hears them, too. Laughing.

Don't look back, she thinks. And she doesn't as she stands and walks the last few hundred feet.

And there is a woman at the very first table with a smile and a kindly face who looks up at her and says, "There you are."

"Yes." She's trembling.

"I'm Aiko," the woman says. "Can I ask your name?"

She blinks, remembering. "Hamida." Savors it. "I'm Hamida."

"Welcome, Hamida." Kindness in the woman's voice. "What's your baby's name?"

She looks at Eve. *My baby.* Looks at the woman, Aiko, smiling expectantly. "Eve," she says.

"Pretty. And a daughter. It must be nice to have a daughter."

"It is," she says, voice croaking. "It's the most wonderful thing in this world."

"You're safe now," Aiko says. "You and your daughter."

Her head pulses with pain. Her heart fills. "Thank you," she says, because she can think of nothing else to say. And then it's raining, softly. A gentle summer shower pattering all around them.

"Finally," Aiko says. "And you can remove your mask. It's okay. Really."

Hand shaking, faltering, she peels the mask away. She lifts her face to the sky, lets the rain wash down her dirty cheeks, dribble off her chin. Lifts Eve up. Eve squeals in delight or distress. She hugs her tight.

Aiko says, "Can I see your comm-plate? I'll return it right away. Promise."

She passes the device over. Aiko presses the screen, studies the result, hands the comm-plate back. "You better get inside. Follow the orange line." Smiles. "It was lovely seeing you. Good luck."

She smiles, and again can think of nothing else to say but "Thank you."

Inside is a hub of activity. Eve is quiet, alert. Rain drums a melody on the dome, melodious and haunting. And she's so tired, fatigue shackling her. The pain in her head is unceasing, vibrating through her like an electrical current. Her vision is dimming, dark edges closing in.

She follows the orange line to a medical tent, and is greeted and welcomed and placed on a cot, where she collapses. Someone reaches for Eve, but she finds some small reserve of strength and holds her tight.

She thinks she hears a voice, far off. "All right," says the voice. "We won't harm your baby. We'll take care of her."

Her voice is thick and choked. "P-Promise?"

"Yes."

And she believes it. Can feel it. "Hungry," she says.

"Feed your baby. We'll check back shortly."

She pulls Eve to her, and Eve feeds, her tiny body a comforting weight. She closes her eyes. The darkness now is a comfort. And soon she must be sleeping, then dreaming, because the pain is receding, her fatigue lifting, her hunger diminishing. In the dark in her head she pictures another child from some other time. *I'm sorry,* she whispers. *I love you.* And now she feels only the small presence of Eve, resting and sleeping too. Does she dream?

She gently squeezes Eve, strokes her back. *There you are,* she thinks. *Look at you.*

Above her she can hear the rain, a steady rhythm like the beat of a heart. And then the cadence slows, slows … and … stops.

She's finally at rest.

TO THE PROGENY FORSAKEN

GWENDOLYN KISTE

It's Saturday morning when the thing without a soul shows up at my door, her lips curled into a devious smile.

Barbed wire twists in my chest, and I'm almost too dizzy to stand. "Hello, Stevie," I say at last.

"Hi, dad," she says, and slips into the kitchen for some milk and cookies.

I stand aside in the hallway, my back pressed into the wall, thinking how I should warn her that the skim milk's long gone sour. But then I remember she won't notice either way. That kid can consume anything. Rotten scraps, a still-beating heart. Hell, she could probably swallow a galaxy if she ever got the chance.

"I just can't deal with her anymore," her mother says when I call her. "Plus, it's your turn. Consider this payback for all the weekends you didn't come pick her up."

And with that, the line goes dead.

Stevie's in the kitchen doorway now, looking pretty as a picture. Looking nothing on the outside like she looks on the inside.

"Can we order pizza?" she asks, as a crack in the plaster opens up wide, and the entire building trembles a little.

"Sure," I say, not wanting to argue with her, not knowing what she'll do if I say no.

Stevie's thirteen. An impossible age under the best of circumstances. An age made even more impossible by who she is. What she is. As though any of us has ever figured that out.

No school will take her, not anymore. Not after the last place where in a single afternoon, she shorted out the entire electrical system and turned a gymnasium to ash.

The principal tried to sue us, but since nobody was killed—and nobody could quite explain how a little girl could be responsible for tying every wire in the walls into heart-shaped bows—they let the whole thing slide, provided we never let her set foot on school property again.

"They already taught me everything they could," Stevie said with a sharp laugh, as she watched me and her mother on the other side of the attorney's long, polished table. Getting the school to drop the case cost me the last of my savings, the last shreds of what I'd made with my band in days almost too long ago to remember now. We had sky-high hair and sky-high egos and not nearly enough talent to match.

When she was younger, Stevie would always giggle and point at me on the faded album covers.

"Look at your fluffy bangs, Dad," she'd say, and I couldn't help but smile.

It's night now, Stevie's favorite time. It's her most restless time too.

"She's fine during the day," her mother would tell me on the rare occasions I bothered to check in. "Sometimes, you'd swear she could almost pass for normal. But not at night. Strange things happen with her at night."

I'd always hold my breath. "Like what?"

"It's hard to explain," her mother would say, and I'd do my best not to laugh, because when it comes right down to it, everything about Stevie is hard to explain.

My apartment only has one bedroom, so I set Stevie up inside the walk-in closet. A nest of old sheets and a moth-eaten sleeping bag I used to take camping, back when I did anything that didn't involve regret and the bottom of a bottle.

I hand her a sweat-stained pillow, at least a month overdue for the laundromat. "This is the best I've got."

"It's fine," she says, pulling the sleeping bag up around her chin.

I leave her alone, but after an hour, I peek inside the closet, and she's looking up at me, wide-eyed.

"Will you read me a story?" she asks, and I stare back at her, suspicion boiling in my chest.

"Aren't you a little old for that?"

She scoffs. "Nobody's too old for a story, Dad."

I don't have any books in the whole place—I hocked them all for pennies a long time ago and then drank down the pennies on my favorite barstool—so I'll have to improvise.

I pick out one I barely remember from when I was just a boy. About the girl with long hair trapped in a tower.

"Does the princess get away at the end?" Stevie asks.

"Of course," I say.

She crosses her arms and smiles, snuggling deeper into the sleeping bag. "Then I like this story."

Stevie looks like a normal girl. That's what everybody says when they find out about her. When they see what she can do with no more than a flick of a wrist.

"I would never have guessed," they say, their quivering hands folded in their laps, their lips pursed politely. They pretend not to care, pretend she's still just a little girl, even as they collect their own children and never let them play with Stevie again, never let them so much as look her in the eye.

It should feel like a lonely life, but Stevie doesn't mind. Or at least she never grumbles about it.

Her mother, on the other hand, has plenty of complaints.

"You need to help," she's said to me more times than I can count, and I always promise to do better, even though I never do.

But that's what I'm trying to fix now. It doesn't matter I have no fucking clue what I'm doing. Maybe even guessing at this parenting thing is better than nothing.

When I go to wake Stevie in the morning, there's something waiting there to greet me, something that stops me cold.

It's webbing, thick as muslin, sticky as honey. And it's covering the entire closet doorway. I take a step closer before I see them there. The spiders, all caught in their own webs, their legs in a tangle, their bodies still writhing in agony. There must be a hundred of them, maybe more, as though in the night, she called out to every arachnid in the building, just to inflict this unceremonious end on them.

I clean them up with an old washrag and flush their carcasses down the toilet. It seems like the most merciful thing to do.

At breakfast, Stevie eats the last of the stale bakery cookies and slurps down the rest of the sour milk. Now all that's left in the house is a flat two-liter bottle of Pepsi and a six pack of Pabst Blue Ribbon.

"Drinking your calories again, I see," she says as she stares into the grimy refrigerator.

I start to sneer, ready to tell her she's the reason, that having a monster for a daughter will do this to a man, any man, even a decent man, not that anybody would ever accuse me of being that. But then her dark eyes flick up at me, and I bite my tongue, thinking better of it.

We sit together in front of the tube TV and watch reruns of *Gilligan's Island* and *The Beverly Hillbillies*. Stevie snickers at every joke, even the ones I don't understand. She probably doesn't understand them either. She just likes to laugh. Everything's so funny when you can crush the whole world on a whim.

The morning gives way to afternoon, our lives dissolving around us, until Stevie glances at me, her eyes bright.

"Pizza again for lunch?" she asks, and I don't argue.

There's a knock on the apartment door, and I try to get there first. Anything to keep my neighbors from finding out she's here. But Stevie's too quick for me. She swipes my last twenty off the counter and skips to the door.

"Hello," she says, and gives the delivery boy a big smile. He can't help but grin back at her. Stevie can be charming when she wants to be.

That's what makes her dangerous.

In the evening, after we've gobbled up a whole extra-large pizza ourselves, I shove the cardboard box into a garbage bag and drag it outside. The landlady catches me in the alley, smoking my last Marlboro.

"You've got a visitor, don't you?" she asks.

I take a long drag off my cigarette. "Sure," I say. "Is there some law against that?"

"No, but maybe there should be." She glares at me, one eye squinted shut. "It's her, isn't it? It's your daughter."

A knot tightens in my throat. "It'll all be fine," I say, but we both know it's a lie.

⸺⸺◆⸺⸺

On Monday morning, all the walls on every floor split from the inside out, and the stairwell grows long, gray tendrils. Like something that's alive. Like tentacles.

By Monday afternoon, the other tenants have fled the building.

"I thought you told us she would never come here," says the old blue-haired lady who lives down the hall, and all I can do is shrug helplessly.

"I wasn't expecting her," I say, as if that's an excuse.

Everybody in town knows about my little girl. Some of them have only heard the rumors, but plenty of them have seen her in action. A bluebird that plummets out of nowhere to peck at the eyes of a cruel teacher. A streetlight that crushes the car of her adversary. (Who knew thirteen-year-olds could have such mortal enemies?)

A condition of my lease here was that Stevie would never be allowed to visit.

So much for that.

Not that this place has any right to be choosy. The heat only works half the time, and the roof leaks like clockwork in almost every apartment. But it was the only building in town that would take me, and while I'd like to blame Stevie for that, it's mostly my fault. It was the same everywhere I went. A revolving door of girls and gin and good times. Holes punched in the plaster, stereos turned up to eleven at three in the morning. It was supposed to be fun. What's the harm in that? For years, I've always told myself I'm filled with good intentions, but let's face it: at best, I'm filled with neutral intentions.

I watch out the window as the last family rushes across the street to their beat-up Gremlin and speeds off into the day.

"Are they all gone now?" Stevie asks, her gaze fixed on the TV screen.

"Yes," I say.

She smiles. "Good."

It's Wednesday when a giant chasm opens in the middle of the living room.

"Oops," Stevie says, as she tiptoes around it.

"You just can't help yourself, can you?" I ask, and she only giggles.

In the afternoon, she's digging under the couch, trying to reach the lost remote, when she finds an old, dusty box.

"What's this?" She flips open the lid, and a stack of Polaroids spills out on the matted carpet, their corners dog-eared and date-stamped.

I sit cross-legged next to her and pluck the photos from the heap, one by one, narrating as I go.

"This is from the day you were born," I say. "At the hospital nursery."

"I know." She brushes it aside, as though trying to forget her own beginning. "You weren't there when I arrived."

"I was on the road," I say, but that isn't true. That's just what I always pretended. In reality, I was holed up in a no-tell motel with some gorgeous redhead whose name I never did learn while Stevie's mother was delivering a baby I never did want.

"She was pretty." Stevie holds up a couple pictures of her mother, all rosy-cheeked and bright smiles, and I nod, because she *was* pretty. At least until I got hold of her and drained every last drop of hope out of her eyes.

There are more pictures here than I remember. Nearly every one of Stevie's birthdays. Sometimes, that was the only day of the year I bothered to see her. Her mother always invited me to the parties, and we always made a spectacle of ourselves, griping or screaming or even just sulking at each other, while our little girl watched, a paper hat on her head, a strange expression in her eyes.

"When did you know you were going to leave us?" Stevie asks, her voice steady and disarming.

I hesitate. "Even before you were born."

"I figured." Stevie thumbs through images of her third birthday, her mother always standing off to the side, a dour look on her face. "Did you ever love her?"

"No," I say.

"Didn't think so."

I fold my hands in my lap and wait for the next question. About whether or not I love my own daughter. But she says something else instead.

"Why do you keep all these pictures?"

I think about it for a second before shaking my head. "Don't know."

After Stevie nestles down for the night in her sleeping bag, I return alone to the broken living room and look through the Polaroids again.

More photos from when she was born. From when she turned two. From her first ballet recital, where I showed up with whiskey on my breath and a barmaid on my arm. I shuffle through a hundred photographs, probably more, before I realize there's no image of me holding her. Not when she was a baby, not when she was older either. Even now, I never get too close. How are you supposed to embrace something that could destroy you in an instant?

At the bottom of the pile, tucked away from the others, is Stevie's sixth birthday party, the one we held at the park. That was the day the first crack in the public swimming pool appeared. The first time we started to suspect what she could do. The same day her mother and I got into a screaming match so loud that somebody called the cops, and I tossed Stevie's Pound Puppies birthday cake at the arresting officer, laughing when he couldn't get the buttercream icing off his navy blue slacks.

Happy birthday, Stevie.

I dump the pictures back in the box and shove it as far under the couch as I can. Then I sit in the dark and wonder how I ended up here.

By Thursday morning, the whole building collapses out from under us. We make it out in time, but only because Stevie wakes me first.

"Come on, Dad," she whispers, the same way she used to when I'd take her to amusement parks, and she'd find a ride she liked.

"This way, this way," she would say, and she says that again today, as she motions me down the fire escape, carrying my boots for me, while I stumble bleary-eyed after her.

We're outside for less than a minute before the place lurches once before turning to dust around us.

"What now?" I ask, my life no more than rubble at our feet.

"Let's drive," she says and tosses me the car keys I never thought to grab.

It's a long road out of town, thin and winding, but Stevie doesn't notice. She just keeps fumbling with the radio, shifting between stations.

"Hey, listen, Dad," she says and turns up the dial. It takes a moment before I recognize it. My voice, the me I used to be. This was my band's only hit single, the slim residuals just enough to keep the lights on in my apartment.

Or it was enough back when I still had things like an apartment and lights and a life.

Next to me, Stevie bobs back and forth in the passenger seat.

At first, I think she's only teasing me. Her silly, aging father with his silly, aging music. But then I see it there. The brightness in her eyes, the sweet grin on her face. She's proud of me. My little girl is proud of me.

Outside the city limits, people don't know about Stevie. It's a small town we left behind, a flea speck on a map, and nobody out here has ever heard about the odd girl with the inexplicable talent.

We drive for hours before finally checking into a dusty roadside motel in the middle of the desert. I don't remember a desert being so close to our town, but everywhere we go, it seems like Stevie is leeching the color out of the land.

"Thirty dollars a day," says the blank-faced woman at the front desk, and I pay with the only Visa I haven't maxed out yet.

The room's got two beds, and Stevie picks the one she likes best, jumping up and down on the mattress, squealing with delight. Within a minute, the wallpaper in the corners is starting to peel, and the ceiling above us is sagging a little. Wherever Stevie roams, destruction follows.

The television in the motel room is all static, and I hit the top of it with my fist three times, as though that will make a difference.

"I hate this place," I say, but we both know it's something else I'm hating right now.

Stevie sits back on the bed, her knees drawn into her chest, all the joy drained from her face. "You want to tell me this is my fault. That what I am turned you into what you are."

I don't say anything, but in a way, that's more than enough of an answer.

Stevie grits her teeth, and I'm sure she's going to break me in two. It takes a long time for me to realize she's not fighting back rage. She's fighting back tears.

"You know that's not true," she whispers.

I seize up, everything in me going numb. "I know," I say finally.

I've blamed her for years, and it's been easy to do. She's an easy way out. But I was always like this, long before her mom and I split up. That's why we split up.

The static keeps buzzing on the television, the past hanging heavy between us.

"You're right, though," she says at last. "I can't help it. I try to stop myself, but it just keeps on happening. Like I'm the weather, and nothing can change that."

I nod, not looking at her. I shouldn't even be surprised. Of course, this is how she turned out. She needs all the defenses she can get in the world I tossed her into. A world where I rarely bothered to leave a forwarding address. I'm not even sure how her mother found me to drop her off on Saturday.

Or maybe it was Stevie who found me. Maybe she ran away to be with me. The way we should have always been together.

It's almost midnight when she asks me for another story.

"I'm too tired tonight, Stevie."

"That's all right," she says, her body coiling up on her bed. She looks so small, no bigger than the little girl from all those ill-fated birthday parties. The little girl I wanted to forget.

The little girl who refused to be forgotten.

In the morning, all the phones in the motel have gone dead. So has my cell, and when I trek to the front desk to find out why, nobody's there. No cars left in the parking lot either, not even ours.

"Where are they?" I ask, a sharp breeze chilling me to the bone.

"They've run off," Stevie says, her eyes set on the horizon. "They're smart."

We've got nowhere else to go now, so together, we walk across the dusty desert. Overhead, thick, violet clouds move in, and the air turns electric and alive. This is Stevie's doing. There might not be any world left beyond this moment. Or if there is, it's not a world she wants to return to.

"We're alike, you know," she whispers.

I nod. "I know."

For years, I've silently accused her of being destruction incarnate, but that's all I've been too. Except I destroyed everything in ways people could brush aside. *Boys will be boys,* they always say, like that's an excuse. Like that makes it all right.

But Stevie wasn't the same as me. She destroyed everything in ways nobody could ignore.

I envy her for it. And I'm proud of her too.

There's a strange, dry heat whipping around us now, and I feel it coming. A blaze that won't be quelled. It's growing stronger by the minute, and this fire isn't coming from below. It's coming from above. Like lightning from the gods. Soon, there might not be anything left.

Stevie turns to me, an arcane flickering in her face. "You don't have to stay, Dad," she says and means it. She'd let me run. As fast and as far as I can. After all, it's the one thing I'm good at.

The flames are here now, and they're climbing higher, the desert turned a brilliant orange, the warmth almost too much to bear. But I won't move. I won't leave her again.

When she realizes I'm not going anywhere, a small smile blooms on her face, and she reaches out for me. With the violet clouds sinking nearer, I hesitate, the weight of my whole life in this moment, the weight of everything I should have done but didn't.

I want to say I'm sorry. I want to tell her that I love her, that I've always loved her, even though it's never been enough. Even though it's too late.

But I don't do any of that. Instead, I reach out for her too, and we settle down in the burning sand together.

"Tell me a story, Dad," she says and curls up on my lap.

"I know one," I say, as the fiery blaze singes the tips of my hair, and the horizon beyond us turns to black. "It's about a foolish king and his little girl and all the mistakes he makes. All the ways she has to pay for those mistakes."

My daughter looks up at me, the darkness of the universe dancing in her eyes. "Does the princess get away at the end?"

I smile back at her. "Yes," I whisper, "she does."

"Then I like this story," Stevie says, her long arms wrapped around me, and as the sky turns to fire, and the world around us melts away to nothing, I hold her a little closer.

THE OTHER CAT

ANYA MARTIN

" *The Other Cat* is on the bed," my mother says, coming into the living room. She's still in her day clothes—at least three layers too many of shirt, pullover, vest, and cardigan with sweatpants and thick fluffy socks. It's November and chilly outside, but the heat is on at such a high temp that I can barely cope in a T-shirt, curled on the couch with my tablet.

I see her eyes drift to her Siamese cat Henry, his back turned towards me on the opposite end of the couch. He never sits on my lap.

"Emma, I worry," Mother adds. I am always relieved when she remembers my name. "If Henry meets *The Other Cat*, they might fight."

I don't answer because I don't know what I should say. I know I'm not supposed to correct her, even if it means lying, not supposed to tell her that there's only Henry.

Mother abruptly heads for the kitchen. Henry leaps down and races ahead of her. I worry he'll trip her, feel relief when I hear her pouring water and Henry meowing loudly, not the crash of human limbs collapsing, leading to the inevitable broken hip, the sharp physical decline, the nursing home. I dread that outcome for the guilt, try to squelch the notion that it also would give me back my freedom.

When after five minutes the electric teakettle doesn't begin its metallic whir, and Henry's meowing becomes ever more insistent, I force myself up. I find her struggling with the teapot's switch, the hungry cat a Greek chorus to her frustration. The problem is immediately clear to me—it's not plugged in. I take the pot from her gently, connect it to the countertop outlet, then remove a cat food can from the refrigerator and place several spoonfuls into Henry's bowl.

Henry now quiet and eating, I turn to see Mother has managed to find a cup, saucer, and teaspoon. I select a bag of decaf Lady Grey from the tin next to the stove and hand it to her. The teakettle sputters to a stop, and its orange light blinks off. She reaches to pour, but I ease in and take the kettle before her hand touches it. I don't want her to accidentally burn herself. I never know exactly what she'll need help with, just that she usually does need help.

I follow her back to the living room, put the cup and saucer down on a tray table. Mother follows and sits down in her leather recliner, winds the teabag around her spoon, squeezing out every drop. She picks up a slim paperback from the bookshelf next to her chair. *The Tao of Pooh*. She has been reading it for weeks. For a little while, she is quiet and I pretend she is the same mother that she has always been. I return to catching up with emails.

"It's really amazing, Emma," she says after a while, the paperback still in her hands.

"What's amazing?!" I ask softly, thinking she is going to tell me about something she read in the book.

"It's amazing that everything looks the same. How is it that *The People* at the hospital can make a duplicate of our house."

"You are at home," I say. The truth slips out this time before I can stop it, habit prevailing over the expert advice. Yet it seems cruel to let her think she's in the hospital. Almost a year has passed since her cancer surgery, months since the chemo and the bloodwork that gave her the all-clear, at least for now.

"It's amazing how *They* paid attention to every detail, how *They* could find an exact copy of the bureau from Grandfather's house, the mirror, the table, Aunt Delia's paintings, all of our family photos," my mother says.

My phone vibrates, notifying me of a text. I glance down to see it's my boyfriend Jeremy sending a silly meme.

I grin and type "Ha-Ha," and realize my mother is staring at me, waiting for some kind of reply.

"Also it's not *our* house, it's *your* house," I say, immediately regretting that I cannot just live in her moment. But it makes me feel uncomfortable, like I am trapped instead of being here voluntarily to care for her after her hospitalization, that I am a middle-aged divorced childless only child returning to my parents' house, relatives few and distant, with a vague future contingent on an unsteady freelance job and a boyfriend across the country. As for friends, I haven't seen any in weeks. A night out means finding a dependable "sitter," usually through an agency, and Mother disliking whoever is sent and refusing to go to bed until she knows I am back "home" safely.

"Of course, it's *our* house, you're going to inherit it when I am gone," Mother says, sipping her tea.

Henry has now crept from the sofa to Mother's lap. She strokes his back, and he purrs loudly—a steady hum that sounds dangerously electric.

"That won't be any time soon," I say. "The doctor said you're cancer-free."

My phone vibrates.

<hey, sweet cheeks what r u doing>

<sitting with my mom>

<you need to <cum> here>

<working on finding someone to look after her>

<just do it Em>

<wish it was that easy, miss you baby>

The text stream ends there. Before my mom's hospitalization, I flew out to see Jeremy almost every month. When my mother was in the hospital, he checked on me ten times a day or more, put heart emojis on my replies, took my calls while she was sleeping. I had hoped he'd fly out after she was discharged, not so much to help, but to hold me at night. But he never did, not then nor later.

My anxious thoughts are interrupted by the soft mumble of Mother reading Winnie the Pooh's philosophy aloud to herself, like a child needing to pronounce each word to understand it. Henry continues to purr, his brown tail flicking back and forth. I follow its twisty motion to his shadow on the floor. Some trick of the light transforms it into two tails, twitching in a parallel pattern.

There is no *Other Cat*.

There is *one* cat.

Henry the applehead Siamese I found in a Craigslist ad who looked so much like our first cat Prospero, he could almost be his twin. My parents had acquired Prospero as a kitten, about a year before I was born, and Mother had always had a special bond with him. Our family had no more dogs since Captain passed just after Daddy. I didn't think my mom could handle a big dog, and she wouldn't have a small one because she was convinced they yapped too much. So I thought let's go back to the beginning, get her a cat again. Henry bonded with Mother immediately, planted himself constantly in her lap, and they became inseparable.

A week later, he bit her hand.

Hard.

From her wrist to her knuckles, it swelled up like a balloon, necessitating the first trip to the emergency room. Eight hours and a slow drip of IV antibiotics, followed by oral meds. She was still my mother when I dropped her back at her house. I hadn't sold mine yet to move in and care for her.

Perhaps I should have insisted that Mother send Henry back to his former owners right then, the ones in the big house who rehomed him because the wife's Pekingese attacked him incessantly. The wife also declawed him, and the combination of these two facts quite possibly explain why he panicked sometimes with little warning, why he bit so hard.

But Mother and Henry had bonded, and when he curled up in her lap, she didn't believe he'd bite her again. He bit her two more times, two more trips to the ER, before I convinced her primary care doctor to prescribe her antibiotic pills to have on hand and dispense immediately.

Henry's arrival occurred six months before the last day I would ever have a normal conversation with my mother. Before she had the sudden fever, spent a week in the hospital, "sundowned" for the first time, came out different. I had never heard the term before, but as a nurse explained to me, it was so named because elderly patients began to act strangely usually late in the day. The nurses did not know why it happened to some people and not to others. Sometimes medications were a factor, or low white blood cell count due to an infection, or maybe simply the environmental change—the hospital itself.

Two weeks later, Mother was admitted again for cancer surgery, stayed 16 more days, *sundowned* every night except the first one when she was still exhausted from the surgery. A big part of her strange agitation involved fretting about Henry. She'd insist she should be allowed to leave the hospital and visit him. Or he should be allowed to visit her despite it being completely nonsensical to think that cats would be allowed in the hospital. She'd hear him in the hallway and would jump up, straining her IV cords, to make sure he didn't get run over by a car, another thing that couldn't possibly happen in the hospital. And on my birthday, she got livid at me for "lying" to her that Henry was at home and became convinced he was dead. While I left briefly to have dinner with friends, Mother got in a physical fight with a nurse. I was told it took two security guards to get her back in bed, where she was force-fed a Haldol, a heavy-duty antipsychotic drug usually dispensed to schizophrenics, without consulting me. It was the worst birthday of my life.

"Have you heard from Mama? I think we should call her."

"It's too late to call," I say. "She'll already be in bed."

"Mama" is her mother, my grandmother. She has been dead for—I do the math in my head—twenty-five years.

"We need to call her in the morning then," Mother says.

"You should change into your nightgown, get ready for bed," I say, setting down my tablet on the coffee table. I know I'm not getting anything more done until she settles down. I hope tonight she won't wander, just sleep.

Mother puts the book back on the shelf.

"Come on, sweetie," she says to Henry.

He meows in mild complaint as she stirs, but leaps off her lap.

When we get to my mother's bedroom, illuminated dimly by the hallway light, I think I see a dark lump on her comforter and wonder how Henry could have sneaked by me. But when I switch on the ceiling light, the bed is empty.

I hear Henry's distinctive meow. He scurries by my legs and leaps onto the multiple layers of quilts and comforters, as Mother trails him into the bedroom.

My mother's nightgown is neatly folded under her pillow. Perhaps her "Mama" taught her to do that. The experts say that the earliest memories will stick around the longest. I hand it to her and she changes on her own, complaining of the cold as she removes layer after layer. I let her retain her sweatpants and socks, and remind her to brush her teeth.

While Mother is in the bathroom, I pick up a complaining Henry and take him back to the kitchen, replenish his dish. I shut the door to the hall, leaving him to wander the main living area safely away from Mother's bedroom. We have an agreement that he cannot sleep with Mother just in case he might bite her at night, though if she wanders, he sometimes slips in anyway.

I tuck Mother in, and she asks me if I can hear "*The People*" singing outside in the neighbor's garden. She wakes me up sometimes and asks me to go out and tell them to be quiet.

"They're just practicing for the opera," I say. "They should be done soon. They need their sleep to be at their best in their performance tomorrow."

Since the experts say it's OK to lie, I am trying hard to at least do so cleverly.

"I love you, Emma," Mother says.

"I love you, too, Mother, now get some sleep."

I can feel her wanting me to stay, searching for words to keep me in her room, as if she is afraid to be alone.

Before Mother can speak again, I kiss her on the cheek and turn out the light because I can't be there any longer. I need this time at night to decompress, read a book, watch a TV show, eventually sleep.

When I get upstairs to my bedroom, Jeremy texts his usual:

<what u thinking about babe>

<more singing outside her window>
<that's too bad because i am thinking of>

He tells me and I heart his comments, even though I want to tell him how mortally tired I am, how I want to cry, and how, as awful and selfish as it seems, my tears are mostly for myself.

"Come and see the fish climbing up the tree," my mother calls from the kitchen.

I find her looking out the window, a bowl of cereal with berry yoghurt and chopped banana in her hand. Breakfast is the only meal she remembers how to make, as long as I make sure the yoghurt cups are always on the right side of the top shelf of the refrigerator.

I glance out the window and see no fish, not even a chipmunk at the bird feeder.

Bowl still in hand, Mother heads to her recliner in the living room. I muse how once one hits a certain age, one chair becomes exclusively yours, always in front of the TV. Both my grandmothers had recliners, and so did Daddy until he passed away, five years ago now. I feel a pang of sadness that Mother hardly mentions him anymore—perhaps memories of her life with him are too recent. But why then does she remember me? Is it only because I am here and she sees me every day? Me and Henry.

I switch on the TV, find a nature documentary on meerkats I had saved on the DVR because she can't really follow any of her favorite narrative shows anymore. Plus any violence upsets her, so she doesn't enjoy the detective series she and my dad used to watch incessantly. Eventually she asks me to switch from the cute playful animals to CNN, and while I worry that the news also makes her agitated, I comply because I need to get some work done. I leave her the remote, and she increases the volume until it's so loud that I want to scream.

I duck out and back upstairs.

I barely log into my desktop computer, when Jeremy sends me a funny meme.

<Ha-Ha, perfect timing>

I spend the next hour googling for an appropriate meme response and find nothing that seems fresh or funny or provocative to send back to him.

"Emma!" Mother calls from downstairs.

I check my phone and realize it's already time to fix her lunch.

"I wish *The People* would stop asking me to give them necklaces," Mother says as I walk into her bedroom.

I was going to heat up a can of ravioli, a comfort food from my childhood and an easy lunch she seems to enjoy. After that I planned to see if she wanted to do a jigsaw puzzle because I'd read online that it could be a good activity for people with dementia. But it's clear how the afternoon is going to go. Mother is in the process of removing her jewelry, piece by piece, from the top drawer of her chiffonier and spreading it all over her bed. Henry sits in the midst of the endeavor, his legs curled under him in a pose that reminded me of a chicken sitting on eggs. Or those Kliban cartoons from the 70s—*is it a cat or is it a meatloaf?*

"Give who your necklaces?"

"*The People*. I don't see why they cannot wait and do this some other time."

"Which people? There aren't any people here. It's just us."

"And Henry," I add.

"Of course *The People* are here. The room is full of *People*. Stop talking nonsense, Emma."

I try a new tactic.

"I can't see any people so they must be ghosts."

Mother seems to puzzle my response, considering it far more reasonable than her previous rational self ever would have. So I continue.

"I mean, think about it logically, if only *you* can see *The People*, then they must be *ghosts*."

Mother stares at me, then back at the jewelry and then at Henry.

"Well, I wish *The Ghosts* would go away because the cats and I need to get some rest," Mother finally replies. "Can you call *The People* who get rid of *The Ghosts*?"

It takes me a moment to fully appreciate what she just suggested.

"Mother, did you really just ask me to call Ghostbusters?"

The joke, however, is completely lost on her. She turns back to fidgeting with the jewelry, mostly costume pieces so at least I don't need to worry about any heirlooms getting broken or misplaced. I take her hand, hoping my touch will calm her sorting frenzy.

"After lunch, I'll help you put it all back in the drawer."

Mother jerks her hand back and picks up a strand of clear glass and black beads. Before I grasp what she intends to do, she starts to put it over Henry's head. Henry sinks his teeth into her arm, catapults off the bed.

"Nooooooooo," I yell at him, chasing him out of the bedroom and all the way to the living room where he seeks refuge under the coffee table.

As I grab the first aid kit and the antibiotics from the linen closet, Jeremy texts:

<whats up?>
<catbite>
<again?>
<yeah>
<sorry babe>

"*The Police* are going to arrest you if you keep this up," Mother says. It's only just past 6 but she's changed into her nightgown and dressing gown already, and up to that moment, I have been thinking tonight I can fix her dinner and she'll just go to bed.

Henry circles her feet, meowing of course.

"What did I do?" I ask, at a loss for how to respond, opening the refrigerator to at least procure cat food and silence one of my sudden accusers.

"You need to be nicer to *The People*," Mother continues. "When you treat them like that, they will call *The Police*."

CNN blares in the other room, and I wonder if her sudden admonition is due to something she saw on the news. I take a deep breath and try to change the subject.

"Would you like a frozen pizza for dinner or shall I make a salmon salad with your favorite dressing—the pear Gorgonzola?"

"You can't talk to *The People* like that and expect them to like you," Mother says.

Henry is back, brushing against her leg. She reaches down and pets him.

"At least I have my beautiful sweet cats," she adds. "You should learn from them."

Mother heads into the living room. Henry looks back at me with a spiteful expression as he trails her. I peek to confirm she's in her chair, cat in lap, and then run upstairs, collapse on my bed.

Voices yell at me in my head.

The neuropsychologist says "you can't do this alone. You need to consider memory care, assisted living."

Mother says she wants to stay at home, implores me that "all I want to do is to spend time with you."

The home care agency scheduler warns "if you don't want full-time care, 9-5, it's hard to find a regular same caregiver."

My own voice interrupts. Now that Mother thinks it's a duplicate house, is it time to reconsider assisted living? But what about the recent articles in the newspaper about elder abuse at facilities.

A random woman at a college alumni event jovially declares: "She's your mother. She was here for you. Now it's your turn to be here for her."

Another stranger: "Caregivers need care, too."

Just as I feel like I am really going to scream this time, my cell phone buzzes. I spontaneously relax.

<jeremy you couldn't have texted at a more perfect moment>

<sorry but I have something important to tell u>

<r u ok?>

<this relationship isn't working>

I stare at the phone, surprised, not surprised, the tension back. This text isn't the one he should be sending me now.

I type furiously.

<wtf>

<know u got it tough with your mom but can't wait any more to tell u>

<if it's about me flying out to see u, really need a break. let me call my cousin beth. she said she wanted to visit, maybe she'd stay with her, give me a few days off>

<met this gal, pretty awesome, we really gel>

<or u could come here. hadn't suggested because it'd be weird with my mom but>

<it's done, sorry>

<i love u>

<sorry em>

I don't know how long I lie on my bed, except it's too long. I need to force myself to check on Mother, make her dinner. Bottle up my emotions, be the dutiful daughter.

When I get downstairs, the living room is empty. I grab the TV remote and switch off the maddening drone of an auto insurance commercial.

I can now hear the faint singing.

Mother's voice.

A lullaby she used to sing to me when I was little.

I follow the hallway to her bedroom, stop at the door.

Mother is sitting on her bed, Henry by her right side.

I blink to make sure I am seeing what I think I see.

The Other Cat, darker just like she told me, with a sleek, shimmery coat, on her left.

My mother is stroking both, one with each hand. Her eyes travel from cat to cat. Both cats are purring.

Henry raises his head and looks at me.

The Other Cat lifts its head, almost like a mirror image except its eyes are shiny silver, unlike Henry's ocean blue.

My mother looks up and smiles.

"Look at them. Aren't my cats beautiful?"

I don't know what to say. Henry is beautiful. *The Other Cat* is something else but I cannot say it is beautiful, and yet as I stare at its ebony coat, it becomes beautiful. Its texture not furry but like a black mirror, as if I stare into it long enough, I'll see my reflection.

I do see my reflection, only in the reflection, I am moving closer. Yet I am standing in the doorway and have not moved at all.

My mother, still smiling, glances to her left beyond The Other Cat as a mirror copy of me sits down next to her and also strokes The Other Cat.

"My daughter," she said. "Let's be kind to each *Other*."

Other Emma smiles, strokes Mother's hair with her right hand, *Other Cat* with her left. Mother starts to sing again. *Other Emma* sings along.

I look to Henry for sympathy, to see if he recognizes me in the doorway. Am I hallucinating, in shock after the upsetting exchange with Mother earlier followed by the break-up texts from Jeremy? Henry closes his eyes and resumes purring, more tranquil than I've ever seen him.

I'm not dreaming. I am replaced. I've given up my life for my mother and now she cannot even recognize me, tell me apart from *Other Emma*.

Should I turn and leave, pack my bags? Am I no longer needed? *Other Emma*, Henry, *Other Cat*, they can surely care for her now. Perhaps I can still salvage my relationship with Jeremy somehow. Perhaps I can again have nights out at the movies, restaurants, parties with friends, travels, work in an office, live in a house of my own, not the house I grew up in, haunted by all the ephemera of my parents' lives.

In the midst of my reverie of reclaiming my life, I realize *Other Emma* is gazing intently at me.

I don't know how long our eyes are locked, but still singing, she gently eases my mother's hand from her shoulder and back onto *Other Cat*, and rises. My mother returns to the reverie in which I had found her, stroking both cats.

Other Emma beckons me with her fingers.

I stiffen, want to run away, back up the hall, out the door, down the street, as fast, as far as my legs will take me, never look back.

Other Emma, this twin spectral sister I never had, beckons again.

And now suddenly I want to stay. I love my mother. I am afraid to leave her, that my decision to leave, to relinquish my protection, will bring upon her injury or death.

I step forward, tentatively at first and then almost leap to take *Other Emma*'s hands. What I grasp is not flesh, not hands as I knew human hands. Her fingers tingle, emit tiny sparks, just corporeal enough to grasp and for her to guide me to sit on the Henry side of (*our?*) Mother. Then she returns to her previous position.

We both stroke a cat and my mother's hair. Henry climbs onto my lap and *Other Cat* onto her lap. And I begin to sing, for I know the words, even those I had forgotten, having not heard the song since I was very small.

My mother turns first to smile at me and Henry, and then she smiles at *Other Emma* and *Other Cat*. And then she looks forward, still smiling, happier than I can remember seeing her in years.

The singing grows louder, joined by many more voices.

The room is full of people, some I recognize like my grandmother who I visited as a child and my grandfather who I only knew from photos, other relatives long dead and if still living, much younger than they should be now. Also figures I don't recognize, appearing, disappearing, mingling with each other, some feet on the ground, some floating, some solid, some bending like reflections in a funhouse mirror.

The People part to reveal a line of *Other Emmas* holding *Other Cats*—Siamese, Calico, Tabby, Persian, all kinds of cats. They each carry their cats to my mother. She strokes each, one by one, as *Other Emmas* present them and then deposit them on the bed, until the bed is full of *Other Cats* and the room full of *Other Emmas*. The cats meow and they all sound like Henry.

And when no room remains on the bed, they still press forward and the cats spill on top of each other, a mass of cats, not fighting, simply wriggling, making room for each other. I wonder how far the procession is lined up in the hallway. Is the entire house full of *Other Cats, Other Emmas*? What will happen when no space remains indoors?

Will they spill into the neighborhood?

Consume the city?

The universe?

I look towards the window, where as usual Mother hasn't drawn the curtains, left that task to me. Instead of night's darkness, a glow illuminates the trunk of the old oak tree outside, and yet it can't be morning already. The glow flickers, flaps, like a quilt in motion—no, not cloth but shiny scales. Schools of tiny fish swimming upwards. Cats leap through the window to catch them. My spectral sisters flex their toes like ballerinas, float up and gently pull cats away from the tree. The fish continue their ascent, replaced by more fish. *Other Cats, Other Emmas* sprout beneath.

The singing drops to a whisper that stretches outwards and inwards, and I sense it deep inside not only my ears but all of me, my bones and muscles transforming into the strings of a harp or perhaps the whiskers of a cat. The soft melody no longer sounds like a chorus of human voices but a harmony of purring cats.

I feel my lungs tighten as all the bodies crush into me. Even Henry squirms, and for a moment I think he might bite, but then he relaxes again. Mother's eyes are shut, her mouth open, wheezing as she does now when she sleeps.

I hug my mother and close my eyes.

LOVENEST

CLINT SMITH

On the pay channel, a man and a woman
Were trading hungry kisses and tearing off
Each other's clothes while I looked on
With the sound off and the room dark
Except for the screen where the color
Had too much red in it, too much pink.
— Charles Simic, "Paradise Motel"

The food here at La Cáscara—unlike the sex during their succinct courtship and brief marriage—was forgivably forgettable. Regardless, it was a suitable location for a negotiation.

Jackie had said that, if he would meet her—to just *hear her out*—that it'd be the last time he'd have to deal with her. *One last favor ... and you'll never see me again.* Neil had agreed under this premise alone. Not that he truly believed this would be Jackie's last scheme. Sitting across from his ex-wife in the booth, he listened to her explain the most recent financial predicament. "It was just a simple misunderstanding," she said, leaning forward. A tea candle set in a chintzy, red bistro globe flickered on the table between them.

The Mexican joint, La Cáscara, was what had once been a diner affixed to the open-air hotel, but now the economy lodging was derelict and undergoing evisceration, visible from the nearby highway.

This had, on several occasions, been one of their clandestine locales—a rendezvous in the nascent days of dating that was arousingly anonymous. Their eventual cohabitation and subsequent nuptials broke that spell. That, and the fact that Jackie simply could not be trusted.

She was now leaning over the table, the flickering light from the red-sconced bistro candle momentarily imparting a hypnotic effect. "Just think," her voice was husky, "do this for me and I'll be out of your life forever." The restaurant was lightly insulated with music, the style of *norteo*—the pleasant wheeze of accordions.

Neil genuinely doubted it. They'd been at this conversational juncture several times since their divorce. Neil knew plenty of people who'd gotten themselves into financial quicksand, but for the most part it was over-ambitious negligence. Not like Jackie. Neil's ex-wife was a fully-sentient grifter within the upper-middle-class milieu. Despite several close calls, Neil was grateful they'd never collaborated on children—an icy mercy, that.

Neil took a sip of the margarita and adjusted his posture on the booth's bench seat. Internally, he was conducting variations of articulating that she'd taken too much already—monetarily and otherwise. *This meeting is over.* But his rehearsed, uncharacteristically assertive script had disintegrated. He looked at his ex-wife. Cuticles of candlelight shone against the slick of her large eyes.

Neil blinked away from the woman who'd once been his companionable accomplice. An entirely different woman. Finally, he returned his eyeline to her and sighed. "It'll have to be cash."

She didn't blink, her words as tacky as nectar. "It's preferable, my love." Neil gave a single, grave nod. With seductive insouciance, Jackie took a sip of her drink.

After a time, the food arrived. Forgivably forgettable.

———◆·◆·◆———

It was only when Neil stood up from the booth that he realized the drinks had been a mistake. The interior of the restaurant listed. Together, he and Jackie wove through the dining room, paid (dutch) at the front counter, exited through the glassed-in vestibule and stepped into the November evening.

The air did nothing to sober Neil, but its bite provided a steadying effect. Night had essentially drawn itself up over the horizon, but there remained a purple pouch of light signifying that fleeting lifespan.

They'd both parked on the side of the restaurant, the parking spaces running parallel to the wide swipe of the two-story hotel. It appeared that the endeavor of gutting the hotel had, quite literally, halted mid-project. Work had clearly stalled out, and Neil had noticed the sign from the Department of Code Enforcement just off the parking lot: ORDER TO STOP WORK: Per Sec. 742-203: This Worksite Is In Violation of State and Local Codes. Pieces of furniture were stacked along the exterior, mattresses slumped against the walls. He could only imagine what violations had been encountered at this hole of a hotel.

Jackie dropped her purse on the passenger seat of her car. Neil was about to say something about making arrangements for Jackie to pick-up the money when his ex-wife briskly moved toward him and wrapped her arms around him.

He'd been here before: Jackie stinging him with some lingering gesture of false tenderness solely for the sentimental poison to remain in his system, engendering his continued pliability. The snare of her lair.

Under similar circumstances, this would be the moment that Jackie would attempt to impart a low-dose of guilt to her diluted solution. *We were so happy once, you remember? We didn't have to end this way.* Of course, by this point, her venomous prescription had grown predictable, and he made no illusions that she'd used similar conditional scripts on other men, and likely a few women, not only in the wake of their breakup but during the marriage itself. But now, there was something in the charge of her body, in her subtly plaintive posture, that signaled something else to Neil—an intimacy of expiration.

When no words emerged, Neil lifted his arms, embracing her with a squeeze he hoped would slacken the tautness of her hug. Jackie slowly slid away, a slim space between them.

Neil gently jammed his hands in his pockets and cleared his throat. "I'll be in touch about the money."

Jackie's eyes were glassy; she squinted against the night breeze. "I'll let you know when I'm coming, okay?" A smile, less predatory than usual. "You can leave the door unlocked for me." Neil snorted. An old joke.

Neil unlocked his car, opened the door and sank into the driver's seat. Engine on, the headlights illuminated the sidewalk which ran along the now-defunct hotel and its forsaken, two-story façade—an autopsy glow revealing details which did nothing to change the situation, but added a nuance of neglected hideousness.

The banks of doors and windows repeated with seedy symmetry. Hanging curtains, all drawn shut, for the most part, their stiff creases of shower-curtain cheapness.

Neil was about to put the car in reverse when he noticed Jackie down at the end of the sidewalk, still standing in front of her car. She stood facing away from him, unmoving, but something in the rigid set of her shoulders gave Neil the sense that she was intent on ... *something*. Neil squinted, scanning the walkway, trying to figure out what had her suddenly preoccupied. And then he saw the door.

Down at the end of the sidewalk, one of the hotel-room doors was slightly ajar, the slender aperture of several inches, the uniformity of the opened door was noticeable amid the identical rank of shuttered barriers.

Neil waited for Jackie to move, but the seconds stretched to an uneasy length; he rolled down his window. "You all right?" Still, Jackie did not move. *"Hey."* A curt jab which he hoped would rouse her from her apparent paralysis. It did not.

Neil stepped out of the car. Loose debris crunched as he stepped onto the sidewalk, approaching his ex-wife. And now when he spoke, he did so like the old days, when she was having a bad dream or had just gotten off the phone after a solemn call with her mother. Tender. "Hey—you okay, kid?"

The *kid* part surprised him. He'd not meant to say it, that long-gone affectionate appellation.

She swiveled slowly, twisting her head over her shoulder. "Do you hear that?"

Neil canted his head—not to hear whatever sound she was talking about, but clocking potential trickery. Jackie lifted her arm, indicating the opened door. "There's someone in there?"

Neil nearly pivoted, realizing that he'd gotten himself into a trap of some sort: one of Jackie's dim-witted consorts, some courtesan from the coterie of her deceptive spheres, was here, set to roll him. The calculus, though, didn't make sense.

He studied her closer. Jackie was uncharacteristically startled. Neil said, "What do you mean?"

"Someone just said *your* name."

Neil was in the initial phase of smirking, his body readying a retreat, when he also heard something—a hush-like screech that might have been words, syllables. The space between the door and the jamb was a slender aperture of blackness. Whatever the noise had been, it had escaped through that slim space. Enough orange light from the parking lot's frail, sodium-vapor lamps powdered the exterior like adobe dust. Offhandedly, he glanced at the room number: *118*.

Neil had inadvertently inched forward—not, he registered in his movements, to have a closer inspection, but to pull Jackie away. He was within arm's reach now when, without turning to glance, Jackie suddenly strode toward the door.

"*Wait*," Neil hissed.

Neil had only taken a step forward when the door swung open, revealing a charged darkness that seemed to hum. The scant light touched nothing inside—not a single detail. But what had he expected to see?—stacks of unused furniture ... the dull glint of a warped mirror. The rectangle of darkness somehow possessed weight—a palpable pressure of black fathoms folding over each other.

And then, from that box of lightlessness, sprang an elderly woman. She wore a loosely-knotted burgundy robe, nude beneath, the thin ribbon of the robe's belt trailing at her sides—the loose lamina of her gray skin jostled over the contours of ribs and hipbones as she sprinted over the threshold.

Glancing at neither Neil nor Jackie, she accelerated. Neil heard the dull flapping then caught sight of the woman's dingy house slippers, perhaps the only impediment to her potential speed. The woman's bathrobe and its belt rippled behind her as she fled across the parking lot, darting directly into the tall corn field, cleaving swiftly into the rows. There came the momentary snapping and shifting of withered stalks.

Neil had pivoted his entire body to follow the uncanny course of the woman. Facing away from the hotel, he flinched when the door slammed behind him.

He spun, fists raised. The door to room 118 was shut. Jackie was gone.

The lethargic oscillation of a year pulsed by.

And in that time the police, for their own apparent reasons, had regarded Neil (to his surprise) with general disinterest.

When the door to room 118 had slammed shut twelve months earlier, Neil had immediately rushed forward, trying the door handle (not budging); he shouted for Jackie, placing an ear against the cold, warped wood; and though silence prevailed, Neil thought he detected something, the tangible pressure of a presence.

He tried her phone. Nothing. He considered kicking at the door but hesitated, bracing himself with a deep breath and mentally reconstructing what had happened moments earlier. *What did I actually see?*

Finally, he'd called the police and, finally, they'd arrived.

He explained everything, including the incoherent emergence of the old woman. *An old woman who moved like a fucking track star.* The police stated that sometimes squatters broke into places like this.

Jackie's car was of preliminary interest. Her purse, which she'd flung onto the passenger seat, contained mundane necessities along with her phone, the only missed calls being from Neil.

Police eventually gained access. And though Neil, in conversation with a demonstratively weary detective, was asked to remain on the margins of the scene, he caught snatches of the room's interior—the swipe of flashlights illuminating the room: bed frames and mattresses propped against the wall, toppled columns of rolled-up carpet. They appeared to be in no hurry, and as such caused Neil to think there was no sign of Jackie.

Neil was barely listening as he gazed past the detective, past the parking lot, out toward the listless hiss of the stalks in the cornfield.

In the weeks and winter months that followed, the police's prying (from what Neil could gather) shifted to Jackie and her string of courtiers, and though Neil could only guess at what they were driving at with their inquiries, it was obviously financial. Money. Always something with money. They abruptly dismissed Neil as a prospect in favor of Jackie's cache of sexual sycophants.

Of course they'd exhausted the security footage. The camera belonged to the restaurant's proprietors, the grainy, closed-circuit footage catching Neil and Jackie inside La Cáscara, exiting into the parking lot, but lost them as they rounded the corner by the hotel.

On a Friday in the fall, and closing in on the one-year anniversary since he'd last seen Jackie, Neil arrived home early from work and, infused with a few drinks, discovered in himself a pronounced aimlessness—a confluence of wholesale boredom and lonely claustrophobia. He went for a drive. He sensed the hum of some emotionally insidious inspiration which was confirmed as he steered east on the interstate, and was validated as he coursed out to the derelict site of their long-gone liaisons.

It didn't help that he was now hungry.

Neil had been aware of the hotel's slow and methodical razing, but now slowed his approach slightly. Though the La Cáscara restaurant remained, its neon sign projecting life into an otherwise lifeless landscape, the hotel had been compartmentally disassembled. What remained around the Mexican restaurant was a concrete skirt of architectural butchery. Crumbled piles to be hauled away. A few walls remained—an imitation of bombed-out civilian centers from war-torn Europe.

The deconstruction had been obviously sluggish, but so too was the annual progress in the surrounding fields. All around it appeared that farmers were waiting to harvest the tracts of corn. The tall, yet sickly, looking stalks appeared to Neil like millions of quills that had been plucked from diseased birds. It dawned on Neil the peculiarity of this: two years of consecutive corn, when the field should have been rotated and set in soybeans.

Neil parked, unable to help a glance in the direction where room 118 had once been but was now a tidy clutch of rubble.

He shrugged deeper into his jacket, sidestepped lagoons of oil and antifreeze, and walked into the restaurant.

In contrast to the deteriorating set piece which collared it, La Cáscara had, over the course of a year, changed very little. With sentimental predictability, Neil was guided to a booth similar to the one he and Jackie had occupied twelve months earlier, this one situated toward the rear of the restaurant. A red-sconced candle flickered in front of him provided solace, a melancholic familiarity.

He ordered a drink, ate some chips and, through the wide front windows, dwelled on the sunset, complicated in its pastel brilliance and in its futile fight with the pushy dilation of night.

Neil was crunching on a tortilla chip when he noticed her out there. The woman had emerged from the cornfield, her gait leisurely, almost drowsy; she strode across the no-man's land between the cornfield and the parking lot. It was evident that her attention was trained on the restaurant, the glassed-in portico leading to the lobby.

Frowning now, he watched her enter the restaurant, a small bell dinging overhead as she passed through the vestibule.

She stood there, eyes trained on Neil, a smirk toying at the corners of her mouth.

She was pale and pretty, and what Neil had initially took as some sort of wrap-style dress was actually a dingy-looking robe. It was the scuffed house slippers that gave her away—nearly impossible to comprehend, but much in the past few years had been uneasy to mentally digest. He'd seen this woman before—the *same* woman who'd bolted from room 118 just seconds before Jackie had disappeared. Her height, the structure of her body, but her features had regained vitality—her hair was a mess but the gray was now honey-colored and thick. If Neil could translate her expression into words, it might have gone like, *You and I know each other*, or perhaps something more simplistic. *Well hello, sweetie...we meet again.*

Neil's mouth hung open slightly. They were engaged, he supposed, in some sort of staring contest across the abdomen of the restaurant.

Just then, with abuela amiability, one of the waitresses approached the woman. As the waitress spoke, and without breaking her eyeline with Neil, the woman from the cornfield slowly lifted a finger and hooked it into the knot of the garment's tattered belt, lithely unfastened it and—in a baroque flourish—swept open the robe.

There came the brief flash of pale flesh, but it wasn't until the waitresses screamed that an urgent sliver of sobriety forked through Neil.

Clinging to her pale, naked body, were dozens of dark, teardrop shapes, some even affixed to the interior of the robe itself. They called to mind similar shapes for Neil: leechy, oblong forms lining the ceilings of caves. But these bat-shapes were bulky, nothing like the smaller bats which populated this region of Midwest—more the size of a full ear of corn, if the cob were coated with black fur.

The waitress shrieked, staggering, stammering in Spanish, her hand catching the front counter, spilling a stack of menus.

There came the clatter of flatware, mumbled phrases of apprehension. Ranchera music continued to infuse the restaurant. Within this rhythm of dismay, there would conceivably come a time when someone—the manager ... the owner, someone—would confront this woman, call the police. But that sort of scenario never materializes. Rather, what happened was this: In a spasmed, black flash, the creatures detached themselves, exploding into flight from the interior of the woman's robe; they streaked into the dining room, wings scribbling the air.

Neil flinched, ducked, getting low along the booth. Some of the patrons had time to get out of their seats in an attempt to make it out of the dining room; but the bat-things attached themselves to these folks quickly, acutely fixing to patches of exposed flesh.

Some of the cooks burst through the kitchen's swinging doors only to be instantly overcome by the creatures.

Neil watched as one of the animals affixed itself to the forearm of a woman; she slapped and scratched with no effect. The woman wavered and collapsed as a variegated, bruise-hued breakout hemorrhaged beneath her skin.

Another man, who must have been attacked seconds before, was trying to make his way to the lobby, his face puffed and purple; but he caught his thigh on a chair, pitching forward and crashing sideways onto a table.

Then came the gunshot—Neil swiveled his focus to its source.

A hefty fellow wearing an oatmeal-colored windbreaker was hunched in a practiced shooter's stance, his large belly hanging over the table. One of the bat-things nestled near his clavicle. The man had a squat weapon which was nearly swallowed in his beefy fists. His eyes fluttered as he appeared to summon enough strength for a final shot, which he did indeed manage, but it went wide, exploding a fishbowl full of candy next to the cash register. He dropped the gun and crashed down in a heavy heap.

The woman's expression never wavered—a smiling sympathy, as if she'd expected all of it.

The aroma of Mexican food was now replaced with cordite, and something low and blood-musty that accompanied the creatures.

Neil glanced around the dining room. All the patrons were now crumpled, unconscious, their skin ivied with a subcutaneous soot. Each person now bore several bat-things, the fleshy suction of those waxy wings fanned out over the bodies. Neil could not tell if they were feeding or—owing to their rhythmic, pulsing hump—pumping the people with some sort of malignant venom.

Neil's chest swelled and collapsed in anticipation of one of those things latching onto him; but he also had an opening, a straight shot through the swinging-doors into the kitchen. He scrambled, boots finding purchase on the worn floor, leaping over one of the bodies as he sprinted into the kitchen.

An old, sauce-spattered stereo played music as Neil coursed through the tight kitchen. Steam rose from a line of stockpots, flames licking up between sheets of charring skirt-steaks on the charbroiler. Neil slowed, passing a cutting board—a knife there; he swept it up, held it awkwardly as he continued through the maze of racks and stainless steel.

He wound his way to the back of the kitchen: a dark corridor back here, a dull green light from an EXIT sign powdering the short hall; he shoved through the door, made it two or three paces, then skidded to a halt.

She was standing just to the side of the back dock by the dumpster, her hands in the pockets of her robe which she'd refastened, the fabric creating a modestly-revealing V along her neckline.

With a ferocious yet clumsy lunge, Neil swept the knife toward the woman. The blade did not make it to any portion of her body, though, as—with an air of indifference—she slapped at Neil's wrist with a sharp swipe, the instrument clattering to the asphalt.

"Seriously, Neil?" she said, her voice tinged with disappointment. "Did you not see what just happened in there?" She jutted her chin toward the restaurant.

Gravel shifted under Neil's boots as his body reset to make a run for it, but the woman spoke: "Stop, Neil. There's no place to go."

Between stitches of rapid respiration, he said, "I can make it...to my car."

She was already shaking her head, a small scratch of a smile on her lips. "No, sweetheart, you can't."

He tugged his phone from his jeans, keying in 911. She adjusted the belt of her robe. "Already thought of that too."

The front doors of the restaurant rattled open as the now-ambulatory patrons lumbered out. Along with them came the black netting of bat-things taking flight. They walked awkwardly yet with purpose; touched by the glow of neon, Neil registered the contusion-mottled quality of their skin, as though infused with inky ichor. They crossed the parking lot—Neil noted the hefty man in the oatmeal-colored jacket, the one who'd managed the ungainly gunshots.

All of them, most bearing bloodstains from their wounds, walked leisurely out of the barrier of light, spreading out as they crossed the parking lot and headed toward the decrepit cornfield. Stalks and withered ribbons rustled as they moved into the rows. And then, with the exception of an errant screech from the unseen things in the sky above them, all was calm and quiet.

Neil looked at the woman. "My *scarecrows*"—she kicked her head toward the field— "for the next hour or so. Come on."

Neil didn't budge, his eyeline ticking between the woman and the sentinels posted in the field. The woman exhaled softly, her lips tightening for only a moment. "Would it help if you knew my name?" Neil was already shaking his head, *No*. "For the purposes of this evening's exchange, call me Marsha."

The smooth fin of her hand was still outstretched toward Neil. "I mean it," she said. "I want to show you something."

After a moment of trying, with no hope, to mentally coordinate an escape, Neil rejected the acceptance of her hand, but made several movements toward her.

"Good," said Marsha, "It's not far."

Indeed it was merely around the corner. Marsha rounded the front of the restaurant, the spill of cheap neon catching the standing spills of oil and coolant leoparding the parking lot.

Neil was only a few paces behind Marsha; he glimpsed inside the restaurant and saw that the glass lining the lobby's vestibule was streaked with red handprints, smears from the ambulatory exodus of Marsha's scarecrows.

The sidewalk which extended along the front of the restaurant elbowed: the familiar path where Neil typically parked his car.

Marsha swiveled to address Neil. There was something unsettlingly pleasant in the motion—two old friends taking a twilight stroll. "I'm certain you have a lot of questions," she said, huffing a little air through her nose as she hissed a giggle. "But I promise this will all be over before the cops show up."

Neil actually glanced over his shoulder, off toward the dark distance. "Cops?"

"Or sheriffs or state troopers or something." Marsha continued walking, though looked closely at Neil. In a discordant registry, Neil saw for the first time that her features were quite pleasant, but while her dark eyes appeared, at a glance, normal, there was constant quivering on the glossy lamina—a static, ocular fluctuation. "There was no way someone didn't call the cops—maybe one of the guys in the kitchen," she said.

He followed her around the acute turn at the end of the restaurant's brick-box extremity.

Neil shuffled to a halt and stared. A wide segment of the hotel had, in part, returned to existence. Bordered by shredded edges, the liminal structure appeared to have been raggedly torn from a photo, its ragged edges vivid and crisp, not the result of some haphazard demolition. It was as though the excavation crew had worked around a 2,000-square-feet portion of the hotel—the two-story portion of rooms and overhanging balcony. The space, with its parking lot-facing windows and crinkly drapes appeared as it had in its previous state: squalid but utile in its mangy incarnation.

Still spiked with adrenaline, Neil drifted forward toward the room nearest him, eyes steady on the door before him. *118*. He took another quick step forward, considered a running kick at the door, but stopped, regarding Marsha. "Is she in there?"

Marsha shrugged. "Sort of." Instead of guiding Neil to room 118, she instead began strolling between the building and the rear of the restaurant. "Let's go," she said. "I can explain."

With a reluctant gait, Neil followed Marsha around the side of the building, passing beneath a stairwell that terminated with an eerie fray about fifteen feet above him.

"Hurry up, slow poke," Marsha said, accentuating the *poke* with a smirk and a wink.

Pulling up behind Marsha, Neil emerged on a facsimile of the outdoor swimming pool, the water illuminated from within, the tumbling bars of opalescent light playing over each other. Even the aroma of chlorine was strong. Cheap-plastic chaise loungers wreathed the pool.

"Pedestrian places like this have a sort of vast utility, you know?"— she spoke as if it were not really a question, rather a reality to be rhetorically consumed. "Travelers, of course. Transients. Energy builds up here like scar tissue. But some people come back." Her teeth glinted. "Some people are … creatures of habit. Repeat customers."

Neil broke his gaze with her and swallowed.

"I'm not a *ghost*," she said, as though the word were tedious, "but the last place I actually existed, consistently, was the 1950s," said Marsha. "Back when this hotel was, oh, I don't know, a prized pivot point in Midwest travel."

She looked at Neil, her eyelids lasciviously heavy. "I probably don't need to bore you with the nuances of my occupation, but this hotel— and that room in particular," she pointed toward room 118, "—were like a hedonistic headquarters for me. I'd see men from all over, and I'd accommodate their requests—most of my specialties were, let's say, unorthodox in contrast to the, let's say, parochial facade of the suburbs. Strangers' peculiar needs were, back then, just a symptom of repression."

Coruscating light from the pool slashed over her features as she closed the distance between them. "One night—I'd finished with my last client; I'd been dozing, someone knocked on the door. I remember yelling at them to go away, that I was done for the night; but they just kept hitting the door. I scraped the blanket off of me, stood up and grabbed my robe," she idly twirled the terry cloth belt, "this little number in fact. I didn't even bother checking the peephole, but opened the door wide enough for the chain to catch. I started in on a *get-the-fuck-out-of-here* but stopped. The person-shape held itself in"—Marsha had raised stiff fingers, her eloquence ebbing momentarily—"just this unnaturally stationary—like a prank: someone had left a mannequin in front of my room. But then it twitched, it shoved the door open, breaking the chain, throwing me backward—I stumbled and landed on the bed. It lurched in then, closing the door behind it. It had clothing hanging off of it, but it was all mismatched, like someone had dumped a trunk of disguises over a human-shaped body." She looked at Neil. "There was also skin hanging off its frame. He—I came to know it as a *he*—reached over and clicked off the TV. And then he was standing right over me." Marsha returned her attention to the surface of the pool. "Maybe he was some roaming serial killer," she shrugged. "Some Midwest masochist. I don't know. But he ... did things to me, in the dark," she continued. "Stuff I was already into, but other things that were ... unfamiliar.

"Maybe you think I should have fought or run; but the truth is, I started matching his masochism, pulling him in deeper to an unexpected, um—transcendence. There were climaxes and then there was an eclipse, and then things just," Marsha kicked one of her house slippers into the pool, splashing Neil's shins, "*slipped.*"

"I woke up coiled in sheets, uncoiled in time." Neil opened his mouth but Marsha cut in. "Whatever had been traded between us, it wasn't reciprocal—things were no longer balanced. It was like watching a movie from the opposite side of the screen. The room was empty. I was just another hustler —another low-level *domme*—that had disappeared. But I remained," her fingers clawed the air, "*here.*" In our inadvertent exchange, I learned to subsist as that night-calling *He* had: there's a vitality in savagery. I'd already grown accustomed to deriving and delivering pleasure from it, but when he showed me that ... *transcendence*—the permeability of this *place* ... I learned how to let it nourish me.

"I roam. I yield to tides of reality. There are other doors, other passages. Sometimes I hear voices behind the walls of these flimsy dimensions. I fuck who I want. I devour what I want. And I go on roaming from one end to the other. It's sort of like this pool—I fell into the deep end a long time ago, but once in a while, I drift closer to the shallow end—close enough to break the surface. It really comes down to this, Neil," he looked up, "I like it here; but *here*"—she swept an arm, indicating the mangled landscape around her—"*here* is *limited*. I have a long chain, but I'm still anchored until someone takes my place."

Marsha reached out, gently clasping Neil's fingers.

"I was in the shallow end when I heard—*sensed*—you and that woman outside the door. It was something in the fibers of that last transaction between you and Jackie," it was the first time she'd articulated his ex-wife's name.

"There was a devious disproportion between you, but you had the opportunity to match her perfunctory sadism, by inverting her cruel calculus. And just like that, the inertia of your lop-sided exchange had made things permeable." Marsha was now nearly cleaved against Neil; she tilted her head. "But Jackie's accidental swap that night didn't have enough … seesaw energy. You're pliant, Neil, but you weren't always that way, were you?" Her grip tightened on his fingers. "Come with me, Neil—let me show you."

Marsha guided Neil back around the side of the building, back to room 118; with her hip, she bumped the door open.

Neil peered into the cumbersome darkness. His expression repeated the question from minutes earlier: *Is she in there?*

Marsha gently towed Neil into the room, and as they entered, the darkness dissipated. The space—the wallpaper … the clunky rotary phone on the nightstand— now resembled a space in the apex of the hotel's lifespan. A boxy television glowed a static transmission. Neil's head felt insulated with a drowsy weight.

Marsha kept her eyes on Neil as she maneuvered him to one of the beds, easing him down, lowering herself to sit on the corner of the mattress.

Blinking slowly, Neil tried to get his jaw working. "Where is—"

Just then, from the far side of the room where the bathroom would be, Jackie emerged. She looked gaunt, beset, and far older than the passage of a single year. But it was her. And for a moment, he felt a pang for the days when their symbiosis was harmonious. Neil flinched to reach out to her, but Jackie—merely giving Neil an idle glance—maintained momentum toward the door. Neil watched her cross over the threshold; Jackie appeared to suck in the night air, her shoulders quaking as if weeping: confirmed when she turned and looked back into the room. Her tear-slick expression was complex. Relief. Maybe remorse. She stared at Neil for a few additional ticks, before twisting and darting out of sight.

"She's made her choice," said Marsha. "She really made it a long time ago. But you knew that, right?"

Neil was still looking at the empty threshold, as Marsha's hand found his cheek, gently pivoting his head to face her.

With Marsha's unblinking gaze trained on him, Neil felt the arachnoidal fidget of her fingers skitter over his pelvis. "Stay," Marsha murmured. Gripping his belt, she pulled him closer to her, and now her lips were working on his neck; shadows in the room flexed and spasmed; Neil's vision had gone to thin slits, but he watched her smoothly slither the robe's belt from around her waist and place the device in his hand. In his ear, she whispered. "Stay. Hurt me. Love me. Set me loose."

With her guidance, Neil found himself coiling the belt around Marsha's wrists. Marsha fell back on the bed, extending her bound wrists above her head and forking a knee. Eyes nearly closed, Neil, his consciousness slowly divorcing itself from his body, felt his hand splay over her sternum, slide past her breasts, and mechanically move toward Marsha's throat, the web of his palm settling on the tender flute of her trachea. Marsha's voice possessed a nectar huskiness. "*Yesssss.*"

With a final filament of cognizance, he thought of Jackie—not with regret, but wry resolve, a lack of surprise in her saving herself. Whether financial or physical, Jackie always had a to-hell-with-the-masses backup plan. What had she always said?: *Try and save your own skin for once, Neil.*

In room 118, the cob-webby miasma had become profound. Between the panels of her open robe, Neil drowsily marveled at the unblemished symmetry of her torso—not the torso of a woman who claimed to have existed over seventy years before.

Save your own skin for once. And almost as if Jackie's departing voice had lent an image: of rippling flesh—

No.

Not skin. Khaki fabric—a Members Only jacket too small for a beefy frame. Neil saw the man fire two awkward shots and then go down with the gun in his chunky fist.

… save your own skin …

It started as layers of apprehension, then Neil was, by inches, withdrawing his hand from Marsha's throat, eventually staggering backwards. With the palpability of a cord being yanked from a socket, the room was now worse than it'd been in its seedy heyday, the walls splotched with fungal discoloration, the carpet and mattresses reeked of water-rot. The television still hummed its static broadcast.

Eyes wide on Neil, Marsha slipped her wrists from the bathrobe's belt and she came up on her elbows, her voice sonorous with disappointment. "Goddamn it, Neil."

Without prelude, Marsha slipped fully out of her robe, while the robe itself sloughed off the veneer of Marsha's skin with it.

The creature that slipped from the husk of flesh was composed of some gray, papery material—Neil's mind immediately bridged similarities to the texture of a fibrous wasp's nest just as even more distracted part of his faculty recognized connection: that wasps used chewed wood and their own saliva to create their papery facades. *I devour what I want.* The rotten, cocoon-crepe exterior appeared grafted to something skeletal and thorny beneath. Despite this, Marsha's slick, owl-like eyes remained lacquered in their papery sockets.

Neil's first attempt to escape resulted in him bumping against the corner of the bed, sending him tumbling to the floor, but after an ass-scooting backpedal, he scrambled over the threshold, gaining traction as he hit the sidewalk's concrete.

Neil drew up on the front of the restaurant; but he'd been so fixated on the possibility of getting the gun that it took him a second to register the sound of a siren. He hesitated with his hand on the lobby's glass door.

In the distance, lights throbbed on top of a single white cruiser approaching at high speed, its headlights jiggling as it jounced over the pock-marked lane. He heard the screams then as the vehicle entered the insulation of light, saw the figures—Marsha's scarecrows—clinging to the car. Several were on top while a pair were splayed over the hood, but at least two had penetrated the cruiser, their legs whipping from broken windows. Neil noted the gore smearing the windshield an instant before suddenly understanding the vehicle's aggressive trajectory.

Neil barreled through the vestibule, swung into the lobby and launched himself over a table, rolling and scrambling to a stop near a booth at the back of the dining room.

Still singing with speed, the cruiser tore through the front glass of the lobby, hitching up as it ramped over the brick of the building's exterior, the half-wall eviscerating the underside of the vehicle. Marsha's scarecrows were flung in a tumble of limbs as the cruiser pitched on its side, skidding to a stop in a sweep of devastation.

Despite the overwhelming damage to the front of the building—along with the mangled, semi-ambulatory corpses slowly creeping from the mounds of glass-glittered wreckage—the dining room's interior was essentially preserved.

Neil slid to his hands and knees, scanning the floor for the gun.

And there it was, across the room—just where the man had let it drop. Neil lurched forward and stopped at the sound of her voice.

"Why are you making this difficult?"

Neil looked over. Marsha was back in her skin, back in her robe. She was standing at the head of the restaurant, not far from the police car's smoking abdomen. Things were moving over there now; Neil could see broken limbs quaking, broken figures attempting to wrench themselves from the wreck.

"We could have loved each other in a way you've never experienced," she said. "There's really nothing left for you beyond this ... *prank* you call an existence."

She was not wrong. Panting, on one knee, he glanced ahead at the black weapon. *Too far.* He blinked, hanging his head a bit. Neil passed an appraisal around the interior of what used to be their beloved La Cáscara. He slanted his eyeline toward the booth next to him—*their* booth, wasn't it? The worn, faded burgundy of the outdated cushions, the tables still warm with hyperventilating light cast from those kitschy, bistro sconces.

Marsha's voice was syrupy and diseased. "You'll never make—"

Neil snatched the red bistro candle from the tabletop, lobbing it at the cruiser's undercarriage with its hemorrhaging a wall of fluids.

The red glass shattered and a fern of flames unfolded, a runner sweeping out and catching a pool of fuel near Marsha. At first she did not scream, she didn't even budge, but rather simply stared at Neil. Indifference shifted to fury, and then … she howled.

Neil thrust himself up, retreating through the kitchen where small fires had emerged on the charbroiler and along the gas ranges. Neil shouldered his way through the back-dock door.

He was in his car. Neil tore out of the lot, screaming past the corn-field-lined lane. In his rearview mirror, he saw an explosion bloom from the restaurant.

In a shredded parachute of road-dust and debris, Neil's car careened onto the nearby highway on-ramp; and just as he swerved onto the interstate artery, a pair of state-trooper cruisers were streaking toward the inferno that used to be a restaurant called La Cáscara.

Each day—as those days turned into weeks, and weeks to months—Neil grew more and more baffled that he was not apprehended. On several occasions, a pair of detectives who'd worked on Jackie's disappearance stopped by his house, clearly trying to bring cohesion to the narrative of their mangled case. Neil didn't invite them inside, but they spoke on the front porch.

"It's a goddamn coincidence," said one of them. "The same property within the scope of a year, don't you think, Mr. Henson?"

Neil exhaled—*a shame*—and looked at the detective. "I really can't say."

Neil accommodated the discussions, answering his questions frankly and soberly. He added nothing to implicate himself and was certain the cops had no interest in hearing about—*What?*—a dimension-dancing creature that navigated the subcuticular landscape of pain and cosmic decay—an obsidian gulf just under their noses. For one reason or another, they eventually left him alone. The story gained a single-night mention on national news stations: "*A responding state trooper was ambushed ... who then executed a number of innocent people within a small restaurant ..."*

Neil spends most of his time tending to the boundaries of his own routines and work-rituals. From time to time in the middle of the night, Neil will wake to a demanding knock at the front door, followed by the simple *ding-dong* of the bell. The icy, two-note chime ricochets off the interior of the house. Invariably, Neil pulls on a robe, shuffles down the hall and inspects the peephole. There is never a figure on the other side, the front porch empty, but the rhythmic exercise seems to stave off a reprisal for several weeks.

It is usually when Neil is in the kitchen, washing up or pouring air-soured wine down the drain, that he sees her through the window, through the blinds' horizontal slats, standing over in the field across the lawn. It's often in the autumn, when the corn stalks are tall. Jackie, his ex-wife, is motionless out there, only a row or two deep within the corn. Her clothes are falling apart, her skin smudged gray, as though shadows themselves have applied cosmetic soot. Jackie's eyes glimmer, her expression is pensive, as though she's waiting for Neil to signal her, run for her, throw a quilt over her quaking shoulders.

Nowadays, Neil dwells on these sightings with dwindling hesitation and contemplation. Nowadays, Neil has adopted the habit of reaching out, tugging the cord taut, and allowing the blinds to fall, obliged by the mercy of their compassionate occlusion.

THE STRANGLER FIG

JEFFREY THOMAS

Trees shared a symbiotic relationship with the city of Haikan. It was a balance between nature and human being. Perhaps not a fully harmonious yin and yang, but as much of a balance as was possible in any relationship involving human beings.

Downtown buildings faced onto broad flagstone sidewalks through which grew rows of trees, like weathered wooden pillars left over from some antiquated city upon which this one had been built, by later generations influenced by the West. Most of the tourists who came here from the West didn't know that this country's name translated as "the Unnamed Country," or didn't care to know.

The roots of these street-bordering trees displaced the nearest flagstones, their trunks painted white halfway up to make them more visible to motorbike riders at night...while in sweltering daytime, parked motorbikes found a shady rest under their leafy awnings.

Further out from the modernized city core, the trees grew more lushly abundant, profuse and wildly tropical in character. They crowded the small mildewed houses as if to camouflage them protectively. They leaned out precariously over the languid, broad green river that abutted the city, reaching their fronds desperately for more sun than their fellows could grasp. They bulged sensuously with fruit for the humans: coconuts, bananas. Their crowns provided homes for birds. Their trunks were adorned with the shed husks of cicadas. They were each one a habitat within this habitat, its own microcosm of life and death and renewal.

With his wife Khim seated behind him, holding him loosely around the waist, Zhon slowed his motorbike and turned it off the street, drove through an archway with the address *B-2 Lido Street* stenciled beside it. Through a short tunnel-like passage, then on into the courtyard of the Banyan Café. Potted plants and flowers abounded throughout the open-air café, and trees that might have been planted there or that the café might have been built around. The café possessed multiple levels, accessed via steep staircases. Khim had been here before a few times, though not for some years now, and she knew the uppermost level provided a nice view of the city in general, and in particular of the tiled rooftops of the temple next door. The café did a good business attracting the temple's worshipers – though maybe too, the café helped draw people to the temple. Another symbiotic relationship.

Khim's paternal and maternal grandparents had been of a mountain tribe, and it showed in her composition. Her face was broad, with strong cheekbones, squared jaw, ruddy cheeks, eyes more slanted than most of her countrymen's, with only single eyelids. Her full-lipped mouth was sensuous but held in tight lines. Yet her black eyes shimmered with emotion, as if through the slitted holes of a mask. She was short in stature, not quite five feet, but her body conveyed strength. Tendons and veins stood out clearly on her arms. Her four grandparents had never once in their lives seen the sea. Zhon had joked to Khim that she had come down from their mountain realm as an emissary to the fluid world. Early in their marriage he had given her a nickname that in their language referred to a kind of female water spirit that somewhat corresponded to the Western notion of a mermaid, though he hadn't used that pet name in a long while.

After adding their machine to a row of slanted bikes parked to one side of the courtyard, Zhon and Khim were approached by a hostess. Zhon explained that they were here to meet with a couple who were planning a wedding reception to be held at the Banyan Café in several weeks. The hostess turned and pointed them toward the rear of the ground floor level. Zhon thanked the young woman and he and Khim moved past her.

Khim followed a little behind Zhon, quiet, like a good wife of old. She knew he'd be doing all the talking. Over her shoulder she carried their waterproof duffel bag.

At a table in the rear left corner sat a young couple, quite obviously the future bride and groom, and a man Khim figured must be the Banyan Café's owner. This was confirmed when the trio looked around to watch Zhon and Khim approach.

Introductions were exchanged. Zhon was charming, as he always was professionally, this effect enhanced by his good looks. Khim only nodded pleasantly at these people, smiling with lips closed. The husband and wife water puppeteers were invited to sit, and the owner motioned over one of his waitresses to take their order. Zhon requested iced coffee with sweetened condensed milk for them both.

Right away, in her strong voice the bride-to-be started asking questions and making her wishes known. Normally, the parents of either the bride or groom — depending on which side was footing the bill — would be present to oversee all wedding arrangements, but immediately Khim could tell this was a modern woman with a strong personality. Her husband-to-be was content to mostly just grin and bob his head in agreement, either cowed by his fiancée or just grateful to be marrying such a beauty. With his round baby face, he looked even younger than she.

Zhon leaned across the table to turn his phone around and show the couple photos on its screen: numerous shots of puppet shows he and his wife had conducted in the past. "I would recommend," he suggested, "that we perform the classic tale of the wedding of the God-Scaled Dragon to the Silver-Scaled Dragon."

"Of course, of course," the doll-like beauty agreed. "Oh yes...these puppets are beautiful." Then she exclaimed, "*Oh!*" and pointed at the image Zhon had just scrolled to. "I like that! Can our dragons spit fireworks, too?"

"Uh," Zhon said, straining his handsome grin, "that effect is used in the performance of Cholukan subduing the Gold-Scaled Dragon. It's, ah, perhaps too violent an effect for a wedding. But look here..." He scrolled to another image and showed her: a dragon puppet spouting a geyser of water from its jaws. "In the wedding of the Gold-Scaled

Dragon and the Silver-Scaled Dragon, when their marriage is culminated they spray water into each other's mouths."

"Oh, okay, I like that," the young woman said. She turned to her man, who was bobbing his head, and gave him a cocked smile. "At the culmination of our wedding, we can spit into each other's mouths, too, right?"

Khim's closed smile edged wider. Everyone else laughed outright. The waitress came with the coffees. As she set down Zhon's glass, she noticed his phone and said, "Oh! How beautiful! Are you a puppeteer?"

Khim looked away. She was used to women flirting with her husband, and her husband flirting with them. Well, familiar with it, if not used to it. She wouldn't have said anything about the waitress leaning in closer to Zhon to get a better look at his photos – those days were long past – but the bride-to-be was getting irritated, and noticing this, the café owner sharply sent his waitress away.

The table they sat at was right up against a wooden railing, and just beyond the railing was the river. Under the heat-hazed sky, the river was mercury bright, but in the shade of the great banyan tree after which the café was named, the water was a murky green.

The banyan tree, looming right beside where Khim sat, stood between the café and the temple, all but hiding one from the other. Studying it, to distract herself from her husband's charming flirtations and ramblings, Khim wasn't sure she'd ever seen a larger banyan tree. Well, it wasn't just *a tree*, was it?

The parasitic plant that had colonized and overwhelmed the original host tree was a variation of strangler fig, but a singular type indigenous only to the region of the Unnamed Country. The original tree at the heart of the organism was all but lost from view behind dense layers of woody vines, and besides that probably dead for a few hundred years, its core hollowed out, a mere support column. Now, what might be considered the main "trunk" of the gargantuan plant was composed of innumerable cords that in their entirety formed a single mass as wide as a house.

Massive boughs extended far out from the main body, slung low over the water, arched like the necks of dinosaurs with their grazing heads lost in the canopy of glossy green leaves – this canopy so thick and dark that the sunlight glinting through it was like stars in a night sky. From these heavy boughs, stray tendrils dangled down into the water.

Khim briefly observed the antics of two shirtless, browned boys in ragged shorts, maybe eleven or twelve, who had ventured out onto the boughs and balanced there as deftly as monkeys, jabbering and laughing and prodding the shaded green water with long sticks. What were they doing? Trying to retrieve something from the water? Khim saw only small rafts of fallen leaves sailing past them.

She let her gaze shift away, toward the tree's base. While above, limbs were weighed toward earth like thick streams of candle wax, melted then hardened, in a complementary effect the tree's aerial prop roots looked like they had grown from the bottom up. Khim noted this because she remembered a religious passage that mentioned the banyan tree in this very way – the branches that grow downward, the roots that grown upward – and she recalled that this mirrored condition was used as a way of addressing the balance of the spiritual and the physical. Especially since, if a banyan tree were seen reflected in water, it might look much the same; just the branches and the roots switching places but serving the same function. Physical tree and reflected tree meeting at the water line, seeming to both grow toward and away from each other.

Now that she remembered that religious passage, she also recalled another in which the banyan tree was referenced. The manner in which the strangler fig's web of vines enveloped and consumed the host tree was likened to the way in which carnal desire in a human could over-take one and suffocate their spirit.

The base of the tree rose up from the water, as if a titanic wizened dragon had thrust its great leg into the shallows in coming to shore from the river. Around this base were thick, floating mats of shed leaves. Cupped between the thickest of the roots that showed above the wa-terline were miniature pools. Trapped in these miniature tide pools between roots were numerous colorful plastic bags, Styrofoam food containers, old rags, cigarette butts. Trash carelessly discarded over the café railing. Also bobbing down there: small red figs dropped from the canopy. Wasps buzzed low over the water, maddened by the figs' sickeningly sweet rot.

Khim's gaze lifted from the floating trash, something higher up catching her attention. At first she just stared at it without comprehension, though it was actually quite clear what she was seeing.

Partly covered in a mesh of vines, as if it were fossilized in the flank of the immense banyan tree, was the mummified-looking body of a huge river rat. How long had it been snared there, as if caught in a spider's web? Many years, and that was why it was so shriveled, desiccated? Or had something, that metaphorical spider, sucked all the juices from it more recently?

A cry startled Khim and she jolted, looked over at the pair of boys balancing on a bough over the river.

She realized now what they had been trying to do with their sticks: poking at the tendrils that hung down from above into the water, whacking at them from the side, trying to get them to react. One of these tendrils had been triggered, had contracted, bunching itself up. In so doing, it was revealed that the end of the tendril had coiled itself around a large catfish. Dangling, exposed to air, the fish slapped its tail at the water. Blood sluiced from its gills; was it being that badly constricted? The boys scrambled to hook the tendril, now, with barbs at the ends of their sticks where they had been careful not to entirely pare away lesser branches. One of them snagged the vine and hauled the suspended fish closer. The other boy set his own pole aside, unfolded a pocket knife, and firmly clutching the fish against his bony chest, sawed it free from the end of the tendril.

The fish almost flopped itself out of his arms, but he managed to keep hold of it. The other boy dropped his own stick and took away his friend's knife to free up his hand so he could get a better grip on the fish.

Whooping, triumphant, they made their way back along the bough, to a spot where between two roots they had wedged a plastic cooler. They thrust the fish into this and slammed its cover shut.

Khim looked back at the severed vine that had caught the catfish. As if it were infuriated at being cheated of its prize, it thrashed and whipped in the air.

"*Khim...*"

Soon enough, though, the knotted-up vine allowed itself to relax and straighten out again...to lengthen enough that its end, however shortened, still managed to disappear into the green water.

"*Wife,*" Zhon said, more loudly.

She looked around at the others, startled, to see that her husband, the young couple, and even the café owner were all staring at her.

Zhon laughed, but she could tell he was annoyed and embarrassed. He had always warned her never to embarrass him in public. To the others he said, "You'll have to forgive her...sometimes we water puppeteers get too much water in our ears."

The others all burst into laughter. Khim smiled again, again and always with her lips closed over her teeth.

"I was asking you," Zhon went on, "to show these kind people the puppet we brought with us, so they can get an idea of just how exquisite our puppets truly are. I was bragging how much work you put into the costumes you dress them in, after I craft their bodies."

Khim bent down, unzipped the duffel bag she had set by her foot, and carefully lifted out a small figure. She held it up, like a newborn child displayed for the first time to excited in-laws – though she herself, alas, to the great disappointment of her own in-laws, had never gifted them with a grandchild.

The figure portrayed the Monkey God, Cholukan, that great trickster, mischievous but powerful, scribe to the Gods, blond-furred and dressed in a golden outfit that she had indeed spent hours sewing together and embroidering. The Monkey God's eyes were red glass marbles, in imitation of the special gift of sight granted to Cholukan by the goddess the Ruby Empress, who so loved her pet. The Ruby Empress herself would appear at the very end of the play, to bestow her blessings upon the dragon couple, and hence the real-life couple.

"Of course," Zhon said, "our friend Cholukan will officiate over the wedding of his great friend the Gold-Scaled Dragon, to his bride the Silver-Scaled Dragon."

"Oh, it's lovely, lovely," the strong-voiced bride-to-be gushed, thoroughly won over.

"You won't be disappointed by our performance," Zhon assured her.

"And you can do it here, right here for my wedding party, instead of where the river passes the park?"

"Yes, yes, we can do this. Granted, in the past we've only ever put on our shows there beside the park, but anything to please you." Zhon with his big charming smile, as if he thought to seduce this beauty away from her passive would-be husband.

But then he already had a beauty waiting for him in the city, didn't he? Khim knew this only too well. He barely tried to hide it anymore.

Jinh…

While Zhon and the woman continued to converse, Khim lowered the gold-attired monkey into her lap and glanced back behind her, at the shriveled rat clutched possessively to the banyan tree's body.

———————⋄———————

Over the past fifteen years Khim and Zhon had grown overly familiar with each other's scents. Small imperfections like snoring or sour morning breath, once overlooked, had become annoyances. They farted in each other's company without apology or redeeming giggles. Khim knew her crying face had once wrenched Zhon's heart. Now she understood it was only a red and ugly thing that he hoped would resume its more composed aspect before too long.

Once during lovemaking he had told Khim that her skin smelled of water. Maybe he had thought she would laugh, but the comment had turned her cold that night. He had tried reassuring her that his skin smelled of water, too, but she had remained self conscious about his words to this day. Water polluted with factory chemicals, she thought. Tainted with sewerage.

Zhon's lover, Jinh, was only twenty, looking even younger. As small as Khim but soft and wispy, where she was solid and tough. Jinh smoked. Khim wondered how Zhon could tolerate that. He had always told her he was repulsed by the smell of cigarette smoke on a woman… the way the smell adhered to their hair, their clothes, imprinted in their very flesh. She supposed he had overcome that…had even come to associate that smell with Jinh's youthful body, so that it was not only tolerable but exciting. When he smelled others smoking, did thoughts of Jinh alight? Would the longing for her flutter in his guts? Jinh was ashy and dry, Khim reflected, the opposite of herself, yin to her yang.

Elementally earthy, a little statuette of dusty stone, firm in Zhon's grasp (however soft and weak her actual limbs), whereas Khim was a liquid thing, to her mind smelling more and more of algae and mud, and dribbling away through her husband's hands.

Zhon was thirty-five; fifteen years older than Jinh. Fifteen years. Fifteen years ago he had married Khim, when *she* had been twenty. Jinh had only been five then.

Of course, no matter how brazen Zhon had become about going to see Jinh, and spending time away from home, Jinh never came to their house. However, sometimes Khim and Jinh would accidentally see each other about the city, and when they did Jinh would look away with a clenched angry look to her face, as if she were the wife...she the one who was being cheated on.

Jinh was a bar girl, and Khim had spotted her several times wearing a form-fitting short dress entirely covered in shimmering dark blue sequins. Once, after returning home from a weekend visit to her parents' house in a little rural village in Haikan's orbit, Khim had discovered a blue sequin in her own bed, like a shed scale. She hadn't shown it to Zhon. She had flushed it down the toilet. *How do you like swimming, imitation mermaid?*

⚬⚬⚬

Today the puppeteers had returned to the Banyan Café to plan out the upcoming performance. They brought the puppets they would use, and the rods they would attach to the various articulated figures to put them through their motions. On that day they would have a CD of traditional music to be played over the café's speakers, to accompany the performance, but for now these speakers only emitted disco-like pop music for the regular patrons.

The husband and wife donned the black rubber fishing bibs they would wear, and the tall rubber boots. Usually they didn't go more than chest-deep, so their upper bodies were visible, but that was why they would both wear a long-sleeved black shirt, black gloves, and a black hood with dark mesh in the front. The audience would *unsee* them, but if they did happen to notice them, they would accept them as the personification of the Fates that directed all beings in their actions, along their life courses.

It was late afternoon; the reflection of the lowering sun bobbed in the water like a buoy. A little one-man fishing boat chugged past, not very far off, a cooler strapped to its roof. The man waved to Khim. She raised one hand slightly.

They stood at the edge of the terrace that looked down upon the water, Zhon gazing in thought as he gripped the rail. He pointed to the right. "I'll be there. Of course, I'll do the Gold-Scaled Dragon, Cholukan, and the Curious Fish. You'll be over there." He pointed to the left. "You'll be the Silver-Scaled Dragon, the Ruby Empress, and the Black Stork."

"Of course," Khim echoed quietly. The female characters, as was traditional. He didn't even need to tell her, but perhaps it helped him organize things in his mind to say it aloud, or perhaps it was just part of him acting his role as director. Khim said, "But isn't the water too deep right here, even this close to shore?"

"I tested it with a rod...didn't you see? Or were you distracted again?"

"I'm sorry...no, I didn't see."

It was true: she *had* been distracted. She had been looking for that river rat, fixed in the net of the banyan tree's serpentine lianas. It was gone. Well...perhaps its remains had finally decayed enough that they had come apart and dropped down into the water? Maybe some scavenger had come along, even other rats, to feed on it?

"Why do you daydream so much?" he asked her. "I really do think you have too much water sloshing around inside your skull."

"So you don't think the water is too deep? The floor too muddy down there?"

"The mud will help to hold you in *place*, you know that. The water is a bit deeper here than beside the park, okay, but even if you do go under now and then...it happens. We train for that. I can hold my breath like a pearl diver. Look, I'm not much taller than you. If I can do this, you can do it. That little bitch has money...this is a better payday than we've ever seen."

"Should we go through a full rehearsal?"

"*Why*, Khim? We've done this play a hundred times, haven't we? We could do this in our sleep."

"So why did we dress for it?"

"I changed my mind, all right?" he snapped. "I told you, I tested with a pole. I've looked it all over. Everything looks good!" He pushed back his black sleeve to expose a cheap waterproof watch, and glanced at the time. "Anyway," he said, preoccupied, "we look business-like if the café owner notices us."

A small group of men sat at a table nearby, and they'd been watching the puppeteers while they drank beer and snacked on tiny crunchy octopuses. Abruptly, one of them barked a cry, startling Khim. She first looked around at the man, then in the direction he was pointing.

One of the tentacle-like creepers that dangled into the water had, for whatever reason — maybe a wasp had alighted on its length? — suddenly retracted. Khim noticed this time, where she hadn't consciously the last time, that these tendrils bore tiny sensitive hairs or bristles. They looked spiny, actually. Were these bristles hollow, she oddly found herself wondering, like straws that could draw up nutrients?

The contracting vine lifted a dripping beer can out of the water. It had crushed the can through the middle in its coils.

"Ha!" the pointing man laughed drunkenly to his friends. "It's thirsty!"

Evening had come, the sky purpling, and strings of little green lights festooned about the café — even in some of the banyan tree's overhanging branches — came on. They made its leaves seem to glow with an uncanny illumination of their own. There were other, far smaller trees spaced throughout the grounds of the Banyan Café, their bushy tops reaching to the upper levels and also jeweled with flashing green lights, but they were dwarfed by that looming, weighty shape off to one side. That tree was like a spot where the very substance of night had solidified.

Khim had ordered a popular Western beer, and she nursed it at a little table where she sat alone, near the railing on the café's third and uppermost level. She gazed off into the shimmering black water.

She understood now why Zhon had come here in a taxi, and asked her to follow him on their motorbike. He had said it was because the taxi was too full of the bagged puppets and bundles of rods and the rubber bibs and boots they would need for the rehearsal that had never manifested. She understood now why he had glanced at his watch. Running late to go bring all the equipment back home, and then go on to meet Jinh at her bar.

He didn't hold his liquor well. Had he slapped Jinh in the face yet, after a drink too many? Khim doubted it, even though the woman served it to him in a greater abundance than he had ever indulged before he'd met her.

Khim wondered why he hadn't just told her he was going on to meet Jinh tonight. It would have been just the same.

From up here she could see past the tree's cloud-like mass of leaves, could look upon the swooping red roofs of the temple next door, like a series of stylized ocean waves. She could see the temple's little wharf, the end of which was flanked by two stone pillars topped with stone lanterns in which candles burned. The pillars were gripped in the coils of snake-like vines that had strayed, had blindly groped, in that direction. When worshipers at that temple passed away, their cheap coffins were loaded onto a little barge that the monks took down the river, to a crematorium.

Khim had only just learned that the temple had been built here because of the banyan tree, and what it symbolized to her religion. She had heard that the tree might have loomed here for hundreds of years before the temple's construction. Probably before most of Haikan's construction.

She smelled incense wafting toward her from the temple. She smelled the river, its stench of life and decay. It was as if the very water itself were rotting.

From out of the gloom a man leaned close to her, and she flinched. Looking around, she felt a little stab of excitement, as if Zhon might have come back for her. She next felt angry at herself for that. She looked into the face of a middle-aged man with beer breath. He smiled yellowed teeth, nothing like Zhon's dazzling smile, and asked her if he could buy her another beer.

"No thanks," she said. "I'm waiting for my husband."

That discouraged him. He mumbled something and tottered off.

After this beer she'd go home. He'd either be there or he wouldn't. Maybe the dry fake mermaid would have left another scale in her bed, maybe even purposely to taunt her.

A rustling sound drew her attention back to the banyan tree. She saw that its restless sea of leaves was rolling, tossing. She realized, though, that no breeze passed across her forearms where she had pushed back her long black sleeves, or stirred her long black hair.

———— ◆ ————

They came just before dusk, well before the wedding party would arrive at the Banyan Café, so as not to feel rushed setting up. This time Zhon had them both ride in the taxi with their equipment, despite the car being no larger than the one he had ridden alone in the other evening.

He had come home late and in a sour mood that night, and Khim had wondered if he and Jinh had quarreled. She had pretended to be asleep, even when he began rubbing her back under her pajama top, something he hadn't done in a while. Maybe it was just that Jinh was on her period? Whatever the case, Khim didn't roll onto her back for him as she once would have, and Zhon had muttered a curse to himself and rolled away from her.

Today he was less surly but they spoke little, all business, like puppets themselves lacking for an animating force.

Some water puppeteers erected a screen upon supporting floats (or if the body of water was small enough, stretched entirely across it), this screen perhaps being entirely black, perhaps painted or embroidered with a brightly colored scene, which the puppeteers would hide behind while manipulating their figures. This was more easily accomplished with a small pond or man-made pool, but Zhon and Khim usually performed at the park, at a certain inlet where the river became calm. Not only that, though; they practiced the more traditional form of the ancient art, where the puppeteers were hidden in plain sight. They would, however, both of them set up a little raft of sorts with something like a miniature pop-up tent of black nylon atop it, these rafts weighted in place near the spot where each of them would be performing. Like moored houseboats, these floating tents contained the various puppets, with their series of attached wooden rods, that would be switched out during the performance.

Khim had waded out through a sucking, ankle-deep bed of slime to her spot, and was mooring in place the raft she had dragged behind her, when she heard an excited exclamation and looked back to see a small boy at the terrace railing, pointing toward her. His father stood beside him, carrying a baby girl on his hip, all three of them watching her. When the boy saw that Khim had noticed him, he waved. She waved back.

She heard the boy beg his father that they stay to watch the puppet show. His innocence spiked Khim. Could Zhon really have once been a boy just like him, thrilled by puppets acting out dramas and comedies, history and folklore, in inky pools lit magically by torches or colored spotlights? Thrilled at the idea of one day projecting life into such puppets himself? A fresh red fig on its fragile stem…before falling, before bobbing in the water and rotting.

What were the puppets to Zhon now? Just tools of wood, like the handle of a scythe or shovel? Blistering and resented?

And that baby girl, dark eyes wide, wondering, uncomprehending as she stared at the woman shoulder-deep in the water. Had Jinh truly once been such an innocent? When did that change, and why? When had she first decided not only to betray another woman, but in essence her entire race of sisters? What was wrong with people? And most of all, Khim wondered just then, what was wrong with herself? She thought she could more easily understand, and control, her puppets than she could her own life.

The father patiently told the boy they had to go meet his mother now, as she got off work, but he promised to take him and his sister to the park one day soon. There were often puppet shows at the river alongside the park, he told him.

"Yes!" Khim called. "That's us – I perform there often! I'll see you there one day soon, okay?"

Khim's words seemed to satisfy the boy where perhaps the father wouldn't have succeeded as quickly. They turned to go, waves were again exchanged, and the father smiled back at Khim in thanks, not lasciviously. She was left feeling somewhat uplifted, and fleetingly she was reminded of why she herself had once loved this strange vocation that had been fated her. She doubted the audience she would be performing for soon would make her feel any warmer than this.

Stay this way, she wanted to cry after the boy.

"Are you ready over there, or what?" she heard Zhon call to her, across the slowly darkening water.

Under the constellation of strung green lights, waiters brought trays of 777 brand beer, which the guests poured into plastic mugs into which other waiters with tongs had dropped big chunks of ice to keep the beer cool in the evening heat. No one sipped beer on their own without first raising a toast to the others at their table. "One…two… three…*cheers!*" they all chanted, the plastic mugs clunking together, and everyone drank as one.

A salad was brought, bowls of rice wafers in pastel shades, deeply red goat's blood soup with gelatinous blood cakes. Soon there would be venison, and the main course would be river fish that tasted of the muddy water in which they lived and from which they had been plucked to die in the air.

Water puppeteers who worked with indoor pools often used complex lighting setups with colored filters and strobes, lately even lasers, plus fog machines, but outdoors such artificial fog might blow anywhere, into the crowd, obscuring the performance. Out here, tonight, all the cigarette smoke wafting from the tables would have to suffice for that mystical effect. But Zhon had at least set up a few strategically positioned floodlights to illuminate their liquid stage, and with darkness having fully descended, one of the waiters switched these lights on as Zhon had instructed him. The guests looked up at this, alerted to the show's imminence. This waiter then went to the café's music system to hit play on Zhon's CD of music and prerecorded dialogue. Zhon had mixed the music from tracks he had sampled online from various movie and TV soundtracks, such as the famously mournful theme music from the popular soap opera *B-2*. The voices for the various male characters in this play had been recorded by Zhon (cackling and speaking in a high pitch as Cholukan, and being silly in another way as the Curious Fish who would provide comical relief throughout, popping up now and then to interrupt the proceedings) and his uncle (who had nicely affected a deep, resonant voice for the Gold-Scaled Dragon), but Zhon had always complained Khim's delivery was too flat and soft, so he had hired an attractive karaoke lounge singer to read the female parts. This had been before Jinh, and Khim had no doubt he had slept with this singer, too.

Now with the CD's opening music track coming over the café's speakers, the wedding party guests – seated at tables abutting the terrace railing, and more tables on the two upper levels – truly focused their attention down on the floodlit patch of water, still chewing and smoking but greatly subduing their raucous chatter.

The play began with a (recorded) introduction by Cholukan, the Monkey God, whom the Ruby Empress had made scribe to the gods. Therefore, the story that unfolded would be like one of the tales that Cholukan had transcribed and now related. And so, the puppets began to go through their motions, skimming the surface of the water, their colorful glittering forms doubled in reflections that broke up into glistening fragments like darting schools of fish. The puppeteers were chest-deep in that oily black water, manipulating in their black-gloved hands the rods that like external skeletons put their beautiful puppets through the motions of mock life.

Near Khim floated her little raft with its tent hiding the other two puppets she would switch with the one she currently operated. Nearby her, too, she noticed a rotting fig bobbing past like the half-submerged head of some stealthy imp. She ignored it, as she always ignored floating trash and even big black leeches that might be attracted to her in the course of a performance. They couldn't get in through her boots, fishing bib, and other garments, anyway. But they still tried, sensing potential prey.

The comical Curious Fish wove its way through the narrative, eliciting laughs from the audience upon every appearance, and the melancholy Black Stork appeared throughout here and there, too, causing the audience to go quiet and somber as if out of respect for her misery. For what is a love story without some comedy, some tragedy? The Curious

Fish, a large golden carp with metallic orange scales, mistook the tail of the Gold-Scaled Dragon for its own tail and exclaimed in surprise, whipping around and around in splashing circles in an effort to get a better look at itself, setting off drunken guffaws. Zhon manipulated both those puppets at the same time in this scene, an admirable feat from a veteran puppeteer.

The Black Stork's tragedy was that she had fallen in love with the Gold-Scaled Dragon, and in one scene she lurked blackly in the shadows to spy on him (though, to make this puppet pop out from the dark water, she was highlighted with touches of blue and purple, her neck was iridescent, and her eyes and long bill were brilliant red). She eavesdropped on the Gold-Scaled Dragon and heard him talking to himself passionately of his great love, but the Black Stork didn't realize it was the Silver-Scaled Dragon he was speaking of, and not herself.

Khim knew from having performed this play before, down by the park, that in the scene where the Black Stork realized the truth and opened her wings for the first time in the play to flap away alone – thereby disappearing from the story – it was not unusual for children and even women to shed tears. While this was always gratifying to her, that she had produced this effect by manipulating a doll she and Zhon had created together like a substitute child, at the same time she would find it funny that people might weep more for a fictitious character in a story than for some suffering real-life human being.

And now in fact it was time for that scene where the Black Stork eavesdropped on the lovestruck God-Scaled Dragon. Sloshing the puppet rods rhythmically through the swampy-smelling water as if paddling a kayak, Khim was making the bird's long legs creep toward the spot where it could listen to its beloved. Over the sloshing sounds she made, she heard something heavy drop from above into the water behind her. She couldn't turn to look, occupied as she was, but guessed it might have been a fig...or from the heaviness of the splash, a clump of figs, perhaps loosed by a monkey.

The smell of cooking food was carried to her from the wedding reception, and the scent of incense came wafting from the temple hidden behind the bulk of the banyan tree, as if rites might be underway for a funeral to occur tomorrow.

Khim felt a pressure insinuating itself along the outside of her right leg. It was hard to define its cause through her thick rubber boot. It might be a plant rooted in the muck she stood rooted in herself, but more likely was a catfish. Nothing to be nervous about. The "Iridescent Shark" catfish could grow four feet in length in this river, but even that wasn't a threat, and crocodiles were not seen along the river where it bordered the city, being nearly extinct in the Unnamed Country from overharvesting.

Then, another heavy splash, this one startling Khim, because it was more to her front and a shorter distance than the one behind her; so close the spray struck her. This time, through the mesh of her hood, she'd caught a glimpse of what had fallen from above. It was one of the tendrils of the banyan tree, that had apparently been coiled up into the canopy of green-lit green leaves. Khim now assumed this was what the first splash, behind her, had been as well.

She tried not to falter in her performance, but no sooner had the second tendril dropped into the water than she felt its pressure firmly against her right leg, where the first tendril had only brushed against her, apparently. This second tendril, to her revulsion, was encircling her leg, and tightening as it did so.

She tried to shake the limb off her own, but the coil only tightened all the more, and now she realized there were two tendrils looped around her right leg and squeezing. The first one hadn't merely brushed her, after all.

An image flashed into her mind, horrifying her – of that catfish drawn up into the air, where the two shirtless boys could get at it. Was that what they intended to do, these two limbs; pull her into the air to hang upside-down as if snared in some boobytrap? Might two of them be strong enough to accomplish that? But then she remembered the spiny-haired limb hadn't decided to lift the fish out of the water on its own (as if to drown it in oxygen); that action had been triggered by the boys. Left to its own devices, the tendril would have had its way with the fish below the surface of the river. There, to leech it of its nutrients. Of its blood.

Khim darted an anxious look over at her husband, as if to ask him what to do, afraid to disrupt their performance, but at that moment came a tug on her right leg so strong that her knees buckled and she slipped down into the water more deeply. Right up to the mesh of her mask. She saw the river's black, glistening skin on level with her chin, and she let out a sharp cry. But was it drowned out by the deep-voiced, romantics musings of the Gold-Scaled Dragon over the speakers?

Another tug, either from the second tendril or maybe both of them working in concert. She was a puppet herself, now, and her master grew impatient. The limbs sought to pull her down entirely under the water. Why? Did they know in their mindless, mechanical way they would have a better advantage there, with their prey out of its own element? Did they prefer the privacy of the darkness down there in which to feed?

Khim's head went under, but she thrust herself back up. She tried to yank her leg away from the coils again, but it was as though men were on the other end of two ropes drawing her down. Her left foot came out of its boot, still mired in the mud. She thrashed her arms, and in so doing accidentally opened the wings of the stork puppet a little prematurely. The wings beat at the water, and the stork seemed ready to flap up into the air and disappear into the night, forlorn and forsaken.

A good number of women in the audience, and even some men made maudlin by beer and rice wine, stifled sobs as the Black Stork prepared to take flight.

"Zhon!" Khim cried out, before her head went under again. She let go of the puppet's rods, finally abandoning her duty, finally not caring if the river's current bore the beautiful puppet away, to reach down and try to extricate herself with her hands.

Fully submerged, she saw nothing under the surface, her gloved fingers clawing blindly at the coils. She was beginning to panic, but behind the panic was a blaze of fury. Had Zhon the director planned this? Had he not been as oblivious to the tree's behaviors as he'd seemed when she had glimpsed hints of them? Had he positioned her just so, in the hopes that this very thing would happen? That she would be vulnerable here, be attacked? She, trapped…him, freed?

No…no…the *bride* had chosen this spot, she reminded herself…

As she sought to free her leg, holding desperately onto twin lung-fuls of air, either a third tendril or one of the first two coiled around her wrist.

She could no longer straighten up.

Then, she also felt human hands taking hold of her. Grasping her around the waist, pulling her backward, or at least trying to. She was at the center of a tug of war, and she knew the arms around her belonged to Zhon. He held her the way she clung to him when she rode behind him on his motorbike.

For a moment she had thought he had planned all this. Of course not. But at the most, she might have expected that he would hang back in horror and cry out for someone to summon help, the police perhaps, or maybe just beg a guest with a knife from one of the wedding reception tables to dive in and swim to her.

But here he was himself, fighting to rescue her. He had heard her cry, and come. She wanted to twist around in the black void to see him, but she couldn't turn, not with more vines wrapping around her. Pulling her down toward the muck. She felt Zhon against her, being drawn down to the bottom, too. She could tell he had let go of her waist to swish his own frantic arms, but he was still there, his body against hers as the tendrils snared him as well. Perhaps the vines would bind the two of them together.

The members of the wedding party would soon weep in a different way.

They would cry out, at first in confusion. Later in horror. The confusion began when the Black Stork stopped flapping its wings and slumped into the water. In place of its flapping wings, thrusting out of the water were flapping human arms. Then, the Gold-Scaled Dragon toppled sideways to bob upon the river's surface, as its puppeteer abandoned it to thrash toward the first operator's side, then ducked down under the surface in search of her.

Neither of them resurfaced after that. Realizing this wasn't part of the performance, drunken guests shouted for help. Could someone summon the police? A few wives begged their husbands to dive into the water with a food-encrusted knife to go to the puppeteers' aid, but what had hold of them? A crocodile? Several crocodiles, however rare? No matter how desperate they felt, no one in the party was willing to venture into the liquid blackness.

Eventually they realized what had happened, when a tendril that had been hanging down into the water all this time suddenly coiled itself up, and in so doing lifted a prize from the river's surface. This vine had hold of the puppet of the Black Stork. Though the wings hung down limply, for a few moments as the puppet was raised, dripping, higher and higher toward the canopy of leaves, it seemed almost as if the Black Stork meant to fly away into the night, after all.

But apparently having realized, at last, that there was no nourishment to be had from the inanimate object, the tendril's coils tightened bitterly and crushed the beautiful puppet through the middle, and it hung there swaying above the now still and silent water.

STILL PACKED

SIMON STRANTZAS

Florence didn't want to explain to Duane that it was over. She'd fallen into bed with him easier than she would have guessed, and it felt so good and natural that she forgot completely about her husband, Sebastian. Luckily none of her nosy coworkers had seen her slip out with the young waiter, all six muscular feet of him. She'd been drunk, but not drunk enough she didn't know better. Just drunk enough not to care. While she rode Duane part of her floated disconnected, wondering how she could have forgotten how it felt. Wondering when was the last time Sebastian had made her feel as good. She ground herself harder against Duane and soon forgot what she'd been thinking altogether. Afterward, after he fell asleep on his stomach, glistening body highlighted by the moon, she gathered her things and took an overly fragrant taxi back to her hotel. She thought about how the door of the cage she'd been locked behind had just swung open. She thought about how now that the conference was over she and Duane had to be over as well.

He gave her a queer look when she told him.

"Uh, yeah, sure," he said, retrieving her empty glass off the bar. "If that's what you want."

"I don't know if I do. It's just, you know. I just don't think it would work out. I'm sorry."

"It's cool."

She gave him one final kiss goodbye from which he pulled away early, then indiscreetly wiped his mouth afterward. As though something tasted off. Florence rolled her eyes; she hadn't tasted anything.

The plane didn't land until an hour after it was supposed to, but she didn't mind. She felt buoyant, cruising high above the earth. The freedom of the preceding week had been like a dream, and she struggled to hold onto it, keep her momentary respite from ending. The rise of the familiar jagged city skyline below reminded her though that nothing had changed. Because nothing ever changes. And when, later, the taxi pulled up to her tiny two-story house, one of so many other tiny two-story houses on the brightly lit street, she felt the choke collar tighten round her throat.

She slipped inside quietly, praying Sebastian would already be asleep.

Then the living room light clicked on and she withered in place.

"You were supposed to call me when you landed. I would have picked you up," Sebastian said, eyes swollen from exhaustion. In his lap, a book he'd obviously fallen asleep while reading. He looked like a pudgy balding turtle, a far cry from the sinewy, wild-haired punk he'd been when they met.

"There was a problem with the engine. They swapped the plane at Newark. I didn't want to bother you."

"Well, I'm glad you're finally home. How was your trip? Did you get up to anything exciting?"

She sensed his eager stare was a trap.

"Just the usual. Seminars and talks. Dinners with other reps. Nothing exciting."

He looked anxious, as though about to say something but not sure if he should. Then he seemed to change his mind.

"Well, I'm glad you're home," he said as he stood, moving the earmarked book to the end table. "I'll bring your carry-on upstairs for you?"

"It's okay," she said. "I can do it."

"I don't mind."

"Please, just leave it."

His face dropped. She tried to smile to spare him hurt feelings but it didn't feel right on her face. It felt like a mask. Like one of those suffocating French iron masks. When Sebastian reached over and touched her she was surprised. His skin felt cool.

"Flo, what do you want?"

The question threw her.

"What do you mean?"

"I mean can I get you something? Anything?"

Was that really his question?

She shook her head. "No, I'm okay."

"You don't seem it. You seem tired," he said.

"And you seem like you want to say something."

"No...not really," he said. Then, after a moment, "But will you tell me more about your trip tomorrow?"

I'm not telling you anything, she thought, then nodded. He looked relieved.

"Go ahead and go to bed," she suggested. He smiled and stepped toward her, arms raising for a hug. She shrank away. "I need to take a quick shower. I stink."

"I don't care."

"Well, I do. Besides, I'm still wound up. I'll join you upstairs later."

"Okay," he said, unsure, then collected his book and made a feint toward kissing her forehead before stopping himself.

She watched him climb the stairs to their room.

When the bedroom door closed she sighed and fell into the worn couch, more exhausted than ever. He was unbearable like this. So eager and needy—it made her feel as though the walls of their overstuffed living room had moved closer while she was away. Their popcorn ceiling, lower, like storming rain clouds. Somewhere outside a neighbour's dog growled and whined. A reminder that it was all endless, and that frustration more than anything finally drove her to her aching feet.

Even the shower felt constricted. She felt sad washing away the last of Duane and the freedom she'd barely tasted. It was all so final. Were those his remnants spiralling down the drain in an opaque gluey wad? Could the massage of the hot jets on her back dispel the ghosts of his fingers drumming along her spine? By luck she noticed the thumb-sized bruises he'd left on each of her hips, bruises that might take weeks to heal, which meant she had to be careful undressing in front of Sebastian. She should have paid better attention and not forgotten herself in the drunken heat of the moment.

It had been years since Sebastian left a mark on her like that. He used to have the air of danger, unpredictability. So when had he become safe? So loving and pliable? His wildness tamed? First he stopped playing music, then stopped listening to it, and slowly he transformed in increments while she wasn't paying attention. He no longer even fought with her, never bit at her. No matter what she tried, no matter how she prodded, he was always the one to apologize. Always deferred to what she wanted, even though what she wanted was to bounce him off the walls.

Florence waited until she heard his droning snore before entering the bedroom, but she only made it one barefooted step past the doorway. From there, she saw round Sebastian boxed by the sliver of light from the hallway, and couldn't push herself further. So she stepped back and quietly pulled the door shut. Across the empty hall was the extra bedroom Sebastian mistakenly believed they would one day need. Not ideal, but it would do. Her feet dangled over the edge of the cramped miniature bed, but if she curled her legs the right way she could make herself fit. Once settled, she pulled the woven blanket over her head and turned everything dark and unfamiliar.

She woke on the uncarpeted floor, sweating and facing the ceiling, a cry still ringing her ears. Had it been real or the vestige of a dream already receding into the murk of her subconscious? There was no clock nearby, but the window was so lightless and black it had to be well before dawn. She sat, rubbed her face, confused how she'd ended up in the spare room, then closed her eyes and groaned. Something in her gut shifted. She considered standing but knew it would be too much work. Instead, she pulled down the blanket from the bed above her and covered her face. It wasn't enough, though. Despite her exhaustion, she couldn't fall back asleep. She spent the rest of the night drifting between two unwelcoming states.

Morning failed to improve things; she only felt worse. Her back bruised from the hard floor made rising to her feet a challenge. Everything was swollen; everything was stuck. Nothing that seemed sensible in the middle of the night made sense in the light of day. It was all beginning to feel far too familiar.

Once Florence worked up the energy, she trudged down the stairs and into the bright kitchen. Sebastian stood at the sink, staring out the window into their green backyard, and when he saw her his rosy cherub face and warm round eyes lit up. It was comforting and she utterly despised it.

"Good morning," he said, letting the sheer curtain fall. "You didn't come to bed last night?"

"I didn't want to wake you."

"I wouldn't have minded."

"No," she said. "You probably wouldn't have."

He returned to the breakfast he was preparing on the stove. Over the years, he'd discovered a love of cooking and experimentation with new dishes, but Florence couldn't help but miss the old Sebastian, the one who once called putting milk in his sugar cereal *too bougie*.

"Tell me what you want me to make you."

"I'll have whatever."

He paused, mouth pursed.

"But...what do you want?"

"I don't know. Nothing. I'm fine," she muttered. She couldn't look at him as she poured a large mug of coffee. "What were you looking at?"

"Nothing. I thought I heard an animal or something. I noticed your carry-on is still where you left it. Should I bring it upstairs for you?"

She quietly groaned. Dealing with unpacking was not something she wanted to do, but she couldn't bear the idea of surrendering to Sebastian.

"I'll move it before I leave."

"All right," he said softly. Then pulled out the chair beside her and sat. "Now that you've slept there's something I need to ask."

Her mug trembled.

"What's that?"

"I think," he said, nervously. "I think we should get a dog."

"We should what?"

"A dog. We should get one. I want to get one."

"A dog?" The word, if it were a real word, made no sense.

"You go to conferences and work late and I'm left at home by myself. It would be nice to have some company. I know you don't like animals—"

"I don't?"

"—but it doesn't have to be a big one. It can be a little dog. Like a terrier, maybe. Or a corgi."

"You want a little dog because you're lonely?"

"No, not really. No. Only sometimes. But with you gone the house feels empty. I thought a lot about this and I'd like to do it."

She closed her eyes. Rubbed her forehead to soothe it. Was there anything worse than an aging punk rocker walking a tiny dog?

"I don't know, Seb. Can we talk about this later? I need to get ready for work."

"Sure," he pouted. "Later."

———————

A court of narrowed eyes watched Florence slip into the office, the voyeurs whispering gleefully to one another. She ignored them and plopped behind her glass desk, careful not to make eye contact. The thought of dealing with their gossip made her queasy. Another day in prison. She sighed and wished she were anyplace else.

A sudden memory, Duane's stubble on the inside of her thigh, made her shudder. She resisted the urge to scratch at the phantom.

"Still figuring out what you want?"

She turned, found Jane standing over her. Jane, whom she hadn't seen in a week. Jane, who was a wreath of scarves masquerading as a department lead.

"Pardon?"

"The mock-ups," she said, pointing at Florence's desk. "You still haven't picked one out?"

Florence looked down at the spread of designs in front of her. They all looked equally turgid.

"Not yet. I haven't had the chance."

Jane laughed uninfectiously.

"You look hungover. It's marvellous."

"I'm perfectly fine."

Jane winked. Adjusted her large-beaded seafoam bracelet.

"I know how these things are, you don't have to tell me. Marty had me fly to Washington a few months back and a group of us broke into the hotel spa at three a.m. to use the hot tubs. Now *that* was a crazy night."

"I didn't do anything like that. It was mostly early nights."

"Oh really?" She leaned in and inhaled, then made a strange face. "Well, you certainly seem as though you got into all sorts of trouble."

She smiled knowingly. Florence refused to acknowledge whatever she was implying.

"Well, I should get back to these," Florence said, holding up one of the horrid designs.

Jane touched her finger to her lips. "I get it. What happens in Vegas or wherever you are. Mum's the word. We'll catch up at lunch. My treat. Wash up and think about where you want to go."

"Go?"

"For lunch."

"I honestly have no idea."

"You must want something. Think on it. I'll see you at noon."

But Florence had no intention of thinking on anything, nor of spending her lunch being interrogated by Jane. When five minutes to twelve approached, Florence hurriedly collected her purse and fled down the back stairwell, past the yellowed I.T. staff huddled around their unfiltered malodorous cigarettes.

As soon as she stepped through the mesh gate into the chilled outside air she realized she couldn't stomach going back, and the admission washed her in overwhelming relief. Her trip, her encounter with Duane...these things *changed* her. There was no denying it. Everything in her life had become a snare, and she no longer wanted to feel miserable, distracted. Was that wrong? She wasn't sure, but she couldn't deny she felt her spirits buoyed and her step lighter, and soon enough she found herself wandering through the Fashion District, and then taking a left off Queen Street toward the lakeshore boardwalk. The sun rolled out from behind the clouds as she rounded the corner, and though the air was crisp she removed her jacket so she might enjoy the feel of the breeze against her bare arms.

I'm so light, she thought. *I might just float away.*

She turned to face the sun and shut her eyes to its warmth just long enough for her cellular phone to ring. Her smile dimmed.

"It's me," Sebastian said. "I wanted you to know I saw your carry-on was still by the door but I didn't move it."

"Thanks?" she said. "Is that why you called?"

"No, of course not," he said. "I was just trying to help you."

She could hear music playing in the background. Something soft-tempo, folksy. She gripped the phone tighter. He'd become so soft, both inside and out. She struggled for breath.

"Seb, I'm a little busy at the moment."

"Sorry, Flo. I know you said we'd talk later, but I wanted to know if you had a chance to think about it yet."

"Think about what?"

"About getting a dog."

She scowled.

"I haven't. I'm not sure it's a good idea. Having it underfoot, constantly whimpering for attention? I don't know, Seb. I might go mad."

He didn't say anything, but she heard his disappointment across the line.

When he spoke again, his voice sounded different. She wasn't immediately sure why.

"Well, anyway...something weird has just happened."

"Weird?"

"Yeah."

There was another wordless pause. She squeezed her eyes shut. Her clenched jaw trembled.

"Are you going to tell me or should I guess?"

"I just got a phone call."

Florence opened her eyes. Stopped walking. The sun slunk behind a neighbouring cloud.

"Who from?"

"That's the thing. I don't know. But he asked for you."

"He who what?" Her stomach tightened, flipped. Something inside cried but she stifled it.

"He said something about a hotel?"

"Seb, I—"

"I could barely hear him. The line was bad. I'm not sure I heard him right."

She felt unexpectedly shaken but did her best to hide it. So many thoughts raced through her head, so many possible lies. She put her hand on her stomach to quell the churn.

"Well, if he calls again, tell him I'll call back."

"Is that what you want?"

"Why wouldn't I?" she asked, though she already knew that was the wrong question and rushed to end the call before he could answer.

Florence wasn't sure where she was going but kept walking—along the boardwalk, past the rollerbladers and joggers, around young women pushing baby strollers. She felt flush, her heart beating faster, her skin growing cold and prickly, and she resented it. Nothing looked familiar. Where has she taken the wrong turn? When? At the end of the Leslie Spit she turned left once more and headed away from the water, up along a wooded path made of flat grey stones until she passed a dark brown sign with "Lancet Park" painted in bright yellow letters. It was a small hidden lawn with a single scuffed and chipped metal playset over which children teemed. She stopped to watch them press their ruddy faces against the bars and against one another, while she observed from behind the smattering of seated adults that encircled them on benches like sarsen stones.

They were animals. The way the messy children climbed and tore at one another, the volume and pitch of their screams. It was impossible to believe they were human, let alone that she had once been one herself. She scanned their round features and pudgy shortened limbs and wondered if she'd once looked as grotesque and misshapen, wondered if a body so small and twisted was the germ for whom she became.

Stranger still was how familiar the children looked. As though she'd seen each shrivelled, dried-apple face before. There was a miniature Jane, all dark hair and darker eyes, shoving her way through the throng. And there were her parents, a pair of runted cherubs, locked hand-in-hand an arm's reach from the fray. Ducking in and out of the group was a Marty, constantly chattering, constantly ignored, his thin ginger hair flattened against his head. It took only a moment to find her little

Sebastian, the wild-haired boy patiently awaiting his turn at the slide. And of course there was a Duane, because there was always a Duane, dead centre of everything, drawing all attention without effort. It was uncanny, the similarities—all roaming free and unhindered around the playset—but more uncanny was how many doubles she saw. There was only one face she couldn't find in the ruddy preschool swarm, but it had to be there, somewhere. Maybe if—

"What do you want?"

The voice startled her. On the bench sat a woman, probably in her early thirties, dressed in an oversized grey wool coat with a green patterned scarf wrapped around her jaundiced head. Stray hairs peeked out haphazardly, giving the woman a harried appearance. She glared at Florence, wrinkled her nose.

"I was just—" Florence offered. "I guess I was just watching the kids." The woman's eyes narrowed. Florence realized how her behaviour must look. "I was just walking by," she added hurriedly. "The children distracted me. I...well, I didn't mean to make anyone uncomfortable. I should go."

The woman's shoulders loosened, her sunken eyes softened.

"No, you don't have to. It's all right. I was surprised because I've never seen you before, and strangers don't usually stop in here. Sit down, please. Is everything okay?"

Florence cautiously accepted the woman's invitation, worried if she didn't the woman might call the police. She glanced at the other parents on the other benches, sitting alone or in stoic pairs. Everyone watched the children dashing through the playset and across the fine sand.

She rubbed her wrists.

"So," Florence offered out of politeness. "Which is yours?"

The woman pointed lazily toward the group of children climbing over one another precariously for their chance to travel down the slide. Florence's miniature parents looked close to tumbling off the edge of the platform.

"Is that safe?" Florence asked.

The woman shrugged. None of the other observers appeared concerned either, even as the writhing mass of little bodies grew larger. If anything, they seemed bored by it. The woman in the green scarf most of all.

"And where are your kids?" the woman asked. Florence mumbled, still distracted by the danger and the lack of concern about it.

"I haven't any."

The woman nodded.

"That explains a lot. Just let them be. Once you have kids you'll realize you can't make their choices for them. They have to learn from their own mistakes."

Florence turned to the woman more baffled than ever.

"I don't think it works like that."

The woman smirked. Made a noise through her fleshy nose. The children grew rowdier, tore at one another. Florence saw teeth. Heard whimpers and barks. Howls.

She stood. "Please. Aren't you going to do something?" Then raised her voice to the disaffected observers. "Aren't any of you going to do something?"

As she spoke, the first of the children crashed through the fleshy jam and shot feet-first down the slide. Behind her, the tiny Duane followed, orderly accompanied by the flush-faced little Sebastian. Or was it the other way around? She couldn't remember.

"See? Nothing to worry about. I knew they'd eventually figure out how to untangle themselves. You'll see one day," the woman continued.

Florence swallowed. Shook her head.

"I'm not having kids."

"No?"

"I—my husband Seb and I decided a long time ago."

She shrugged. "I guess he would know."

Yes, he would, Florence thought, but kept it to herself. She didn't like how her head felt. As though simultaneously stretched in multiple directions. The children's running in circles only amplified her unsureness.

"Sorry. Which one did you say was yours again?" Florence asked.

"Oh, does it matter? Whichever you want. Pick one."

Florence shook her head. Put her purse under her arm.

"I should get back to my walk."

"Just pick one. Any of them. Please. Just pick."

Florence's legs grew more unsteady by the moment.

"I can't. I have...I have to go," she said.

"Don't." The woman tried to sound disappointed. It didn't fit her right. "You still haven't told me what's wrong. I wanted a chance to help."

"Nothing's wrong," Florence said, waving her away. "I'm fine."

The woman stood, too. She came up to Florence's collar but was still tall enough to take her shoulders.

"I don't believe you," the woman said. "But it's okay. I'm here every day. I can wait."

"Thank you?"

The woman smiled. Florence turned and strode away, knowing if she looked back the woman would still be there, watching her go, same smile plastered to her round jaundiced face.

It wasn't until the park was long out of sight that Florence felt like herself again. Even so, she struggled to process what had happened. Each detail she recalled of Lancet Park, of the little yellowed woman there, pushed out the one before it, leaving her with only a few scattered and fractured moments.

More amazing was how little time had passed since she left them all. Time appeared to be dilating—each moment stretching too long. In contrast to the week before, she supposed, which sped by far too fast. It was only on the return to her dreary gated life that she could process and reckon with what she'd done. Each memory of Duane lingered—his glazed eyes when he wanted her to be more interesting; his knobby scarred hands as they took hold of her, flipped her over. Her own sense of release. She reached down and rested her hand on her quivering stomach. Duane was quiet, taciturn, open. Nothing like the staid, confining Sebastian. And she realized she didn't care if what was germinating inside her was a seed of guilt. At least guilt reminded her she could still feel. And what she felt was a desperate longing for the sense of unencumbrance she'd left at that hotel.

Returning to her tiny cellblock home mid-day was strange. The sun shone uninterrupted on the cramped cul-de-sac like an enormous searchlight. Were it not for the choked barking of some neighbour's dog she might have suspected she was trapped in a frozen moment of time. She disliked the unnerving solitude, and yet when she hurried into the house, almost tumbling over her still-packed carry-on, she couldn't deny a sense of relief when she called Sebastian's name and he didn't answer. That would make what she did next much simpler, albeit no less crazy.

But *was* it crazy? To call Duane? It had to be, especially considering how they'd left things. Yet she also felt more certain. Calling Duane was imperative. She couldn't explain why, but he haunted her and she knew no other way to exorcise him from her thoughts.

She raised the phone's receiver. As soon as it made contact an extended high-pitched wail like an animal crying overwhelmed her ear. Florence immediately dropped the receiver back on its hook. After a few moments nursing her shattered nerves she braced herself and tried again. Tentatively she placed the receiver back against her head and found the screech had gone. Only the empty dial tone greeted her. She exhaled. Crossed wires, she assumed.

Only at that moment did it occur to her she didn't have Duane's number. She'd never needed it. He'd simply been working at the bar each night, and only too happy to take her home when his shift was done. Did his apartment even have a phone? If so she couldn't remember it among the dirty dishes and laundry, but she'd been understandably distracted. A quiver rippled through her as she recalled those nights together. And, then, the obvious answer struck her. The bar. Of course she'd find him at the bar. Of course.

Dialling the hotel's number was easy. Knowing what she'd say when he answered was not. But she'd figure it out. What choice did she have? Florence's hand gently came to a rest on her stomach. The feel of it was soothing. She closed her eyes and imagined she was miles away from anything.

"Welcome to the Sheehan Hotel. This is the Front Desk. How may I assist you?"

Florence's panicked eyes flicked open. Suddenly, she doubted her plan.

"I was a guest there last week," she improvised. "My husband said you called looking for me?"

"Happy to help. What name was it under?"

Florence told him, and when that didn't work she told him the room she'd been staying in. She listened to the clatter of his keyboard for long enough to worry it wasn't they who had reached out to her. If they hadn't, did that mean—

"Here we go. Yes, it looks like we called you earlier today. Our staff wanted to make sure you enjoyed your stay with us."

"Yes?"

"That's great to hear. And did you have any suggestions about how we could make future stays better?"

"No, I don't think so."

"Wonderful. I'll put your comments down in your file for our team. They'll be happy to hear them. Is there anything else I can do for you?"

She hesitated. "You could—I mean, would you connect me to the bar? I need—"

"Certainly! One moment, please." There was a click and after a moment another, followed by a tinny ring that drilled a beat too long. She rubbed her palm hard against her slacks.

"Adobe. Can I help you?"

"I hope," she said. "I'm looking to speak with Duane."

"Duane?"

She panicked. Did Duane have a last name? Did she know it?

"He's one of your waiters?"

There were muffled sounds on the other end of the phone line. Voices she couldn't make out. Calling had been a tremendous mistake. It felt as though doors were closing around her. Florence started to hang up when the voice returned.

"I'm sorry, he's not in yet."

It was the middle of the day. Why would she think he'd be working? Through the receiver she heard a sound like popping. Or laughing.

"Should I try back later?"

"If you want," the voice said, curtly. She started to ask when but before she reached the end of her question he'd already hung up.

Florence sat down. That was not how the call was supposed to go.

In a way, she'd been lucky. She'd avoided the humiliation of realizing she was making a mistake while on the phone with Duane. In her cold newfound clarity she now saw he was not the key to her freedom. He was barely a person. Just a stack of muscles and a youthful cock costumed in overpracticed disaffection. She'd have to open that door some other way.

Without realizing it, in her distraction she'd been scratching the inside of her thigh, and when she lifted her hand she was horrified to find her fingers were tacky with some viscous fluid. Its pungent odor, sour, like something unwashed. It was stomach churning, and she immediately fled to the bathroom; first to scrub her hands, then to strip off her clothes and hurry into the shower. She set the temperature as hot as she could stand then scoured herself raw. It took longer than expected to clean off the residue, but eventually, thankfully, the gluiness gave way.

Her clothes, though, were unsalvageable. The stain had spread from her slacks to her blouse, fusing them together in a vile wad. Just the feel of them made her gag, and she struggled to cram the congealing mass into the white wastebasket before her stomach revolted. Drawing closed the liner was not enough; she had to toss the bundle out the window.

Her head followed after it. Bumps appeared instantly along her naked wet skin as she immersed herself in the cold air and breathed deep, clearing the sour nausea that lingered in her throat. As her illness faded, her ears rang with a muted sound almost like an infant's babble.

The telephone's ring interrupted her. She pulled in from the window and caught a glimpse of her face in the bathroom mirror, twisted with equal parts shock, eagerness, and dread. She knew who it was on the line. Who it had to be. It was carved into the grooves that cornered her eyes. Florence dashed naked from the bathroom to the phone in the bedroom, lifting the receiver despite her mounting reluctance.

As she placed the speaker against her ear she wished she had clothes on. The call would be so much easier with clothes on.

"Hello?"

"Florence?"

She was dizzy. She dropped onto the edge of the bed.

"Yes, it is."

"What are you doing home?"

"Sebastian?"

"I called your office. They said you disappeared. Are you okay?"

Was she? She didn't even know. Everything was so confusing. Everything felt smaller, more claustrophobic.

"I don't think so. I might have caught something. Where are you?"

"Coming home. I'll be a few minutes. Do you want me to bring you anything?"

"I don't know, I just need to—"

More muffled noises interrupted her. Was his hand over the receiver? She waited and when Sebastian finally returned he was breathless.

"Listen. I have to go. See you soon."

Then a click. No time for "I love you" or anything else Florence expected. Just a click. She set the receiver back in its cradle.

Then dashed back to the bathroom to be sick.

Florence dressed slowly, her balance growing more affected. Thinking became difficult, thoughts colliding and entangling. She felt Sebastian out there, somewhere, making his way home. Her mouth was dry, her hands clammy. He was closing in on her.

What did he want?

What did she want? She didn't know. Not really. After everything that had happened, she'd avoided thinking about it. But that was no longer an option. It didn't matter how ill she felt or how dreadful. It could no longer be avoided.

What did she want? She asked, over and over.

A voice, barely audible, growled.

To leave, it said. *To open the door and leave.*

But she couldn't. Could she?

And suddenly Florence realized nothing was stopping her.

Her packed carry-on, waiting by the front door, zipper hanging open like a smile.

She staggered out into the afternoon with a plan. She'd tell Sebastian she'd been sent last minute to an urgent out-of-town pitch meeting, then assure him it would only be for a few days and she'd call him when she landed. It didn't matter if he believed her; she'd already be long gone and out of reach. Thoughts of both Duane and Sebastian swam through her head, co-mingling with one another, pulling down on each of her arms as though she were a parade balloon. She felt as light as one, too—disconnected from solid ground—and had to take care not to look at her feet as she fled to avoid losing balance as the world teetered out of control. She made it almost halfway to the gate before her stomach convulsed painfully around its knot, but now that the decision was made she was determined to ignore it, to escape. She had to before the sickening feeling pinned her permanently in place.

But she made it only to the end of the drive.

Because that's when she heard it. Pitched so high and loud it was like an awl driven into her head. Some instinct stopped her legs from working. What was that cry? It reoccurred, a wailing summons from behind the house.

Beckoning her.

Ignore it. She had to ignore it. Sebastian was almost home.

She had to be gone before he arrived.

Instead, Florence set her carry-on down. Started her walk back toward the house. The ground ahead looked askew, as though it had been painted on a wide cotton sheet and that sheet was slowly being twisted. She stumbled once but caught herself. The air thickened and coagulated around her. She pushed through even as it filled in the void behind her, preventing retreat.

A carefully placed hand against the side of the house provided her support as she moved forward. The wail was getting louder, and as she urged herself closer she felt the sound in the back of her trembling chest, exacerbating the sourness she tasted. It was only when turning the corner into the back yard that the world suddenly righted and the resistance she felt evaporated.

But by then it was too late. She was stuck.

Stuck, and staring.

It sat in the middle of the yard, small and pink and whimpering.

The grass around it brown—which made no sense as the lawn had been fine when Florence looked through the kitchen window earlier. It raised its head when it saw her, large wet eyes with irises so wide everything appeared black. It reminded her of a baby bird, if that made any sense, because those eye bulged and blinked under veiny lids. However it was nothing like a bird at all. It appeared to be on the edge of life, and when it coughed while scratching its face Florence jerked away. How had it gotten into the backyard? Where had it come from?

"Oh my God!" The words were in Sebastian's voice. In her momentary confusion she thought it had said them. Then she turned and found her husband standing across the yard, damp and short of breath. He was holding her carry-on, the size of a small child, claim ticket tied around the handle. "What did you do? Flo, what did you do?"

She could barely speak. Her mouth was so dry.

"What did I do?"

"You got us a dog!"

A what? She stared at it, unsure. It stared back.

"Is this why you left early? To surprise me?"

"To surprise you?"

Sebastian carefully approached, his excitement noticeably welling. He knelt and pressed its wrinkled pink skin. It made a sound like laughing. Her hand found her clenched stomach.

"I can't believe you kept this a surprise! Without a doubt this is the most amazing thing you've ever done for me. For us!"

"Sebastian, I—"

He picked it up. It squirmed in his arms as he pressed it close to his chest. He closed his eyes. Florence smelled the clear jelly being smeared on his stained shirt.

"This is the start of something," he said. "A beginning. I can *feel* the change taking place."

"I don't understand."

Sebastian smiled as he slipped his finger into its mouth and it began suckling, reaching up for him. His eyes lit up.

"This is going to be so great, Flo. You'll see. Taking care of it is going to help a lot. Both of us, I mean. Everything is different now. We're different now."

"I am?"

He turned and looked at her, cradling its squirming pink flesh. Sebastian's eyes were wet and his smile had faltered, but only slightly. "This is a good thing, Flo. Trust me. This—all of this—is going to take work, but we'll figure things out together."

The pain in her abdomen grew sharper. Like a knife, sliding in. She flinched when her hand found the turgid flesh, her palm came away sticky with that murky sour fluid. There was a cry from Sebastian's arms. He started rocking it.

"Are you okay?" he asked her. "You're really pale."

"I need—" she started, her legs wobbling. "I need to sit down."

Sebastian replied but her ears stopped working. The world spun upside down then like a popped balloon spiralling away.

Florence opened her eyes and saw sky. Smelled the pungent odor of what coated her. Sebastian's one hand held hers, his other acted as a cradle. She heard it simpering as he helped her to her feet.

"You need to see a doctor."

"No," she said, clutching her stomach. Waves of nauseating cramps rolling in. "Not yet."

"Flo…"

He drew his hand away so she could find a wobbling balance.

It watched her from his arms. The noise it made was not describable.

"I need," she murmured, "I need to go. Just for a while. I have…" She swallowed. "There's a meeting…"

"What are you talking about?"

She heard a distant ringing from inside the house. She looked up at the window.

"I just have to go."

"Don't."

"I have to."

But when she turned she couldn't see her carry-on. The only thing nearby was her husband. Her husband, and what was in his arms.

"Just look," he said. His eyes watering, his mouth little more than a slit. "It loves being here with us already."

She stared at it. It stared at her, glassy-eyed, blubbering.

In the distance, the telephone kept ringing.

WE DON'T LIVE HERE ANYMORE

BROOKE WARRA

A ghost is not a haunted house.

Divorce is a haunted house. The purple specter of a grape juice stain on the countertop, lingering there since your toddler learned to pour her own breakfast. The nick in the living room doorframe that's always looked a little like a watching eye, there since you and Lonnie tried to move the old couch out but instead had to hack the thing to pieces with an axe before ditching its remains in dumpsters all over town because there's no large trash service in this neighborhood.

The creaking floorboards you know by heart, the dilapidated cobwebs in every corner, the bad smell in the second bedroom carpet. These are your ghosts. If you stay very still, sometimes, from the corner of your eye, you can see Darby, four years old, running through the living room, tripping, and bashing her head on the edge of that coffee table your mother-in-law dropped off on her way to Goodwill, and Lonnie scooping her up while you fetched a frozen pack of peas for the bruise.

So, sometimes, you stay very still.

Last night, that commercial for that mop, the one with the annoying suburban family and their dog—the one Lonnie and I used to impersonate every time one of us cleaned the floors—played during a movie I was trying to watch and I cried on my knees on the floor, making long keening noises until I retched and snot poured down my face.

When I met Lonnie I was 18, already a wife and mother. Darby was at home learning to walk while Adam, my high school sophomore sweetheart and Darby's father, played the new first-person-shooter, and I went to a bonfire where a band was supposed to be playing.

The twin towers had come down that day. It felt like it might be the end of the world.

A group of us had met up in a friend's backyard to burn things, drink beer, and discuss "American Exceptionalism" like we knew what we were talking about. We were wise and oppressed the way only free, privileged American children can be. At the time, I was reading a lot of Dostoevsky between folding loads of Adam's work shirts and underwear. Lonnie was wearing a Pixie's concert t-shirt. We sat in the grass near the fire. I showed him my favorite scar—a crescent moon-shaped knot of skin from a bike wreck in my cousin's gravel driveway. He showed me the scar his teeth had made going through his lower lip from a spill off the monkey bars at school.

When I woke at sunrise, I was topless in a field, Lonnie next to me. We wandered back to the house, searched amongst the sleeping bodies of the party-goers until we found a half-full bottle of wine and a roach to share for breakfast. We talked about our mutual love of specific cereal brands and golden oldies music and a shared hatred for cops and specific ice cream flavors.

"What's your *name?*" he had finally asked me and I told him, "Just call me Ray."

That half-full bottle of wine lasted the next several years. We stayed half-drunk and half-dressed, intoxicated on each other, on fights, glorious rows that began with throwing each other's shit in the front yard while the neighbors watched and only ended hours later in bed.

Darby grew into a serious little girl, learning to start the coffee before we woke and how to scramble eggs with a trick in the microwave, cleaning up after us and rolling her eyes. By the time the twins came when she was eight, she was practically their mother. We teased her about her self-imposed bedtimes, her habit of eating green beans straight from the can when she got tired of our penchant for fast food. But secretly, sometimes, especially in the afternoons when she sat hunched studiously over her school books and tossed cheese crackers to her brothers underneath the table—I would feel so overwhelmed, so in awe of her, or at the sight and smell of her, the soft baby curls at the base of her neck, and the fact that this perfectly grim, earnest little human had come from my own body that I would have to throw my arms around her and cover her face in kisses until she slapped me away.

The twins were an abomination—a healthy set of boys, an exact blending of mine and Lonnie's looks and dispositions. They were unruly, thoughtless, destructive, and adorable. We allowed them to commit various murders.

I resented everything about motherhood. From the first signs of pregnancy, my body's willingness and determination to get on with things without my participation or permission. The sickness, the swelling, the exhaustion. The gestational diabetes. The sobriety. And after, the runny noses and teething, the endless piles of laundry where the love seat used to be.

By the time I realized I was loving every second of it, it was too late. They were growing up, all of them. Darby was driving the car to her shifts at the animal shelter, the twins were down the street playing hockey in the cul-de-sac until dark and insisting I need not tuck them into bed as they tore past me, up the stairs to their shared bedroom, door slamming.

We worked and starved and made art and told ourselves we were a thousand times more interesting than we were. Lonnie took third-shift as a security guard at the water treatment plant but sang in a punk band on the weekends, wrote every single one of their songs, playing house parties until the cops came. I charmed every trucker passing through town who ever stopped for a sandwich at the convenience store where I cashiered but on my days off (just Tuesdays), I painted grotesque portraits, hellish landscapes, and the odd still-life.

I don't remember when Lonnie's bandmates stopped coming around the house, littering our garage with beer cans and profanity-laced political rants—sometime around the explosive popularity of social media and the birth of their own kids. No one had time or a reason to meet face to face anymore. When had my painting dropped off to nearly never? These things happen. Life happens. We still talked about doing these things, maybe more when the kids were older. When we retired (do convenience store cashiers retire?) and the kids were off on their own and we were living out of an RV, traveling the states, playing pubs and selling paintings at Saturday markets, that would be the life we were meant to live, that's when we'd really be free.

We started a collection of coins in a jar on the nightstand. Every *clink* of a penny, a wish in a well, a dream.

Of course he cheated.

Of course I knew it and pretended not to. It was a rot in our marriage. The stink of it was on everything. It was gangrenous, a sickly sweet bruise I poked at only when no one was looking. I'd go through his phone, delete every contact, or give it to the twins to dunk in their apple juice. The nights I waited up for him and he would waltz in just before dawn, I'd tell myself I was going to set all his clothes on fire. I was going to set him on fire. I was going to take the kids and leave for my mother's. I was going to make him leave. But when he came home, I'd lap up every word of the lies he told me like they were water in the desert. I'd make him breakfast and make a fool of myself trying to get him into bed with me. To reclaim him, to take back land that had been stolen from me.

I stared at myself naked in the mirror a lot during those years, looking for flaws, fingering the soft, doughy skin of my belly, tracing the stretchmarks my babies had left on their way out. I did crunches and planks in the nude, whatever was wrong with me, I would fix it. I would find the fault and close it.

I should have been taking photos. I should have been dressing myself in silky, lacey things, laying across tables and countertops, documenting my youth, my sex, the bounce of my ass. I should have known how beautiful I was; the dark purple of my nipples from all the breastfeeding, the dimples in my ever-thickening thighs, the leg hair I was too tired to shave after chasing after the kids all day. That's a thing that no one tells you—the hair on your legs stops coming in as you get older. It starts coming in other places.

That, and that you should take naked pictures of yourself.

<hr />

When the fibroids came and wouldn't stop, they told me I needed a hysterectomy. I cried at night, alone in bed. Lonnie came home more often at dawn, his car refusing to start after a long night of "playing poker at Jonny's".

Darby's friends liked me then. I was younger than most of their mothers.

"Yeah, but, you're not like, a regular mom," they'd tell me, a compliment of sorts.

I didn't tell them how Darby, finding me making breakfast, pantsless with a mug full of coffee and rum, would scream, "Why can't you just be *a normal mom, Ray?*", slamming the door as she left for work, dragging the twins behind her.

"Being a woman has nothing to do with your uterus," they told me, and Darby nodded, so I did too. "It's literally got nothing to do with it."

I would have liked to have had friends like these when I was young. They were like a spectacular eclosion, these kids, all of them, shedding their cocoons. I was happy just to feel the breeze coming off of them, their beating wings. They didn't take shit off anyone and were the ones to teach my daughter about taking a "mental health day," how to say "no," and how to ask for money she was owed. I took notes.

They showed me how to shape my eyebrows, how to tape my breasts into a tank top, how to practice witchcraft and pay homage to the divine feminine without the burden of my pesky uterus. We shaved Darby's head and made poppets out of her hair, named them after people we knew, wanted to take care of, or wanted to keep away. We made altars and left offerings to Hecate in the wintertime, to death, to dismemberment, to rebirth.

"There's all kinds of women in the world," they said and took me to marches, to protests, to night clubs where I learned to love the body I was in, the body I didn't owe anyone, dancing with it pressed against all the other kinds of bodies I met out in the world, holding hands with strangers in clouds of pepper spray, gorging on drive-thru tacos with the top button of my pants undone in parking lots at 2 a.m.

They told me not to wait up for Lonnie anymore and to watch more porn.

The landlord keeps calling me now. To ask when I will be ready to hand over the keys. I *do* have both the house keys, right? Per the lease we signed (over a decade ago), I need to turn in *both* of them or pay a fee. There is a young couple wanting to move in the first of next month and of course the carpets (the twenty-year-old brown shag) will need cleaning if I want my full deposit back. They're an ever-so-nice young couple with a little girl on the way and they can't wait to utilize the creek in the backyard this summer.

It's embarrassing that Lonnie has left me, that the twins are staying with Darby in her studio downtown, that I can't stay sober long enough to make them a proper dinner these days. That Lonnie won't come help me pack up the house, our life, *our whole life*—the broken toys that need to be thrown out, the little clay bird paperweight Darby made him in second grade he's left behind, the t-shirt and book collections we should divide up. It's embarrassing that we are pushing forty—parents, grown-ups who are still renting. It's all so juvenile and predictable: he met someone new and I haven't seen him since. He doesn't call the kids. Our friends don't tell me where he is.

I don't tell the landlord that. I promise to get the house cleared out in time. I lie and say I've signed a new lease.

I went and looked at apartments, near Darby, near the college. I thought about taking a few classes. Reading more Russian literature. Starting something new. But the apartments felt obscene. The white walls, the beige carpets, the speckled counters. Not a hint of life in their sterility. No notches in the doorframes for growing children. No missing window screens from the comings and goings of errant teenagers. Nary a mysterious smell in the carpets, a scuff mark on the linoleum, a fist-sized hole in the dry-wall. How could I live there if I couldn't even breathe?

Instead, I went home and sat in a lawn chair with the sprinklers on, smoking from a bong with a sign in the grass that said, "free to good home" and all of our shit in the yard. And just like that, our whole life was carted off piece by piece, on to new adventures, bigger and better things, until even the lawn chair was gone.

I kept the bong. And the paperweight.

That damn creek in the backyard.

Every spring it's flooded the yard and basement and every spring the landlord ignores my texts and emails about the water drowning my tomatoes, seeping in through the concrete walls, frying two different washing machines until we just started taking the laundry to the coin operated machines up the street.

There's mold. I didn't notice it before. But it's started creeping up the walls.

When Lonnie left me, you'd think there would have been a magnificent fight. We were neighborhood-famous for them, after all, even laughing at the good-natured impressions of ourselves at every Fourth of July barbecue.

That day, I came home from work—a double shift at the convenience store. I smelled of fried foods from the hot case I'd cleaned out before leaving and peeled off my shirt as soon as I walked through the door. The twins groaned to see me making egg-drop ramen, topless, sweaty, and for the thousandth time.

"I don't care," I said both about the traumatizing sight of my starched white bra to their virtuous eyeballs and about the ten cent ramen. "Get your homework done, nope, don't you dare run out that door—I don't *care* what Jacob's mom makes him for dinner—seriously, put the cat down, sit down, no you can't call grandma, no, we aren't ordering pizza, oh, fine, I'll put a shirt on—there, *happy now?* Get your math out."

I'd fed them and Henry (the cat), swept the mess from under the dining table, left the mess on the stove, thought about (also for the thousandth time) starting a new painting and instead sat on the couch with a package of sandwich cookies, watched half a talk show and fell asleep. When I woke sometime later, it was dark and the boys were back from hockey at Jacob's, fighting over (of all things) a nearly empty jar of jelly before I sent them to bed. I paired and folded several pairs of socks, my next day's work shirt and pants, and grabbed a thrice read thriller off the bookshelf and went upstairs to my own bed.

It wasn't until the next morning when I was having my coffee at the kitchen counter, I started to suspect.

Lonnie still wasn't home.

I flicked the curtain above the sink and saw the empty driveway. He still had the car. I could walk to work, sure, but he usually drove me and I only walked back home while it was cooler weather and after he had left for his shift. Did he have the night before off? Had he gone out? When was the last time he hadn't stumbled home at least by sunrise? Come on, think.

The boys had crashed down the stairs then, fighting (now over a filthy t-shirt) and demanding blueberry pancakes despite the fact that I had never in their lives made blueberry pancakes. The animals. How could Lonnie stay out all night and not come home? How could he leave me here alone with these animals? I made them pop tarts and shooed them out the door toward their bus.

I stood there at the counter for a long time after that, maybe hours, watching the car not pull into the driveway, examining a glob of strawberry jelly on the formica, rinsing a single fork from the pile of dirty dishes, letting Henry the Cat circle my legs and cry for food, wiping crumbs into the sink and running the garbage disposal. It gave a throaty belch and I hacked at the smell of mold. There was rot in this house then too.

———————

After the yard sale, Darby's friends had come by, told me I could do anything now, be anything now, that this was all pretty exciting if I thought about it the right way. They asked if I wanted help painting the walls for the landlord's inspection. I had stared at the grape juice stain on the kitchen counter and thought, "The landlord or the new tenants will bleach that or tear it out," and the idea had sent me into tears. Darby's friends braided my hair, made me a grilled cheese sandwich, told me, "Lonnie's not shit, really, Ray," and left. It was the first time I had cracked a smile in weeks. So there was that, at least.

———————

I tried cleaning up the backyard, the places where the weeds and sticker bushes swallowed up the fence and at least one tricycle the twins had abandoned years ago. My boots sank into the soggy ground. One got irretrievably stuck and I fell in the mud trying to yank it loose. I gave up the idea of doing any landscaping after that, deciding to tell the landlord we had let it "rewild". That's a thing people do now. I can show them the benefits of this, the wildflowers and moss covering the ground, the squirrels and rabbits that make a home in the old plastic playhouse, the bees that have nested in the carport. Bees are endangered, you know.

Now, I only venture into the backyard to collect dandelions and wild strawberries to eat since I spent the last of my cash at the dispensary besides what I give to Darby for the twins. I haven't been to work lately and I know that's going to cause a fight between us. She thinks I'm being dramatic.

But I'm not.

People look at me. The neighbors, my mother, my children, and they think, "She's depressed because Lonnie left her."

They see the dirt I've let collect underneath my fingernails. The mats in my unwashed hair. The shiny, buttery coat of sweat on skin. The absolute stink that is wafting off of me. They take all that in, and they think *I think* I can't live without that man.

They don't know that I know better.

"You really need to do something about the mold," my mother says. She wants me to let her in, to see that I'm okay, that I'm eating, that I'm bathing like I promised. That I'm done with my pity-party and have at least three (at least three, for chrissakes) boxes packed and ready to take to her house or a new apartment, she doesn't care where, but they need to be ready to go because she is leaving the car running.

I have only let her see a little, just half of me through a cracked door and no porch light (I told her some neighbor kid's shot it with a BB gun but the truth is I smashed every bulb in the house last week). I tell her there are no boxes to take, and mercifully she doesn't want to stand on the porch and fight about it (that car is running, after all), but waves a hand in front of her face and tells me the mold is really a stench and why don't I let Gary come over and take a look at the basement before I move out.

I don't tell her that I like the smell or that I can hear the mold spores—hear them—whispering past me and all around me, that they sound like Darby when she was baby, her laugh, that rolling, belly-laugh that babies have when you blow raspberries on their tummy or they discover they have feet. I don't tell her this but I want to tell her other things. I want to grab my mother's hands, those soft, papery hands that all my life have smelled of dish soap and garlic, the hands that held me, soothed me, and occasionally slapped me as a child and press them to my face and breathe them in. I want to throw myself at her, throw my arms around her, feel the stable, solid weight of my mother against me and tell her how beautiful she is, what an incredible woman she is, that I admire her gray hair and her varicose veins and her sensible shoes.

I am on the verge of doing this, opening my mouth to say these things when she plants her hands on her hips, frowns, and says, "Jesus Christ, Rayanne, you are positively ripe, take a bath," before turning sharply on her heel and heading back to her car where Gary is waiting.

I also don't tell my mother about the mushrooms that have started sprouting in every corner of this house. How I've started eating those too. How they grow in clusters, in the dark, pregnant, fat, and bursting before they rot, leaving behind found things, things I thought were lost. Photographs, a note Darby scribbled on a scrap of notebook paper once ("Went to Piper's, be home by 8-ish"), report cards ("the twins are bright boys but need to practice sitting still during class"), my engagement ring, a single cubic zirconia on a plated band that Lonnie bought at Walmart for $15 before we got the gold bands our fifth year, thought to have been accidentally donated years ago (oh, the tearful fight that had caused). I bit into a mushroom just this morning to find it. And every day more are sprouting from the closets, the outlets, in the shower, and even on the ceiling.

Every day, more treasures are erupting from their desiccated remains. A kitten—the little black kitten Darby got for her eighth grade graduation present, who had run away just a few days later, never to be seen again—crawled out of a cluster of fungi, mewing, and hungry and slick with a mildewed, amniotic slime. Henry The Cat had taken one look at him and bolted out of the house like his ass was on fire but I'd picked him up and cradled him and promised him saucers of milk.

Of course I smell terrible.

The moss and mold will do that to you. At first, when I was still afraid of it, I had tried scraping it out from underneath my fingernails, tried scrubbing it out from between my toes and other places. That was before I stopped bathing, stopped grooming and preening in front of the mirror, back when I still thought Lonnie would show up any day, back when I cared if he did. I practiced long, cool stares to his imagined groveling and steadying my voice for when I would tell him I would think about letting him move back into the house.

But then the mold had really taken hold, really gotten quite out of hand.

I would wake up mornings and a blanket of moss had grown over me, wrapping me, swaddling me like a newborn while I slept on the mattress on the floor in our bedroom. After a while, I stopped trying to brush it off, stopped trying to dig it out of my skin, my eyes, my ears, my hair. It was dripping from the ceiling fans, crawling over the windows. It was inside me, even.

See, everyone thinks I lay down every night and cry about him, but they're wrong. They think I'm lonely but I know I'm not alone. How could I be alone when even my own body is a thriving eco-system of cells, of bacteria, of larvae, spores, and creatures I can't begin to name, they are so many? Sometimes, I'll pick a scab out of boredom and a butterfly will unfurl from the bloody wound underneath.

A spectacular eclosion.

My body is rewilding.

The landlord called again asking for the keys. She is really hoping I can turn those in by Thursday or *(sigh)* she will have to send me the bill for the new locks and you know, she really doesn't want to have to do that.

I tried to tell her to go fuck herself and just send me the bill but the strangest sounds were coming from my mouth. In the place of my regular, somewhat still-childish voice with the inexplicable hint of a Tennessee accent (I've never been anywhere near there, it used to drive Lonnie and the kids nuts to hear it), my words came garbled, gravelly, and bubbling like rocks tumbling in a riverbed.

To be honest, it scared me and I hung up the phone but I spent hours afterward wailing at the walls of this empty house, listening to my new voice swimming back to me.

Am I making sense anymore?

I have this fear that I'm losing my mind. I know that's not true, mind you. I'm not losing anything. I know that. It's like, okay: when I was nine years old and I was crying in the broom closet at the church my favorite aunt was getting married in after her boyfriend got her pregnant at prom, and my mother found me there, sniveling all over my flower-girl dress, pulled me into her lap for a rare showing of affection and said, "Ray, oh Ray. You're not losing an aunt... you're gaining an uncle. And a cousin," before swatting me on the butt and telling me to blow my nose, the whole church was waiting on me to go throw those goddamned flowers.

And I told her the same thing when I married Adam and then later, Lonnie. And again, when I had the twins.

"Just more to love, Ma."

And that's it. I'm not losing myself, my mind, or anything really. I'm gaining. I'm multiplying, dividing, replicating, *changing*. I'm growing. There's so much more of me now.

This morning, the new tenants came with their moving truck, full of all their stuff, their whole life packed inside, their whole life ahead of them. I watched them carry in lamps, chairs, a baby's crib (they'll never use), and a playpen (that they will). I wondered which of these things will become their ghosts, which will haunt them the most. I wanted to tell them this house is already haunted but I couldn't speak, not yet and so I just peeled myself from the ceiling, and slithered between their belongings, touching a boar's hair brush, a decanter, a throw pillow with a stain, took an engraved, heirloom spoon with the name "Emma"—a baby gift, surely, from one of the mothers in law—and swallowed it whole.

I think about the children, of course. My children, who are waiting for me to come and usher them all into their grown-up lives, hold their hands through heartbreaks and child rearing, or the absence of children, through all the ceremonies, losses, and promotions of adulthood.

Who need me to be someone I've never been before—a woman in sensible shoes, with silver hair, and a long litany of unsolicited advice.

And I will be. I will sit alone at their graduations and the christenings of new babies, I will not have Lonnie there to remember with me the first days of Kindergarten (when somehow both the twins came home without shoes on their feet), or Darby's last Tooth Fairy visit (when instead of a dollar bill, we drunkenly hid a slice of cold pizza under her pillow and she threw it at us the next morning), or all the snow days, fevers, try-outs, and failures that led up to these moments. Perhaps, someone new will be at my side, someone who will smile and clap with me but who won't *know* these things the way we knew them together.

And that's okay.

I am making my peace with that.

But for now, I am watching these new people move into *our* house and wondering how they aren't bothered by all these ghosts, how they don't trip over the avalanche of legos that erupted out of a cluster of pluteus villosus just this morning.

I watch them for a long time, my mouth hanging open, clouds of spores pluming forth with every breath before I remember:

I don't live here anymore and I wander into the backyard, lay down in the tomato garden and give my body to the earth and wait.

WE SPEND WEEKENDS WITH DAD

MICHAEL GRIFFIN

1

Eddie and I were so excited, with Dad pointing out everything along the road and telling funny stories while he drove. I didn't even think much about exactly where we were going until we were almost there.

"You didn't tell Mom you were taking us to the beach."

As soon as I said it, I worried it might have sounded like I didn't want to go, but I wasn't complaining. It was just that we were all getting used to the idea that whenever we went with Dad on weekends, there were certain rules since he didn't live with us any more.

Dad slapped his hand on my leg, which made a big smack, but it didn't hurt me any.

"I didn't want to give away the surprise. You boys like surprises, right?"

"Right!" Eddie shouted from the back seat.

Between the city where we lived and the beach, there were so many miles of hills all covered with trees, where it always rained, even on days that were sunny back home. When we drove back down out of the hills, we could start to smell the ocean, even before we could see it.

Eddie and I had been to the beach lots of times, but it was always with Dad and Mom, all four of us together. All those times before, we always went to the beach place where Grandma lived. This was some other, different beach I didn't recognize.

There was a little town where everybody drove their cars really slow, and a roaring sound in the air, like a bunch of airplanes always flying way up, too high to see.

"Where is it?" I asked Dad. I meant to ask, were we going to a house or a hotel, but I also wondered about the strange foggy little town where everything was gray and slow.

Dad pointed like there was something just up ahead that would explain everything. I looked where he was pointing but I didn't see anything, just one empty field after another, nothing but sand and beach grass blowing in the wind. The roaring sound got even louder than before.

"Right up here a ways," he said.

Eddie leaned forward from the back seat. Dad never made him ride in his car seat, because Eddie was nine, which was pretty big. The deal was that Eddie had to promise not to take off his seatbelt and mostly stay put like a bigger kid, like me. "Where?" Eddie asked. "Where is it?"

"Are there hotels?" I asked.

"No hotel, don't need one," Dad said. "We'll be staying at this house belonging to my friend. It's my friend's house."

"Friend?" Eddie asked, like he hadn't heard the word before.

"What friend?" I asked. "Do we know him?"

Dad looked at me, not looking at the road at all, and he made this big crazy wink, being funny. "What makes you say him? Could be a her, couldn't it? Could be a lady's house."

Eddie looked at me, wide-eyed. "Lady's house," he said.

"Anyway, you'll see."

"When?" I asked.

"Dad, what will Jim and I do while you're playing with your friend?"

"You boys can run around outside. How often do you get a chance to build things in the sand? Make yourselves a huge castle. Dig tunnels all the way to China."

"It's raining," I said.

"No, it's not." He pointed out the windshield. "Look up. Beautiful blue sky, heading this way."

The sky was nothing but roaring, rushing gray clouds. Raindrops sprinkled all over the windshield so Dad had to run the wipers.

"Anyway, I brought you some books and comics. You like to read that stuff, right? So that's what you'll do."

2

There were more streets without sidewalks, where sand on both sides spilled in so it seemed like the pavement was being eaten up and undoing all the roads. Maybe it was really far, or maybe it just took forever and ever because Dad was driving extra slow, the same as all the other cars, barely moving at all.

We pulled up in front of a strange, wide house. It was really low, like all the sand in the yard kept getting piled up higher and higher by the wind, so you could walk up to the front of the house and climb right up onto the roof without a ladder. I guess almost the whole house had to be underneath the ground.

The drift had been dug away outside the big front window. There were no curtains but we couldn't see much inside. No lights were on. The house looked empty.

Dad pulled as far into the driveway as he could, before the tires bogged down and we had to stop. The back part of Dad's old car was still hanging out into the street.

We got out and Dad went to the trunk for our luggage. Eddie and I ran to the side yard, which was a big, wide-open field with no features but that same spiky beach grass.

When Dad had all the luggage out, Eddie and I ran back toward the car.

"I told somebody I'd stop by," Dad said. "Take care of some business."

"Business?" Eddie asked.

"Whose house is it?" I asked.

"Told you before, my friend owns it," Dad said. "Work friend. A business friend from work."

"But who?" I asked. Eddie and I had been to Dad's work a million times. We knew all those guys, all the architects and engineers and boss guys.

"Never mind," Dad said. "I'll take our bags inside. You should want to play outside, go ahead. Look at this lot over here, it's empty. Whole thing's yours, like having your own private beach."

"It's not beach without ocean," I said, not really trying to complain.

"Where's ocean, Dad?" Eddie asked.

"Ocean's a few blocks down there. Maybe we'll take you later. For now, play in that field. Stay nearby."

"Can't we come in?" I asked.

"Of course you'll come inside, but only later, later," Dad said. "We're staying here, I told you before. But not just yet. Play outside for now."

"I have to go to the bathroom," Eddie said.

Dad looked at the house, like he was trying to figure out how to break some bad news. I thought he was about to tell Eddie he had to go pee in the field next to the house, then his face brightened and he snapped his fingers like he just remembered something.

"Hey, there's a toilet in this garage. Half bath, that's good enough, right? You're not planning to take a whole bubblebath, are you, Eddie?" Dad winked and grinned at his own joke.

Eddie nodded and made a point of grabbing himself down there, so Dad knew how serious he was.

Dad grabbed the handle on the garage door and tried to lift it, but it wouldn't budge, probably because of the big drift up against it.

"Wait out here," Dad said. "I'll run inside, open it from there."

Dad went in the front door, which wasn't locked. Pretty soon the garage door started going up, and when it was about halfway up, the dry sand spilled into the open garage. Eddie climbed down the sand dune into the dark garage and for a second I thought I might never see him again. Then a light flicked on in a tiny bathroom in the back wall, and I saw it really was a garage. That was where Eddie was going, nowhere bad.

I waited out front.

3

When Eddie was done, he climbed back up the little dune until he stood beside me.

"Remember your little private beach next door," Dad reminded us from the garage. Now that the bathroom light was off, everything inside was all dark so I couldn't see him. "I'm just going in to check on some things. You boys better stay outside for now, both of you. Got the whole neighborhood to yourself, practically. That's paradise for a young kid, right? Oh, and here."

He stepped forward until he was visible in the light from outdoors, and held out a folded-over brown paper bag with something flat in it.

"Here's some of those funny books I promised you."

I took the bag he offered, figuring it was those comics he'd mentioned.

"If you have to be on your own for a short little while, this'll keep you entertained."

Dad looked kind of sorry for a second, but didn't say anything else. He went away into the dark in the back of the garage. I heard the door open, not the door to the tiny bathroom, but the one that led inside the house. When he opened it, no light spilled out. The door shut. It was like Eddie and me were alone, not just alone in this garage, but like we were the only ones in this house, or this neighborhood.

I went down the sand dune into the garage, further back until there was no more light. I fumbled around until I found the door Dad just went through, beside the little bathroom. I grabbed the doorknob and tried it, but it wouldn't turn.

Back outside I told Eddie it was locked. I felt like I was telling him bad news, or something scary was happening, so I tried to smile.

Eddie grinned. "Let's go play," he said, and ran off toward the side yard.

I couldn't think of anything to do but run after him, but first I left the paper bag of comics inside the garage, so they wouldn't get wrecked in case it started raining again.

The field next door was really big. I guessed there was supposed to be another house in between this one and the next, but for some reason it was missing.

"While you were in there, I saw two other kids playing next door," Eddie said. "Girl kids."

"When I was inside? I only went in for like two seconds."

Eddie shrugged. "Maybe they want to play."

The next house was pretty far, and I didn't see any kids there. "There isn't any girls, Eddie."

"Uh huh, I saw 'em," he insisted. "They were throwing a red ball back and forth."

"Sure you did, a red ball."

"It was long like a football, but skinny." He demonstrated the shape with his hands, like a noodle or a hot dog.

"There's no such kind of a ball like that," I told him.

"Uh huh," Eddie insisted. "And they're both wearing jerseys like for playing a game. Red and white ones but without numbers."

I went a little closer and looked through the row of thin trees against the black house next door. There definitely weren't any kids or any red ball.

4

We had nothing else to do, so we ran around, chased each other, tackled each other, threw sand, made up games, dug holes and talked about what we could build if we dug really deep. We both wanted to make a house big enough to live inside with no parents or any grown ups.

"What are you boys doing there?"

The voice scared us.

A lady had come through the hedge from the black house, and she was shouting like we were really far away, even though she was standing right in front of us. I could see the bright red shiny polish on her toenails.

I stood up before I answered. "Just playing."

"Don't play there," she said, not in a mean way, just like she knew her idea was right and she thought we'd agree with her even if she didn't explain why, because we were kids. "Nobody plays in that yard since what happened there."

Eddie stood up too and was beside me.

"What do you mean?" I asked. "What happened?"

"The kids, what happened to the kids," she said, as if she thought we knew and we'd just forgotten. "Nobody's allowed in that house."

"We're not inside. We're out here," I said.

"Are you alone? Two boys, unsupervised?" She looked like she didn't approve, but still she didn't seem mad at us. More like she was scared or worried or something.

"Our dad's staying in that house. We're visiting. It belongs to his business friend."

She made a look on her face like what I said was really funny, like I was trying to make a fool of her but she didn't fall for it. "What kind of friend?"

"We don't know his name. Dad didn't tell us yet."

Her face changed a little. "There's nobody staying there, nobody for a long time. You boys should play somewhere safe. Where did you say your father went?" She looked around the field like she might have overlooked Dad before.

"You're right," I said, just wanting to get away. "We'd better get our dad. We'll go find him."

"You boys might get hungry later," she added.

"Our dad will be back," I told her, starting to pull Eddie away. "Don't worry."

"Maybe, but if you do get hungry, I'll make extra meat. I'll make enough so you can share."

"Our dad's here," I said again. "He's inside, we should really--"

I stopped talking because her face changed even worse. She made a new expression, like she'd just remembered something burning on her stove. She turned away and slipped back through the hedge onto her own property.

5

I felt funny being out in that empty field, like we didn't belong. Even though the lady neighbor had gone back to her house, the whole thing made me feel like this wasn't our place and we might get in trouble, just playing outside like Dad said for us to do. Eddie didn't say anything but probably he felt the same way. He stuck close to me without saying anything for once, and followed when I started back toward the house.

We went inside the garage, thinking it had been long enough, maybe Dad would be coming out, or might finally let us in. I checked the door again. It was still locked, but this time I heard sounds inside.

I put my ear against the door and Eddie saw, which made him want to listen too, so he hurried over.

Inside there were sounds of laughing, Dad and somebody else. The laughing I could hear just fine, like they were sitting right on the other side of the door, but the words they were saying sounded muffled so I couldn't tell what they were talking about. I couldn't really even tell their voices apart. There was another sound like slapping sometimes, slapping and laughing. They were playing a slapping game, I thought.

"Somebody's getting in trouble," Eddie said.

I pulled him away from the door. "Come on."

We went toward where the sand from the driveway spilled in, where there was enough light and we felt like we were on the border between inside and outside. It was the place where Dad had left us, so I thought we could stay there without getting in trouble.

Here was the paper bag. I unfolded the folded-over part and looked inside. On the top of the pile there were a few really old, worn-out comics with ragged edges. They were the oldest comics I'd ever seen.

"They must be from when Dad was a little baby," I told Eddie. "Like you."

Most of the pile was magazines, even older ones, wet and curled-up from sitting outside, and smelly like they'd gotten moldy or something. I pulled two of them out.

"Wow," Eddie said. "Naked lady pictures."

"Playboy," I said, reading the covers. "Penthouse."

Eddie's mouth was open, a pink circle.

I nodded like these were something I knew all about. "A whole bunch of 'em."

I forgot about the comics and opened the first magazine.

"Don't," Eddie said. "Don't look. Dad says don't look at that."

Pictures of a smiling lady, a stewardess on an airplane. Her pink costume was missing different parts in each picture. Even with some of her clothes missing, she was doing her job, bringing things to men on the plane. She carried a tray of drinks, without her white shirt on, for a man with a big mustache. She brought a little baby-sized white pillow to give to some business guy, while her skirt was pulled up to show what was underneath.

"Jimmy, no," Eddie said beside me, but that didn't stop him from looking at the pictures too.

6

I felt more nervous looking at the magazines in the garage than I'd been feeling out in the field with the weird lady yelling at us, so after a few minutes I put everything back inside the bag, with the comics on top like they were before. Eddie and I just stood in the garage, looking out at the road where nobody ever drove by.

After a while it was raining again and then I wished we'd gone outside before it was raining, so we could've messed around in the field some more without getting wet. I didn't know how long we were going to need to wait out here.

Eddie just stood beside me, not saying anything.

Finally someone came walking in the street, an old man walking a three-legged black dog. The dog was limping just a little. Really he walked almost like if he had all his legs. Maybe he was born that way and got pretty good at it. Eddie tugged my hand to make sure I'd noticed.

The old man saw us and veered over until he was standing where the road met our driveway, right at the edge where Dad left the car. That was when I saw Dad had left the trunk wide open when he'd gotten the luggage out.

The old man definitely noticed us, because he was making faces and gesturing like trying to get our attention, until he was sure we saw him.

"You boys like jokes?"

"We're not supposed to talk to strange men," I said.

"Who's talking? We're not talking. All I said was whether or not somebody likes jokes."

I didn't say anything else, because we were definitely talking, which we weren't supposed to.

"Never mind, you seem pretty serious for ones so young." He shook his dog's leash and started off.

"Hey, old man!" Eddie yelled after him.

I was pretty surprised, and I didn't know what Eddie was getting at. I thought the old man might get mad about being called old.

"Nobody old here," the old man said, but he was chuckling, not angry. "I'm forty-one."

Forty-one was the same age as Dad. This man looked a lot older than that.

"We saw two girls playing next door," Eddie said, and pointed at the black house where the lady had come from.

The old man made a face, like what Eddie just said about the girls made him want to run off. "The girls, nobody mentions those."

"What does that mean?" I asked, even though I wasn't supposed to be talking to him. I hadn't planned to start, but now we were already talking, and I wanted to know what he meant.

"Something terrible," the old man said. "Two young ones next door, about your ages. Horrible." He kept shaking his head and shivering his whole body like he was all upset.

"What was it, though?" I asked. Now I had to know.

"You don't like to hear," the old man said, but he seemed exactly like he planned on telling us, and just didn't want to jump right into it without building it up first, like the way you told a scary story.

I just waited, and Eddie did too, even though he'd been the one who started this, talking about two girls next door.

"Young mother, left alone," the old man said, with something shaking in his voice. "Left alone, husband disappeared. Couldn't care for her young ones, not on her own."

He stopped but I didn't know what to ask, so I just waited. Eddie waited too.

"Maybe something went wrong with her, I don't know. What happened was she left them alone so long, they got hungry, got cold, got wet. Those girls were in trouble, maybe they were starving, maybe something worse."

"What happened to them?" Eddie asked.

"She came back, did the little mom, cut the girls to pieces, and disappeared again," the old man said.

"I saw the red ball," Eddie said. "I saw the red shirts they both wore."

The old man looked really mad or sad, like he didn't want to remember, or maybe he was trying to seem like he didn't want to talk about it, even though he kept talking about it and wouldn't stop no matter what.

"That's right," he said. "That's how they found them, only those were white dresses made red with blood. How did you know?"

I tugged on Eddie's shirt. "Come on, Eddie. Let's go in."

"I'm coming," Eddie said, but he was still standing there, staring out at the old man with the three-legged dog, like he was waiting to hear something else.

"We'll ask Dad about it," I said. "Come on."

Finally Eddie waved goodbye to the man and his dog and came back into the dark part of the garage with me, up against the locked door.

"What does it mean," Eddie asked me, "when a mom or a dad doesn't want to take care of their kids anymore?"

7

There was nothing to do in the garage, so after a few minutes we went back toward the driveway and looked out to make sure the old man and his dog were gone. Eddie climbed up over the soft sand, which kept spilling more and more into the garage until I wondered what stopped it from just filling the whole place up.

"Let's go outside," Eddie said.

I climbed up and out. All the blowing around had made sand build up around the car even more, so everything looked way different from a little while ago. So much had piled up, I wasn't sure the car would be able to move or drive. It was super deep behind, like a ramp leading into the trunk with the lid still up.

Also in the big field, the drifts had blown up to make a big mound in the center. It looked like the ground was inflated like a giant balloon, so it bulged up. Eddie raced ahead and tried to climb the little hill, so I chased him. The dry sand kept slipping out from under my feet, so the harder I tried to run, the more it slipped away. I was getting nowhere, and I couldn't catch up to Eddie, even though my legs were burning, like really tired. I kept gasping to catch my breath, running faster and faster, trying to make headway, but not getting anywhere, just slipping down. It wasn't such a big slope, but I couldn't get up. I felt myself getting heavier and heavier, the harder I tried to run. My arms and legs were tired and I wanted to give up. I guessed I couldn't do anything against so much gravity.

I didn't really want to be in the big field anyway, but we couldn't go in the street, and I didn't like the garage. That field was the only place to stay. I was just starting to think I hope we don't see the neighbor lady, so maybe we need to stay quiet, then I saw her slip through the hedges just like before. She looked at me and walked straight toward us. Now she was beckoning toward us like she had something important to tell us right away. Eddie went ahead, surprising me by going on his own. He was four years younger, and usually just acted like a little scared kid, but now he was acting like he knew the lady and wasn't scared of her.

When we got closer, I could see she was wearing something different, a nightgown made of thin white material with pink flowers all over it. It left her arms and shoulders bare, like a big, loose tank top.

Both her hands were full of big chunks of steak or liver or some kind of meat. She was holding it up so the blood ran down her arms and dripped off her elbows and made drops in the sand. The nightie was really thin and every step she took, it kept blowing up and sideways, like all her skin wanted to be out from under what she was wearing. I wasn't trying to see her naked but I kept seeing parts.

She smiled, just for me, like she could see me looking and not wanting to look.

"I don't need to be shy around you. I know the kinds of magazines you read." She winked.

"Our dad doesn't want us looking at a lady who's not dressed all the way." I felt like I had to tell her why I kept looking away whenever I saw something. "Even an old lady."

She laughed. "I'm not old. At your age, you think everyone's old."

Aside from the blowing-around nightie, what was really bothering me was the raw meat in her hands. There was all this blood. It was raw blood.

"There I was, standing in my kitchen trying to guess how much meat to make for two growing boys," she said.

"We don't need meat." When I said it, I realized how hungry I was. I felt like I had to say we didn't want any, even if maybe I really did kind of want it.

"I can't tell exactly how mature you boys are, just like you can't tell my age. I'm young, I'm a woman in my prime."

That reminded me of the old man in the street saying he was the same age as Dad. I wanted to ask how old she was, but I was afraid she would say thirty-seven, same age as Mom.

She was grinning at us and swinging her bottom, and like doing her own little dance in the sand. Her smile was mostly on one side of her mouth.

"I bet you boys are at that stage of growing where you can just eat and eat, no matter how much you pile on your plate. Building up all that muscle and bone."

8

I didn't know what to say to the lady. Whatever had made Eddie rush out here into the big sandlot, he was acting like a little, shy kid again.

"Music," Eddie whispered, then I realized what he meant. There was music behind us, coming from back in the house where Dad was.

"We've got to go back inside," I told the lady, and pulled Eddie away.

Even before we slid down the sand into the garage, I could tell something had changed inside. Light and music from inside the house poured out, like there was a loud party going on. Even the door leading into the house from the garage was hanging open. That was how we could hear the song.

All this time I'd been wanting the door to be open so we could find Dad, but now that it was hanging wide open I felt funny about just walking in. We hadn't been invited, not exactly. Eddie was staying back toward the entrance to the garage, so I went forward on my own, taking little steps toward the inner door until finally I could see in.

Just within the doorway was a big room with red and yellow lights flashing. A naked lady was sitting in a chair, covering different parts of herself with her hands and her arms across her body. She winked and smiled like she thought it was funny, seeing how I reacted when I saw her.

Eddie came up behind me and I thought of warning him off, but then he went past me inside.

That music was playing so loud, and the naked lady stood from her chair and danced a little bit, shaking her bottom and shuffling her bare feet. It reminded me of the dance the other lady was doing out in the field a minute ago. Maybe that lady had heard the song too.

"Why are you naked?" I asked. "Where are your clothes?"

"She looks like that stewardess lady," Eddie whispered.

"Where's your clothes?" I repeated.

"Oh, I had them," the lady said. "I was wearing some for a while, but now I guess you could say I'm between outfits."

Eddie grabbed my hand.

"Where's our dad?" I asked her.

She tilted her head and stuck out her bottom lip, kind of acting like a little kid, even younger than me. "Not here. I think he went down to the beach."

"He did?" Eddie asked, whining like a baby. "Without us?"

I looked at Eddie, then at the lady. "We wanted to go. We told Dad we wanted to."

She laughed and did a little cha-cha dance. "He's not here for playing games with a couple kids. He's trying to catch something."

"Catch?" I asked.

"You boys like fresh fish?" She winked.

Eddie and I looked at each other but I couldn't think of what to say.

"Now that we know each other a little bit better, I'm ready to tell you the truth about my current state of undress," the lady said.

"Uh huh," I answered.

"I'm naked because I'm painting. I'm an artist, a painter. Have you ever heard of life studies?"

I shook my head, and Eddie had shrunk behind me and was hiding behind my legs.

"That's what I'm doing. I study whatever body is at hand. Either of you young gentlemen ever consider life modeling?"

"You mean like, pose?" I asked.

She smiled this big smile, like she felt really thrilled about something. "Fresh out of the ocean. That's the best."

9

Eddie went to sit in front of the old TV, even though it wasn't turned on.

"Doesn't work," the lady said. She went into the kitchen, where she had a wooden stand with a painting she was making. Right next to that was a big mirror. She stood in front of those and picked up a brush and this board with squirts of paint on it, and started poking the brush at the picture. It didn't really look like her. There were all kinds of shapes, like slashes of red and yellow, like she was really painting the lights in here. It might have been a picture of anything as far as I could tell, but since there was a naked lady standing in front of it, looking at herself in the mirror, then looking back again at the picture, that made it seem like the picture was supposed to be her.

"My boy-os!" Dad surprised us, bursting into the room, talking really loud and moving fast. I didn't see where he even came from.

"Dad!" Eddie said, and ran to grab Dad's leg.

Dad pried him loose and went into the kitchen. He set a brown paper bag on the counter, then went up to the naked lady and gave her a smack on the bottom. She stuck out her lips, then he put kisses on her neck and grabbed her all over.

My face felt hot and I didn't want to look any more.

"We'll rustle up something for food," he said for us to hear, "but first, drinks."

Eddie was back to sitting before the dark TV so I went to sit by him. It made me feel weird, looking toward the kitchen with the naked stewardess-looking lady, especially with Dad acting all different ways I wasn't used to seeing.

In a minute Dad brought me and Eddie drinks, big heavy glasses of Cokes with ice, but with something smelly in it too. It tasted sweet enough like Coke, but also kind of like spicy or something.

Dad went back to the kitchen and clanked plates and silverware.

Eddie sipped from his Coke and coughed. "Hey Jimmy, wasn't that the biggest owl you ever saw?"

"What are you talking about?" I asked. "Where was there a big owl?"

"Outside, right when I saw those kids and their ball. It was a real big one, bigger than you even. Maybe bigger than Dad."

"What, an owl? No way, Eddie."

"It was hooting and hooting at me, when I kept trying to see the girls. It was looking right at me and then it tried telling me something."

"Eddie."

"It was trying to scare me." He took a gulp from his Coke and coughed again and stuck out his tongue. "Maybe it wasn't trying to scare me, but I was scared anyway."

"Eddie, that's dumb. A talking owl and it's supposed to be tall like Dad?"

"Not exactly talking. But saying stuff."

"Hah. What did it tell you?"

He shrugged. "Kind of like a warning. He said, it's the wrong place. You're at the wrong house."

I smelled food, and I was hungry, but I felt real tired too, and the Coke made my stomach feel sick. I was so tired I could barely sit up. I wanted dinner and I thought it sounded like Dad and his lady friend were already eating. They were having dinner without us.

Eddie was flat on his back, asleep in the middle of the floor, right in front of the dead TV. I wanted to get up and see if the TV could work, but I thought first maybe I'd shut my eyes for a minute. Rest my eyes and maybe soon Dad would remember and wake us up and we can have dinner.

10

In the dark I was awake but I didn't know where I was. My face itched and I felt carpet stuck to my cheek.

The room was all black and cold, and outside the windows everything was black and wet. I could tell how wet it was. The night was really deep like water, and then I remembered the ocean.

I thought everyone was gone but me and Eddie, sleeping on his back. He looked like he was dead.

Then I heard a clink of ice in a glass, and looked up. There was the kitchen, and in there wasn't all dark. I could see the lady sitting at the table. It was the same stewardess-looking lady from before, but now in a robe. She was watching me, swirling her Coke in her glass, with her head lolling to one side like she was really tired or sad.

She kept swinging her legs back and forth, and moving her knees apart and together. The robe she was wearing was that slippery, shiny kind of red cloth. Her bare legs were sticking way out, like she wanted them out in the air like that, like she was too hot and needed to cool off.

"Where's Dad?" I asked, once I was sure she could see me awake and sitting up. I wished my voice didn't sound scared.

"He's gone out," she said, and then she had a bunch of her drink.

I nudged Eddie, even though maybe he would've been better off if I just let him sleep. I kept nudging and pushing him, but he didn't wake up, didn't even move. It kind of scared me, but I could see he was still breathing. His throat was making a moaning sound, like when Dad snored after drinking beer.

"He's not gone," I told her, because I didn't want him to be.

I stood up and tried to look around, but everything was really dark except the kitchen which I was trying not to look at, so I kept hitting into things. I cracked my knee on a table, and bumped a corner hard. I felt tears in my eyes, not because it hurt so much, but I felt pretty scared and nervous.

Maybe she was right, Dad was gone. Maybe he was hiding from us. But why would he do that? We were still here, me and Eddie. Also his friend was still here, too.

"Go back to sleep, kid," the lady said. "Sleep away."

11

Another time, I wasn't sure what time it was, but everything was darker and blurry and felt like still being asleep but I kept seeing and hearing.

The sand piled higher against the house. Outside that curtainless window, I could only see a sliver of the sky, because the sand was heaped almost to the top. I knew the sky should be black, because night was supposed to be dark, but I could see, or at least I knew the dunes had blown so high.

In that little gap at the top of the window, two faces peered in. Little girl faces. Their mouths were open, like if they were crying, but there weren't any sounds I could hear. It was too dark.

12

When I woke up, Eddie was already awake, staring at the dead TV. Now it was daytime, and the house wasn't dark any more. The sand hadn't yet piled as high as the tops of the windows, so light streamed in the gap where last night I'd seen the small, white faces of the girls peeking in, watching me.

Eddie was sitting on the floor, rocking back and forth like his stomach felt sick. I was about to ask where Dad was, then I heard Dad's laugh in the kitchen. He was sitting at the table with the lady, just like before. I got up and went in there to ask why he let us go to bed without dinner.·

"Where'd you go, Dad?" I didn't like how my voice sounded whiny.

"What do you mean?" he asked, but I couldn't see his face.

"Last night."

He turned, kind of smiling, and messed up my hair with his hand. "I didn't go anywhere, slugger."

I looked over at Eddie to see if he could see what I saw. Dad wasn't being like Dad. Eddie looked like he wanted to say something but couldn't say it. His eyes looked like he might be going to cry.

I got really mad and scared. The more scared I felt, the more mad it made me. I knew we weren't safe anywhere here, me and Eddie, but I didn't know how to get away to any place where we could be safe.

"You were too gone," I said to dad. My voice was loud. "You were."

Dad was surprised. I was afraid it would scare Eddie, me getting so mad, like maybe he could tell I was acting mad because things were scaring me. Eddie made these huge eyes.

"Okay, champ." Dad laughed like it was all a funny joke, and now he was letting us in on it. "I went to visit my other friend."

"Your friend?" I asked.

"Sure," Dad said. "My friend next door." He pointed in the direction of the black house.

"I don't get why you left us outside while you came in with this one friend lady, then you left us here while you went over to see the other friend lady." My voice sounded like a young kid's voice.

Dad laughed like he wasn't worried because he didn't care if I could tell he was lying. "Boy, so many questions." He went out of the kitchen, past Eddie in the living room, then down the hall.

When I sat beside Eddie, he nudged my shoulder. "Be quiet, Jim."

I was trying to figure out how to explain why I was mad, because Dad wasn't taking care of us.

Eddie changed the subject. "I forgot to tell you about after the owl. When I was outside before, those kids said they saw our dad other times. In the night times, here."

Down the hall a door slammed.

I jumped up and rushed toward that sound. In that hall, the same one Dad went down, all three doors were closed. I didn't know what to do, so I tried the first one. That door opened, and the room behind it was empty and really cold because the window was wide open to outside. I shut the first door and went to the second, and I was about to see if it would open when I heard sounds behind the next one, the third door at the end.

I went to that one instead and grabbed the knob, but it wouldn't turn. That door was locked.

There was a sound, a lady laughing, then a scream, really loud. It was a scared scream.

Before I could figure it out, somebody else laughed. A man.

After that came all kinds of hitting sounds, like people bumping into each other and against the walls. Not just that, but skin slapping, like last night. There were bumps, really heavy ones like somebody moving around furniture.

Eddie yelled from the living room, so I went back to him.

"He went," he said, pointing. The front door stood open, with outside air blowing in. Now the whole house was cold like that first empty room.

I figured Eddie was being dumb, like maybe the door had blown open by itself, so he made up some reason why it was open. Sand kept spilling in, so I had to climb up to see what was outside.

Dad's car was gone from the driveway. That left a big, open space where it used to be, no tracks or anything.

I went back inside to the hall, trying to figure out what to do. A minute ago had been all that slapping and laughing. He had to still be here, at least I hoped, but now all three doors stood open. The outer two were empty, but in the middle room was the lady from the kitchen, the one who painted pictures of herself. Her fingers were covered with sticky blue paint and she was smearing it on her throat.

"Don't you hear what they're telling you?" she asked. "Don't you know how to listen? You're in the wrong house."

I ran back to the front door to look out again, because I couldn't believe the car was really gone. Maybe Dad was still here somewhere, buried under that sand.

But there was for sure no car.

"I think I saw a telephone box on the road when we came here," Eddie said in a small voice. "We can go find the telephone and call mom."

I did want to call Mom, but even if we could get to the phone and call her, I wasn't sure how she could find us. We were in a place it seemed like nobody could ever find. We might never get back. I couldn't tell Eddie we might have to stay in this place from now on.

"Was that phone something you really saw?" I asked Eddie. "Are you making it up, like you made up the girls in the red costumes?" I didn't have any reason not to tell Eddie the truth, that I'd seen the girls myself. I guess I didn't like to think about what that meant.

"I didn't make it up," Eddie said.

"This time he's really gone," the lady said, now in the living room with us, barefoot in her nightie. She smiled, but it was a mean, nasty smile. The bruises around her eyes were purple, so I felt sorry for her. Her lips were all bloody and cracked. Maybe she was only mad because somebody made her hurt, too. I hoped that was all, that Dad wasn't gone. He wouldn't leave us here, even though his car wasn't outside anymore. I could see how it was, but that didn't seem like it could be real, so I kept doubting.

I grabbed Eddie's hand. "Come on," I said. "We have to go try to find that phone box."

We climbed the drift spilling in the doorway, dry and loose, sinking away beneath our feet.

"There's no Dad for you here," the lady yelled behind us. "You have no parents."

I didn't look back. I kept climbing, holding Eddie's hand really tight.

The drifts outside had piled higher than the roof of the house. A road had to be there, somewhere.

I couldn't see how we'd make it, not as far as the phone Eddie saw when we came. Every step, we kept sinking. Home was impossible. The world wanted to stop us, not only dad and his friends, but this empty town being slowly buried in dry sand. So much distance between us and anything, and we weren't moving. All I could do was grab my brother's hand and keep trying to pull us out.

THE CRYPTIC JAPE

MATTHEW M. BARTLETT

CAST OF CHARACTERS (in order of appearance):

The SCOUT
The CROWD
The COMEDIAN
The VAMP
The BARTENDER
The REPORTER
The COMIC
The HOSTESS
The EMCEE
The SERVER
The CHAUFFEUR
The FACE

A side street blue with dusk light. Evenly spaced smudges of sepia from dust-dimmed streetlamps. Brick walls inked with graffiti tattoos, crowned with barbed wire. Battered trash cans, their mouths full to overflowing. Acrid fog billowing like winter breath from sewer grates. The sound of highway traffic, and also, distant, but growing louder, the percussive throb of a copter's rotors.

Derelict automobiles line the west curb, corners propped up on concrete blocks or sunken by puddled tires. Gas caps dangle like fractured appendages. Black bags billow from side windows, duct-taped flags of negation. In one decrepit sedan, two dark shapes huddle, a small orange light bouncing between them like an indecisive firefly.

On both sides of the street, buildings loom: silent sentinels, pristine, unlit, the lack of signage or graffiti rendering them innominate. In the space between two high-rises, a blemished moon drowns in twilit murk. Above, V-shaped klieg lights slice grey clouds.

A red Lamborghini Aventador limousine pulls onto the street, trailing purple smoke, its engine purring. Its hood ornament is the sleek, long-snouted skull of some unknown animal, with a pair of spiraling horns that form a sight for a custom-retrofitted hood-mounted SIG Sauer LMG-6.8 machine gun.

The orange light in the derelict car stops moving. The sewer grates draw in and hold their breath. The clouds overtake the moon from both sides like black-coated assassins. The helicopter's rotors fade.

The car door opens upward, a lopsided shrug accompanied by a high-pitched mechanical whine. Out steps the SCOUT. He is clad in a black suit and a stockman hat. Mirrored sunglasses perch on his thin nose. His mouth is wide, bisecting the bottom of his face. His neck is a nest of blisters. He leans back into the car for a moment. Then he approaches the club, a squat black-brick afterthought situated between a ramp-fronted stone church and an unlit parking garage. Its red-glowing windows cower behind steel bars. Above the double doors, a scribble of blue neon tubes spells out The Cryptic Jape. The SCOUT opens the door and enters.

Inside, red, blue, yellow, and green stage lights pointing this way and that. Servers in black tights and t-shirts winding their way around crowded tables, ponytails jouncing. Recessed lighting in the walls and under the set of stairs leading up to the bar. On the tables and along the bar, shapely flames shimmying, a large fire divided into small glass chambers. The CROWD, seated at the tables or wandering about, chattering and tittering and rustling and rumbling. Business deals, romantic arrangements, promises and covenants.

On a wall-wide screen runs a video loop of a bus accident filmed by frame-mounted interior cameras. Passengers sail like angels up from their seats, clothes billowing, eyes wide, mouths open in O's. They crowd together at the ceiling. Through the back window the scenery rotates, a kaleidoscope of greens and browns. Emotive opera plays over the sound system, a woman's voice, shrieking, chirping, tittering. Glasses clink over the competing sounds of conversation.

In a black-brick bathroom, a COMEDIAN in a blue suit and tie kneels before a red toilet, vomitus flowing like water from his mouth. Through teary eyes he sees the bowl is now full of glinting minnows swimming in strange patterns, ancient patterns, patterns of portent, he knows not of what. He reaches with a trembling hand and flushes. The fish swirl down and away into the black aperture at the bottom. Slowly, trembling, the COMEDIAN stands. He washes his hands in the red sink. The foam coats his hands like fat cartoon gloves. He rinses them and wipes them on a brown-stained towel wound into a stainless-steel wall fixture. In the red-framed mirror he regards himself, lays stray strands of dark brown hair back over his ears and tucks them behind.

He steps out into the dim, graffiti-strewn hall. As he walks toward the door that leads to the seating area and the bar, his back straightens and his stride grows confident, almost a swagger. He pushes the door open and winds his way through the lily-pad tables to the bar. Only one drinker sits there, a VAMP at the far end in the shadows, twig-thin, in a blue dress no thicker than a shirtsleeve, a Fedora hat sunk low on her brow, disturbing with a bony crooked finger a ring of condensation on the polished oak. Her features, crooked and sharp, are twisted into an expression suggesting exhaustion, resigned perplexity, presumably due to the glass in front of her, which is too full of blood-red wine to safely lift.

The COMEDIAN hoists himself up onto a stool. The BARTEND-ER, clad all in black—fatigue pants, t-shirt, ballcap, and sunglasses—approaches and places on the bar a curvaceous goblet half-filled with dark blue liquid strewn with black flakes. The COMEDIAN hefts the goblet. He sips carefully, wincing. He glances at the VAMP, who is still stymied by her wine glass.

The COMEDIAN (with great bombast and gusto, to the VAMP): *Ablute thyself.*

The VAMP lifts the glass as though responding to a hypnotic suggestion, and pours its contents down the front of her face. Then, gasping, blinking away the red dew on her long lashes, she departs the bar, knock-kneed, stumbling, weaving, waving her hands in front of her face.

The VAMP: *Oh! Oh!*
The BARTENDER (to the COMEDIAN): *Good one.*

As the BARTENDER commences polishing the glassware, the COMEDIAN turns his attention to the television behind the bar, which flashes scenes of an urban neighborhood in fading daylight. Police vehicles, fire trucks, and ambulances, their crowns of lights rotating and blinking, block access to short, weedy streets. Yellow police tape twists and flutters. They cut to a REPORTER, a young woman in a headscarf holding a microphone.

The REPORTER (unheard, via subtitles): *Police are investigating an incident downtown. This is an active scene. The incident is ongoing. Family members are on the scene. It is a very emotional scene. It is all unfolding in the area of this beige house off of this quiet street in a neighborhood in the part of the city you see behind me. Police have been canvassing the area. Through the window we have seen police taking pictures and cataloging alleged evidence. This incident is still unfolding. Neighbors have gathered. Information is limited. The police are not sharing much at this time. We do not know the circumstances that led up to this incident and we don't know the identities of any of the individuals involved. We do not know the nature of the incident. We have reached out to police on the scene and are working to confirm more information. We will stay on top of this story and provide more information as we receive it. Again, an incident...*

A COMIC approaches the bar. He wears a thrift shop blazer and an untucked white shirt with a yellow collar. His too-short necktie sways like a steel pendulum, his lank blonde hair mirroring the movement. He and the COMEDIAN shake hands, and the COMIC points out a HOSTESS seating a tall, gaunt man at a table at the back of the room—the SCOUT. Once the SCOUT is settled, the HOSTESS reels away from the table, her hand over her mouth, her eyes wide. The SCOUT beckons a SERVER and says a few words to her. He then lifts between two long fingers a folded bill. The SERVER hesitates, then plucks it away and heads to the bar.

The COMIC: *D'ya think?*
The COMEDIAN: *Could be.*
The COMIC: *This could be big for me. For you, even. One of us, maybe all of us? Movies. Situation Comedies. The talk show circuit. Big for me, this could be. Maybe even for you. Or maybe not. Maybe neither of us. Maybe he won't see anything he likes. Oh, lord. What do we do? What will we do? What should we do?*

The COMIC continues in that vein as he wanders off, nearly colliding with the SERVER, who glances at him with distaste and leans on the bar.

The SERVER (to the BARTENDER): *One Smoker's Cough. In a hurricane glass.*
The BARTENDER (looking across the room at the SCOUT): *Cutty-eyed buck fitch.*
The SERVER (rolling her eyes): *If you say so.*

The music stops short. The house lights flicker and fade. The chatter sinks to a murmur, then to silence. Small salvos of applause scatter like the popping of firecrackers. The COMEDIAN swivels on his stool to watch. The curtains part and slide into the wings. The stage spans the room, too large for its purpose, furnished at its center with only a metal-legged yellow stool, an accent table with a glass of water on it, and a spotlit microphone on a stand. The COMIC walks from backstage and approaches the stand. He blinks in the punishing light. He clears his throat into the microphone. Someone in the CROWD boos and he winces.

Then it is silent, the hungry kind of silence. A beat. Then another. A third.

The COMIC (stridently): *In September, when the sunflowers die.*

The CROWD jumps, then laughs at their own reaction. One person shrieks in startlement.

The COMIC (seductively): *In September when the sunflowers die.*

Again and again the COMIC repeats the phrase, changing the tone each time, angry, amused, fearful; never stumbling nor stuttering, faster and faster, emphasizing syllables in order, then in reverse order, then either at random or in patterns too complex to discern. He prowls the stage, pumping his fists, stomping like a giant, shimmying, his clothing bouncing on his body. One of his teeth shoots out and spins toward the edge of the stage like a skimmed rock. Another follows it. The CROWD roars with laughter, one person braying, crying, falling to the floor, taking his chair, his drink, and his silverware with him.

The COMEDIAN swings his gaze from the commotion over to the SCOUT, who is staring at the onstage COMIC with an inscrutable expression—grin or grimace, the COMEDIAN cannot say.

The COMIC: *Thank you very much, thank you, you're very kind.*

The COMIC backs away through the red curtains that flank the stage, arms and middle fingers raised. The EMCEE steps out in his place. He is dressed like a barber who's gotten separated from the rest of his quartet.

The EMCEE (in a lugubrious baritone): *Ladies and gentlemen, ladies and gentlemen, I beg your brief attention.*

The CROWD clamors and boos and barrages the EMCEE with expletives and invective.

The EMCEE: *It's time for response and call!*

The CROWD cheers.

The COMEDIAN (to the BARTENDER): *On a dime, they turn.*

The BARTENDER ignores him, continues to run a rag over and into a long-ago wiped off glass.

The CROWD (as one): *Gigayacht!*
The EMCEE (in sing-song): *Gigayacht!*
The CROWD (as one): *Excreta!*
The EMCEE: *Ex! Cree! Taaaa, ha haaaa!*

The SCOUT does not participate. He pulls a black cigarette with a red filter from a red and black pack and pushes it between his lips. He produces a long wooden match from an inside pocket. He strikes the match on the side of his neck. The flame lights his face up hellish red.

The COMEDIAN also does not participate. Instead, he watches the SCOUT. He considers his newly written act, which he has spent sleepless nights memorizing. He will discard that act tonight, he decides. That act, all his old acts, they seem so juvenile now, when he thinks of presenting them to the SCOUT. So he will improvise, ad-lib. He opens his wallet and produces a playing card: a three-armed, skull-headed Jester clad in an Elizabethan corset, a fool's cap with squirrel skulls for bells, arms bent, fists on cocked hips. He places the card in the tip jar and rises.

Backstage is stenciled in red on the frosted glass door. The COMEDIAN enters. The COMIC paces the floor. His eyes are raw and red, hair soaked. His shirt lays open, unbuttoned, his chest a sweaty tangle of matted hair.

The COMIC: *Did he laugh any? Hey, don't ignore me. Did he laugh any? Did he laugh any?*

The COMEDIAN, ignoring the COMIC, walks to the curtain and parts it slightly to peer out at the CROWD. The house lights cast a gauzy glow that obscures their features, though some are revealed by candlelight, and they look like the faces that gather at an execution, rapt, hungry for the sight of gore, the aroma of the lash when it scores flesh. He can't see whether the SCOUT is at his table. He waits to be announced.

Outside. The street is dark now, the moon secreted away to some unknown province, perhaps not to be seen again. The limousine idles in the center of the street, its doors up like the wings of an insect in flight. Thrumming bass shakes its frame. The CHAUFFEUR stands by the car's side, large arms crossed over a large stomach.

A police cruiser turns onto the road from the alley. Its blue lights flashing, rotating, crawling like bugs over the buildings, the parking garage, the cars, the church, the club. Then the side-mounted spotlight comes on, lighting the road up in sharp relief, every crack, every flaw, every discarded cigarette and shell casing, and the CHAUFFEUR, whose eyes disappear when the glare hits them. His head opens vertically, ejecting a bulbous grey brain with distended eyes and a mouth full of malformed fangs, trailing a skein of purple intestine.

The spotlight extinguishes. The blue lights stop spinning and shut off. The police car backs up carefully and, spraying gravel, speeds off back down the alley.

The COMEDIAN steps off the stage, cold from the CROWD's hostility despite the heat of the stage lights. By rights, the act should have killed. He made connections, ad-libbed callbacks, went where his mind took him. What is he doing here? Why this life, where every utterance is a trial, the jury a bunch of stiffs, the judge a gaunt and spectral SCOUT...but is the SCOUT still here? He hadn't looked at the table the whole time. Not that he would have seen anything. But he might have. He might have.

The COMIC approaches. He is shirtless now, reeking of alcohol.

The COMIC: *Oh, brutal. That was so brutal. I'm sorry, man. Oof. So brutal...*

The COMEDIAN turns and walks back to the curtains. The house lights are on, the CROWD just starting to rise and gather their belongings. He has a clear view of the SCOUT's table. Empty. His act drove out even the SCOUT. At least the CROWD had stayed. But his career was over. Or it wasn't. There are other scouts. Or it was. He had done what he considered his best, his most freewheeling and effortless and cutting. He needs to think. He needs to tune out the demented babbling of the COMIC. He needs to go home and sit in the bathtub. He needs to crawl under the ground and go to sleep with the worms and the grubs.

He leaves by the back door. The promised alarm fails to sound. His beat up two-seater car slouches bereft by the torn-up chain-link fence, wedged between a white SUV and a dark sedan. The SUV rocks slightly; the sedan bounces on its springs. Bass vibrates from the road out front of the club, and an odd light illuminates the narrow path between the side of the club and the parking garage.

A footstep crunch on gravel, then several more, as though the entire CROWD has come to confront him, to demand their money back, maybe to hurt him. The COMEDIAN whirls around to see the SCOUT stepping out from the shadows into the light of the path, his arms behind his back. The SCOUT now has many legs. His hat reaches heavenward, tall as a skyscraper. A half-formed second face, swollen and scrunched, drools at his neck. The FACE addresses the COMEDIAN by name.

The FACE: *Your mind was once a fist, and tonight it opened up into a hand.*

The COMEDIAN feels that hand now, cold, grabbing the cobwebs from the inside of his skull, shaking loose the spiders from his spine.

The SCOUT: *We can use you for our ongoing concern.*

The COMEDIAN realizes now that he is face-to-face with everything he has ever wanted, since he first stepped out onto a stage as a teenager and was humiliated, everything he continued to want as he learned and grew and turned his act around and forced sweet laughter from hostile audiences. Movies. Situation comedies. The talk show circuit. The COMEDIAN turns to flee and comes face to face with the CHAUFFEUR. The CHAUFFEUR's smile and the CHAUFFEUR's hand become his whole world, and then he's lifted, dropped, locked in, and spirited away to meet his dreams. He feels the limousine bounce as it rolls over the body of the COMIC.

IMPZ

CRAIG LAURANCE GIDNEY

The final straw for Ms. Whitt was when we set her weave on fire. It was DiAundre that did it, but it could have been any one of us. We were all terrible, and we were proud of it.

Azalea Heights had set up a free afterschool program for the tenants. Calling it a program was a stretch. It was more like jail, with some government paid lady acting as warden. There were six of us in the program, in all age groups. At fifteen and a half, I was the oldest. Then there was Charmaine and DiAundre at fourteen. Big T was twelve. And the twin eight-year olds: Thelma and Ray. We weren't the only kids in AZH. There were lots of them. But we were the only ones our parents forced to attend. Mostly because we were problem kids. At risk. And, after a few months, we ended up being the only kids.

At first, it was hard to get along with each other. For instance, I hated Charmaine. She was a C-cup, and I was still in my training bra. Not that I had enough tit to put in there. But still. Also, she was so thirsty for attention, acting all stupid in front of boys. Tyrone, aka Big T, had horrible temper tantrums that happened for no reason at all. He was maybe 200 pounds, and once he got in one of his moods, it was impossible to control him. He was like an outta control Humpty Dumpty. DiAundre was the clown. I think he had ADD or something cause he literally couldn't sit still. He was always fidgeting or doodling or making smart comments. He was like the Tasmanian Devil, bursting with energy. Thelma and Ray were strange kids. Half the time, you couldn't understand them. They spoke to each other in another language that sounded like a mixture of cricket chirps and Pig Latin.

We bonded over a mutual love of chaos.

The first time we teamed up, our victim was Becky. Actually, her name was something else. Ashley, or Skylar. But she *looked* like a Becky. Fresh outta college, before she went to law school or whatever. Brown-blonde hair, almost transparent skin, and perky as hell. A white savior type, like that stupid Michelle Pfieffer movie. White girl swooping in from her high horse, to uplift us savages. Becky had a nose ring and wore Hello Kitty t-shirts with sparkles. She thought she was cute. She even tried to speak to us in Ebonics. *No bueno, bitch.*

Becky talked to us about Black Liberation, and how she was determined to break us out of the cycle of poverty. The boys could escape the Prison Industrial Complex pipeline, and we girls could learn how to be Strong Women of Color. Becky bought a paperback library of mostly used books. *The Autobiography of Malcolm X*, stuff by a lady named Zora and another one named bell, lowercase. She had heart, Becky. I'll give that to her. But we were bad down to our bones. We destroyed things cuz we could.

Charmaine and I bonded over messing with her.

One day, Becky pulled the girls aside while the boys played hoops on the black top.

"Who are your role models?" she said, bright and fresh, like she'd just fallen off the turnip truck.

Little Thelma said, "My favorite model is Tyra, but I like Naomi even though she's mean."

I rolled my eyes, sucked my teeth and said, "She means role models, not super models. Is you retarded?"

Becky tutted. "Eudora, don't use that term. That's not a nice thing to say."

Thelma stuck her tongue out at me.

Becky said, "Who is your role model?" looking directly at me. It was creepy, her gaze. Babies look at you the same way. So trusting that it was stupid.

At that moment, behind Becky's back, I saw Charmaine rifling through Becky's purse. I was impressed. It was the first thing I saw her do that didn't have nothing to do with boys. She pulled out Becky's phone. I could have let the white girl know what was going on, but she annoyed me. And I wanted to see what Charmaine was gonna do.

"I'm really interested in that Zora chick you mentioned. She sounds so cool, studying magic and writing books. I want to be like her," I said.

Becky beamed. God, she was so stupid. I expected her to squeal. "You know, she lived not too far from here, when she went to college...."

"Really?" I said. I made my voice go higher. Charmaine slipped the iPhone into her pocket.

Becky left for the day and the six of us looked at her iPhone, which Charmaine had somehow unlocked. We scrolled through her email (boring), her music collection (even more boring) and finally her pictures.

"Hold up," said Big T.

"Hells yeah," said DiAundre.

Both boys hogged the phone, and began furiously scrolling and swiping.

Thelma and Ray said, "What you looking at?" When they spoke English, it was always in unison, as if they shared a brain.

"Naw," said Big T, "ya'll is too young for this."

Charmaine and I shared a look, one that said *Of course, it's titty pics.*

After maybe five or ten minutes, I said to the two boys, "Hand it over. Stop whacking off to her pictures."

Right then, the phone rang. The boys dropped it like it was on fire.

"Jesus," said Charmaine.

I picked it up, and answered it. An older female voice came on: "Becky?" (Or Ashley or Skylar).

"She's not in," I said.

"Isn't this her phone?"

"It sure is. She must have left it here by mistake. This is one of the kids in the afterschool program."

"Ah. I see... This is her mother..."

"I'll be sure to let her know you called when she comes back," I said. I did my best to sound sweet. I aimed for sugar, ended up as High Fructose Corn Syrup.

Becky's mother swallowed it down, though. "Aren't you a dear?"

When she hung up, I clicked into Becky's photos.

"She a freak," I said after seeing all of them.

Charmaine peeped over my shoulder. "I bet she was on the pole at one point."

"Let us see," the twins said.

I shrugged, handing the phone over to them. What did I care? They weren't my kids. They began talking in that weird chirping language. They spoke fast and laughed. Us older kids were all like WTF?

They seemed to come to an agreement of some kind. Thelma held the iPhone and Ray apparently instructed her.

They sent the XXX photos to all of Becky's contacts.

Becky never did retrieve her phone. By the end of the week, though, it was deactivated. It seemed that the city wasn't sending a replacement. But next week, there was Ms. Whitt. She was a big woman. Not fat big. More like bulky, like an athlete. This made sense, as she was ex-military. She didn't have any makeup or jewelry and only wore tracksuits with steel toed boots. Shit kickers is what DiAundre called them.

The first day she made us run laps around the AZH complex before she watched us do our homework.

When DiAundre fidgeted, she got in his face, screaming at him like he was a new recruit. She made him do ten push ups for every infraction, and said that in the future, if any one of us was out of line, she would make all of us do 50 push-ups. Thelma and Ray were always separated from each other. She couldn't stand their secret language or the fact that they always spoke in stereo.

On the third day, after she left but before we went to our homes, I gathered the group in a huddle.

"She has got to go," I said.

"How," asked Big T. She had been merciless with him as he did the laps, calling him Fatboy and telling him to "leave the Tastycakes alone."

Charmaine, who had her ever-present makeup bag confiscated, said, "She's a tough nut to crack."

DiAundre said, "I bet she's a bulldagger. A stud. Maybe she's in the closet and we can—"

"Fat chance," I said. "She ain't in the closet. If she ever was."

The twins began chirping amongst themselves. Then, they said, "Booby trap her desk."

"An oldie but goodie," I said.

DiAundre, though, fucked it up. He'd volunteered to set the trap since he hated Ms. Whitt the most. He had made a kind of bomb out of a shoe box, spring loads, and realistic looking plastic snakes and cockroaches. DiAundre stumbled into the room later than we'd bargained for. Ms. Whitt was, as always, punctual. He only had three minutes to set the trap.

"Teacher made me stay late," he said breathlessly as he fiddled with the box. He finished in the nick of time. Whitt stomped into the room just as he was scurrying back to his desk.

She looked slightly different this time. Instead of a faded natural, she now wore a weave. It reached her shoulders and had blue streaks. She had long eyelashes and just a touch of make-up, including some reddish-brown lipstick.

"DiAundre," she hollered, "what have you been up to?" She walked behind the desk, peering suspiciously at the drawers.

"N-n-nothing," he said, and fidgeted. As usual. Charmaine and I rolled our eyes so hard they almost fell out of their sockets and rolled down the hall.

"You sound guilty as hell, boy," Whitt said. She walked right on up to him and leaned into his face. The blue streaks in her curly weave looked like the plastic snakes. She pushed her face right in front of his own. He could probably smell her breath. I imagined her breath smelled like tuna fish and cigarettes.

Poor DiAundre leaned back, like a trapped rat cornered by a mangy cat.

Then two things happened.

I swear I saw the air around Whitt's hair blur, like one of those stupid picture apps filters. The rest of her face and hair was in focus. It was just a section of that blue, blue streak. There was the smell of gas. Heavy, overpowering. Then, Ms. Whitt's weave lit up. She shrieked and began beating on her head, trying to put the flames out. The flames weren't red. They were *blue*. The same color as the streaks in her weave. They danced about her head, and there was the smell of singeing flesh— which smells like that really bad lunch meat that passes for hamburgers at the school cafeteria—and she ran out of the classroom.

Then, the desk, where the booby trap was, violently popped open. The box of snakes detonated. The snakes were plastic. But the cockroaches were real. And they flew.

<hr />

We were at the AZH rec room the next day. We knew that Ms. Whitt wouldn't be returning. That was a given. I didn't even think that a replacement would be sent. But we met up anyway, excited and terrified about what happened yesterday.

Charmaine said, "I saw a movie when I was little. It was starring that girl from those *Charlie's Angels* movies. Anyway, she had the power to burn shit up. It was like that...."

"Except," I interrupted, "the flame was fucking blue. And besides, DiAundre ain't no Negro with superpowers."

"Yeah," said DiAundre, "I had nothing to do with it. That fire—and them flying cockroaches—that was some straight up Harry Potter shit."

Big T said, "You mean, you *didn't* light up her hair on purpose? Dawg, I thought you were slick...."

He was interrupted by the twins as they burst into the classroom. They looked as if they were being chased by something and had frantic expressions on their faces. When they caught their breath, they said, "There's a new lady coming."

"Hold up," I said. "How do you know that?"

"Mama told us." Their mother was on one of the AZH community committees, so she would definitely have the 411. As they babbled on, Thelma and Ray revealed that there had been complaints from downtown about the mistreatment of the people they sent. The one they were sending out today would be the last one. After that, the after school program would be discontinued.

We cheered after the twins told us the story.

"I'm gonna miss you guys," said Charmaine, wiping away a fake tear. "Psych! It's been real, though."

I said, "Don't get too comfy. We still gotta get rid of the new bitch—"

"The new bitch is here," said a voice from the doorway to the classroom, "and she can hear you!" The voice was high and babyish, like Betty Boop or Pikachu.

I almost pissed myself. Everyone else froze.

The new classroom supervisor stepped in the classroom. Our jaws dropped. She had on a hot pink velour tracksuit that hugged every inch of her slammin' body. Her booty was as big as Nicki Minaj's and her boobs strained against the fabric. I swear I could see her nipples. Her hair was cornrowed in a tight spiral so you could see her scalp. It must have taken forever to do that style. Her ears were pierced multiple times with gold rings that were stacked up the curves. It looked like she had slinkies on her ears. Best of all, she wore transparent acrylic stripper heels, at least 5 inches high. They looked like hooves. I know that the boys in the group were springing boners. I knew that *I* had a ladyboner and I wasn't even sure I was Born That Way.

She sashayed into the room like it was a runway.

"Children," she said in that helium-balloon voice of hers, "sit your naughty asses down."

Each of us looked in each other's eyes. It was a look that said, *Is she for real?!?*

She said, with a little bit of an edge in her voice, "I ain't fucking around."

She looked like a Video Ho, but there was something nasty lurking beneath her demeanor. She would cut a bitch. I knew it, and probably all the other kids knew it too. We scurried like roaches to our desks.

When we were seated, she smiled. Her lips were painted a red that was almost orange. There was something about her mouth that wasn't right. It was too wide, too plastic. It was like a shark's grin.

"Hello, class," she said. She practically *sang* it. She turned to the blackboard and—

We all saw it.

We all heard it.

We all wished we had captured it on our cell phone cameras.

She scratched her name out on the board with her frosted pink nails. The sound was something terrible. It was like the scrape of bone on bone. We felt each letter's creation, a squeal that rattled the back of our teeth.

When she was done, her name was billboarded over the blackboard: LILITH BAYLOCK

When she finished, she sat down behind the desk. She said, "You may call me Lilith or Miss Baylock. Don't ever call me bitch again, though. There will be consequences. And you won't like them. Why don't you introduce yourselves to me. You go first." She pointed a French-tipped finger at me.

I stood up, even though I didn't want to. It was weird. What was even weirder was what I said. "Good afternoon, Miss Baylock. My name is Eudora Robeson, aged fifteen. I attend Marshall Junior High and I am in the 9th Grade. I live in Unit 3C with my mom, her boyfriend and my little brother Eugene. Eugene is on the Autistic Spectrum. I'm not sure, but I think I may like girls."

Everyone else giggled at this.

It spilled out of me. I had just wanted to—grudgingly—give the new bitch my first name. After I finished, I sat down and shut my mouth.

She pointed at DiAundre. He stood up, stiff as a soldier, and began reciting: "DiAundre Washington. Live with my parents and three sisters in Unit 4A. I have ADD and I'm on Adderall, but sometimes I sell my pills to this college kid. I bought a PS4 with that money! Still in the fifth grade at Morrison cuz I had to repeat. I can't read too good."

Charmaine was next: "I go to Morrison, too. But I'm in seventh grade. I live in Unit 6A with my grandparents cause who knows where the hell my mom is and my dad is stationed at the naval base in Bahrain. I was messing with Kenyatta over in Unit 7A but no-one knows because he's 18. He broke it off. He was just a fuckboy."

Lilith Baylock stopped Charmaine with a hand gesture. Charmaine froze, like we were playing Red Light, Green Light. "How old are you, girl?"

Charmaine said, "Fourteen." Then froze again (Red Light!).

Baylock said, "Too young for that shit. But we'll fix it." She waved her hand, and Charmaine sat down. It was like she was a puppet. I found that I could barely move.

No. That's not right. More like, I could move, but I didn't want to and I didn't know why I didn't want to. Every time I thought something like, *She has some weird power over us*, or *Lilith Baylock is a straight up witch* like those basic Beckys on that *Charmed* TV show, I would feel strange.

Big T popped up out of his seat like a jack-in-the-box. "Tyrone Spencer, aged twelve. I live in Unit 8A with my folks. Dad's a security guard at the Walmart on H Street, and Mom is the dining room manager at an old folks' home. She always brings me leftover cakes and cookies home from work. That's why I'm so big."

His whole family was fat. Eugene, my little brother, called them The Klumps, after the fat family in *The Nutty Professor*.

Then it was the twins' turn.

Thelma and Ray stood up as one, and held each other's hands. Then, they began talking in that weird-ass language of theirs. They were speaking at the same time, but they were saying different things. Ray sounded like he was talking one of the made-up *Stars Wars* languages— like whatever the hell that big slug spoke. Thelma, by contrast, buzzed. Like a cicada, or a thousand flies. It was horrifying. It made me itch and shiver. I felt the tiny, ticklish scrape of insect feet beneath my skin.

That was weird enough.

But then, Lilith Baylock answered them back. The same way. Yes! She managed to speak like a space alien *and* buzz like cicadas in high summer.

She and twins chattered on and on. It lasted forever. It didn't help that all of us were more or less frozen to our seats. I began to get itchy. I decided that I couldn't take it anymore. I was going to move, goddammit. I focused on my forearm.

Move!

Fingers made of stone. Hands underwater. A million pinpricks as it woke up. And then I felt it. The invisible clamp of Baylock's spell. It was made of crystal. But crystal can break, can't it? I'm not no damn mineral scientist, but I'd seen crystals shattering in movies. I remember seeing a science fiction TV show where they killed an evil being that looked like a mountain of crystals by sound vibrations. I imagined Mariah Carey singing her highest note.

I felt the invisible vise shatter. I heard the crack. Everybody did.

Even Lilith Baylock.

All of the eyes in the classroom were on me. But I only felt the heat from Baylock's gaze. I thought she was fixin' to zap me. Cuz I had no doubt that she could shoot energy beams or whatever at me.

Instead, she smiled. Wide. A real shit-eating grin. It was charming, really. Until you noticed the points on her teeth.

"Very good, Eudora. You're growing into your power," she said with a giggle.

"What do you mean, 'my power'?" I said.

"I've been keeping my eye on you all for a while now," she said as she stood up. "I haven't felt such delicious naughtiness concentrated in one place for a long-ass time. Separately, you can only be so effective. Hindered by family or school. But together, as a unit…hot damn! Six little imps, good and ready to unleash chaos."

Charmaine said, "You talking about demonic stuff. I'm a— Chris—chris…" She began stuttering. "I mean, every Sunday, I go to ch-ch-chu…"

"What you mean, you been watching us," said DiAundre. He was up and twitching and blinking.

"Oh, my little pyromancer." She walked up to him, and stroked him under his chin, like he was a cat. He stopped twitching. She continued: "I can smell black magic like a pig can smell truffles underground. You've developed in this soil, like a fine wine. A combination of raw talent, Oppositional Defiant Disorder, poverty, and groupthink. You've flourished in this environment. And now, I'm here to mold you into your full potential!"

Big T said, "How could you watch us? Did you have, like drone cameras or some shit like that?"

"Oh, my dear Greedigut, where do you think I watched you from? We have no need for human technology where I come from!" She giggled, her ridiculous breasts jiggling like jello shooters.

I knew where she came from, even if the rest of these triflin' kids didn't. I knew it like I knew that water was wet. I knew that Lilith Baylock wasn't no human female. She was just pretending to be one. She was put together all wrong. I knew that beneath her Lil' Kim skin suit, there was something with teeth, horns and claws. I could imagine her watching us from some ratchet corner of Hell, like that green witch in the *Wizard of Oz* spied on Dorothy in her crystal ball.

"Today, we must learn to calibrate ourselves, so we can function as a unit. We're getting all Guantanamo up in this bitch!"

She clapped her hands, and suddenly, Kenyatta Burress from Unit 7C was in the room. He was all, "Da fuq?" He was trying to grow a beard, but it was straggly and his face was full of razor bumps. What Charmaine saw in him, I'll never know.

Lilith Baylock said, "Charmaine, my sweetest! Did this nigga break your heart?"

Charmaine looked like she was fifteen, going on eight. I could see her eyes fill up with tears.

"Charmaine, what the hell is going on?" said Kenyatta.

"I was just a jump off," Charmaine said quietly.

Baylock grabbed Kenyatta's chin in a vise grip. "He played with your heart. This fuckboy here. I can see it in your eyes. I can feel your heartache."

"Get offa me, you bitch," Kenyatta said. He squirmed like a naughty toddler out of her hold.

The world turned silent. The flickering hum of the overhead lights stopped. Us kids stopped breathing. It was as if the world was covered in plastic bubble wrap. The look on Baylock's face was the look I imagined Dahmer or Gacy gave to their victims just before slicing them to bits.

"Don't. Call. Me. A. Bitch." Each word dropped like a stone.

Then, Baylock changed before my very eyes. The Minaj/Lil' Kim stuff oozed right off of her in a pink velour wave. What she was and what she wasn't is hard to describe. Spikes erupted everywhere from skin that had the texture of cockroach bodies. Her mouth was a ring with a spiral of teeth the color of cigarette butts. Her eyes were lips that winked with little stalky things snaking in and out.

She didn't make any sense.

I looked around, to get everyone's reaction to this reveal. But I didn't see any shock or fear in any of the faces. Not even Kenyatta's. It was as if they didn't see what I saw.

"Class!" said Baylock, her voice as bright and chipper as Mary Poppins. Her disguise was back on, just like that. "Let's turn this fuckboy into a fucked-up boy!"

I turned around to glance at my classmates—

They had *changed*, too. They still had their faces and their clothes. But they were also something else. Goat horns sprouted and retracted like cat claws. Charmaine had batwings one moment, and none the next. DiAundre burned with fire that disappeared if you looked at it too long. Big T looked like one of the monsters from *Where The Wild Things Are*. And the twins were iguanas one minute, birds, the next.

I wonder what I looked like.

I ain't gonna lie. We fucked up Kenyatta real good. By the time we were done, he was a hot mess. He had burns all over his body, scratches on his face and was bleeding from multiple wounds. Nigga looked like MS13, the Bloods and the Crips all had turns with him. Baylock whisked him away somewhere to die.

I know what we did was wrong. I know that Lilith Baylock is some kind of demon that we summoned from some dark corner of Hell. But it felt *good*, embracing who and what we were. Finally belonging, having a purpose and all that shit.

We became a gang that day. Guess what we called ourselves.

PROTECT & SERVE

CODY GOODFELLOW

Trainee Madrigal had been riding with Sgt. Albright for a week, and tonight was the first time the older cop let the rookie drive, when the 10-999 call came in. *Officer down, all units respond—*

"Before you can call yourself a policeman," Albright said, "you need to see this."

Big John Albright was pretty cool for an old white cop. Madrigal's dad, who retired last summer after twenty years prowling La Mirada, had warned him about cops like Big John, who should've been promoted to plainclothes eons ago, but stayed in uniform to "keep a lid on the younger guys." But Albright seemed to buck the profile. Over and over, Madrigal watched him de-escalate situations between other cops and people of color. The rookie asked him once, after they backed a traffic stop with racial profiling stink all over it and Albright braced the other cop to let him off with a warning, if he was the only non-racist cop on the force.

Albright had said, "Hell no, I'm as racist as any cop. If you're not blue, fuck you." He'd laughed as if it was a joke, and not the funny-be-cause-it's true kind.

Yeah, he was cooler than shit in the clinch, and the other cops were scared of him. Maybe his dad would have made an exception for Big John, but his dad dropped dead less than a month into retirement, cursing his new electric lawnmower.

They pulled into a mini-mall parking lot on Euclid and Curlew. Dissolved in a blue and red acid bath from nine patrol SUV's, two ambulances and a fire truck surrounding a squad car parked at the curb, draped in yellow tape.

It was something you only see on TV, all the shaken witnesses and loved ones wailing and embracing, pounding on things and coming apart at the seams. But all of them were cops.

Albright put a hand on his shoulder. "You feeling it?"

Madrigal felt stirred at the reminder, but he knew this kind of thing could happen, it had been foremost on his mind since his first day at the academy. Madrigal just nodded.

"I better go over there," Albright said, climbing out. "Stay put."

Hours after the sun went down that sweltering late September evening, the heat of the day seemed to seep out of cracked sidewalks and molten tarmac. You could almost wring sweat out of the air by making a fist.

Albright climbed out and ambled over to the knot of angry cops. Madrigal watched, fascinated. These guys seemed to have bought into the idea that they were the Law, invincible, and to find one of their own could be killed had taken away their last spoon.

A civilian in a cheap tracksuit came over and talked to the cops. One of them threw a punch, knocking the civilian out of one of his sneakers and pounced on him before he hit the ground, taking his head in both hands like a coconut he was about to crack open. Albright wrapped an arm around the cop's neck and dragged him away.

Madrigal was still watching when Albright came back over and tapped on the roof. "Slide over. I'm driving."

Of course, the console on the drive train made it impossible, so Madrigal got out and went around the car. Albright got in his face, took his arm. Breathing hard. Eyes hooded. "Terry Gafford," he said. "Say his name."

Madrigal said the name. It left a taste like a penny on his tongue, conjured a ruddy face he'd noted once or twice in the locker room. Hooded, greasy eyes sizing him up, writing him off.

Sweat off Albright's brow dripped on his uniform. "Everybody's pretty worked over when this happens. The older guys especially, they feel like they've gotta take it out on somebody, even when we already got the guy."

Madrigal pointed at the tracksuit, still sprawled on the sidewalk counting his teeth. "Is that him?"

Albright let out a violently compressed sigh. He looked almost angry now, a weary blankness that made his face a silicone mask. "Just the property owner. Wants to know when he can reopen. Just got in the wrong guy's face at the wrong time." Albright looked at Madrigal and realized the rookie hadn't asked a stupid question.

But now he did.

"So do we? Got the guy?"

"He got away," Albright said.

"No shit?" Madrigal felt a twinge of shame at the excitement in his voice.

"Get in the car," Albright said.

For the next two hours, cruising the streets in an old-school Crown Vic prowler with recessed light bars on the roof instead of the highly visible up-armored SUVs the rest of the force was driving, they were like a one-car goodwill tour, seeking to undo all the wrongs of policemen past.

936—Intoxicated person. Albright stopped a trio of bouncers pounding a drunk outside a meat-market sports bar on Lardner, near Mission. "Shame on you," he said to the bouncers. "His bad habits pay your salary." After he refused medical attention, they dropped the drunk off at his residence.

947—Suspicious Person. Responding to a call about a young Black individual loitering outside an apartment complex carrying stolen property. The complainant was highly agitated without probable cause, and Albright gave her a brisk but polite dressing down not only for wasting the department's time, but for infringing on the civil rights of a solid citizen who was behaving in no reasonable sense suspiciously. The suspect explained that he had just bought the keyboard under his arm on Craigslist from a tenant in the complex, and was waiting on a friend to pick him up. Shaking the young individual's hand, he urged him to avoid the neighborhood after dark. "It's dangerous, man. Full of white people." Albright honked and waved as they pulled out of the parking lot and floored it northbound on Custer.

"You know why they like to wear their pants like that?" he asked at the next red light.

Oh shit, here we go... "I grew up in Van Nuys, Sarge." He cleared his throat, watching the young black guys cross in front of the cruiser. "But I heard stories."

"Tell me one."

"Uh... Okay. Every kid in the projects used to wear hand-me-downs, so it was a way of showing you had a big brother at home who'd back you up... or... It's so they can carry without making a bulge, or just trying to make it look like they're strapped... And there was some bullshit about how it meant you were down to fuck in prison, I think white people were saying that cuz of Rush Limbaugh or something..."

Albright nodded, tapping on the steering wheel. "You wanna know who started it?"

"What, the rumor?"

"No, the style, if that's what you wanna call it." Albright goosed the siren and jumped the red light, nearly clipping a camper. "We did."

"Who?"

"Cops. Undercover cops in the Eighties."

"Get the fuck out of here. Why?"

"Got tired of chasing 'em. Think of how many we'd have to shoot if they wore belts."

Madrigal cracked a dutiful smile, hoping it was another joke.

Watching the traffic, Albright said, "To get a license in this town, you have to obey twenty-four traffic laws. The average cop knows about forty-six. But there are 112 laws on the books. Everybody's doing something wrong all the time, and nobody stops them." He fingered a medallion hanging out between the buttons of his uniform, like the St. Christopher's medal Madrigal got from his mother when he joined the Marines.

The radio would chirp and crackle to itself, then unleash a digital scream, sandblasting their ears with static and garbled speech, trailing off into dead air that made the whole city feel like a haunted house.

"This is the job," he said. "I get it, we're all victims of circumstance. Products of our environment. You give a kid a script, he's gotta read it.

So do we. Last mayor thought he was another Giulani with his tough-on-crime bullshit. Had us racking up quantity arrests, but the quality was shit. Beating heads in over dime bags, rolling retail thugs out of bed with guns to their heads. It brought out the worst in us. We don't need to be like that. But *this*… this isn't that."

"What is *this?*"

The radio made a querulous squeak like a hungry stomach. Albright seemed to hear something more in it, distracted. "Suspect is a retail coke and meth dealer," he said. "Two Intent-To-Sell beefs and an Illegal Firearm. Clarence Hooks, a.k.a. Clancy Hooker, a.k.a. Clee Hop, a.k.a. C&H, like the sugar. 42, 5'8", one-eighty, dark skin with vitiligo patches on face and neck, wearing black pants and a white hoodie. Suspect is armed and driving a white '09 Acura sedan, #V471FU2. Deadbeat dad twice over. We never got him on it, but during the last white powder drought, we believe he and some other dealers switched up on their clientele and turned them on to fentanyl. If we could tie him to it, he'd be on Death Row twice over.

"11-58," Albright said into the radio. Madrigal wracked his brain… *Radio traffic is monitored… Phone in all non-routine calls…*

"Terry was a good cop," Albright said. "Never harder than he had to be, but never any softer either, if you know what I mean."

Madrigal figured he did.

"Not like it matters. He was a cop, that's enough. Your dad would've liked him. He would've liked you, eventually. Kind of guy you know has your back. Did two tours in the Marines. Went to Iraq the first time, for Desert Storm. Lot of cops can't get upstairs fast enough, but Terry loved shoe-leather police work. Overtime, double watches. He lived for this shit. Helping people. Fixing problems. Christmas toy drive every year, he ran it. If another cop got it, he collected for the family. I guess I've got the duty, now."

"So what happened?"

"Hooks works on his car in the mini-mall lot by his apartment, been using it to front for slinging grams for years. Terry calls in for a meal break when he spots Hooks and codes 10-59 to see what he's up to. Must've been bad, because Hooks caps Terry in the neck and groin before fleeing the scene. A witness called 911 and we responded."

"So… Terry's the big bald guy who sits in the front of the day room, right?"

"Yeah. What about him?"

"Just… dude looked like he was running on a treadmill sitting still, tonight. If I was to keep my eyes open like you're always saying, I'd wonder about his last piss test."

The turn signal lever snapped off the steering column in Albright's hand. "Fuck are you saying, trainee?"

"Just… Terry wasn't responding to a complaint, he rolls up on this guy… I mean… Terry *reeks* of it, Sarge. I'm just saying, he went on break, but then he did this stop… What about his body-cam?"

"You bucking to be Hooks's lawyer? Because this is no trial, and you're no fucking judge."

"I'm sorry, Sarge, It's just…"

"We wouldn't last a week on the street, if every cop had his own personal meter to decide whether the cop next to him is worth protecting."

"*117… 248…*" the radio croaked. "*Copy anyone in vicinity… Suspect's car spotted at Betty's Bubble, 17501 Burr, northeast corner of Burr and Crater.*"

"10-4," Albright replied. "117, we are en route."

Albright ran Code 3, lights and siren in full effect, blowing through three major intersections and hitting the siren as he threaded the gaps between speeding cross-traffic. In less than ten minutes, they were halfway across town, three blocks below Imperial, what old-timers like his father used to call Indian Country.

The Bubble was a funny kind of bar. No sign out front. Whatever you ordered, you'd get a dirty glass of Mad Dog or warm beer and charged like you were on Park Avenue, if they served you at all. All the bottles behind the bar had tiny notes bearing the names of the players who put them there. It was a front for local retail drug runners and pimps, its continued existence an enigma that Madrigal would have asked about, any other time.

"Go in," Albright told him.

"What, by myself?"

"Bring your fairy godmother, if you need to. Flush him out."

Madrigal stepped out of the car. The gaggle of lanky underage punks smoking around the door scattered, mumbling and texting "popo" and "five-oh." He felt like he was walking into an ambush. His right hand strayed to his sidearm as he reached for the doorknob with his left.

Inside was dim and choked with cloying blunt smoke like someone was freebasing Fruity Pebbles. Maybe a dozen individuals looked up and hissed through electroplated grills, covered their faces or spit on the floor. The hostility was like microwaves, cooking him from the inside out.

Someone got up from a booth in the back and made for the back door. Madrigal saw a spotless white hoodie, a dark face with a paler splash of skin shaped like a keyhole over the left eye.

"Hooks! Police! Stop and drop!" Madrigal charged. He fumbled his gun out of its holster. Two men crossed in front of him, headed for the restroom. Madrigal threw an arm to shove them out of his way and hit one in the throat, knocking him flat on his back. The suspect rammed the back door and slipped into the alley. His white hoodie was so bright it left a flare on Madrigal's dilated retinas.

He stepped over the man he'd clotheslined, brandishing his sidearm in the face of his friend, running for the back door swinging shut in his face. He hit the push-bar with his gun-hand, nearly squeezing the trigger. Out in the alley, his night-vision ruined, but he saw the white hoodie through red fog. He planted his feet and shouted, "Police! Stop or I'll shoot!"

He sighted the fleeing suspect down the barrel of his gun. His finger twitched on the trigger, his brain spinning out of his skull. He shouted again. The suspect reached the mouth of the alley, swimming in iodine streetlight and then he was flying as a car swooped into view and knocked him off his feet.

The cop car swerved sideways to block the alley. Albright jumped out just as Madrigal came running up. "Why didn't you call for backup?"

The suspect lay prone on the sidewalk holding his ribs. Albright knelt down and put a knee in the small of his back, bent his arms behind his back and zip-tied them.

"You almost got your cherry popped," Albright said. "Why didn't you?"

The suspect was trying to say something. Madrigal stood over him, the gun still in his hand. Suddenly, it felt very light.

In the car, the radio squawked. Madrigal thought it was screaming his name. He could barely make out what the suspect was saying into the pavement. "Why you chasing me, Five-Oh?"

Albright bent and turned him over. "Why you running, Pepe? We're not even looking for you."

"You looking for C&H. Ain't seen him."

"We don't need your help finding Clee," Albright told him. "We don't need you for anything."

Madrigal felt like he was going to puke. Gutter grime caked the white hoodie. In the streetlight, it looked like dried blood. Pepe was a light-skinned African American with a spray of freckles across his cheeks and a badly broken nose, but even now, Madrigal's fevered brain was trying to paint the suspect's vitiligo on his face.

"You good?" Albright asked him.

Madrigal had to try three times before he could holster his gun. "I'm good..."

"Are you, though?" Albright told Pepe to go home and Madrigal to get in the fucking car, already. They left the suspect squirming on the pavement with four broken ribs and his hands zip-tied behind his back.

———◆◆◆———

They drove. The radio spat like a geiger counter. Sometimes the noise got louder when Albright turned or hit the brakes and reversed. Sometimes it got quiet and he sped up, head swiveling, reading the street. *Warmer, colder, hot...*

"You think you know what we are. You think we're just another gang."

"I didn't say that—"

"But you believe it. You saw what the Job did to your dad, yet here you are. You're maybe the one in ten who wants to make a *difference*. You look down on the rest of us already. Maybe you're right. Those guys who think our authority comes from being feared, who feel invincible because they can kill anybody who looks at them cockeyed... but you almost capped the wrong guy just because he was getting away. Maybe you're more one of those guys than you think. Those guys who don't know the truth about the Job were the ones freaking out back there."

"What do *you* know, Big John? What's the truth?"

Albright fingered his badge as he drove. Madrigal noticed two of the points on the star-shaped shield were bent. "You're not a cop your first day, you'll never learn to fake it, and you'll never really *feel* it. If you're here to find your father, you'll lose yourself first." Albright touched his shoulder. "Were you raised Catholic?"

"Yeah… sort of…"

"Have you ever wondered why the Archangel Michael was also a saint?"

"Honestly… no. Should I?"

"It's religion. You're never supposed to ask. But you can see the twists and turns it took, like the weird bones in whales that tell you they used to walk on land. When Christianity went from being a cult to the law of the land, they had to sell it, and a weakling who took it on the chin for our sins was good enough for regular jack-offs, but the soldier class wasn't buying it. Most of them were into Sol Invictus, or the bull-god Mithras. They needed the wolves to become shepherds to watch over the sheep, so one of those old blood-and-thunder gods, they made him an angel. The flaming sword in the darkness, the tip of the spear. The one who watches over those who have to go through the doors, and avenges them when they fall.

"And maybe it's a sin, but I've been praying to the God of the sheep all my life, and I never got nothing from it. But I know who's looking over my shoulder. I know who lifted me up, when my life was hanging by a thread. I know who answers my prayers, and gives me strength."

He held something under Madrigal's eyes. The medallion he'd been playing with all night. A crooked coin with a sigil in deep relief minted on it: what looked at a glance like a cross was really a flaming sword.

"He used to watch over us, but we forgot to honor him, and now we're dying in the streets, dying unavenged and unremembered, and nobody's afraid to shit all over good men who do a job they never could. But all that ends tonight."

"Why, what's tonight?"

"The night of the Feast. The archangel cast a third of the heavenly host into the pit, purging the enemy within. His blood cries out for justice. Him and all the unavenged. It's Michaelmas, and we have a chance to put it right. Give them peace, at last."

The radio squealed, making them both jump.

"Sighting on his car," Albright said.

Madrigal asked, "What did you hear?"

"He changed cars." Albright pointed out the maroon Hyundai Elantra two cars ahead of them. "He's right in front of us." Traffic was sleepy and sparse, the neighborhood more vacant lots, liquor stores and check cashing places than anything else.

"You heard that over the radio?"

"I'm not telling you what I heard. The question is, what kind of cop are you, that you *can't* hear it?"

The Hyundai turned right on Encanto and Albright floored it. Out of the clipping and crackling, Madrigal heard voices. It sounded like someone reciting a rosary while being boiled in oil.

"Corner of Quorn and Graas. In the name of Sol Invictus... for the blood of our brother."

Madrigal's eyes went so wide, they almost fell out. "Did you hear that?"

"I *always* hear it," Albright said. "Whenever I look at somebody on the street, I hear it telling me all the evil that individual's done, and how they should pay for it. I hear it in my sleep, telling me all the evil shit my neighbors are doing. That's what it means to be a *real* cop. That's what it means, this job. We keep the secret that all of this is a lie that wouldn't last a day without us."

After Quorn, the city just seemed to give up—boarded-up storefronts, burned-down houses, wrecks up on blocks and folks living in campers and cardboard boxes. When there was no one else on the road, Albright goosed the lights and siren. The Hyundai accelerated, wailing at the top of its four-cylinder lungs, but the squad car overtook him before the next light. Albright sideswiped the Hyundai's rear wheels, sending it into a spin. The smaller sedan jumped the curb and clipped a telephone pole, coming to rest pointed the wrong way, rear wheels up on the buckled sidewalk.

In the Hyundai, the suspect was punching the half-deflated airbag and stumbling out of the car when they rolled up on him. Albright parked and put on his sunglasses. "Any idiot could see Terry had a problem, but you don't judge a man when he's saved your life. His heart was all fucked up from that shit. He quit more than once. Whatever he was doing with Hooks, even if he was shaking him down, he deserves—no, he *demands*—payback."

When somebody waved a gun at police, giving them no choice, they called it suicide by cop. When a cop got himself killed so his family could still collect his pension without a shameful autopsy, they call it heroism.

As they got out of the car, every streetlight on the block burned out. Madrigal heard the voices. They weren't coming from the radio. *Sol Invictus... Archangel...*

Hooks was halfway down the street, running for his life. Albright drew down and squeezed off one round. The suspect face-planted on the sidewalk. Albright and Madrigal took their time walking up on him. No cars passed, no light shone on them but the moon.

Hooks was up on one knee panting, trying to make the other leg move, but his kneecap was gone. Albright reached him first, standing tall with his gun out. "Come here," he said. "You need to do this."

Madrigal's gun was in his hand and he was looking at the suspect, and it was like there were six of him, begging and fighting and saying something about self-defense and praying to the wrong god and reaching to pull a gun or a knife out of the hole in his leg.

There was nobody around, but Madrigal felt surrounded. A chill wind raised goosebumps on his skin, shriveled his balls and made the fillings in his teeth sing in harmony with the radio. *Unconquered Sun...*

He fumbled for his body-cam. The light was blinking red and wouldn't activate. The world would believe whatever they said, about what was about to happen.

A crowd gathered close about them. He could hear them drowning out Albright, heard the sound of them coming out of his own mouth, and now, he could see them.

They were cops.

Worsted wool tunics with brass buttons, gold braid, jodhpurs, Sam Browne belts, white gloves, patent leather jackboots, peaked caps, motorcycle helmets, truncheons, batons, nightsticks, blackjacks, tear gas, tasers, revolvers, tommy guns, manacles, handcuffs, nameless, numberless black-banded badges, and no faces. Featureless black glass masks cracked and melted into mouths that demanded obedience and blood.

They were ghosts, he knew it in the marrow of his bones, but of *what?* More real than anything alive, but their emptiness promised nothing like an afterlife, only hunger and punishment. Effigies of fear and anger so poisonous they'd created their own hell, their souls dissolved in the acid-bath of the Job. But in their eagerness for human sacrifice, they were something worse than ghosts. They were almost gods. Their hate must be protected, their rage must be served.

"It's righteous," Albright said. "Do it, and you're untouchable."

With the immortal anger of the unavenged silently howling at his back, Madrigal just stood and shook his head.

"Thought I saw something in you." Albright pointed his gun at the back of Hooks's neck.

Madrigal's gun came up to point at Albright's center of mass, the muzzle nosing between the plates of his body armor. He grabbed his radio and shouted over the voices, "248, 17, 10-15, suspect in custody. I repeat—"

"So it's like that," Albright said. Holstering his gun, he took a knee in the small of the suspect's back, cuffed him and informed him of his rights. "You have no idea what it's really like, but you will."

The voices got fainter and higher in pitch and Madrigal heard every siren in the city coming for them. Albright knelt beside Hooks to whisper in his ear, "You're gonna be a legend, Clee. Everybody's gonna know you took out two cops in one night."

ZONES WITHOUT NAMES

DAVID PEAK

"You're all being lied to," said the pamphleteer, a man named Sloke, thrusting his poorly printed literature at the people who passed him by. "Everything you see. Everything around you. None of it is real. None of it can be trusted."

The snow-swept air was cold and the masses were bundled up in heavy coats. They kept their hands in their pockets and avoided eye contact, heads down on their way to the employment offices and soup kitchens. Sloke was easy to ignore in his threadbare overcoat, with his long hair and untrimmed beard, his dirty fingernails and wild eyes.

Somebody kicked the cardboard box at Sloke's feet, and his remaining pamphlets were sent fluttering down the sidewalk. He went after them, bumped into someone, screamed at the next person to get out of the way. Just as he grabbed a fistful of slush-soaked paper, he was shoved from behind. He stumbled into an alley and fell onto a pile of garbage bags, gagging on the garlicky stench of rat poison.

They had their hands on him then, a couple of kids, or so he thought. Sloke couldn't be sure, couldn't get a good look. It happened too fast. They dragged him onto the concrete. One of them clapped him on his ear. Another one kicked him in his thigh. Then they were kicking him everywhere, his ribs, his arms, his legs. He curled into a ball and tried to cover the back of his head.

Just like that it was over. One of the kids called Sloke a parasite. Another one spat on him. They took off running, their shrill laughter echoing down the alley.

Sloke sucked air through his teeth as he rolled onto his back. It hurt to breathe. He stared at the sky, a sliver of gray shifting between the buildings. He couldn't remember the last time he'd stopped to look at the sky, how the strange gasses glimmered in its gossamer folds. Snowflakes seemed to emerge fully formed out of thin air, sticking wet on his face.

He closed his eyes. His consciousness started to fade. In that moment, suspended just beyond the black pull of sleep, Sloke saw a dome of white light expanding over the horizon, heard the rush of whipping wind. He saw a ruined cityscape, a city he didn't recognize, nothing he'd ever seen in waking life, all sloping skyscrapers, bent rebar, and broken glass. Down in a deep explosion crater, countless black threads emerged from a tangled heap of blue-gray bodies, pulling taut in a perfect grid. The grid rose into the sky, a razor-sharp mesh, slicing the corpses into quivering, bloodless cubes.

He woke gasping for breath and was surprised to see a man in an expensive suit and overcoat squatting next to him, a concerned look on his face.

"Are you okay?"

Where to even begin? Sloke coughed as he sat up, leaned against the brick wall. Snow had accumulated in the creases of his overcoat.

"Come on, let's get you on your feet. You look like you could use a warm cup of tea."

The morning rush had slowed and the snow had stopped. Sloke followed the well-dressed man to the nearest government checkpoint. Tight coils of razor wire gleamed in the cold light. Soldiers wearing facemasks and carrying heavy machine guns patrolled their observation posts. A train whistle sounded in the distance, quickly approaching.

"They see everything these days," the well-dressed man said, pointing to a CCTV camera mounted near the tracks. "The many eyes of our government. And us, caught in its nefarious web."

The signal bell rang and red lights flashed as the two men ducked the barrier. An ominous sign posted on the security gate warned that trespassers would be fired upon, that the grounds beyond contained pockets of scrambling gas.

They entered a dreary café and sat at a table near the window. Glasses and dishes clattered as the train slowed into the station, shedding a noxious cloud of coal-black smoke. The stock cars were crowded with emaciated horses, their long necks strained over the railing.

The grease-thick air of the café smelled of melting plastic. Sloke couldn't help but notice the cook watching them from the ticket window. A waitress sat at the counter, talking to a distorted face on some sort of handheld screen, a technology Sloke hadn't seen before.

"No one reads the news anymore," the well-dressed man said. "All anyone wants to see is a reflection of themselves."

After a moment or two, the waitress sighed, put down the screen, and approached their table. One of her legs was much longer and thicker than the other, and she swung it in a wide circle when she walked. She was young but not pretty.

The well-dressed man ordered two cups of tea, whatever they had, offered to cover the cost.

Sloke waited for the waitress to limp and thud away. "Why are you doing this?"

"Doing what?"

"Showing me kindness."

"I guess you could say I'm indebted to you." He reached inside his coat and tossed one of Sloke's pamphlets onto the table. The blocky lettering on the cover said, WE ARE PUPPETS DANCING AT THE ENDS OF THEIR STRINGS!

"My name is *Gird*, like *grid*." He made a movement with his first two fingers. "But with the middle letters swapped."

"Like *grid*," Sloke said, recalling his vision of the ruined cityscape, the black threads slicing through the pile of corpses. What did it mean? He picked up the pamphlet and aimlessly flipped through it. He didn't recognize the words. "Where did you get this?"

"From you, of course."

"From me?"

"Not too far from where I found you today. You wore the same coat, only it wasn't so threadbare. Your beard was shorter too. But I recognize you well enough."

The waitress brought them their teas. They were pale yellow, lukewarm, and the bags looked like they'd already been used. Gird waited for her to leave and revealed a silver hip flask. He unscrewed the cap and added a splash of brown liquor to both cups.

Sloke couldn't remember the last time he'd had whiskey. Or even seen it. Alcohol, cigarettes, coffee—those were premium commodities. He quickly took a sip, welcoming the pleasant burn. The smell of it alone sent him reeling. He used to love the stuff. Too much. It had almost cost him everything back when things still held value.

Gird kept his voice low. "When I found you in the alley you looked like you were having a seizure. It sounded like you were choking on your tongue. Your eyelids were fluttering."

Sloke looked around. The cook no longer lurked in the ticket window, and the waitress was once again fixated on her screen. "I was having one of my visions."

"About what's in control?"

Sloke said nothing.

"You were muttering about black threads."

"I don't know anything about that."

"I think you do." Gird tapped the pamphlet on the table. "You mention them here. The strings that control us, you say. Only you don't say who's pulling them. Still, I get what you mean." He leaned forward. "It's what you don't say that's important."

Sloke wondered if this man was crazy.

"You think I'm crazy. I can tell. Let me ask you, do you think you're crazy?"

"I think everyone else is crazy. They want to keep on pretending like everything is normal when it's not. That makes them crazy to me."

"Well, two people who agree on a vision of the world can't both be crazy, can they?"

Sloke thought about this for a moment. "I just try to make sense of what I see. I don't know what that makes me. I see things—I notice things that other people don't seem to notice—and I try to relate those things to other things. That's all. Like recognizing patterns."

Gird sipped his tea. "My wife and I were recently married." He held up his hand, displaying the gold band on his finger. "In exchange for paying for our wedding and giving us an apartment, the government enrolled us in a procreation program. It's our civic duty to have children, they say. You read in the news how people are executed for producing and distributing birth control? Too many parasites, they say. Not enough workers." He took another sip. "I don't know if I can bring a child into this world. I lie awake at night thinking about it."

He tapped at the pamphlet again. "In here you say the only way for people to survive is to stop having babies. Aren't you worried about how the government will react to that sort of thing?"

Sloke thought about the kids who shoved him into the alley, who punched him and kicked him. They were desperate. Hungry. Scared. They'd called him a parasite. That word was always creeping into things, *parasite,* poisoning things.

People could sense there wasn't much time left. There wasn't enough of anything to go around, and soon there'd be even less. So they lashed out at people like him, like Sloke, people with vision, because he was out there saying the things they didn't want to hear.

Sloke felt the booze. "I'm a nobody, so they let me run my mouth. If someone like you—someone with an apartment, nice clothes, a wife—if you stood in the street and said those kinds of things, they'd put you on the first train to the tar sands."

The waitress asked if they were ready to settle their bill. "This isn't a social club," she said. Instead Gird ordered two more teas. Out came the hip flask again, the musical sound of the cap being unscrewed, the heavenly burning sensation. Sloke started to forget his pain. He started to feel like a human being again. The two men talked about the way things used to be, the old world, whatever they could remember, but then Sloke had to stop himself before he remembered too much. His head spun when they stood. Gird dropped a few heavy coins onto the table and they were back out on the street, Sloke and Gird, back out in the cold.

"I'd kill somebody for more whiskey," Sloke said.

Gird laughed and clapped him on the back. "That can be arranged, my friend. This way."

They returned to the train tracks and stood before the no trespassing sign.

"You heard what the scrambling gas does to you?" Sloke said. "Messes with your genetic code. Fuses your bones. Liquefies your organs.

Two people fall into a pit together and they come out sharing the same kidneys."

Gird flashed what looked like a government badge. "Don't panic."

Sloke took a step back away from the gate. "I've done nothing wrong."

"Relax."

"I didn't even—"

"I'm not going to arrest you. I couldn't even if I wanted to. I'm just a drone who works in surveillance." He gestured to the CCTV camera. "Those cameras you see everywhere? Those are my eyes. They're connected to a network, which I built. They call me the webmaster. From one zone to the next I can see everything."

Gird turned a small black object over in his hands. It was smooth as polished stone. "That red light near the lens? That means it's recording. Now, watch this."

He swept his thumb over the object and its top half fanned outward. The pieces clicked into place and it made a tight whirring noise. He pressed a few tiny buttons. A moment later the red light on the camera blinked, once, twice, and faded. The camera dipped down as if it had fallen asleep. Gird snapped shut the controller, or whatever it was, and returned it to his pocket.

"All that stuff you write about how nothing is what it seems, you're more right than you know. There's a program on my computer at home. I can show you things you wouldn't believe. But first I need your help with something. A special favor between like-minded individuals."

Sloke hesitated.

Gird held up the hip flask. "Plenty more where this came from."

"What do you need me to do?"

They didn't have to wait long for the next train to roll through the station, and when it did they crept alongside it, hidden within all that heavy smoke, and slipped through the open gate. They followed the tracks for a while—Gird deactivated any cameras they came across—and arrived at a tight passage between two bullet-flecked buildings.

Gird warned Sloke to mimic his movements exactly. And in this manner, Sloke following Gird, they passed through a series of small, hastily constructed structures, all plywood, plastic tarp, and sheet metal, and waded through a sea of waist-deep grass. They climbed over piles of crumbled stone, rusted machinery, burned-out cars. They squeezed through a hole cut in a chain-link fence and entered a darkened warehouse.

As they reached the exit, Gird turned to Sloke. "We need to make sure you blend in." He opened a makeup compact, brushed chalk-white powder on Sloke's face, and applied several layers of waxy red lipstick. Then he did the same for himself.

Sloke didn't need to be told where he was. He'd heard all about the government zone. The streets were swept and lined with cobblestones gleaming in the warm glow of gas lamps. By then it was early evening. The men wore nice suits, nice coats, nice shoes. The women wore fur coats, heels, pearls. Everyone was caked in white-powder makeup, heavy rouge, their mouths painted red.

A horse-drawn carriage swept by, hooves clopping, its coachman yelling, cracking the reins.

Gird seemed to relish Sloke's reaction. "When the future arrived and people decided they didn't like it, they retreated to the past. They adopted a nostalgic vision of the world."

Sloke could not have felt more out of place, yet no one took notice of him. He followed Gird beyond the brightly lit shops and stately homes and climbed a steel staircase. There, the streets opened onto a wide square, a bronze statue of the grand general at its center. Everything was lit with flood lights for maximum effect.

"Take a seat," Gird said, gesturing to a bench near the fountain. They drank more whiskey, staining the flask's mouth with lipstick. Sloke noticed how Gird's demeanor had changed. He seemed pensive, on edge.

"Why did you bring me here?"

"Just a moment." A few minutes later he nodded across the street. "There."

A man descended the stone steps of an official building. He was older, with silver hair, and he wore a black coat and a red scarf. When he reached the sidewalk, he lit a cigar, its tip glowing orange as he puffed on it. Then he made his way up the street and turned down an alley.

"All right," Gird said. "Let's go."

He kept his voice low and spoke rapidly. "Those lies you write about? They originate with that man. He's the governor of truth. He's the one who told us we needed to build giant spaceships and drill other planets for their resources. You remember what happened next? What they brought back? They poisoned our air, our water. The wars that followed. Now they say our only hope is to build more spaceships and spread life to other planets. The complete opposite idea. We need to start over, they say. This planet can no longer sustain life. Well, whose fault is that?"

The smell of cigar smoke still lingered in the alley. Sloke caught a glimpse of the silver-haired man just as he turned the next corner.

"Here." Gird extended the grip of an antique handgun to Sloke. "That man will walk two more blocks and then pause on the footbridge to finish his cigar. He does it every night. I want you to shoot him in the back of the head." He pressed the gun into Sloke's chest. "Take it, you fool."

Sloke did as he was told. The gun was heavier than he thought it would be. He contemplated what it meant to end a man's life, tried to see it from different angles. Would it really be so bad if the world had one fewer person in it? One fewer government rat? If what Gird said was the truth, then countless lives had already been lost because of this man. How many more might be saved by his death?

"I've turned off all the cameras. No one will ever know you were here." Gird grabbed Sloke's arm, spoke through his lipstick-stained teeth. His breath reeked of whiskey. "Think of the message this will send. A murder in the government zone. No one will ever feel safe again. They'll know exactly how it feels."

Sloke was smart enough to know when he was being manipulated. He was also smart enough to know that it didn't matter if what Gird said was the truth. Gird could be anybody at all, a government agent using a fake name. A regular person with a fake government badge. An anarchist. An environmentalist. Another person who had lost everything.

He thought about what it meant to survive in the years after the white light broke over the sky, cordoned off into increasingly small, increasingly crowded zones, forced to live off less and less, eating rats raw, children left to starve in the street. The sights had been horrific. Funeral pyres ten feet high. Exposed hearts growing on human faces. Hands replaced by crab claws. A baby ripped in half by a dog with two heads—a mutant fighting over a meal with itself. The thing that made people human—whatever it was, their spirits, their souls—was all but destroyed, replaced by the all-controlling black threads.

How else to explain the unthinkable things people did to one another?

Sloke saw Gird's face in the low light of the alley. Even under all that white-powder makeup, he saw how this man, this human imposter, lacked a soul, how the threads rose up around his head like a crown of wild snakes.

The gun kicked hard. There was a concussive pop, sliced through with a high-pitched ringing noise. Gird dropped out of sight, revealing a spray of brain and bone slipping down the wall.

Sloke tossed the gun into the snow. He rifled through Gird's coat, found his government badge and the weird black controller, and pocketed both. Gird's eyes were still open, remote. The bullet hole in his forehead glistened. Sloke took a moment to study it, to see if he could detect one of the black threads trying to hide themselves away. But no, they would never reveal themselves that easily, not when they knew they'd been detected.

He left the alley. The streets going one way were ordered according to the alphabet, while the streets going the other way were numbered in sequence. Everything was built on a perfect grid. He checked the names and numbers against the address on the badge, and soon enough he stood before a high-rise. He pulled the collar up on his coat, entered the lobby, flashed the badge to the person behind the reception desk, and quickly shuffled onto the elevator.

Sloke pressed the badge to the eyeball-shaped scanner and the doors slid shut. He got off on the second-to-last floor, made his way down the hallway, found the right door, unlocked it with the badge, and entered the apartment.

The foyer led to a spacious glass-walled living room. Sloke had never been this high up before. He'd never been this close to the sky. He crossed the room and placed his hand on the window. He wished his body could pass through the glass, that what he saw did not simply exceed the reach of his physical form, but rather that his physical form could cross any distance uncovered by his eye. He wished he could join with the pure energy pulsing through the clouds, to live purely. But then the overhead lights turned on, darkening the glass, once more exposing him as a guilty man in a world that was unforgivably angled, all too constricted.

A beautiful woman stood in a doorway off the side of the living room, her hand on the light switch. She had long hair, wore a silk nightgown, and was visibly pregnant. She said something, but Sloke couldn't hear what it was. His ears were still ringing.

"What? I can't hear you."

"I said you're the one who writes the pamphlets. The man from the street corner."

"You know who I am?"

The woman crossed her arms over her belly. "Who did you think you were writing to all this time? You think the people in your zone spend a lot of time thinking about the ethics of having a child?"

Sloke didn't know what to say. He wondered if she could see his crime written on his face.

"Your makeup is running. You have blood on your face." She pressed her lips together. "My husband?"

Sloke said nothing.

"I told him it was a stupid idea, but he never listens to me. He probably took you somewhere and pointed out an old man, made him seem like some terrible monster." She pointed to the ceiling. "He lives upstairs, you know. The old man. His name is Hincken. We hoped to move into his apartment."

"The governor of truth is your neighbor?"

"Hincken? The governor of truth?" She laughed briefly before clearing her throat. "I'm sorry. I've already taken my mood boosters for the night." She seemed to consider this for a moment. "You're real, right? You'd tell me if you weren't?"

Sloke looked around the room to see if anyone else was there. He half expected security to start pounding on the door, a dozen soldiers to come rushing into the room with guns drawn.

"My husband was convinced you were writing to him directly, leaving little hints in everything. Just for him. He said that at every marionette show there's one child in the audience who is doomed to see only the strings."

She glided closer to Sloke. She smelled fresh as scrubbed metal.

"I have nothing but time on my hands," she said. "Time to sit and think about the problems of the world. How people can come together to solve those problems if only they would stop hurting one another. It's really rather simple once you think about it."

A bolt of crooked lightning lit the sky. And for just a moment, Sloke thought that maybe he saw the form of a massive object partially hidden in the clouds, something beyond his comprehension, some kind of spaceship or astronomical object. He closed his eyes and tried to imagine what this object might look like, but instead saw only the negative impression of the lightning. The whiskey was starting to give him a headache.

"Weird weather tonight," the woman said. "Weird light. You see such strange things this high up. Once I saw a man fall upward from a hole in the sky and into another hole. He looked like an overgrown child."

"It's the radiation. One of the bombs went off in the atmosphere. Or at least that's what they say. The people who tell us what's real. People like your neighbor, Hincken."

"Hincken said that? You know him? I'm hoping to move into his apartment. It's got a better view than our place on account of its being one floor higher. He's all alone up there. I'm sure he'd want us to have it."

"You shouldn't trust him. He lies."

"Well, you know what they say. One lie leads to another and pretty soon you don't know what's what. Not knowing what's true and what's false. Pretty soon you're stuck in a sticky web of your own creation."

"Like a spider."

"Not exactly." She spoke like a teacher instructing a small child. "The spider can always leave its own web and make another one, but its prey gets stuck there forever, or at least until it's eaten." She ran a long-fingered hand over her protruding stomach. "Waiting for death is its own kind of forever, I guess."

"Can I use your husband's computer? Your husband said he had a computer."

"Wow. He must really trust you if he told you that. It's top secret. Come on, I'll show you."

She led Sloke down a long hallway, her bare feet silent on the pristine carpet. The walls were lined with framed oil paintings, things Sloke vaguely recognized. Many of them showed horses. Magnificent images of horses. At the end of the hall stood a marble statue of a naked man, again something Sloke vaguely recognized, or thought perhaps he should recognize, if only he could remember how or why.

The library was a narrow room with a high ceiling. Books filled shelves along the walls, though none of them looked like they'd been read. A computer terminal was set up on a small desk, and next to it were a dozen of Sloke's pamphlets. He grabbed one off the pile. *What terrible crimes will they force us to commit against our fellow man?*

The woman leaned over the desk and booted up the terminal. The hard-drive fans kicked on, whirring loudly. "They call my husband the webmaster." She clicked on a few files, then gestured for Sloke to sit. "He's got eyes everywhere. Fleets of drones. Satellites. He's got all sorts of secrets locked away up here." She tapped the side of her head with her finger. "He's going to be an incredible dad."

A window on the screen appeared to show security footage of an empty street in the government zone. Sloke didn't recognize it. She showed him how to change the image by pressing a button on the keyboard. He saw the outside of a factory. He pressed the button again and this time saw the façade of an old building.

It went on like this for a few minutes, with Sloke pressing the button, changing the screen, and studying what he saw. He saw building after building, each one in worse condition than the last. Mere ruins. Piles of rubble. Then he was looking at the same cityscape he'd seen in his vision, the same sloping skyscrapers, bent rebar, and broken glass. The city he did not recognize, only this time he did. He couldn't believe it. This was it.

He pressed the button again, hoping to see the explosion crater, the place where the black threads had first emerged. Instead, he saw an endless black ocean, its surface rippling with ghostly moonlight. And there, a large cylindrical ship stranded on a jetty of craggy rocks—something truly massive—its hull badly breached, corroded by rust, half submerged in the water. Was it a tanker? No, it was too big to be a tanker. The more he tried to see of the object, the less he understood it, as if it were an impossible formation.

"Do you know where this is?" He pointed at the screen. "What zone is this?"

The woman looked over her shoulder—her attention had been taken by something near the ceiling, something in the shadows that Sloke couldn't see—and shrugged. "Probably doesn't have a name. Which I guess means it wouldn't be a zone. Zones without names aren't zones at all. They're just whatever else is out there. The great outdoors."

Sloke studied the screen. Something moved in the ship's exposed hull, a small black shape thrashing in the foamy waves. It went limp, appeared to pulse like an artery, almost imperceptibly extending and receding, a raw nerve exposed to the light.

Sloke nearly pressed his face against the screen, trying to get a better look. The tiny pixels on the screen seemed to form a perfect grid. Then the screen seemed to shift and contort. The pieces no longer fit together, suddenly scrambled.

The woman yawned. "You're just like my husband. You lose yourself in that thing." She moved toward the door. "It's past my bedtime. I'm afraid I won't remember any of this come morning." Then she slipped away into the darkness.

Sloke turned back to the screen. The image appeared to show yet another nondescript building. A building like any other building, like so many other buildings. He pressed the button on the keyboard again and again, trying to get back to the shipwreck. He needed to study it more closely. His thoughts had been so close to coming together. He was getting so close to adding everything up, to finally making sense of it all.

Then he remembered Gird's controller. He removed it from his pocket, held it in both hands. It was smooth to the touch, perfectly formed, like some sort of black egg.

He swept his thumb over its surface, tried to mimic Gird's movements exactly. If only he could remember what to do. He tapped on its hard shell, shook it, tried to pry it open, but it stayed shut, closed off from the inside.

The computer terminal went to sleep, and the screen went dark. The hard-drive fans quieted. Sloke wasn't sure how to wake it up again. He pressed the button on the keyboard but nothing happened. He wondered how long he could stay in this room until someone came to take him away. Surely he had until morning, when the woman woke up and put the pieces together. He continued fumbling with the strange black egg. If he was lucky, he thought, it would be just enough time to figure out what in the world this thing was hiding from him.

EX ASTRIS

ERICA RUPPERT

The brushed brass sign on the heavy door said *Wallinger, Merrill, and Littlejohn,* and nothing else. Castaigne looked down the empty corridor to the bank of elevators, wondering at the quiet in such a big building, pushing down his unease. Then he swung the door open, and stepped inside.

The office he entered was bland, its carpet and walls tastefully neutral, the art on its walls soullessly abstract. Beyond an empty reception desk was a short hallway ending in another door. He coughed into his fist, and waited.

Someone moved behind the far door, and eventually a tall, narrow man emerged.

"Peter Castaigne?" the man said as he crossed the room, holding out his hand. "Aaron Merrill. Thank you for coming."

Castaigne nodded, and shook hands with him. Merrill's skin was cold and papery, and Castaigne broke his grip quickly.

"Please, come into my office," Merrill said, pointing to the far door.

"Seems private enough out here," Castaigne said, but followed Merrill all the same.

The inner office was as plain as the first one, except for two guest chairs and a straggling plant on the windowsill. Castaigne got the impression that these were temporary offices, short-term rentals. He wondered where the sign on the door had come from.

Merrill settled himself behind the uncluttered desk. He seemed even taller there. Castaigne took a seat opposite him, and waited.

Merrill picked at a corner of the empty desk blotter.

"You already know, I'm sure, that I want you to find someone. Find out what happened to her," he said at last.

"Who are you looking for?" Castaigne asked.

"Jennifer Littlejohn." Merrill paused. "Are you going to take notes?"

"Don't worry about that," he said. "Just tell me what's going on."

Merrill looked oddly happy, as if he were remembering something pleasant.

"It's been difficult since Jenny's been gone," he said, glancing down at the desktop.

"Did she die?" Castaigne asked.

Merrill shook his head quickly. "Oh, no," he said. "Jenny's not dead. She's just—gone."

Castaigne waited, but Merrill did not continue.

"So, Jenny Littlejohn, like the name on the door, left you?" Castaigne prompted after the silence stretched past his patience.

"She didn't leave me," Merrill said sharply. "She's gone."

"So who is she to you?" Castaigne asked. He scratched absently at the bandage on his palm. Merrill didn't respond.

"That's the big question," he said, shrugging.

Castaigne lit a cigarette, took a long drag from it, flicked ashes onto the floor. Merrill grimaced as Castaigne scrubbed the ash into the carpet with his foot.

"What do you have to give me about her?" Castaigne asked. "Your relationship, her known associates. You have that information, don't you?"

Merrill smiled without mirth.

"I can tell you something about who she was. But who she is…" He let the sentence trail off.

Castaigne leaned back into chair, and stretched out his legs. This was a tired, old game. He was in no mood for it.

"Look," he said. "If you're going to make me guess, I'll just make some crap up that sounds like it could be true."

Merrill smiled again.

"She's the daughter of an old friend," he said. "I kept an eye on her after her parents died, when she was still a teenager. We spoke almost every day."

Castaigne nodded.

"Okay. When did you last speak to her?"

"A few weeks, now. I had hoped she would respond to my messages, but there has been nothing."

"What else have you done to try to contact her?"

Merrill shrugged, steepling his fingers.

"Drove by her apartment. Called her job. The usual."

Castaigne stared at Merrill until he looked away, shifting his gaze to the wall behind Castaigne's head. Castaigne tamped out his cigarette against the sole of his shoe, and tucked the butt back into the pack.

"Okay," he said, standing up. "Anything else? A picture?"

"I have that," Merrill said, opening a drawer. He looked at the photograph in his hand for a long few seconds before handing it to Castaigne.

The woman in the photo was caught in three-quarter profile, her mouth open, her eyes focused on someone outside the frame. Her messy hair stuck to her flushed face. She looked as if she'd been dancing. She appeared to be in her mid-twenties, pretty enough, but not striking. She reminded Castaigne of his daughter.

When he looked up again Merrill slid an envelope across the desk toward him. Castaigne picked it up and pocketed it without opening it. The price Merrill had agreed to was high.

"I'll be in touch," he said.

Merrill rose to walk him out of the offices.

"By the way, how did you hear about me?" Castaigne asked, before they reached the outer door.

Merrill waved his hand loosely in the air.

"Oh, people talk."

Castaigne narrowed his eyes. He'd convinced himself that no one knew about what had happened out west. But he'd never had a clear reason to believe it.

"What people?" Castaigne asked. He felt a prickling along his nerves. He had tried to keep a low profile since he had left California.

Merrill looked him in the eye, and waited until Castaigne had to blink.

"Show me your hand," Merrill said.

Castaigne cursed under his breath and peeled away the wide adhesive bandage before extending his right hand, palm up. He would never escape what had happened no matter how many quiet years passed, never escape the sense of being followed, observed by something always just out of sight. It was a relief, in a way, that someone had finally made contact. At least he was done waiting for it to happen.

Merrill looked cursorily at the twining pattern scarred into Castaigne's flesh.

"You don't even know," Merrill said.

Castaigne opened the door and turned his back on Merrill.

"I'll be in touch," he said again over his shoulder, and headed for the elevators.

———————————

Castaigne knew before he dialed that Jenny's number was disconnected. He drove over to the address Merrill had given him, and found a spot on the street to park, hoping for better luck. This was an old neighborhood. Gentrification had barely gotten a toehold in it, yet.

He checked the building number, and climbed the worn steps up to the door.

The name on the bell was J. Littlejohn. He didn't press that one. Instead he pressed several of the others, waiting to see what response he would get.

After a few seconds the intercom crackled.

"Minute," a staticky voice said, and then whoever was behind it buzzed him in.

Castaigne yanked the door open and stepped into the too-warm vestibule. He paused to look over the row of mailboxes on the wall. Of the dozen, only four had names in addition to apartment numbers. None of them was J. Littlejohn.

There was no elevator. He headed up the wide staircase to the third floor.

An old woman in a floral housedress peered around the edge of her open door, watching him as he came up the stairs.

"You're here for Jenny," she said as he walked down the hall toward her. "But she's not here anymore."

"I know," he said, stopping at a respectful distance.

Through the thin walls, he could hear the chatter of daytime television and the occasional burst of laughter from a small child. He had lived in buildings like this.

"But you're here anyway," she said.

Castaigne nodded.

"I'm an investigator," he said. "I've been hired to find her, if I can."

The woman looked him up and down.

"Well, you're honest about it," she said.

"So there have been other people here, looking for Jenny?"

"One," she said, after a moment to think about it. "Hold on."

Castaigne waited outside Jenny's door as the old woman went back into her apartment. He heard her rummaging around inside, then the soft scuff of her slippers as she came back out.

"Here," the woman said with the beginning of a quaver in her voice, handing him a business card. "Somebody stuck it in my door by mistake, Figured I'd give it to Jenny when I saw her. But I never saw her."

He looked at the smudged square of cream paper. He flipped it over.

In tight scratches of blue ink was written, *Jenny—I'll be back on the seventh. Be ready for me.*

"How long ago did you find this?" he asked her.

The woman closed her eyes as she thought. When she opened them again she said, "About a month. It was toward the end of last month."

"And you haven't seen Jenny in all that time?"

"No," she said, her voice growing softer, shakier.

Castaigne looked at the card again.

"Did you happen to see the person who left this?" he asked.

The old woman stared at him, her pale grey eyes wide, searching his face for an answer.

"I–I don't know," she said.

Castaigne put a hand on her arm, gently.

"Are you okay?" he asked.

She shook her head.

"I can't remember," she said. She looked up at him, her face crumpling into deeper lines. "I should remember."

"It's okay," Castaigne said. "This card is a huge help."

He took out his wallet and pulled out two twenty dollar bills, and pressed them into the woman's hand.

"Go relax," he said.

She looked at the money she held.

"Let me know if you find Jenny," she said. "She was a nice girl."

Castaigne smiled, trying to be reassuring.

"Of course," he said.

He waited for her to go inside and chain the door before going back to Jenny's apartment. He unfolded the filed-down pocket knife he kept on his keychain and slid it into the lock. He turned it slowly, tested the door, turned the knife again. With a dull click, the lock opened. He eased open the door and slipped into the apartment.

It was more spacious than he'd expected, a relic of an older style. The living room was separated from the kitchen by an archway, with tall windows filling one wall. There were only a few sticks of furniture, a dinette set, an upholstered armchair, a lamp. It didn't look as if Jenny had actually lived in these rooms. He checked the barren bedroom and bathroom before circling back to the kitchen. Aside from a few plates in the cupboard it was as bare as the rest. The refrigerator hummed quietly in its corner. He opened it. It was empty, and smelled of mold. As he closed the door again he noticed a slash of color wedged between the refrigerator and the cabinets, near the floor.

He pried out a fabric-covered journal, the kind bookstores used to sell. The spine was water stained and the covers had been bent and straightened again. He flipped it open. A few loose sheets drifted to the floor. Other pages had been torn out, leaving only jagged, fragmentary words behind on the ragged edges. But the remaining leaves were covered in dense, angular script, a mix of words and patterns he recognized, and almost understood. An intimate ache began behind his eyes. He turned more pages, hoping to find plain writing.

On the inside back cover was a looping, girlish scrawl distinct from the rest.

I have tasted stars
have swallowed whole a failing sun
It tasted of nothing
the edge of the universe is always just ahead
a line scarcely lit against the wider dark

He read it again, his heart sinking. Jenny and he had seen some of the same things.

———— ◆ ◆ ————

Castaigne tucked the journal into his waistband, under his jacket, and made sure the apartment was locked again when he left. He tried not to hurry as he walked back to his car, but the press of the cover against his back was uncomfortable, like a cold, wet stain. He tossed the journal into the glove compartment as he slid behind the wheel, glad to shut it away. Its mysteries would wait, for now.

He sat in his car for a long while, studying the card the old woman had given him, turning it to see if anything caught the light. The paper remained plain, the ink opaque. He fiddled with the card, and reached for a cigarette. He sighed.

———— ◆ ◆ ————

Castaigne watched Jenny's building for the rest of the week, becoming familiar with the people living there and their daily routines. He didn't notice anyone unusual coming or going, at least not unusual enough to raise his suspicion.

While he watched he searched the web for Merrill, whose scant online presence identified him only as a consultant, and listed his office at the address where they had met. But when he searched for Wallinger, the last name on the office door, he came up with a full name and an address that caught his attention—Esther Wallinger, with an apartment listed in a building on the other side of the block from Jenny's.

Castaigne digested the new information. There were no coincidences. He could only keep going, now.

He left his car where it was and ambled around the corner, his head slightly lowered, trying his best to be unobtrusive and unnoticeable. He knew he was walking into a trap. He just didn't know what kind, yet.

The address was an empty building, its windows boarded and its door padlocked.

Castaigne climbed up to peer through the door's chicken-wire reinforced windows. The vestibule beyond was dusty and littered with crumbling plaster. In the middle of the floor was a clean white envelope with Peter written across it in wide block letters.

He froze. His vision narrowed to the envelope, to his name.

They knew his name.

He tried to calm himself. Merrill knew his name, and Merrill didn't owe him any allegiance.

He looked around. The street was empty. It felt as if the world was empty. He turned, and an envelope with his name on it lay at his feet. He did not look back into the building to see if it was the same one. He bent to pick it up, his fingers trembling and cold.

The paper was heavy and smooth, but it tore like tissue as he opened the envelope and took out the folded sheet within.

Peter, it read, *What took you so long? Come talk to me.*

Below that was a new address, and her signature.

Esther.

Castaigne went home. He felt vaguely ill, his head fuzzy with the pressure of what might come. He wasn't ready to meet Esther Wallinger in the flesh. Any delay was a reprieve.

As much as it unnerved him, he brought the journal in and set it on the coffee table. His hand hurt where he had touched the covers, the lines of the scar tracing a dull fire into his skin.

He peeled off the wide bandage to look at his palm. The scar had never healed properly, the lines writhing red and white across his skin like worms. It shouldn't still be so sensitive, years later. He washed his hands with warm water, trying to ease the pain, then ate his dinner standing over the sink.

After he pulled the shades down over every window, he settled on the couch to reluctantly read the journal.

Despite the deep ache inside his head, he forced himself to try to understand the choppy, sharp script. Only some of it was in English. There were passages he thought might be Spanish, or Italian. He could pick out a few words, but not enough to discern more than the broadest meaning. Other sections were in alphabets he could not read at all. He did not try to decipher the symbols. He didn't want to know what they meant.

Hours passed. His vision began to blur, but he kept reading.

The sections he could understand made little sense to him, but he had an almost instinctual awareness of what they could mean. Close, in sight but just outside his reach, lay what they were trying to bring forth, to lay bare. It made him nervous to think about why he knew what little he did. He would rather never have learned any of it.

He turned on more lights, giving in to the primitive need to cast out the dark. He closed the journal, exhausted and off balance from its convolutions.

He stretched out on the couch and closed his eyes for a moment, before he sat up again, restless. He couldn't clear his mind of what he had read, couldn't forget what he almost grasped. He rose, and paced back and forth across his small apartment. He stopped at the side table where a picture of his daughter sat in its plastic gilt frame.

He missed her. Sarah had been twelve the last time he saw her, just before he moved away. The phone calls had gotten more and more infrequent, the trips back east postponed again and again. He had made mistakes he would not be able to repair, even though his ex badgered him to try, for Sarah's sake. At least he hadn't started over with a new wife, a new family. He had failed once, and he hadn't changed. There was no reason to put anyone else through it.

Outside, the night was big enough to swallow the city whole. He could feel it.

In the morning, Castaigne wrapped the journal in a plastic bag and took it with him when he left, hiding it under the carpet in the trunk of his car. He thought it would be safer than leaving it unguarded in his apartment, but he doubted it was truly hidden from what had watched him all these years. He was sure that it would be of value to someone, soon.

He drove to Merrill's office, putting off the inevitable visit he would have to make to Esther Wallinger. She would find a way to bring him to her. He had no doubt of that.

He parked in the garage beneath the building and smoked two cigarettes in slow succession, gathering his thoughts, weighing what he wanted to learn from Merrill this time. When the security guard drove past him a second time, he got out and went into the building.

The brass sign looked dull under the fluorescent lights, not as crisp as the first time he'd seen it. He looked closer. A faint scratch ran through the names, as if someone had tried to strike them out.

When he pulled open the door Merrill was at the reception desk, waiting for him. Merrill smiled thinly.

"Come in, and tell me what you've got so far," he said.

Castaigne walked back to the same rear office, sat in the same neutral chair.

Merrill leaned uncomfortably against the edge of the desk before taking the second guest chair beside Castaigne.

"There must be something," he said. "You have a way with these things, after all."

Castaigne looked at his feet, letting the silence spin between them. He focused on the immediate conversation, not allowing himself to think of all the rest, unspoken, around him. When he judged Merrill had begun to grow uncomfortable, he spoke.

"I know you already knew that Jenny's number was bad, and that her apartment was empty," he said. "I'm also pretty sure you didn't tell me where she works, because that would be a dead end, too."

He paused, took out another cigarette, tucked it back into the pack.

"I smoke too much," he said.

Merrill watched him.

"Did you come to accuse me of holding out on you?" he asked.

"No," Castaigne said. "Because it doesn't matter to me."

Castaigne waited again, but only briefly. He didn't want to be in this room, with this man, for much longer. He rose and walked to the window. Through the sheer curtains he could see crowds of pedestrians crossing at the corner, navigating the crush of rush hour. He wanted to be lost among them.

"What do you know about Esther Wallinger?" he asked, turning to face Merrill again.

Merrill shifted in his seat. He looked away. His face was flushed, but his voice remained calm.

"It doesn't surprise me to hear her name," Merrill said. "She was always one for jumping the gun."

"How?"

Merrill shrugged with an artificial casualness. Castaigne watched him, waiting for him to break.

"She pushed Jenny too hard," he said.

"Who was Esther to her?" Castaigne asked.

Merill blinked, as if he had put it out of his mind long ago.

"Her aunt, I think," he said. "Or some distant cousin."

Merrill stood up, and opened the office door. His hands shook.

"Maybe she isn't, after all. Maybe I've been wrong all these years," he said. "You need to go now. Come back when you have something about Jenny."

He did not follow Castaigne out. Castaigne paused in the hallway and looked at the sign again. There were more scratches than there had been before, curving lines and straight. The pattern was uncomfortably familiar.

Merrill's name was a blur beneath them, almost scratched out.

— ◆ ◆ —

Castaigne drove straight from Merrill's office to the address Edith Wallinger had given him. He knew he didn't have any real choice in it. They knew how to look for him, if he tried to disappear. He couldn't hide what called them to him.

Her home was a tall, neatly-kept townhouse in a neighborhood that whispered of money, its brick face painted grey, its windows and front door guarded by black iron bars. He pulled to the curb in front of it, and got out of the car. He stood there, leaning against the fender, looking for signs of life inside. A curtain shifted at one of the lower windows. He sighed, opened the gate, and climbed the steps to the double entry doors.

He turned the knob on the small bronze plate beside the door, and heard the click of a connection. A bell chimed deep within the house.

The woman who opened the door seconds later smiled warmly at him.

"Peter," she said. "So good to finally meet you. We've been waiting for years, it seems."

"Hi, Esther," Castaigne said. He kept his distance from the doorway.

"You've come this far," she said, stepping back to give him room.

He knew she was right. He went in.

She led him into the living room, and took a seat on the couch. Castaigne chose an armchair nearer the door.

"Where shall we start, then, Peter?"

Castaigne shook his head.

"Why not start with why I'm here?" was all he said.

She studied him without responding. Castaigne swallowed. Esther was following a different thread.

Castaigne watched her impassively, waiting for a hint.

"Would you like something to drink?" she asked. "Coffee, water?"

"No," he said.

"I would," she said, rising. "I'll be right back."

As her footfalls faded away, Castaigne quickly assessed the room. It was comfortable and tastefully done, with the feel of a magazine layout. He peeked out the doorway. There was no sign of Esther, but he knew he wasn't alone. This was part of the trap. The house around him was quiet, breathing with hidden life. He wondered what games she would play with him, now that she had him here.

He ventured out into the long center hall. Across from the living room was what seemed to be a library, although none of the books he could see had any lettering on their spines.

He stepped carefully down the hallway past the front rooms, as silently as he could. The hall was longer than he would have thought it could be, and lined with white-painted doors on both sides.

He tested the handles as he went. Each one was locked, and each made his hand colder, as if he were gripping ice. He wondered if he had tripped any hidden alarms, if Esther already knew how far he had gone exploring. He wondered what would jump out at him to drive him back.

Ahead of him he caught a flash of smooth, fast motion, and he leaned into the narrow shelter of the nearest doorway. Further down the hallway a young woman locked one door, then crossed the hall and unlocked the room on the opposite side. At first glance she resembled the young woman in Merrill's photograph, but when he blinked she had changed. No matter how many years had passed, he knew her face, her profile, the color of her hair. It had to be her, even though he knew he had to be imagining her. He had missed her for too long.

"Sarah?" he said. He wanted it to be her, so much.

She paused with the door half-opened and turned her head toward him, her face expressionless but her eyes bright.

"Peter," she said. "I have so much to tell you."

It was not Sarah's voice. It was deeper, rusty and rough, as if she hadn't used it in a long, long time. And as she faced him, he realized his mistake. She didn't look like Sarah at all, her face more like a doll made to resemble her, or a clever mask. It wasn't natural. He stepped back.

She leaned toward him at an impossible angle, her mouth opening around a grinding laugh. Pale light shone from behind her teeth. She stretched like a snake uncoiling, her head shifting on her neck like a cobra's waiting to strike.

Cold flooded him. He retreated.

"I know the truth," the elongated woman said through her mouthful of light, and then her face collapsed in upon itself, her whole form dissolving into a cloud of black dust.

Castaigne gasped, unable to form words. He fled back to the living room, where Esther sat with her cup of coffee, waiting for him.

"Sit," she said. "Catch your breath."

He stared at her, but sat back down in the armchair, cradling his scarred hand in the other. His heart pounded painfully. Blood roared in his ears.

"That's Jenny," Esther said. "She wants you here."

Castaigne fought to quiet his rapid breathing. He clenched his hand, testing it. Warmth seeped back into his flesh. Esther moved over on the couch, closer to him.

"Aaron sent you to find her, but he was circling, trying to keep us from knowing he was looking." she said. "He's quite clumsy. I don't think he realized quite who he hired."

Castaigne exhaled through his nose, calming the animal fear that still sparked along his nerves.

"He wanted me to think he did," Castaigne said.

Esther finished her coffee and put the cup on a side table.

"We can return your Sarah to you," Esther said softly, laying her slim fingers on his forearm. "It is a small thing."

Castaigne pulled away from her, raising his hands to warn her back.

"Don't mention her again," he said, growing angry, fighting it down. "This mess is about Jenny. Once it's over, I'm leaving."

Esther's face hardened, and her eyes grew cold.

"I thought you understood more than that," she said. "She is infinite—or would be if she weren't constrained. What you saw was her, in one of her forms. There are so many more. But you will cling to the lies you tell yourself."

Castaigne shook his head. The pressure had begun to build within him, again.

"Why would he send me, if he already knew you had her?"

Esther smiled.

"Because Aaron knows he cannot reach her. Not himself. We have taken precautions."

Castaigne pointedly lit a cigarette. Esther wrinkled her nose at the smoke.

"So how am I here, if you 'took precautions'?"

Esther gestured vaguely at Castaigne's bandaged hand.

"You have your own resources," she said. "You can go where others cannot."

He got up, and paced the length of the room.

"What does it mean?" he asked. "Am I taking her to Merrill, then? Am I bringing Merrill here with me to see her?"

Esther's smile faded like an old flower.

"No," she said. "Jenny can't leave, and Merrill cannot come in."

"This doesn't make any sense," he said. "It's a waste of time. Merrill's issue is with you. Whatever you're involved in, my being here doesn't do anything."

Esther looked at him, appraising.

"Such a funny phrase, a waste of time," she said. "Time doesn't work that way. You were given a great gift, whether you use it or not."

She reached out to touch him again, but stopped short.

"Now it is a burden to you. But if you accepted what you could do with it—you could see past all this, you could learn what has watched you these past years, what power you could be part of."

Castaigne closed his eyes for a moment, and took a deep drag from his cigarette.

"I'm going to go now," he said. "I know you can find me. But don't."

He stood, and she stood with him.

"But don't you want to understand what Jenny wrote in her note-book?" Esther asked. "I'd be surprised if you ever slept again, not knowing the whole truth of it."

Castaigne didn't move.

"Let me show you," she said.

He knew he couldn't leave. She wouldn't allow it. But he wasn't sure if it was Esther, or Jenny, who held the leash.

Before Castaigne could respond the doorbell rang, again and again, and a fist pounded on the entry door. Then Merrill's voice came to them muffled, but still loud.

"Esther! Let me in!"

Castaigne could imagine how desperate he was, to make a scene in this neighborhood. Esther brushed past him to open the door on its chain. He followed her, and caught a thin glimpse of Merrill's face, frantic and red.

"I have to see her, Esther," Merrill begged, pushing against the door to try to force it open.

Esther held him back.

"No, Aaron," she said, with a note of sympathy. "You know you can't."

"Please," Merrill asked, his voice breaking. "I need to see Jenny. Just once more."

Castaigne came forward, nudging Esther out of the way. He pulled the chain loose and let go of the door. Merrill spilled into the room, scrambling to keep his feet.

"Thank you," he said to Castaigne. Then he turned to Esther, who waited calmly at a distance.

"She's not ready," Merrill said. "Let me take her back, let me bring her home. It's not her time."

Esther held up her hands, showing Merrill the patterns carved into them. He flinched away from her, as if she had shoved him back.

"This is not the first time, nor the last. This is now. It will always be now," she said. "And Jenny doesn't want you here."

Castaigne let them argue. His hand burned with light, the scar reacting to the strangeness in the atmosphere. He felt adrift, as if the ground beneath him was gone, and he floated in a vast interstitial nothingness. Fear stirred in his belly.

Esther made some small motion and Merrill crumpled, his skin turned to ash as white flame enveloped him. It was over in a moment.

She dusted off her hands. Thin smoke rose from Merrill's remains.

"Are you ready to meet more of Jenny?" she asked Castaigne. "Because she is certainly ready to meet you."

Castaigne nodded slowly, and drew a deep breath. His stomach lurched, and he swallowed back bile. Jenny's want was inevitable. He could only hope that what had protected him so far would still keep him safe.

———◆———

The door to Jenny's room was as plain as any other in the hallway, but looking at it made his head buzz, like a swarm of flies had found their way in.

Esther unlocked the door for him, tilting her chin toward the darkness behind it.

Castaigne gathered himself for a moment before walking through. Esther closed the door behind him. The small click of the latch catching sounded far away.

He stood in the shadow of the doorway, acclimating to the strange, cold air of the room. It smelled of minerals, of dust. It burned his throat as he breathed it. Around him, the room seemed larger than it should be, the air currents swirling from a great and shadowy distance. He stepped away from the door, and felt a surge of dizziness, as if he had slipped sideways under the pull of a wave.

In the dim light he could make out a platform in the distance, with a tall obelisk rising from it. A darker shadow moved against the obelisk with the sound of something scraping over hard ground. He felt for the holster he used to wear, a reflex, but he knew a gun wouldn't do him any good here. He bit down on the fear rising in his throat and moved forward.

Light gathered on the platform in a lazy spiral, revealing the figure waiting there by slow degrees. He crossed the room, aware of the gravity of her presence, the orbital pull. As he climbed onto the platform he could still see the resemblance to the woman in the photograph.

In the unsteady light he could make out the designs carved into the stone pillar, echoed in the patterns knotted into the ropes that bound her to it. His head ached to see them. He recognized them. He could almost understand them.

He stood before her, watching the play of light across her features, watching the slow unveiling of her eyes. At last she looked upon him, and an indecipherable expression rolled across her face. Bones moved beneath her skin, shifting into new positions. He drew in a deep breath at what was revealed.

She had not been human for some time. He didn't think it mattered. Esther had been right. Jenny couldn't leave here. Jenny was beyond such small things.

Her pale, yellow eyes followed him as he bent to examine her bindings.

"I have tasted stars," she said, her voice like the slow grind of stone on stone.

Castaigne glanced at her and quickly looked away.

"Peter," she said. "Peter, the stars taste of nothing."

He cringed. He tugged on the thin ropes tying her to the stone needle, testing their strength. They were pulled tight enough to cut into her cold flesh. He could feel the meanings they made.

Her eyes shone with the glow of the Milky Way.

"Jenny," Castaigne said, drawing her attention, regretting it as soon as he had it. He felt the cold of her eyes fall across him, ice on his skin. He did not want her to see him, not if this was what it was to be her sight.

A rime of silver glittered on her cheek. The pale light inside her seeped out like tears, like mucus, like spittle, dripping off her chin. It ran down from between her legs and spilled across the floor. Ice bloomed where the light fell, ripples of frost lapping at some strange shore.

He stepped back, off the platform, away from the pooling glow.

Her eyes glistened as she gazed on him.

"The sun fails. I have seen it," she said. "I have seen it all."

His skin crawled at the rasp of her voice, repeating what she had written for him to find.

"Jenny," he said again. "What do I have to do?"

Her head swiveled. She looked up, and past him. Light swirled like silt stirred in water.

"I have seen *nothing*," she said, her voice a harsh whisper, her words a promise to something other than him.

With the weight of her attention lifted from him, Castaigne backed away until he felt the solid door behind him. He knocked on it, six sharp raps. After an impossibly stretched moment Esther unlocked the door and let him back into the world.

———————

Esther laughed at Castaigne's stricken face as he emerged. He stumbled on the threshold.

"Wasn't that a revelation?" she asked him. "She is creating this change. It all comes from her, like a seed sprouting, or an insect developing from larva to imago. Surely you understand, Peter. Surely you've seen such things before."

Her tone was coy, knowing.

"Stay with me," Esther said, lowering her voice. "Jenny is going to show us what she is capable of."

"And what is that?" Castaigne asked. He was cold, too cold even to shiver.

Esther looked up at him, her eyes bright.

"I think you know," she said. She reached out and took his hand. "If you don't, you will. Soon."

Esther peeled back the useless bandage and traced the lines on his palm, then looked up at him with the fire of a true believer.

"She is the catalyst. She will make it real. She will make it true, this time."

"Why did you kill Merrill?" Castaigne asked her.

She laughed again.

"Merrill was never more than a hanger-on, an old friend we outgrew. He was too much of a coward to invest in what could be."

Castaigne paused.

"Then why don't you kill me?"

Esther slowly opened her hands to him. The scars scrolled across her palms were different than what marked him. They were dark, almost as if they swallowed light.

"I told you, you have your own resources," she said. "Jenny made sure."

He leaned back against the wall. He was exhausted. A low vibration moved through him, bending the air around him. Jenny knew where he was. She could see him. Her awareness hurt like a rotten tooth, like a torn nail.

"She's coming. Now," he said, and it was the truth.

Esther's mouth opened in a surprised circle.

A noiseless wave pulsed through the house, and Esther abruptly fell back, her hands twining in the air, her eyes wide and dark with rising panic.

Castaigne's head felt as if it would burst, the pressure of the air around him suddenly crushing. He fought to breathe. His vision warped, lines and forms becoming unstable.

Esther cried out once, an invocation, but her voice was cut off instantly in another pulse.

The silence within the house was staggering. A thin film of light seeped under the door from Jenny's room, spreading, soaking the rug, staining the floorboards. The door dissolved in its glare.

Esther's mouth moved, but Castaigne could hear nothing. Nothing.

The light reached her. Instead of moving back, Esther stepped confidently into the shining pool. Her hands moved in rhythm with her silent mouth, displaying her scarred palms to the light again, and again. Then the light slid up her legs, and Esther was no longer speaking. She was screaming, but her voice was lost to the void.

Castaigne did not want to see what the silent light did to her. The pain of her threatened to swallow him. He scrambled backward, clumsy, his feet soundless on the floor. He fled. Jenny let him.

Outside the house the world returned, full of traffic noise and the orange glow of sodium-vapor street lights. Castaigne stopped on the sidewalk to catch his breath. The windows of the house were dark, as if there were nothing behind them.

Nothing.

He knew what nothing was, now.

He moved out of the way of a group of pedestrians heading toward the main street. As soon as they were past him he longed for the comfort of any human company.

Above him, past the streetlights, he could feel something moving between the invisible stars, bright and soulless. Jenny had called it down. It frightened him, that awareness, that intelligence, that shining nothingness. It knew who he was.

His hand ached. The scar he carried was both a beacon and a ward against that knowing void. White light seeped from the curves and angles of the scar, burning with cold, reacting to the change in the world. He pulled his sleeve down over his palm and shoved his hand into his jacket pocket, trying to cover what shone through.

More people passed him as he stood there, trying to find his bearings in the bright, empty space he moved through, now. He huddled into himself, wishing he could speak to them, hoping to be ignored. He started walking, knowing he would eventually draw mundane attention if he stayed.

A silence began to settle over him. He was safe from it, but he would never be free of the void still spilling from Jenny, bound in her room and boundless. He kept walking. Maybe he could buy himself another few years before Jenny looked upon him again. He would have to read her journal, to be certain.

He would understand it, now.

THE INTERCESSOR

RICHARD GAVIN

The sound of raindrops splattering against the roof alerted Janice to the fact that the thunderheads she'd seen pressing over the lake at lunchtime were at last making good on their threat. She hurriedly stirred the cream into her evening coffee, then carried the mug and a paperback to the backdoor. Her ambition was to reach the boathouse before the sky fully opened. Few things were as exhilarating to her as experiencing a storm from inside that rustically cozy shelter.

But her plans were dashed the instant she saw the door to her private boathouse, which Janice unfailingly kept locked whenever she was not by the waterfront, being pulled back from its jamb.

She halted in her tracks, blinking a few times, hoping that the image of the parting doorway was a mere trick of the senses.

It was not.

A figure emerged from the gap with unnerving swiftness, pushing itself out of the unlit boathouse. The shape was like some huge, peculiar flower blooming from black soil in a time-lapse film.

The storm instantly lost its allure. Janice could only watch dumbly as the intruder began to make its way across the dock.

The figure was distressingly tall and bone thin. The antique ball gown it wore was too heavy to be seasonal and too authentic looking to be a costume. It was a drapey rococo affair of periwinkle velvet. The gown's hem reached past its model's ankles to sweep the ground like the drooping limbs of an old willow tree. Dirty lace frothed out to cuff the long sleeves. The figure's face was obscured by an ornate wide-brimmed hat.

Janice stared as this unbidden guest ploddingly made its way toward her lawn, which sloped down to meet the lakefront. The lawn was inlaid with a crude staircase of oiled timber that snaked up toward the rear porch of the main house.

The figure began to scale these timber steps, shakily, yet with fey determination, not yielding until it reached the porch. Once there, the figure calmly gripped the back of one of Janice's outdoor dining chairs and dragged it until it was positioned directly before the backdoor.

The visitor settled onto the furnishing, then sat in mute meditation of the woman on the other side of the screen.

What Janice had been presented with was beyond her ken. She gawked at the seated figure, her mind racing to identify it, to catalogue it, to slip it into some niche where it might make sense. But nowhere, not even in the murky region of dream, had Janice ever encountered such a being.

What crowned this creature was not a wide-brim hat. Its head was an old-fashioned carousel, complete with carved mares, gryphons, and dragons, each painted in colours vivid and rare. The carousel's drop rods were spiralled and golden. Bevelled mirrors sparkled from the cresting around the canopy's edge. The centre pole extended down past the carousel's platform to serve its secondary purpose as the figure's neck.

Each time the gowned shape drew breath or exhaled the trilling notes of a calliope filled the air.

Her brain torpid from shock, Janice found it a sound thing to do to slip the tiny chrome hook on the screen door through its eye on the frame, as if this primitive latch might protect her.

An unpleasant sticky wetness began to warm the top of her sandalled feet. Only then did Janice realize that her hands had gone limp and had sent both the brimming mug and the book to the floor. She glanced down and saw her cherished paperback of daily affirmations swelling as it absorbed some of the pooled coffee. Lifting her eyes slightly, Janice felt queasy as she studied the visitor's hands, which were large and calloused and hirsute; the appendages of a labourer, not the aristocratic lady for whom the periwinkle gown had been designed.

"I know you aren't real," Janice said thinly. The statement felt juvenile and weak. Still, she repeated it twice more. She needed to regain her footing in truth. "I know I'm imagining you," she continued, "I just need to figure out *why* I'm seeing you. And I will figure it out, you know…whatever it is you represent." Her tone had grown firmer and more confident.

Meanwhile, the figure's head continued to spin. The wooden beasts that were its facial features rhythmically rose and fell, the atonal bleating of its calliope lungs came and went in cycles. Janice's threats were apparently not impacting whatever game this apparition was playing.

For the span of two deep breaths, Janice kept her eyes closed. It was a technique taught to her when she'd been but a nervous schoolgirl, and it had never failed to rinse her mind of anxieties. She was a grown woman now; savvy and strong. Her life coach often referred to her as a warrioress of the heart.

It was time to invoke her inner power, time to purge this intrusive negativity.

'I exist in the light of Now,' Janice muttered to herself, paraphrasing one of her favourite affirmations, *'the shadows of my past are powerless against the me of today…I am present in the present…I am a loving expression of the universe…'*

With that, a feeling of serenity moved through her like a gentle breeze. Lightened by this newfound peace, Janice opened her eyes.

The carousel-headed shape remained vivid and close.

Janice felt the tears as they began to run down her cheeks. "No…" she pouted, wiping them away with unneeded force. "I know you're just a negative projection. I know that."

As if in response to her conviction, the wind outside suddenly shifted, ushering a pungent scent into the sunroom, one akin to spoiled meat. Clearly this guest was too much of flesh to simply be a projection, a thought.

Instantly the danger became unbearably real.

"Leave right now or I'm calling the police!" Janice cried, her voice faltering.

The guest was wholly unresponsive.

"Fine," she said, then turned on her heel.

Her race to the phone was plagued with the awful expectation of hearing the backdoor being torn from its hinges, of the thing on the porch charging in after her.

But the house remained still.

Any relief that Janice may have felt by reaching the kitchen unharmed was erased once she discovered that the telephone had melted. Her throat released a noise not unlike a cat's mewl, then she braced herself against the edge of the sink, for her legs had lost their strength.

The phone drooped in a useless mass from its wall-mount, an abstract sculpture of yellow plastic and wires. Janice reached to touch it, then withdrew, fearing a burn or some form of contamination.

She then made haste for the house's front door, only to find that it had managed to slip away and hide itself. Her blind charge to where the door should have been ended bluntly and painfully against a solid wall whose cedar panels stood uniformly and without interruption. Janice ran her unsteady hands over the sanded wood, refusing to believe what she was experiencing. She scratched at the barrier, as if her means of escape was concealed just beneath its surface.

'The window...'

Hoisting herself onto the counter, her plan was to open the kitchen window and kick out the screen. The window frame looked wide enough to admit her body. It would be a bit of a struggle, but achievable.

She reached to push back the sliding pane as far as it would go, but her fingers again found only wood. The familiar sights of her surrounding property then revealed themselves to be mere illusion; a painting whose dimensions were tricks of forced perspective upon a flat wall. The artist who had wrought this trick was a master, one whose adeptness at chiaroscuro had managed to fool Janice (for God only knew how long) into believing that what she'd peeked out at so nonchalantly now and again during her daily routine was the objective world.

If this view was illusory, what else in her life might be?

The thought chilled her. Now frantic, Janice proceeded to claw at the painted window-scape until her nailbeds were embedded with curls of oil paint and keen splinters of wood. Looking down at her bloodied fingertips, then around at the similarly false windows that decorated the living room and the bedroom beyond it, Janice finally permitted herself to break down. She crumpled onto the linoleum floor.

Finding a means of escape was the lone thought that obsessed her. In her distress, Janice briefly weighed the feasibility of smashing through one of the cottage's walls. She had very nearly talked herself into trying when the clear image of her tool bench down in the boathouse flashed through her mind. All her drills, her hammers, anything that she might have used to break out of her home like a prisoner from their cell, was down by the water. And the creature on the porch blocked her path.

She sat up and pressed a quaking hand to her breast. Her heart was pounding so intensely that Janice feared this force would soon become too great for her body. Her pulse seemed to be rumbling the lithosphere and the upper mantle as surely as a temblor. She imagined her floor and the earth's crust beneath it simultaneously cracking, and a great fuming fissure then spreading wide to spore her.

But outside of her mind the only quaking was that of the thunder pounding the waterfront, and the great hot summer gales, like gusts from a blacksmith's bellows, thrashing the lake, making it a roiling thing of malice.

Through both the raging storm and the rumble of Janice's pulse, the calliope managed to push its sickly-sweet music into the house. Janice put her hands on either side of her head and squeezed, but the carousel-thing seemed to be piping its merry tune directly into her brain.

Now feeling utterly lost, Janice slinked down onto her belly. With her hands still blocking her ears, she began to commando crawl across the kitchen floor, over the living room's dirt-faded hooked rug, finally nuzzling herself up against the corduroy sofa.

'If it cannot see me, it cannot hurt me…if it cannot see me…'

This childish mantra passed through her head in a loop. She remained balled-up behind the furnishing, straining to not hear the calliope music, or the shrill cry of the carousel's gears pleading for oil as they turned.

She had almost managed to convince herself to just charge past the shape in the chair and go running to the neighbours, but she knew that the cottages on either side of her had been vacant since the 1st, more critically, there was no way of telling how fast her visitor could move. Given its anatomy, it could be capable of anything.

She wondered if she might be able to escape by scrabbling up the chimney, but no; several plates of iron mesh had been installed years ago to prevent stray birds from nesting there. This route was no more plausible than breaking through the walls.

Janice waited her agonizing wait. There was nothing else she could do.

Then, mercifully, miraculously, the music stopped.

Had the creature departed?

With delicate hope in her heart, Janice dared a peek over the back of the sofa.

The shape remained on its throne, its merry-go-round head still turning patiently. A moment later, its piping music resumed. Janice caught herself wondering if the thing had nodded off momentarily, had fallen asleep on the job. Regardless, now it was alert once more.

Janice quickly ducked back down. In a way, Janice knew that she was playing a game of her own, a fatal version of Hide-and-Seek. But the game was rigged, for the seeker from which she was hiding knew precisely where she was. In fact, had it not used its powers to trap her here by melting the phone, by stealing the doorway, by mutating the windows? Janice wondered exactly what type of being she was dealing with.

Her unfocused gaze trailed off into the bedroom. It was as if the vision board that she kept hanging on the wall at the foot of her bed was somehow vying for her attention. From the living room floor, Janice studied the mounted corkboard. Its surface was festooned with pinned-up photos, magazine clippings, and slips of paper bearing her favourite words of personal empowerment. It was a collage of her true self's touchstones: her aspirational dream home, tropical destinations she considered paradisiacal, bright images of Buddha and Athena and Christ and Glinda the Good Witch of the North.

Peering at this homemade mandala caused a sudden shift in Janice's thinking. What if escape was of secondary importance? Perhaps the more urgent issue here was something mystical, a test of her spiritual mettle.

This fresh theory seemed very sound indeed. After all, Janice had already discounted the possibility that her visitor was simply a figment of her imagination, for it was undoubtedly real. Not in the everyday sense of the word, but real on a metaphysical level.

A thing like this had to come from elsewhere. There could be no other explanation. She had been chosen. She was being challenged. Janice felt confident that she could prevail.

Straightening her posture, Janice silently called upon the aid of the angels Raphael, Gabriel, Michael, and Auriel. She could feel them pouring their celestial might into her. Now fortified, she stood, envisioning her body as glittering with golden fire.

She moved to the screen door.

Janice looked at the stoic shape for as long as she was able, but there was something entrancing about the way its head rotated, something at once attractive and repulsive. Did the constant motion soothe or entertain this thing, she wondered? Was this being forever adrift in some midway fantasy?

She must not allow herself to be hypnotized.

Janice closed her eyes, then spoke.

"Spirit, hear my voice and heed me." She very much wanted to sound fierce and fearless. If only her hands would stop shaking. "Why have you come to this realm? I fear you've lost your way crossing over to the other side."

The figure was now thoroughly soaked from the downpour. Its velvet gown appeared a deeper shade of blue. Water ran down the spinning beasts of its face. Beyond the porch, the wind thrashed the evergreens that hemmed Janice's yard. Breaker waves were heaving up to the height of the boathouse before crashing apart on the dock and covering the boards with a skittering foam.

"What do you want from me?" Janice asked at last. She was sobbing now. Her convictions were eroding from the unmoveable mountain of terror and confusion before her. Clearly she was outmatched. If only she could discover why it was happening; that seemed even more meaningful than knowing exactly what was happening. Was this karmic debt? Had she neglected to properly banish a spirit she had evoked during her adolescent dalliances with thaumaturgy?

"O lost spirit," Janice tremulously intoned. She extended the prime fingers of her right hand and onto the air traced an invisible pentacle. "I hereby grant you licence to depart. Leave this place of the sun. Return to the nightworld from whence you came…"

The figure did not vanish. It did not even rise to shuffle off. Instead, it remained shiftless in its chair.

Desperate to fend off the panic attack that was threatening to claim her, Janice talked herself through her predicament. This creature, with its impossible form, was clearly not of this world, Janice knew, but maybe it was something from *in between* this world and whatever realm laid in wait on the far side of the grave. It could be an intercessor, a thing sent to arbitrate the dissonance between this world of the living and the unhuman things that lurked beyond it.

It was as if this being, whatever it may be, existed simply to confound Janice's every attempt at defining, at understanding. Like some ancient trickster god, this carousel-headed debutante with the apish hands seemed to have been sent here simply to test, to confound. It may not have any meaning, any message. It could be just an interstitial monster, a thing oblique to whatever plane it wandered.

Maybe there was no meaning in any of Janice's cherished beliefs either…

The affirmations, the prayer beads, the shrines, they could all be little more than fancy wrapping used to decorate an empty box.

It was feeling more and more plausible that finding meaning was simply not the point. This entire ordeal may simply be about experiencing something Real, even if that Realness was horrifying.

With startling suddenness, two vivid shapes moved into Janice's sightline. They were racing along the lakefront path. One shape was yellow, the other red, and they were gliding along the muddy trail like two fiery comets.

The shapes were those of children, each one dressed in a rain poncho of bright, shapeless vinyl. Their upraised hoods concealed their heads, but Janice could hear them laughing and shouting to one another in the hope of being heard above the storm.

They were almost past her house now. In a matter of seconds these signs of human life, of the recognizable world, would be gone.

Janice paused her musings and began simply to scream, to scream with greater urgency and force than she ever would have believed she possessed. Never had the words 'help me' been uttered more impactfully.

The pair of children stopped in their tracks and turned their obscured faces toward Janice's home. They resumed running, only this time the children were charging toward her back porch, toward the thing in the chair.

"No!" Janice shouted, "No, please go call someone! Tell your parents to send the police!"

But it was obvious by the children's delighted voices, by the fearless way they scaled the porch steps, that they were either ignorant of, or calloused toward, Janice's plight. Dread lined Janice's stomach with ice as the awful revelation came over her: the children had never heard her at all. What had attracted them to her house was not her shrieks, but the appeal of the midway.

She staggered back. By now her warnings to the children were completely drowned in calliope music.

Then, like the visitant itself, like the vanishing door and the painted windows, yet another feat of illusion blossomed before Janice's unbelieving eyes: the children grew smaller as they neared the carousel-headed creature. Instead of becoming larger and more distinct as they approached, the veiled kids shrank as they pulled themselves up onto the visitor's lap. Janice watched them as they scaled the figure's rigid arms. The two were now no larger than a pair of monarch butterflies crawling upon an adult body. Their voices were reedy and thin, as if distorted by helium.

The creature stalled its head long enough for its two fresh victims to bound onto the carousel's platform that was its jaw, and to select their favourite wooden creature. Once the butterfly children were nested on their chosen beasts, the thing resumed rotating its head. Only now it was moving faster, faster. The piping music sped up until it was reduced to a cacophony.

Janice was just able to discern a whirling smear of yellow and red as the rider's ponchos whipped past, and then these smears turned to blotches in her head, ones that seemed to make the entire world spin as rapidly as the carousel beyond her door. Janice felt her body sway briefly before the velocity tossed her to the floor.

The heat of the sun on her face eventually ferried Janice back to the land of the living. She bolted up, her body aching after having spent an indeterminate span upon the unforgiving floorboards. Had it been hours, days, weeks?

Upon recognizing that she was lying in her sunroom, mere inches from the screen door, Janice timidly shielded her eyes with her hands.

For a spell she did nothing but listen.

Where she expected to hear a calliope or hideously shrivelled cries of delight from the shrouded children, Janice encountered different noises: a discordant stream of voices, male and female both, and the scuffling thud of many footfalls. Daring a glance through her flexed fingers, Janice's eyes were met with the sight of a vacant porch.

Bliss shot through her body. Her initial disbelief at first spying the hideous intercessor, if that's what it truly had been, was now matched by her giddy disbelief over being free of it.

She stood and moved forward, pressing her face against the screen.

The patio chair sat empty, but the lakefront path beyond it was crowded. A group of men, children, and women were shuffling in a sloppy procession. Two names were being called over and over, like an incantation that the criers evidently hoped would bring the incanted into view.

That they were a search party was a fact that would have been obvious to even the dullest person. But Janice appreciated that she was in possession of a deeper and more specialized knowledge: she intuited exactly who this party was hunting, and what's more, she also knew where the two missing children had gone.

Janice looked over to see a group of three adolescents making their way up the oiled timber steps in her lawn. She noted that one of these new visitors was clutching a stack of fliers, perhaps ones that featured photos of the two missing kids. She might be able to see their naked faces at last.

This trio was coming to query, to ask about what had happened to the children that had come before them. But how could she possibly share it, Janice wondered? How does one even begin to convey a truth so confounding, so ill-suited to mere language?

Janice's eyes fell to her blood-stained, splinter-ridden fingers.

'Show them...' said a voice in her head, and all at once it became clear. There are indeed some things that words cannot express.

But she could demonstrate such things. Indeed, she could show them.

Janice came bursting through the backdoor before the visitors had even reached the porch. Her bloodied hands were outstretched in the hope that she might touch these new guests and channel, flesh-to-flesh, a little something of what she knew to be Real. Her feet did not even touch the ground as she advanced, so great were the hidden forces that moved her.

She had so much to share, so many ineffable truths. Janice's head rotated fully around and around as she floated between her world and that of the crowd. She could hear a high-pitched song, not unlike a calliope, swelling up all around her.

Only after she had managed to grip the slowest-moving visitor did Janice realize that the raw and primal song she heard arising from everywhere was a chorus of screams.

SONGS WE SING AT SEA
ARE THE LIES WE TELL OURSELVES

KAARON WARREN

Verse 1

I first began recording the folk songs of the cruise ship *Fair Queen* (to give it its official name) in '52, many years after most of the crew had died. There were only five left, and I decided to begin with Roberta Henry, a stout old woman who would not talk to me unless I came armed with grocery bags full of food. If I were an unkind person I would say that she could live for a week on the crumbs scattered across her ample chest, but I am not unkind. She was surprised to see me; the Government has denied the existence of these people for decades, and anyone who might care has forgotten. But I am tasked with helping with the housing crisis, and her an old woman with rooms she never uses in a house she can't maintain.

We were 30 years past the plague by then but still it plagued us, ho ho. People like this one, exposed and not killed; they were finally worth our attention.

I was struck by the lack of nautical design in her place. She lived only four blocks from the sea; as I stood on her front step I could hear that distant roll of tide.

Inside she had thick curtains to keep the noise out. Most houses in the area had names like *SS Stopforgood,* or *Seaspray,* or *Sailor's Rest.* Hers was unnamed. I asked her about that and she said, "It's not alive, you silly man."

And yet she would tell me of the many names they gave the cruise ship in the five years they were trapped on board.

At first they'd believed that once all the passengers had disembarked (enough ambulances for the sick ones, enough testing stations for those not yet sick) the crew would be accommodated. The head chef was forcibly stopped as she tried to leave; police with actual guns stopped her at the top of the gangplank.

"You're a danger," they were told, although arguments were had as to 'a' or 'in'. They were told "Triple pay for every extra day you wait," and that helped. There wasn't one of them who couldn't do with the money. To the credit of the shipping company they did get paid, but not triple pay. They got a pittance, but that built up over the five years and was worthwhile by the time the journey finally ended.

A week passed, or a month; no one is sure. The police stayed guarding the boat, and the crew members waited.

It was overnight they were cut adrift. My old lady, young then and pretty, from the photos she had around the place, vibrant and wild and pretty even in her waitress uniform, she and the others were ten hours into a party. The bartender assured them all opened bottles would be emptied into the sea and the waste! And no passengers? So the rolling party began and continued.

There was no one on the deck that cold night but they felt a different sway. Once you find your sea legs, the old lady told me, you can tell a wave from a ditch without thinking.

"We're moving," the carpenter said. He was the largest of all the men and handsome, the old woman told me, but the stories he told would chill your heart. The stories he told were so awful they burnt the beard off a good man.

She paused then. I didn't want to ask the question; I had a job to do and I was already behind. "That's all lovely, but…"

"Tell me!" her grandson crooned.

But she wouldn't. "Grow a beard and I might," she said.

Her grandson sat on the dining table, cross-legged, and he murmured with her, his voice rising when she broke into song as if some spirit took him. I thought, *he is memorizing the stories for when she is gone.*

His voice was beautiful.

Chorus

"Go to bed, you motherless child," she said to him, and his mouth opened, his face screwed up, a boy both insulted and cross.

Verse 2

The old lady said, "The carpenter, he loved to see how ill we could be. He loved to wait until we had a plate of food then tell us stories to turn our stomachs, like the one about the woman chained to a treasure chest, and she starved to death. She ate the sand, he said, and she tried to eat off her own fingers, but her teeth were soft and black from ill-use so they broke away. Poor abandoned woman." Even now, decades later, the story brought tears to her eyes and I wondered who had loved and left her.

It was the carpenter who said, *we're drifting, I tell ya,* and of course you know a dozen songs were sung on that one.

Chorus

She and the boy sang for me until she told him again to go lie in his bed, but she didn't call him a motherless child this time.

He went nowhere, staying there to stare at me with big black eyes and scratch at his armpits.

Verse 3

They drifted. They had no one to sail the ship (THOSE people got saved, didn't they? The Important crew?) so they drifted. The rolling of the waves and the wake of the cruise ship barely changed. They would gather at the back of the ship and tell stories of islands and other places.

They saw strange lights at sea and if drunk enough imagined magical cities that welcomed them as heroes and people with good songs to sing.

Stories at sea are the lies we tell ourselves, the old lady told me. She said, "They say now we were a phantom ship but here's the thing; we were vanished to them but not to ourselves."

♩ ♪ ♫♫ ♭ ♯ ♮

After six months at sea, the Garrulous Times began. They had read all the books left behind, lost and found, most of them chosen for the easy read but some of the deep stuff as well, like Kahlil Gibran, she told me, but I didn't know the man, and children's books they tore up and remade into other stories.

They'd watched all the movies.

It was time to tell stories and sing songs. It was as if by singing it, turning it into poetry, they were one step away from what most of them believed; that they'd never make it off the ship alive, that they'd float forever and a day on the water, on the abandoned cruise ship.

"The dear *Fair Queen*," I said.

"We never called her that," the old lady said. "We called her *Shit Heap*, and *Fair Queasy*, and others."

"Nicknames are natural human humour," I said, but she didn't listen.

Instead, she sang songs of all the names of the ship, and she actually stood up and JIGGED, and her grandson danced as well, his long foul nails tapping on the dining room table and I could only thank god I would never have to eat there.

Chorus

She puffed out and sat down and her grandson said, "Tell him about the carpenter's dead lover!" and she said, "Go make your bed, motherless child," but he stood so close, his hands on his hips, and seemed to grow larger just standing there so she sang the story, broken-voiced, tired.

Verse 3

"The carpenter told us he didn't mean to, 'It was an accident. I wish she'd understand. I wish she knew how much I loved her and wanted to keep her safe.' It wasn't long before we saw her, that dead girlfriend, all wrapped in white bandages, blood-stained, always a step or two behind him, her eyes barely visible from her curtain of gore-filled hair. An accident? I wondered at the real story, but he swore it was the truth, that he hadn't wanted her to die, she'd done that herself, but by the hunch of his shoulders and the sag of his face we knew the truth. We always knew the truth on *The Borangula*."

"*The Borangula?*"

"We called our ship *The Borangula* by then, after the long-forgotten city. Because we were lost. Forgotten."

I had never heard of that city and was sure she was making it up.

"You mean Bimini?" The Bimini Blocks are man-made blocks of stone found in the Bahamas, remnants perhaps of a sunken city.

"I do bloody not," she said.

"Do you miss the water?"

"I do bloody not," she said.

Nevertheless, she lived in a home too large for her, when a single cabin would do. She would be at home on one of the ships that never sailed far from shore.

"It's not like it was," I said. "Cabinning is different now. You'll be looked after until the day you die. You won't have to worry about a thing." I didn't tell her how long this might take. Weeks rather than months. "You'll have a great time onboard, I promise."

The old woman stamped her foot like a child.

"I will not," she said. Her grandson squatted on the table, his filthy feet bare, toes clenched. I cleared my throat.

"But I'm not here for that regardless. I'm here to hear your stories. Your songs," I said. I held up my small recorder. "We don't want to lose your voice."

There's never been a better way to gain a person's trust than to listen to their stories.

Her face changed as she told the stories and sang the songs. I saw it in the grandson too; it was like they were acting those stories out.

"How did you find me?" the carpenter sang to his dead girlfriend, and he wept as she answered so quiet.

"The beating of your beloved heart, I heard across the waves, and with that a sound like drums, slow and low funeral drums, beating out a warning."

♩ ♪ ♫♪ ♭ ♯ ♮

For a long time they dreamed of dry land. The old lady said sometimes those dreams were so real she could feel the dirt between her toes, or the concrete at her heels. It was so real, when she woke up the ship seemed like a dream and they all had this. Moments of dazzlement as you realize you're at sea, she said. When the waves are gentle and the sea air too, it's only when you smell the brine that you really understand you're awake. They began to believe there was a god of the sea who kept them floating. Who watched over them alive and dead, and sent them crucifix fish, which barely fed them but gave them sustenance. They saw whales in the distance but no desire to battle one of those, and they hauled up fish galore. They hauled up bales of turtles and sieges of herring, and seaweed for the side of the plate, ignored.

"We gathered wood for rafts," the old lady said. "One reason we let the carpenter be. He'd work away, 'more wood' he'd call, 'and nails', and bit by bit we'd pull the chairs apart. And the beds! We didn't need them all!" She winked at me and the boy turned red, not wanting to know. It was that, the sharing of the beds, but also those who'd died. Gone to sleep between the waves, gone to bed, and comfy it is too, they say.

They sang me a song of the raft of the Medusa, singing, "but we had no such desperate need. We had as much wine and beer as we could drink, we had food in tins to last a decade. The laughs we had to think of those rich passengers, supping on lobster bisque from a can and complimenting the chef on the freshness of her ingredients. She laughed herself, our chef, who cooked feasts for us and who would deny she'd never been happier?"

She sang me a song of someone giving them supplies. "Only once," she said. "We lost two men that day, pushed off the delivery boat as they tried to board, squashed between that boat and ours." She winced at the memory. "They delivered us salt and spices, although we had plenty of both because you can't season thin air, and they brought tins of vegetables we fell upon with great delight. We even drank the water they came in." She closed her eyes and licked her lips as if her taste buds still remembered.

One eye opened.

"Who's hungry?" she said, leaving it to me to confess I was, and to go out for chips and pies and cakes. I called the office and they told me to persist.

I asked about the grandson but they didn't know. I didn't want to be cabinned myself so I went back with hot food and my kindest smile.

We ate off plates that surely came from the ship.

They didn't need the rafts in the end. The ship floated close enough to a port that they could get across. One swam and traded enough for a small boat. And they traded more for papers and passports, and they dove into their new lives like waves diving into the ocean itself. Vanishing into the vastness of it all.

Things were very bad on board by then, but I wouldn't mention this. I reminded her of the freshness of the air out there, and the friends she'd made. I didn't mention the sewerage filth that covered one whole section of the ship (they had decided that was better than it spreading everywhere) and the tins of food almost depleted, the lack of fresh fruit, the way they were so coated with salt, their skin was mottled and cracked and dead in parts.

They all took whatever they could carry. They shared it out fairly. Plates, glasses, cooking pots – everything to give them a start.

"I sold most of mine at market. That was a great adventure," the old lady said, and the boy nodded solemnly as if he'd been a part of it.

Chorus

"Go make your bed," she told him. "Go on."

Verse 4

She said, "We had fun and never any troubles to bother us. There were babies born but so early and so wrong you wouldn't recognise them. They looked like the crucifix fish. We gave them the same rewards as our departed companions though, the same songs to see them over-board. The same wishes for a long afterlife.

"I lost a lover to the vagaries," she said, and I thought it was a perfect word for a death with no real answer to it. "Tossed him over the side and he came back alive. I knew it was him by the marks on his arms; tattoos you've never seen before or want to see again. Done beautiful good, I'd say, the octopus and the whale in battle but he never did tell me which one he thought he was."

"What do you mean he came back?"

She rolled her head around on her shoulders as if tiring out. "So long as we sing their songs they'll stay quiet."

The grandson came and sat nearby me. He hummed a tune I already seemed to know; I could feel my tongue beginning to move, wanting to hum it too.

I got up and sat further away from him, next to the old woman. She leaned close to me and she whispered, "And those babies came back grown, crawling up the ladder like they were born to do it." Her grandson bowed, as if this was his own doing. "He's got brothers and sisters galore," she said, quiet. "All crawled out into the world."

♩ ♪ ♫♪ ♭ ♯ ♮

My head was fuzzy with songs, hundreds of them, so fuzzy I could barely speak when I called the office. "She'll go peacefully," I said, no longer caring if she heard me or not. Her face screwed up at me, and she nodded at the boy, and that's when he leapt at me. I hadn't moved far enough away; nowhere was far enough. Up close his skin was like a road map, cracked, salty, crusted with pink. He didn't bite me at all but he held me still and whispered in my ear, hummed and whispered words until I was singing them myself.

"Beautiful voice," the old lady said, her own voice almost gone. She said, "The human body is like a ship. A vessel carrying the souls of millions or at least dozens or one or two, and if we are lucky, remembering who we are. We've all got stowaways."

The boy nuzzled my ear with his nasty wet nose, and the two of them sang songs to me.

"That's where story ideas come from," she said, like a curse.

Chorus

Go make your bed, she said to the boy.

   Go make your bed

   Make YOUR bed, the kid said.

"I'll make your bed," I said. "We'll make your bed so comfy you'll never want to get up again." I felt cruel then, but she'd been laughing at me all the while, stringing me along, telling me stories that were never true.

Not a word of a lie, she swore, but that was a lie as well.

The boy went onto the front lawn and lay down, his arms folded over his chest like a dead boy in a coffin. The van pulled up but the men ignored him; they only wanted my old lady. They only wanted this lovely house and all the things in it, and she'd be happy at sea for as long as she lasted.

♩ ♪ ♫♪ ♭ ♯ ♮

She cursed me, and now I can't stop singing and telling stories and singing.

♩ ♪ ♫♪ ♭ ♯ ♮

I walked away, whistling and singing.

I caught a look at my face in a window and watched it shifting and changing as the stories ran through me.

Unsteady on my feet. I walked with a rolling gait, like a man who spent so long at sea he no longer knows how to walk on dry land.

I've not been to sea, not me.

Not now.

Not ever.

♩ ♪ ♫♪ ♭ ♯ ♮

The audience, ghostly some and living others, clapped and cheered and someone brought me a beer.

"Encore," they called. "Sing us another one, go on!"

ACROSS THE DARKNESS

S.P. MISKOWSKI

In my junior year of college I loaned a classmate some money, and she never paid me back. At first, I didn't want to make a big thing out of it. I waited as long as I could, almost to the end of the semester. Then I called her. I left voicemails five, six times. After that I sent emails and text messages. She didn't call back and didn't reply.

I went to her dorm room, and all of her stuff was gone. I called her family on the west coast, and her mom said she was away. I could have asked her mom for the money. I could have told her why her daughter wanted the loan from me in the first place. But it seemed spiteful. Besides, I blamed myself for trusting the wrong person.

I needed that cash for the next semester. So I started looking for a job, something I could ditch later on.

This company I found on Craigslist seemed okay. I know, I know, but they had good ratings on Yelp and their ad looked professional. No typos, no weird skills needed, no remote settings, no red flags. I gave them a call and the woman who answered the phone was nice. She seemed nice. So whatever, right?

That moment you walk into a room for an interview half-hoping they won't hire you, but then you feel a connection with the interviewer, even if you have nothing in common? I walked out of their office with a job, and it was perfect for the situation I was in. It felt *right*. I felt lucky.

Dana, the woman on the phone, who also handled the scheduling, gave me the exact hours I wanted. And the pay was better than I expected. So that was how I ended up cleaning houses.

One big reason the agency was better than the other places I researched online: they were good about bundling clients, assigning one person or two people to a small geographic area. This way you cut down on the amount of travel. Instead of driving all over town, you might clean two houses on the same street, on the same day, and you were done.

After two weeks of shadowing and training with an experienced employee, then another two weeks of filling in for other cleaners, I passed the probation period, and the Beaumont neighborhood became my basic assignment. Three miles from campus, two afternoons a week, and every other Saturday. Again: lucky.

Okay, a slight downside to working one neighborhood: sometimes one client would ask about another. It might be a polite, casual question, like, "Do you know where she bought those vertical blinds?" Or "Are they planning to set out jack o' lanterns this year?" That kind of thing was harmless. Gossip was a different matter. We were never allowed to discuss the personal lives of our clients.

Well, let's call her Nikki. She was older, maybe forty, maybe too friendly. She was always asking about her neighbors. I couldn't understand why she would care. Her house was gorgeous, modern: marble counters, gas fireplace, polished concrete floors. Nikki had her own business online. She was married to a tech manager type. And she had a stepdaughter, but the girl was always out of the house when I was there.

Nikki usually offered me a soda or a cup of coffee, if she wasn't on the phone or showering or answering email when I showed up. We were told not to accept gifts or to consume any food or drink on the job. So I always said no thanks, politely. When she asked personal questions, I told her I didn't know anything, or I hadn't seen or heard anything worth mentioning. The job was important to me—I really couldn't ask my parents to replace the money I'd loaned to my classmate.

That day you show up feeling a tiny bit hung-over from a party the night before and you just can't turn down a glass of iced soda because it looks like the coolest drink in the world? Although I did accept a soda,

I remembered not to gossip about other clients. No way was I going to lose my position and have to tell my parents what I'd done.

See, my dad's a stockbroker. Self-made, mortgage paid off before he was forty, a real investment wizard. He would've hit the ceiling if he knew I'd just given money away—money he'd set up for me when I was, maybe, nine years old. Money I can't replace without his signature. So.

Clever girl, I decided to get out of the situation with Nikki by telling her a story. It was almost Halloween, why not something spooky? No, not about the neighbors. About me, about something I did on the job one time, while I was still in training.

Before I go on, let me just say: This is kind of bad but not illegal. (I looked it up.) And it doesn't reflect on other employees or the agency, so there's no point tracking them down to voice anybody's outrage. This was just me being stupid, okay?

This is the story I told my client:

My first week of training was all right. No big problems. I did make one stupid mistake, using a solvent on this antique brass blow poke hanging next to a fireplace. Turned out it was stained to seem antique, right, and the solvent I applied stripped the surface. I thought it was supposed to shine!

So, I apologized. The client laughed. Said she hated the blow poke. It was a wedding gift from her in-laws, and she didn't like them or their taste, and she was fine with it being shiny instead of fake-antique. The woman who was training me laughed, too. She promised not to tell Dana or anybody else at the agency. It was no big deal.

Anyway, the next assignment during my training period was a one-time clean-up, not a regular customer. And it kind of freaked me out at first.

An elderly woman had died. She wasn't in the house when we got there. She was at the mortuary waiting to be buried. She wasn't murdered. There wasn't a big mess to clean up, with bloodstains or anything. She just died because she was old.

Someone had stripped the bed and taken away the mattress. The place had that faint odor. You know the one—natural and understandable, nothing to be ashamed of—a lingering combination of urine and bleach, with a hint of violets. Kind of sweet, actually. Whenever I smell them together, they remind me of my grandma.

The woman's son and daughter had gone through the place and taken what they wanted to remember her by. What surprised me and made me feel sad was how much they left behind.

This was a duplex, by the way, over on Shepherd Lane where a lot of seniors live. It's one of the best senior places in town. I know because my mom considered renting an apartment there for my grandma when she was still okay to live alone.

All of the cabinets and storage closets are at mid-range, so even a person with arthritis can reach them. The bathtubs are the walk-in type, with a seat and handles built in. A guy comes around every other day to collect garbage for the dumpster. Everything is quiet and compact, and there's a private garden in the middle of the block with walkways where people can get some exercise without leaving home.

Anyway, this woman had lived in a small duplex, one bedroom and one bath, a tiny kitchen, a living room with a sofa and a bridge table set up. And she had all of these mementos.

The place was full of photos in antique frames, more photos stuffed into albums, tons of them, and postcards and matchbooks from all over the country. Meticulously clean satin and silk vintage dresses, all from the early 1960s, with bolero jackets and car coats hanging in the closet, covered in plastic dry cleaner bags. High heels, at least thirty pairs, were lined up and matched with these adorable purses. It was amazing.

Her relatives had collected the valuable stuff, like jewelry and silver lighters and frames, but they left behind most of her personal treasures. All of the things that said who she was and how she lived, it was just sitting there, unwanted. They had even picked through the albums for a couple of photos and left the rest behind, on the coffee table.

That weird thing that comes over you when you instantly connect with another person, with some indefinable detail in their photo or a story about them, and then you remember they're dead? I couldn't stop thinking how sad it was for her favorite stuff to sit around waiting for the Goodwill truck. The son had given instructions to get rid of it all, donate it. I kept staring at all of these pretty dresses and purses, thinking nobody loved them anymore, and now they would be separated and sold one piece at a time to people who would only wear them at Halloween.

So yeah, I took some things. Nothing worth much money: a pea-cock blue sweater set, a mustard mini-dress with matching scarf, a black pencil skirt, a pair of Capris, a two-piece tweed suit with a silk blouse, a red fur-collared jacket, some slacks, a few cashmere sweaters, an emerald-green clutch, a pair of flats, a pair of peacock blue mules with sequins, cat's eye and leopard print sunglasses, some glass brooches and bracelets, a couple of hats with veils, a box of postcards and photos.

All of it was so cute, and well taken care of, and now abandoned. I couldn't resist. I hauled these things away in a trunk. I was supposed to take it to a drop box, along with a trash bag full of treasures. I figured it didn't matter to anybody, so why not haul it home instead?

When I got back to my apartment that night, I unpacked the trunk. I opened this little white leather suitcase with a monogram on one corner. I studied the older photos inside. I noticed, when this woman was young, she kind of resembled me. Superficially, she could have been me, if I wore my hair up.

At first, I didn't even know what to do with all of these things. I thought I'd keep them for a while, and if none of my friends wanted them, I'd put them on eBay, right?

But here's the crazy part. When I tried on the clothes, they fit. Not loosely or pretty well. Perfectly, as if they were tailored for me. And as if they'd been designed to make me look devastatingly cool. In the Capris my narrow hips took on an edge. Against the fur-collared jacket my hair sort of *gleamed.*

I took some pictures. They were hilarious. I took more, and I tried to imitate the way the woman in the photos was posing. I matched the makeup as well as I could, and pinned up my hair, and it was really something.

You have to understand, this was during my job training. I was a little worried Dana or one of the other employees might catch me and ask why I'd helped myself to this dead woman's stuff. But the fear wasn't enough to stop me.

Anyway, I had a Facebook account I'd opened but never used. I was going to keep in touch with my parents on social media when I started college, but Skype and text were a lot simpler. Facebook is, you know, a whole big *thing.* My mom and her friends love it. They have this mom group where they compare wines and complain about the cashier at the Cheesecake Factory and talk about losing weight.

So, I had this account just sitting there. And after poking around a little I remembered I could easily change my username, right?

That moment, when you're staring in the mirror, and you could swear a light bulb literally pops to life above your head like a cartoon? I used the dead woman's first name and my own middle name: Natalie Hawkins. I posted two of the photos of me wearing her clothes. Inspired by the postcards, I said I was originally from Cape Cod, had traveled a lot, and now lived in L.A. I described myself as "a fast learner in the big city of life."

Stupid, I know. It was stupid fun, like scrapbooking—another thing my mom and her pals love to do. Or maybe it was more like an art project, where I assembled this identity from found materials. Okay, stolen materials, but they would have gone to waste anyway.

It never crossed my mind that anyone would friend me, I mean "me." But within a week the account attracted about twenty friends. Who were they? I didn't care. It didn't matter if they were catfish, trolls, or bots. I just assumed they were drawn to keywords like "fashion" and "travel," and I accepted all of them.

I have to re-emphasize, here, the whole project was harmless. It was nonsense. I was planning to delete the account after a couple of weeks.

My job training had ended, and I'd completed my fill-in assignments. I met my own clients, and figured out what they expected, or at least what I had to do to keep them happy while I maintained an A average at school. I just didn't have time to meet new people in real life. It was a lot easier and more relaxing to post fashion photos between study sessions.

Around this time, Natalie started exchanging comments with a few people on her timeline. I know how it sounds. But I'd tried on more outfits, posted more photos. I was getting pretty good at it, and I wasn't ready to throw out all of this stuff I'd created.

I thought, if my project attracted this many friends, or admirers, how could I throw it away? They were like art patrons. I didn't think of them as individuals. I didn't even check their profiles, for fear of getting sucked into their problems and politics and whatever. I avoided too much contact. All I knew about them were impressions created by their comments.

One friend, whose profile picture was a teenager with a sleek bob and a beret, said Natalie embodied "the boldness and elegance of 1960s style at its best." Another, whose pic featured a bedraggled forty-something smoker, said Natalie could have been a Dario Argento muse, if she'd been born half a century earlier and in Italy.

I mean, of course it was all wrong, but the friend list grew a little every week. Each new ensemble and photo elicited praise. Natalie replied with modest gratitude. None of this felt wrong, exactly, but I sensed I couldn't keep doing it forever.

What most of Natalie's friends had in common, and I could see this in every word they posted, was loneliness. Some had names I didn't really believe, and others seemed true, but who knows, right? All of them were searching, hoping to connect with another person, any person who shared an interest or an opinion. Even someone who wasn't a person at all.

I started to feel sorry for them. And I was afraid to read their profiles or scroll through their photos. Afraid their neediness would be depressing. Pretty soon every comment on Natalie's timeline gave me a tiny stab of guilt.

The day I finally made up my mind to ditch the account, something strange happened. I didn't know what to do, so I just waited.

On Facebook, you never know who might send you a direct message. You can skip messages from anyone you don't know, anyone who isn't on your friend list, but I couldn't figure out how to make them disappear. And I tried. So, the DM from someone named Walter Urbana sat there in Natalie's message queue for two days before I worked up the nerve to read it.

After all this time, dear Nat, I wonder if you will remember me. What a thing it is, to write that sentence! After all we've been through together. All we've been through since.

When I saw your photos, so many memories came rushing back. Paris. New York. Montreal. The best times of my life.

I'm being sentimental, as you always said I would be someday. I'm overcome by thoughts of our last night, last weekend, last words.

Will you meet me, I wonder? Yours. As ever. – W.

This was exactly what I meant about not wanting to find out too much. This was why I'd avoided reading the profiles of Natalie's friends. They were too sad. This poor guy, somebody's demented old granddad, spent his time flirting online with women who reminded him of his first love.

Can you guess why I blocked the guy? I did, yeah. Right then, before I could accidentally learn any more about him and start crying or something. Poor Walter, I know, but my life was kind of busy. I had an exam coming up, cleaning assignments, papers to write. My dad left a voicemail saying how proud he was I'd proven him wrong; I really *could* stay on the budget he'd set up for me. No fucking pressure, right?

For a couple of weeks I had so much going on, there wasn't enough time to even sign on, let alone check messages or post photos. I worked my ass off, studied through lunch, spent every spare minute at the library, and when I got home at night I just crashed.

Once I sort of caught up, I decided to check Natalie's account over coffee. A second DM from Walter Urbana had landed in the message queue in the middle of the night. At least, according to the time stamp.

There's no need to be cruel, Nat. Not that I blame you. What happened at the beach house was my fault. Nothing went the way I'd hoped.

Please think it over. Consider one last conversation. In person, or by phone, anything you wish.

Yours. What more can I say? – W.

Look, I'm not someone who gets scared, or angry, just like that. In fact, my mom says all of my reactions are "slow burn." She finds it funny. I used to think it was funny. Now I wonder if it's a kind of emotional flaw, an unwillingness to get involved with people if I think they'll cost too much time and effort. Like the classmate I'd loaned money to. What had I known about her, beforehand?

Maybe this is the real reason I signed on to clean houses. I was given a schedule. I went in with supplies and instructions. I completed a list of tasks and then I left. Unless a client turned out to be really nosy, like the one I told this story to, I never had to engage in conversation.

I thought about my decision, in my second year, to leave the cramped and smelly dorm room I'd shared with a Felicity lookalike and live alone in the tiniest apartment I'd ever seen. (At first glance I thought it was a walk-in closet with a window.)

Sleeping on a lumpy futon, eating breakfast cereal standing over the sink, watching tendrils of ivy crawl across the window, lacing vines until the window couldn't be opened. All-night study sessions. Lectures and labs and exams. And in my spare hours—cleaning houses.

Posing in cute, innocent selfies wearing the vintage clothes of a dead woman had become more than my hobby. It was my only social life. But at some point, it stopped feeling harmless, although I couldn't say exactly what I was doing wrong. Nothing. Everything. Blocking an old man who was lonely and reaching out to strangers to fill his time. What I called nothing meant the world to this guy. It meant enough for him to create a second Facebook account under the same name, just to pursue Natalie.

Right about now I guess you're in one of three groups. You think I should have let true love take its course and fade away naturally. (Assuming Walter had no stalker tendencies.) Or you think I should've been kinder, helping him find what my mom's friends call closure. (Which always makes me think of sutures.) Or maybe you're thinking: *WTF is wrong with this girl? There is no Natalie!*

If you're in that last group, I agree. Which is why I decided to go ahead and delete the whole account. Which is what I should've done without delay. But this is what makes Facebook insidious, right, the way a comment or a photo can hook you? Curiosity keeps people coming back for more.

As soon as I spotted one of those adorable selfies of Natalie—me with my hair swept up in a French bun, both put-together and casual in Capris and a sky-blue cashmere sweater, leaning against the windowsill with a cigarette in one hand—I forgot where I was. Absolutely lost track of the room, the time, everything. It was like swooning, or fainting, without falling down.

I just sat there, imagining Natalie and Walter sipping martinis and dancing barefoot at a rooftop party. Moonlight spilling down in a wide arc across the brickwork. The aroma of tobacco and grilled steaks in the cooling air.

Just like that, without another thought, I clicked on Walter's profile. Fully intending to write a DM—although, of course, what the hell would I say? Should I offer condolences? Confess that Natalie didn't exist? Confuse the guy even more by suggesting he had me mixed up with someone else? Make a date to meet for coffee, and watch him have a complete meltdown when he realized I wasn't Natalie—either his or mine?

I have no idea what I might have written, if I hadn't stopped to read the post at the top of Walter's timeline. It was dated October 9th. Six years earlier. A note of regret and farewell, with thanks to his friends who had persisted in hopes and prayers. How the final stage wasn't as bad as he had anticipated. How he wished he had ten more years he could throw away exactly like the previous 70.

No one was maintaining the account anymore. All of the posted material was out of date. Walter's profile was one of those set adrift by its owner's death. No one had claimed it. The last items added were several heartfelt tributes, all of them tacked on to the last post but about a week later. Scrolling through them, something seemed vaguely familiar. The phrasing? The clichés about a better life after this one?

I checked the names again. That was it. Two of the people who'd left comments were friends with Natalie.

Clicking on the first name I recognized, I held my breath, waiting for technology to bring me a larger image: the face of a teenager sporting a sleek bob and a beret. The sly expression, turtleneck sweater, stubby fingernails painted sea green. The cache of poems, some of them two lines long; the fashion icon tributes; the screenshot of a message of encouragement from a famous designer; the bleak early morning posts about depression and loneliness.

Then the bedraggled middle-aged smoker. Almost all of his pics were giallo posters. Garish yellow light and ketchup-red blood spatters. The torn blouse of a screaming victim. Discussion threads dissolving into vicious debates about who did what better—Argento or Bava? His final post was eight years old, an apology to all of his "colleagues and acquaintances" for some unspecified misdeed, a prank carried too far, a joke that ruined him and got him canceled by his fellow film fans.

My first thought was: How can all of this sorrow just *live here,* like deserted houses? Why hasn't anyone noticed these people? Why didn't anyone take care of their accounts, their last words, their cherished photos? How many people have died and left their final words there, a last, failed attempt at reaching across the darkness?

I checked ten of the names on Natalie's friend list before I lost my nerve. All dead. All left to linger in the form of electronic data, a shimmer, an outline of whoever they once were.

I sat there for a while, shaken, scared. Then I deleted my account, I mean Natalie's account. I didn't want to investigate any further. I didn't want to know how all of these "people" were drawn so quickly to Natalie, or to me. I only wanted them to go away.

That same night, I left voicemail for a couple of friends IRL, inviting them out. I just wanted to pretend none of it had happened. I felt this overwhelming need to be in the world again.

Well, the day I had a hangover and accepted a soda, I told this story to my client, Nikki. I left in all the stuff about creating an account and posting selfies and getting all of these friend requests. I left out the part about the friends being dead.

I was hoping my client wouldn't be freaked out by what I'd done. It occurred to me that she might see me as a potential thief, or a creep. Instead she sat there at the kitchen counter with this faraway expression until I thanked her for the soda and went back to my work.

I didn't think about it again after that. I just showed up on time and did my job. The client never tried to make me talk to her again.

Only about a month later, I was wiping down the kitchen surfaces when I saw she'd left her laptop open on the counter. One of those crazy moments. You're there. The computer is unlocked. The client is upstairs in the bathroom.

Well she had a bunch of discussion threads in progress on the Facebook page for this import company she works with. These suburban ladies buy stuff handcrafted by women living in poverty in remote parts of the world, and the company puts out a catalog with cute names for all of the products, and women like Nikki sell them online or at parties. Basically. I mean, I could see right away it was a pyramid scheme but it's none of my business.

The thing is, on this group page, she had her own profile with her name, Nikki, listed on her account. But then she had this other profile for a younger woman with long, dark hair and amazing cleavage who kept complimenting her and thanking her for bringing these bracelets and purses and soap dispensers into her life so she could make a real contribution to the world. It was a phony dialogue. First, she would say what a godsend she was, and then she would thank herself and say it was nothing.

It's funny, right? I could see how funny it was. I guess it's hard to sell stuff online. Hard to set up parties and meet people and promise some kind of miracle. *This lotion will make you young again.* (No, really!) *This dress will make you feel sexier and happier than you've ever felt in your whole life.* (Try it! You'll love it!)

Yeah, it was funny. But I got a chill, too, when I saw the name that she was using for the second account, the woman who kept paying her compliments. Natalie Hawkins isn't the most common name in the world. Not common enough to be a coincidence.

I told myself she used the name because she figured it wouldn't matter to a dead person. And I considered telling her the part of my story I'd left out. The weird part.

But you know what? I decided not to. After all, she stole the name from my story without asking permission. And it's hard to convince anyone of something they haven't experienced yet. I don't know why. Most people just believe what they want to believe.

INTO THE GREEN

A.C. WISE

The trees click and hum then immediately go *shhhhh,* correcting themselves for giving a secret away. Rose squints as Nate kills the engine and the boat makes a hollow tocking sound against the dock. Even with her eyes shaded, it's a moment before Rose can see the island properly. And even then there's not much to see. Only the green.

Jo nudges Rose's shoulder.

"Angel Island. What did I tell you? Isn't it perfect?" Her cousin grins.

A one-two punch of excitement followed by the tiniest bit of annoyance that Jo found the place, not her, knocks against Rose's heart. But excitement wins out and she scrambles onto the dock. Jo is right; Angel Island *is* perfect. Founded by a weird, rich recluse who used it as a bootlegging base, then had some kind of vision, moved his family here, built a house, which later burned, after which some kind of cult moved in, and now it's been abandoned for nearly forty years. Perfect. Really.

"Tell me I'm the best cousin ever," Jo says.

"You are the best," Rose echoes dutifully, the call and response of their youth.

She's still grinning, barely paying attention to Jo, and already lifting her phone to film. The long dock arrows straight to the base of a gentle slope before giving way to a beaten dirt path disappearing through the trees.

"Your subscriber count is going to go through the roof," Jo says as Rose pans the shot searching for any glimpse of the compound buried deeper within the island. "Sponsors will be banging down your door. Is that a thing? Do urban explorers get sponsorships on YouTube or does that only happen with those weird unboxing videos?"

"Shit. No signal. So much for the livestream idea." Taylor holds his own phone above his head.

"Were you seriously expecting a signal out here?" Rose slides her own phone back into her pocket. "It's fine. We'll shoot, edit, and up-load when we get back."

Nate ties off the boat then begins handing up bags. Rose shoulders two, lets Taylor grab what's left.

"Are you sure this is okay?" Taylor wears doubt, an expression Rose isn't used to seeing on him.

Usually he's the first to lead the charge into abandoned factories, desiccated amusement parks, the ghost of subway tunnels, and unfin-ished hotels.

"The developers aren't going to have us arrested for trespassing or some shit, are they?"

"Relax. Jo's being paid to be here, and we're her assistants." Rose's mouth quirks upward – it's the fact that they almost have permission to be here that has Taylor rattled. He'd be more comfortable straight up trespassing.

Technically, Jo didn't mention bringing her cousin and her cous-in's friends on her advance scouting mission to see what needs to be done before the place is torn down to bones by developers to build an exclusive luxury spa. But also technically the developers didn't specify she couldn't bring anyone along. After all, it's not a one-person job and if their cameras just happen to be running as they work? Easier to ask forgiveness than permission..

Rose moves up the dock toward the apron of soil and leaf-rot trail-ing from the tree line. An optical illusion makes the shadows step clos-er for a moment before they fall back again. The click-burr-shushing sound returns, then stillness, deep and complete.

In her bag is a thick book Rose has only skimmed, detailing the history of Angel Island. Or at least the history of its legends, rumors, and hearsay. Ghost lights, spooky noises, unexplained disappearances, phantom buildings and strange rituals. As they pass between the trees there's an oppressive, back-of-the-neck, someone-is-watching feeling. It makes sense. If even half the stuff in the book is true, then the island can't help but be haunted as fuck.

"Best cousin ever." Rose grins.

Shadows layer themselves thick, the temperature dropping as soon as they're out of the sun. Rose's skin goose-pimples, but her smile stays in place as she climbs the gentle slope to the compound.

Flakes of paint cling to the raw concrete walls. Rose hasn't even been inside yet, but she can already tell the compound is a maze. No one was held here against their will, supposedly; the only trick if you did want to leave, Rose thinks, would be finding your way out.

Already she's lost track of the path back to the dock. Everything on the island looks the same, except this one spot, where the trees hold the line all around the edges of the building as if by some unspoken agreement. She looks at the wall again, zooms the camera in – a fleck of turquoise like a polished stone, another in yellow as bright as sunshine. Colors more suited to an elementary school, or a children's library, than a cult compound. Rose scrapes at a bit of startling violet with her thumbnail and it comes away like peeling skin.

"You have to come look at this," Nate shouts from inside.

Rose ducks as she enters. Despite being just over five feet and the door being an average height, the impulse is uncontrollable, as if the top lintel might suddenly drop on her if she doesn't crouch. Her foot immediately comes down in a puddle in the middle of the floor.

"Ewww."

"It's just rain water, don't be a baby." Taylor's voice echoes weirdly. Even though he's standing right beside her, he sounds as though he's in another room.

Rose looks around for Jo. She must be deeper in already, doing the job she was paid to do while they mooch and film. She turns her attention to the light from Nate's phone playing over the wall as he records.

"Holy shit."

The mural is barely faded, despite forty years' time. The image wavers as the light passes over it, and the figures stretch though they're already tall. Featureless, pale as the birch trees around them. They make Rose think of a corporate-designed logo for some sort of charity – like a hands around the world kind of thing – but subtly wrong.

Their clustering draws her eye to the center of the painting where a single figure, smaller than the others, lies on the ground against a square of darkness. Not a square, a grave. They're looking at a burial.

Rose startles and the reflection of the scene catches in the puddle at her feet, shivering. At any moment, one of those faceless painted figures will turn and shush her. They're intruding on something sacred. A ritual they weren't invited to witness, and certainly not to film. She almost pulls Nate's arm down, makes him put his phone away.

They shouldn't be seeing this. No one should have to see a funeral for a child. Heat builds beneath Rose's skin, as if delivered by a slap, dizziness in its wake and the sense of panic rushing in. She looks around for Jo again. Does she see what Rose sees? Is this some kind of sick joke? The mural here just for them?

But it's only Taylor and Nate, who have been her friends for years and know almost everything about her, except this one thing. Only her cousin knows. Only Jo would understand the utter terror of small fingers slipping out of Rose's hand as she tries desperately to hold on, eyes flooded with fear, and a mouth stretched wide to call her name.

She wheels around, almost crashing into Taylor.

"I'm going to take a look around outside." She pushes past him, not giving him the chance to protest.

One of the first rules they set when filming – never wander off alone. She should apologize, explain, but she can't. She needs to get out of this room, right now. Rose ducks again, back into the sunlight, blinking and blinking and letting the brightness excuse her tears.

She hauls in a breath, striding away from the door before Taylor or Nate can call her back. As long as she keeps the building at her shoulder, she can't get lost. Rose puts one foot in front of the other, heel to toe, head down, refusing to let her chest hitch into hyperventilating sobs.

The bridge wouldn't have held either Rose or Jo's weight, even at twelve years old. But Theo at seven and small for his age should have been light enough to cross.

He'd been scared of the rushing water, terrified, but they'd dared him. They'd also promised him it would be fine. They were his big cousins and they'd always looked out for him.

Their parents had rented a house for a week, right on the lake. Like a mini family reunion, but just the members of the family we like, her dad had said with a wink. Rose and Jo had taken to the water immediately, but Theo refused. He wouldn't even get into the boat tied to the dock behind the house.

He was convinced there were monsters lurking under the water where he couldn't see. The first night in the house, Rose had woken to Theo's screams. She'd tumbled down from the top bunk, Jo on her heels, and they'd found their little cousin with his face mashed up against the sliding glass door leading out onto the deck that eventually stepped all the way down to the shore.

The glass fogged where he breathed against it, a wild, animal sound. His eyes were fixed, wide, wide, wide, and in her memory, Rose sees the reflection of the water pooled in them, like the lake had gotten inside, crawled beneath his skin. Even though he'd been screaming, staring at the lake, he'd been asleep. His mother had come and wrapped him in a blanket, guiding him gently back to bed.

"What do you think he saw?" Jo had asked.

She and Rose had pressed their faces where Theo had, but there'd been nothing to see. Just still water, bruised blue-purple-black, ringed by trees, and far on the distant side of the lake, another house throwing out glittering coins of light.

Back in their room Rose hung her head down from the top bunk. Jo was convinced she would roll out in her sleep even though as long as Rose had known her, Jo had slept like the dead and never moved.

"What if it's a prehistoric beast, like a crocodile?" Rose asked.

"Or a witch who drowned," Jo countered.

"I've heard there are places where whole towns are flooded to build lakes. Maybe that's what Theo saw, streets full of drowned houses and the ghosts of the people who used to live there walking around."

As much as they'd enjoyed scaring themselves, they'd been good big cousins. They hadn't uttered a word of their stories to Theo. It didn't matter though; he still wouldn't go near the water. Jo and Rose had taken him on a hike through the woods instead. They hadn't known the river was there, with its rickety and fraying bridge. They hadn't intended to cross, but something had grabbed hold of Rose, like a hand around her heart, fingers squeezing hard, hard, hard, the other hand pushing the words of the dare out of her mouth and she couldn't stop them.

Three steps in, the bridge had given way. Theo's legs hadn't been long enough to let him jump back or move ahead to safety. Rose and Jo had tried to grab him, tried to pull him back, but the current had been too strong.

The small body in the center of the mural burns behind Rose's eyes. With Theo, there'd been no body to bury. Once the river had gotten hold of him, it had never let go.

Should she find Jo? Warn her? But there's a chance Jo won't even see the mural, or react the same way as Rose. Telling her would just upset her. She should let it go.

Rose glances through one of the windows as she passes, and almost chokes on a breath. The mural is still there. The same, attenuated figures, almost indistinguishable from the trees flickering as Rose passes like she's looking through a slit in a kinetoscope so figures jump to follow her. But the figure in the center of the mural, the one being buried, is gone.

She stops, forcing herself to look head on. It's not the same mural. A different room. A different painting.

Rose considers turning back, but as she pivots to look behind her, she has to steady herself against the wall. Everything tilts, panic scrabbling at her again. If she turns back, she'll get lost. Even though it's one narrow track all the way around the compound. She has to keep going. She has to complete the circuit.

She turns around again and the fist squeezed around her heart, around her throat, around her gut, eases off. But now the light through the trees is wrong, low and gold as though it's late afternoon, as though she's been walking for hours, not minutes. Sweat sticks her shirt to the small of her back. She should have brought water with her. But then she hadn't intended to be gone so long.

How long, though? Shouldn't she have come back around to where she started by now? She listens for voices – Jo, Taylor, Nate. She must have circled the compound at least five times. It just keeps going.

She's almost running now. The green blurs in her peripheral vision, making her think of a kinetoscope again. She saw one in a museum once, the repeated image of a horse galloping past the slits in the paper shade. Only she's the horse now, running and running and getting nowhere. The trees are the slits dividing the light, the skin dividing her from the world.

Something gray keeps pace with her. Jumping from place to place. Or it's the light playing through the trees. If she doesn't look, it won't be real. It can't be real.

She rounds a corner of the building, jutting at a weird angle, and stops as if slammed into a concrete wall, breath knocked out of her. A panicked wheeze escapes a throat gone too small and her eyes sting. A path cuts through the trees – too neat, too perfect, too maintained. As though countless feet have kept the dirt pounded down for forty years even though the island is abandoned.

They're still here, Rose thinks, and it's an absurd thought. *They never left. Nobody ever left even though they all disappeared.*

Rose shakes her head. Shakes away a buzzing sensation like a wasp flying close to her ear. The trees whisper *shhhh*. Through them, there's an outline suggesting a house, a mansion, except she knows the compound is the only building here.

But there was a house here once. The one built by the rich man who made his fortune bootlegging, then had some religious epiphany and moved his family here away from civilization to the island where he claimed he met an angel. Something he couldn't explain. It opened his eyes, changed his ways. And eventually he brought friends, families of friends, the first roots of the cult or the commune, living in small houses – huts almost – scattered around the mansion he'd built, which doesn't seem very communal to Rose at all. But that house burned. A long time ago.

That had been in the book, the one she'd only leafed through. The kids who lived in the commune claimed the house still appeared sometimes. They would dare each other to stand where it burned and summon it like a ghost.

Rose shades her eyes, peering. There's no house. No outline. Just the strange configuration of the trees suggesting architecture.

But below those lines something squat and gray sits at the side of the path. A gravestone. No. A statue? But that doesn't mean it doesn't also mark a grave.

Rose takes a step away from the solidity of the concrete behind her. No dizziness assails her this time, but her mind screams a warning. She knows what happens to characters in fairy tales who leave the path. She knows what happens to idiots in horror movies who wander off alone.

Just one step closer. Not all the way off the path. Just close enough to see the statue's features are worn smooth by years of hands touching it. The figure isn't human. Except maybe it is. There's a suggestion of curling horns. It reminds her of a matryoshka doll, pregnant with the sense that there's more hidden inside. Its shape is an egg, except not like that at all. An urn. A sarcophagus, but only as tall as her waist, and from this distance she can't see any sign of a seam, no indication it opens. She'd have to go closer to be sure. Lay her hands on the stone and feel for a crack to know if there's something folded up inside.

She reels back and collides with the wall behind her. The statue grins. There's no way she could see that at this distance, especially as worn as it is. It has no mouth, no lips, no teeth. Even so, it grins.

She wheels around, places her shoulder to the wall of the building, not caring that it scrapes at her skin as she does.

"There you are!" Jo steps from what looks like a blank wall into bright sunlight, and in her panic, Rose almost hits her cousin.

"Whoa, hey, are you okay?" Jo catches Rose's shoulders.

Rose blinks. Hauls in a breath. Makes herself nod.

"Yeah. I'm just…" What can she say? "I'm good."

"We found a dry spot to set up camp. Come help me with our tent so we can eat. I'm starving!"

Jo waves the way and disappears back inside the compound. Rose follows, the shadows of the building falling over her. The ceiling presses down. She resists the urge to look back over her shoulder. To see if the path has followed her here. To see if the woods have shifted and brought the squat gray statue closer. She doesn't want to see it again. Doesn't want to think about what may or may not be inside.

"So what kind of cult was it? A sex thing, or a suicide thing?" Nate holds a hotdog over the campfire's open flame. With the concrete at least they can't burn anything down.

Nate gestures toward the book on Rose's lap – *Angel Island: A History*. The spine is cracked, the book almost swollen, its pages fanned. Did it get wet on the boat ride even though everything else in her bag remained dry? She could swear she only skimmed it, but the book in her lap looks well-read, well-loved.

"Neither?" Rose shrugs, a full body motion, feet going up onto her toes and tipping the book closer to the center of her body.

She hates the uncertainty in her voice. She hates, suddenly, being here. She tries to remember – did she find the book in a second-hand store after Jo mentioned the island, or did she already know about it, one of her bucket-list destinations for her and Taylor and Nate to shoot? She's barely even finished half of her beer, but her brain feels foggy.

"It was more like a commune, I guess?" Again, the uncertain lift in her voice, and Rose straightens her shoulders, tries to put more confidence into her tone and ends up sounding to herself like a drunk person over enunciating their words to prove they're not drunk.

"They were kind of like hippies. They wanted to live off the grid, so they moved out here. There was some kind of ritual they used to do, like a mock burial so their members could be born anew, but that was the closest thing to weird religion stuff. Mostly it seemed like they just wanted everyone to pull their weight and not be dicks to each other."

"Sounds pretty great, actually," Taylor says. He leans slightly into Nate, their shoulders touching.

"It's the guy who founded the island who had all the wacky beliefs, but really the commune grew up after him," Rose says. "William Angel Bryson – he claimed to have met something here. An angel, or at least that's what he believed. That's why he named the island the way he did and took Angel as his middle name."

Rose taps the cover of the book, warming to the subject. Jo, Taylor, and Nate listen, rapt as the words spool out of her. She isn't sure which ones are true, or at least which ones she read. The words are just there, pushed onto her tongue; all she has to do is open her mouth to speak them.

The firelight warms her. Her cheeks especially feel flushed and she drinks in the sensation. There's a pleasant, light-headed feeling, like she's buzzed, the kind of happy drunk where she talks too much and can't stop herself.

"Bryson's wife had some weird ideas too. Something about mesmerism and trees? She supposedly brought some expert out to the island after her son died to transfer his spirit into the woods. She thought the island was haunted, that her son's ghost was trapped here. Really, she was probably just grief stricken, you know? Like, did her grief cause the haunting, or was the haunting the cause of her grief? Either way, you can't blame her. Her kid was the only person who ever died on the island—"

Rose blinks. That isn't right. Her hands stray to the book's cover, passing over it as if to pull the words up through her fingertips.

"I mean, he died shortly after Bryson moved his family out to the island. He was only ten. Some kind of accident."

He drowned.

The words are a jagged splinter forced into Rose's mind. She coughs, choking on them, taking another swig of her beer to wash them away. The story tries to twist itself away from her, make itself into something else and she fights to get it back under her control. The boy didn't drown. He fell. Climbing. She remembers reading that in the book. Somewhere.

"He broke his neck." She says firmly, like she can hammer the words into being the truth.

The image that comes to her mind is no better – a small body with limbs bent the wrong way, neck *folded,* and she can't shake it free.

"Didn't some other kids die here though?" Nate asks, chewing.

Rose turns her head away so she won't have to see his jaw work, his throat swallow. Her stomach turns, and she takes another sip as if the beer will settle it. The shadows outside the windows – empty of glass, just black squares cut in the raw concrete – feel solid, more like boards nailed over the gaps, even though Rose can feel the breeze swinging through them. Insects, or some kind of night birds, make a sound like *k-k-k-k-krrrr.* If she looks, she'll see a face peering in at them, squat and gray.

"No. I mean yes." She grips the book, which feels thicker, crammed with far more pages than just moments ago.

"It's not clear," she settles on finally, a nervous smile sketching over her lips. "You know. Ghost stories, right? People disappeared, but none of the accounts agree and for all anyone knows, the people who vanished just took a boat and left, sick of living in the commune, but…"

She lets the words trail, shrugs. Jo flashes a smile, mischievous, her cheeks flushed too. There are several empty beer bottles next to her foot.

"Tell us a ghost story, then." Jo gestures with the bottom of her current bottle before necking it empty.

Rose immediately regrets her choice of words. And at the same time, she feels the need to tell a tale clogging up her throat. The words rising, clawing their way up to force her lips open. She is in the woods again, by the bridge over the river. A smile that isn't hers opens and she says the cruelest words she could to her little cousin: *I dare you.*

Around the fire, the others shift closer and give her all their attention. Rose tries to clamp the story down, but it comes anyway, unwinding out of her.

"The kids on this island used to play something they called the Daring Game."

She hears her own voice, at twelve years old: *You gotta do it, Theo. It's a dare. A double dare. We can't leave until you do.*

Rose wants to stop. She can't.

"They would go to where the old house used to be, the one Bryson built and lived in until it burned. They said – they believed – you could summon the house like Bloody Mary in a mirror. They didn't say how."

Rose grips the book so hard her knuckles ache. She can't look at Jo, but she feels her cousin staring at her, hard as well.

"They would go to the spot where the house used to be and dare someone to stand on the other side of the door, where they would be inside the house if it appeared. The youngest kid on the island, they made him stand in the house one day. He was terrified."

A catch in Jo's breath. The tension in Rose's hands gripping the book travels up her arms, digs into her shoulders so that her entire body hurts.

"They called the house and it came. It came and went again and the kid they dared to stand inside was gone. Swept away." Rose's own breath hitches, catching on something like tears. Shame burns through her.

"Rose—" Jo reaches to touch Rose's arm, to stop her. The word *don't* is on her lips, but doesn't pass it, because Rose cuts her off, turns to face Jo with tears hot behind her eyes but invisible in them and a terrible grin stretching her mouth.

"The house came and carried him away, just like a river."

Jo's eyes go wide. Her mouth too, a shocked 'o'. As if Rose had slapped her. In a way, she has. Jo's eyes shine, and she stands fast enough to knock over bottles, which roll away with a glass-scraping-on-concrete sound.

"Jo!" Rose jumps up, finally released from the spell of her terrible words, her cousin's name a gasp now that her body is under her control again.

The book falls from her lap, dropping with a heavy thump. If she tries to pick it up, it will be stuck. Like a curse. It will never move again. She reaches for Jo.

"Don't." Jo pulls free and out the door.

"What was–?" Taylor asks, rising, but it's Rose's turn to shrug him off.

She snatches up one of the flashlights near their bags. At the threshold, she almost expects to meet resistance from the line of dark sealing them in. But the door is only a door. Rose switches on the flashlight, bounces the beam across the trees.

"Jo?" Her voice barely reaches past her lips let alone to the path where her cousin must have gone.

Rose sweeps the light again and something jitters between the trees. Her heart jitters in response and she tries to pin the motion, hoping to see her cousin, shoulders hunched in anger, turned away from her. There's nothing there at all. Something trills and *krrrrs* in the dark, almost a chuckle. When Nate touches Rose's shoulder, she can't help but jump.

"She'll be fine. Just give her space to cool off." Nate doesn't push for an explanation, but guilt still clots Rose's throat.

She steps back. Clicks the flashlight off. She listens, hoping for Jo's footsteps, crashing angry through the bush.

Nate's hand on her shoulder guides Rose back inside. She lets him. Nate is right. Jo will be fine. She'll be fine. She just needs a moment, some air, then she'll be back and Rose will explain. It wasn't her. She didn't mean it at all.

Rose jerks upright with a snarled sound like she was choking in her sleep. *Drowning.*

She turns to look at the humped sleeping bag beside her. The way it's twisted around, she can't tell if Jo is inside. She reaches, then lets her hand fall. She tells herself she doesn't want to wake Jo. She's being stupid. Really though, she doesn't want to know. She doesn't want to know for sure if Jo never came back, because that will be her fault too. She drove Jo away, like she drove Theo over the bridge. She can't be responsible for her big cousin too.

Rose crawls to the tent door and unzips it. Nate and Taylor's tent sits across the room. She imagines them snuggled close, Nate's arm slung around Taylor's chest, safe and protected. She feels an irrational stab of jealousy. An irrational loneliness. She's in a haunted house and she wants someone to comfort her, to tell her she isn't really alone.

Her gaze drifts to the window. Something peers in. Rose swallows a shout. A tiny, hunched man, gray and grinning. The statue she saw earlier, come to look inside. Then the shape spreads wings like a cloak and lifts into the air. A heron, just a heron, gliding silently through the dark.

She reaches back into the tent, drags her sleeping bag out. She builds the fire up again and drapes the unzipped sleeping bag around her shoulders. Her eyes ache like she's been crying. Her head aches too – hollow and full.

The book, the one that dropped from her lap earlier, lies where it fell. Rose nudges it with her toe, wanting it to be farther away from her. Part of her hoping a spark will jump from the fire and the book will burn.

"You're up early!" Jo's voice, chipper behind her, startles Rose awake.

She must have dozed by the ashes of the fire. There's a camp mug of coffee beside her foot, poured from the presumably full pot she has no recollection of making.

"You're not—" Rose stops at Jo's quizzical look.

Nothing in her cousin's body language suggests anger. Nothing suggests she slept anywhere other than in their tent, or spent the night stomping through the woods. Rose's mouth dries and she takes a swig of too-hot, too-bitter coffee.

"Never mind." Rose shakes her head and indicates the pot. "I made coffee."

She watches Jo pour, and even manages a neat one-handed catch when Jo tosses her a breakfast bar. The story she told last night, did she really tell it? Rose remembers back in high school how she accidentally ruined one of Jo's favorite sweaters and Jo didn't talk to her for a week. She wouldn't forgive Rose that easily. Then what? Rose thinks of two separate worlds – herself in one, talking to doppelgangers of Jo, Nate, and Taylor, telling a terrible story from a book she didn't read, another version of herself sitting quietly with the real Nate, Taylor, and Jo, enjoying the campfire. The thought makes her skin crawl.

How can she ask without bringing up Theo, without hurting Jo? Nate emerges, sleep tousled, Taylor behind him. The space around the campfire bustles and Rose wants to shake them all. Can they really not see how utterly fucked up this place is, how wrong?

"I thought maybe we should split up, cover more ground?" Taylor plunks down beside her, unwrapping a breakfast bar. He refills her cup when he fills his own and Rose nods, distracted.

Taylor glances back at Nate and flashes him the thumbs up. He lifts his mug. "I'm going to finish this then get started."

"Okay." Rose barely looks at him.

Jo slides into the place Taylor just occupied, bumping Rose with her shoulder so that Rose looks up.

"Seriously, are you okay?" She gestures. "You look...not like you."

Rose can almost feel dark, bruise-like rings under her eyes. Her body is an ill-fitting suit. Maybe she isn't her after all.

"I—" She opens her mouth and is cut off by a terrible sound.

A piercing cry that goes to the heart of her like a bolt and Rose shoots upright, shedding her sleeping bag, running for the door.

"Rose!" Jo calls after her.

Bright sunlight slices Rose's vision and she stops, heart pounding. She waits for the sound to come again, still hearing the echo of it. It's a sound she knows in her bones, one she couldn't stop hearing for days, weeks, months after the river pulled Theo down.

Jo touches her shoulder. Rose swings around, wide-eyed.

"Don't you–?"

But what can she say? Don't you remember the way he cried as we tried to hold his hand? And even with both of them, the current was too strong. Even with both of them, together, both of them issuing the dare, both of them trying to drag him back from their mistake, Rosie was the heartbroken name on his lips as the river stole him.

The sound comes again, closer, and its source, a bird, hops forward, cocking its head. Its bright eye finds Rose like it's making a point. Like it's mocking her. The sound again, high and piercing, but not a child's cry. Then the bird clatters its wings, disappearing against the sun and it's gone.

Rose stands at the window, leaning her upper body over the sill, as if to catch a secret about to be whispered to her.

Tk-tk-tk-tttttt. Krrrrr.

Taylor and Nate split off on their own. She's meant to be filming outside, but she can't make herself step through the door, though she's no safer in here than among the trees.

They shift, almost hypnotically, lulling but not soothing. The light between them is wrong. Umber, like a sunset, but too intense. Like something burning.

Rose shoves herself away from the window, lurches out the door. Her chest tightens, gaze pulled to where she knows the old house used to be. Was there a map in the book she read, or didn't read? She can't remember. There must have been.

The light is only afternoon deep gold, not ruddy, not burning. But even that doesn't make sense. It can't even be noon yet. Except. The outline of her phone presses against her pocket as Rose slides it out with mounting dread. Her photo gallery is open and she forgets to even check the time, scrolling through shots of the trees, videos of herself climbing over fallen logs, shimmying under things, recording all the broken pieces of the island.

She spent the day alone, wandering through the woods taking pictures she doesn't remember. Cataloging the statues - weird, squat shapes like eggs, like coffins. She tagged them in her gallery with names. The Sleepy Goat. The Grumpy Frog. The Gryphon.

Rose pivots, aiming her phone at the trees where the house is and is not. She takes photos and videos both, then shades her screen with a cupped hand. The illusion in the still photographs is faint, but in the video, the way the wind shifts the treetops – even though Rose never feels it down nearer the roots – the branches suggest a roof, gables, a door she could almost step through.

I dare you. I double dare you.

A footstep behind her and Rose drops her phone. She spins to find Jo standing in the door to the compound, looking troubled. A pulse of selfish relief – if Jo feels it too then maybe they can leave. Maybe she's also being haunted and Theo isn't Rose's to carry alone.

Rose scoops her phone up to shove it back in her pocket. A spider-web crack runs across the screen and an edge of the broken glass catches her thumb.

She sucks at the wound and thinks of Theo, standing in the hallway of the rented house, thumb in his mouth, afraid to go to sleep because of what he might dream. Shadows swamped him, making him look small, lost in a tunnel of darkness. Making the hall seem longer, like there was an impossible distance between him and Rose.

She remembers the plate glass window leading out to the deck behind him, more than a doorway, a gate to another world. The lake framed him – sick green-blue like a bruise starting to fade. She could almost believe something under its surface *had* risen up to touch Theo in his sleep, laying its claim on him.

Not a witch or a prehistoric beast, just a sadness, a grief that had found a boy too sweet and trusting, too raw and open to the world. It had crawled inside him like crawling into a wound.

"We should have protected him." It's barely a whisper, but Jo startles as if struck.

"What?"

But Rose sees it in Jo's eyes. She knows.

"We should find Taylor and Nate," Rose says. "We should go."

Jo nods, stunned. This place is bad. It's reaching out to them. They may not be as pure and innocent as Theo, but they are still raw. There are still spaces for the ghosts to get inside.

"Come on." Rose grabs Jo's hand, tight, tight, tight. She has no intention of ever letting go.

She pulls Jo behind her, onto the path, leading away from the compound. A cloud chooses its moment to cross the sun, and they're somewhere else – polished wood floors, crown molding, plaster medallions, and buttery wallpaper dripping down the walls. Rose moves faster. They have to get out.

"Nate?" Jo calls. "Taylor?"

The green swallows the names. Crown shyness. The words pop into Rose's mind – the way trees give each other space, so the sky looks like a river dividing them. Except when she looks up the green is solid; she can't tell where one tree ends and another begins.

Don't look up. The opposite of Theo stepping onto the slick, swaying bridge and Rose promising it would be okay. *Just don't look down.* The swollen river rushing below, an arm snaked free from that fathomless green lake haunting Theo's dreams, just waiting to snatch him away.

The Monkey Standing on Its Head should be just there around the bend, but when they round the corner it's…*wrong.* The statue is different, its face shifted. It looks more like a man now, a leering court jester.

They change their faces. We didn't put the statues here, they were always here. They move, and their faces are different sometimes.

That was in the book too, wasn't it? She'd read that somewhere in the swollen pages. She should go back, for the book, for their supplies. No. They should run. She and Jo, hand in hand. But they can't leave Nate and Taylor behind.

She watches for the Pelican with Its Beak Under Its Wing, but what she sees sliding through the edges of her vision is something else entirely. Rose digs her heels in, wanting to look and not wanting to look. Jo pulls ahead, now leading her, until she stops so suddenly Rose crashes into her.

"Oh." A single exhalation of breath.

It's a moment before Rose sees what Jo sees, longer before she can even begin to make sense of it. Her eyes and brain duke it out, trying to piece the picture together. It won't piece.

Nate crashes through the trees from the opposite direction. He stops as suddenly as Jo did, mouth open, eyes wide. They all stare. At Taylor.

Taylor is at the crossing and branching of several paths. *Folded.* There's no better word Rose can think of to describe it. Pieces of Taylor are tucked inside that should be outside, all of him made to occupy a much smaller space than should be humanly possible.

"Ah fuck. Fuuuuuck." The word becomes a howl, a sound of grief and Nate lunges toward Taylor, but Rose breaks free of Jo's grip to hold him back.

She doesn't know what will happen if he touches Taylor, like whatever folded him might be a communicable disease.

"Don't." Rose tries to hold him, tries to hug him, even though her eyes sting too.

Nate shoves her away, hard, eyes red and burning.

"Fuck!" He kicks the leaf litter. Punches the nearest tree and swears again. "We can't just leave him."

The words are so helpless and Rose hears them doubled, in Nate's voice and in Jo's, but the way Jo sounded at twelve years old.

We have to go back. We can't just leave him.

And Rose's answer: *We have to get help. We can't. There's nothing we can do.*

Sobbing. Choking on breath and tears and holding Jo's hand, dragging her away from the river. To get help. Not to flee Theo's anguished screams. His mouth and eyes dark smudges in his face as he disappeared.

It's not my fault. I didn't. I didn't. I did.

"Should we?" Jo's voice is soft, catching. Rose hears the words her cousin doesn't say: *bury him.* "We can't leave him like this?"

Rose wants to say they need to get the fuck out of here, there's nothing they can do, but a weight drags at her, a small, insistent hand, river-cold, pulling her to stay. She moves, an awkward sideways crab shuffle toward Taylor. Jo is right. She's always been right. They can't just leave him.

Rose touches him, the barest pressure of fingers against Taylor's shoulder. She isn't sure what to expect. That he'll tip over? That he'll unfold? That something will change so they no longer have to look at the horrifying thing he's become.

He doesn't move. Not an inch. It's like shoving solid stone. Like something rooted in the ground. Not placed, grown, as though this is where Taylor has always been. Rose pushes again. Nate grabs her wrist, grip crushing hard for a moment, the sorrow-red in his eyes a glare full of hurt, full of anger that needs somewhere to go. Rose bows her head.

He lets her arm go roughly, shoving it away. He turns to Taylor and wraps his arms around him. The shape is wrong and Nate rocks them both, as if he could rock Taylor free, but he's the only one who moves. His muscles strain and he screams again, but there's nothing, nothing he can do. In the end, he buries his face against what is no longer Taylor's shoulder and sobs.

"We should go." It's barely a whisper, but Rose turns around. She says it again. She pushes Jo, turns her forcefully on the path and shoves her cousin ahead of her.

"But—" Jo stumbles and her words break as Rose shoves her again.

Jo's mouth, her eyes, are shocked smudges in her face. She looks over Rose's shoulder, at Nate, at his grief. He's drowning in it, the green, and there's nothing they can do.

"I know," Rose says. "I know."

And she pushes Jo again. She won't let her stay behind. A hollowness gnaws at her with teeth like green leaves, chewing their way out in concentric circles, leaving her empty inside. Taylor was a friend. Nate is a friend. She'll mourn them later. All she feels now is numb. They need to leave. She cannot let Jo go.

The forest screams. Rose pushes Jo again and again, hauls her up when she slips and bangs her knee hard, ignores her and keeps shoving when Jo tries to push past her, to go back, to wade into the green. A sound like cicadas droning and a mosquito's whine and the wind hushing all at once roars in Rose's ears. Jo's face is a mess, blotchy from crying. When Rose allows herself to glance back, even knowing she should not, she catches sight of Nate – of what she thinks might be Nate – crouched in the doorway formed between two trees. His head to one side, his knees jutting up at sharp angles, his arms dangling too long between them. Like the Grumpy Frog, but made of skin and bone.

The sight pulls the breath from her lungs, cracks her ribs and makes it impossible to breathe in again. Run. Keep running. Nate turns his head to track them. It makes Rose think of an owl. He'll twist his neck all the way around. Like Taylor, folded and folded. Tears blind her as she stumbles on.

"Have you ever thought about how you can't really see into the green?" The flatness of Jo's tone startles her.

Despite pushing her cousin ahead of her, Rose had almost forgotten she was there. It doesn't sound like her cousin at all. She almost glances back again, almost looks to see if Jo is behind her with Nate and Taylor, framed by the doorway of an impossible house.

Just the thought disorients her for a moment, as if she has turned back, and then Jo is planted on the path in front of her, turned away, shoulders hunched. Rose steps around her. She needs to see her cousin's face, and she's afraid of what she'll find. Is it Jo? Does Jo have that scar there, just off center on her top lip? Were her eyes always that shade?

"It's like deep water," Jo says. "You can't see under the surface, but anything could be there, waiting."

The signs of grief and fear have been erased from Jo's face. Her cheeks are smooth, like stone worn by too many hands, by years of rain.

Rose does the only thing she can think to do. She rears back, doesn't give herself time to doubt, and punches her cousin right in the face. Crimson blood spurts and Jo makes a choking sound, staggering back. It's enough, she's moving again and that's all that matters. Rose doesn't have time for mercy. She grabs Jo's wrists when she tries to put her hands to her wounded face and drags her toward the shore. What she hopes is the shore.

The trees sing, a high and piercing sound. The leaves sway and fracture the light and Rose feels something too big – like a breath, like a sob – rising in her chest and threatening to break her wide.

She's running, with Jo's hand in hers, stumbling with branches and leaves whipping at her skin, the trees trying to close the path up like a zipper around them. She's running with her cousin's hands in hers, except it's Theo's hand too as they pelt toward the water. If Rose can manage not to look back, then he will be there behind her, and Jo too, all of them fleeing together this time.

Their feet pound the earth. Three sets of footfalls, not two. She has to drag his ghost out of here with them, keep carrying him as long as she's alive. She can't leave him behind, as much as she might wish she could. Guilt doesn't work that way, grief either.

Roots twist across the dirt, trying to trip them. Overhead and behind, leaves rattle. Just ahead, a break in the green. Water glinting in the sunlight. Rose almost sobs in relief.

Then something jerks her backward, her arm wrenched at the shoulder, and she skids to a halt. Jo stands frozen at the edge of the green.

"Jo." Rose is breathless, can't form any words beyond her cousin's name.

"I can't." Jo shakes her head. More tears stream down her cheeks, she looks terrified. "I can't."

"Just step forward. Just…" Rose holds out her hand.

Don't look down.

Jo shakes her head again. She looks down, and Rose follows her gaze, expecting to see vines or roots or leaves tangled around her cousin's feet. There's nothing. Only an invisible tide, dragging them both backward, a river come to sweep them away.

Kek-kek-kek-krrrrrr. The trees snicker their victory.

"Please. Don't leave me." Jo's arms hang slack by her side.

The green crowds closer, or Jo is farther away, the space between the woods and the shore folding. Shadows swamp her even though the sun is piercing bright now, even though the island is burning, everything on fire. Just behind Jo, Rose sees Theo, lost against the trees. A worn shape, barely even human. Smooth. Like an egg. Like a tomb. There's a crack in his skin, something terrible hidden inside.

The shore's mud sucks at Rose's feet. Theo shifts, impatient, waiting to see what she'll do.

"Rose." A creaking sound, not like Jo's voice at all – even though her lips move – like branches in the wind.

Rose snaps her attention back to Jo's face, her gaze still pleading. She's never seen Jo this frightened before, except…

"Do you remember, when Theo was little and he burned his hands trying to help us build a fire?" Rose swallows around the words; they hurt. She keeps her gaze on Jo's face, ignoring the shadow at the edge of the trees, at the corner of her eye. Theo isn't really there. There's nothing she can do.

"Rose, what—"

Rose ignores her, goes on. They've never really talked about this, about that day, the bridge, the river, the dare.

"Aunt Ellie was so mad, but she didn't want to yell at us, so our moms did. Remember? We were grounded for a week. We were his big cousins, and we were supposed to look out for him. He always wanted to do everything we did, even if it was stupid and dangerous, even if he was scared."

The wind in the trees sounds like humming, like a thousand insects chewing all at once. A green tide, a river.

"Do you remember?" Rose hears her voice, desperate, hitching.

"I remember, Rose." Jo's voice is a whisper, very far away.

The wind picks up, whipping leaves from the trees, cutting sharp. All the people who lived here, they're still here. Rose feels them, crowding close. If they stay another moment, their hands, their voices, will fold her and fold her, infinitely small. The statues will change their faces. The green will swallow them whole.

"Why did we let Theo come with us? We knew he was too little. We should have made him stay behind."

"He was scared of the lake." Jo's voice breaks. "He was scared. We couldn't leave him alone."

The hum is inside Rose now, the scream. She is too small to contain all the things nested within and any moment now, they will break free.

"We dared him. It was like something else was in my throat, but…" Rose's voice breaks now too. "But not really. I don't know. It was my fault."

The words are like a dam breaking, everything rushing out, but it doesn't feel good. The water, the grief, the green, pouring out of her endlessly. It will never stop.

"If it's your fault, then it's my fault too." Jo's voice is raw, shaking.

She's too far for Rose to reach, and she's right there. She stretches out her hand.

"Rose, please." Jo's voice fades under the buzz, under the hum, under the green.

Rose throws her arms around Jo. She wraps her and she pulls and this time, she won't let go. The green is a sucking current. It fights her and the trees chitter and laugh and scream and Rose screams right back, a wordless sound that leaves her throat scraped bloody.

Then somehow, she and Jo are on the dock. They're falling into the boat. Rose looks back at the island, at the trees, all of their leaves shaking and shaking around a house aflame.

Rose feels herself there, the walls around her – the crown molding and the polished floors. Did she step through the door? Is she here or there? Which one is her?

The boat's engine roars, the sound punching Rose's chest, starting her heart up again. She sits hard and the boat lurches, Jo steering wildly so they almost crash right back into the dock. But at the last moment, she jerks the wheel and they shear through the water, sending up a spray.

Rose expects the trees to haul them back, the island to block them somehow. For a moment, it feels as though they're caught in the water, not moving even as Jo opens the throttle all the way.

Then time snaps forward, and Rose hears a *tsking* behind them, a disappointed sound. She looks back, though she shouldn't. The trees are right down on the shore, the dock invisible. The scent of smoke drifts toward them. If she looks any closer, she'll see a house where the compound stands. She'll see bodies, long and tall and glowing pale, making the trees bend without wind. She'll see a small, smudged shadow, mouth open to wail her name.

At the wheel, Jo turns, but it isn't the island she's looking back at, it's Rose. There's something in Jo's eyes like fear. Rose opens her mouth. She wants to apologize. She wants to say they share the burden. That it will be okay. Don't look back, don't look down.

But her throat only clicks, a dry, rattling sound. Underneath her skin, leaves hush and whisper among themselves, and over the din of them, Rose can't say anything at all.

Bb MINOR
or The Suicide Choir: An Oral History

GEMMA FILES

B major: harsh and plaintive
B minor: solitary and melancholic
Bb major: magnificent and joyful
Bb minor: obscure and terrible

— Key and mode descriptions from Marc-Antoine Charpentier's
Regles des Composition, ca. 1682

KAYLA PRATT, HELP-LINE VOLUNTEER

Tell me about the call.

How it happened was, I was volunteering on the Keep It Street-Safe vandalism tip-line, the one they set up to find out who's been knocking out all the RESCU cameras in the area around where King Street East turns into Cherry Street, past Front Street down to Lake-shore—you know, that big development where they're building what's gonna be called the Canary District. Red light cameras mainly, but they've also knocked down a couple of traffic monitoring cameras, some ATM cameras ... it's like they're trying to turn the whole area into one big dead spot. It's hard enough to get an idea of what's happening down there anyhow, because it's pretty much either construction sites or a whole lot of old, semi-industrial spaces like the areas under the Gardiner Expressway, buildings no one's bothered to demolish yet.

I didn't get the call myself, because I was monitoring for control that night, but I saw out of the corner of my eye that Sam seemed to be having trouble, so I cut in, took it over. It took a minute to figure out what was going on, because it was two people and they were talking really quietly, whispering right up close to the phone, like they were afraid somebody was going to hear them. There was a lot of echo, a lot of noise; they told me they were in a bathroom, but I could hear stuff coming in through the walls too, like people singing, or—you know that thing really hardcore Baptists do, like at that church up near Pearson International Airport? Speaking in tongues—glossolalia, they call it. It was like that, but singing. Singing in tongues.

These people, these *girls,* they sounded really young, like kids. One of them had a bad cough, really wet, rattling in her chest. The other one sounded stronger, but her voice was still so hoarse I could barely make out what she was saying.

What was she saying?
Uh, like…"Help us, please send help, we need somebody. Our Moms are going to die, the Mouth says they have to do it to themselves. She says everybody has to." Just like that, over and over again. She never stopped. Not even when the phone cut out.

Didn't you think maybe it was a prank? I mean—
—if it was real, why didn't they call 911? Yeah, that's what my boss wanted to know, too. "Why would they call *us,* Kayla?" Like I could give a fuck about *that* question, right then… not that I said it out loud, obviously. Not like *that,* anyway.

Because you believed the call—the callers.
You'd've believed it too, if *you'd* heard it.

I have, actually. The recording.
Oh yeah, okay. Well—she sounded pretty fucking convincing, right? Like they were both scared out of their minds, like they were gonna start crying any minute: A hostage situation, somebody being held against their will, maybe a bunch of people being coerced into…murder, suicide?

Mass suicide?

(PAUSE)

Minute I heard the one with the cough talking like that, I knew we needed to kick this up to somebody who was a lot better equipped to deal with it than us.

The Emergency Task Force.

That's what they're there for.

ETF STAFF SERGEANT ARSHAN NAJI, SPECIAL WEAPONS TEAM SUPERVISOR AND NEGOTIATOR, TORONTO POLICE SERVICES

Tell me about what happened next.

Well, we couldn't get a hold of the landlord immediately, because it was a weekend, but the building manager said they'd been there since before she applied for the job; it was a condo, fully paid off, and the owner lived there, along with a bunch of her friends. Zusann Groff, that was the owner's name—and she was a lawyer, too, so there was nothing they could do to force them out, not even with the occasional complaint about noise or overcrowding ... well, *suspected* overcrowding. Nobody really knew *how* many friends Groff was cohabiting with, exactly, 'til we got inside.

Why not?

Because pandemic, that's why not. Remember how fast people started inviting other people over, basically the minute they could prove they got vaccinated? No big parties, just keep it to one or two at a time? Well, it took a pretty long time for Groff's neighbours to figure out none of the people coming to "visit" ever actually left, especially when we went into that second lockdown, the Rho variant scare one. She was the only person who ever came and went, the only one anybody actually *saw*—when you knocked on the door, she was the only one who ever answered. But when you live close by you can tell when there's people next door, even when they're hardly talking to each other, at least not very loud; lots of moving around, lots of flushing the toilet. An incredible amount of food deliveries. And that was a long time before choir practice started up.

Choir practice?
That's what Groff's nearest neighbour called it, uh...Ada Sagao. Groff was the last unit on that floor, down a little hallway, just past the stairs; Sagao was right around the corner, but she could hear it through her bedroom wall. She was working out of her home, like everybody else— said she asked Groff and her guests not to do whatever they were doing in the evenings, so she could sleep, but then they started doing it in the mornings instead, which woke her up way too early and gave her panic attacks. Then she asked Groff if she could maybe not do it every day, and Groff said they had to, because they had something coming up—Sagao thought it was a performance of some kind, but when we interviewed her later on, she couldn't say for sure Groff ever really called it that. So Sagao complained to the manager, and Groff told the manager she'd do something about it, make alterations that'd help them keep it down.

Did she?
Brought a bunch of guys in, almost immediately. They worked quick. Things did get quieter after that.
(PAUSE)
Until we showed up, I guess.

ADA SAGAO, COMPUTER TECHNICIAN

Tell me what Zusann Groff's choir sounded like.
I don't know if it was a choir, as such. Not officially.
It's...hard to describe. Singing, I guess. If you could call it that.

What else would you call it?
I'm not a music expert. All I know is, it was disturbing. It disturbed me. And—no, forget it.

What were you going to say?

Well...afterwards, when I read about it in the papers, they said there were thirteen people living next door to me; the woman who owned the place—Zusann—plus twelve others. Which is crazy in and of itself, really, considering how small these units are, but...whenever they started singing, it always sounded like more. Like, a lot more.

Was it always the same song?

"Song..." (LAUGHS) Yeah, I guess it was, eventually. I mean...yeah, after a while they'd hit something that sounded...familiar. It always felt the same, somehow. Like—

Like what?

Like—cold, and high, and lonely. Awful. Like everybody was singing in two different keys, two different voices. And one went so low it droned, and the other went so far up it—yelped, shrieked? But it was still music, somehow. And sometimes, when they hit that pitch...sometimes...it was like they weren't even human, anymore.

(PAUSE)

You ever hear of Nusrat Fateh Ali Khan? Sufi devotional singer, did some stuff with Peter Gabriel, back in the nineties? He sang qawwali, this incredible stuff full of yearning and heartbreak, pure vocal pyrotechnics. I think it's supposed to sound like you're in love with God.

Okay.

Seriously, Google him, it's worth it. Well...this was like the opposite of that.

Could you make out any words?

Most times I don't think it even had words. Not by the end.

I heard you recorded some of it.

Not me, no. My friend, Kika—she's a musicologist. You'd have to ask her.

Can I have her contact information?

Uh...sure.

ETF STAFF SERGEANT ARSHAN NAJI

Initially there was some back and forth over right to enter, but we were finally able to push through on the idea of child welfare endangerment. I mean, "push through" sounds like we were doing something shady, but it was a legitimate concern—the threat sounded imminent, plus we didn't have any sort of idea how long we had before things were likely to kick off, just the phone call itself and a whole lot of weird noise from inside the unit.

The choir.
The singing, yes. That was already going when we got there. It never stopped.
    (PAUSE)
    So we knocked, asked for Ms Groff, called through the door that we were there to run a welfare; no response. Repeated it three times, asked for permission to enter: still no response. Eventually, the Crown got a warrant to us, and we were able to move forward.

How so?
We tried negotiation first, obviously—opening channels, etcetera—but...basically, they just ignored us. Kept on singing, louder and louder, to the point where we thought we heard screaming. That's when I gave the order to breach.

Was there any resistance?
No. It was a clean entry, minimal damage. Nobody anywhere near the door. We cleared the place room by room, without incident: Kitchen, living space, one bathroom, two bedrooms. The place was spare, totally stripped down, barely any furniture left. Both bedrooms were nothing but Ikea bunk-beds—that's where we expected to find the kids, hopefully alive.

And did you?

No. There weren't any kids, turned out. There never had been. It was just...somebody, a couple of somebodies, pretending, I guess. I hear some of Groff's friends used to be actors.

Why would they have done that?

Basically? I think to get us to come over and break in on them, in the first place.

(PAUSE)

Anyhow, we were stumped there for a few minutes, still couldn't figure out where the singing was coming from—not until we checked the floor-plan, saw the unit used to have two bathrooms.

The alterations.

That's right. They'd knocked everything out, made a whole new room, hid it behind a fake wall at the back of bedroom number two. It probably used to be an en suite.

So that's where they all were? Thirteen people?

Yes, it was pretty tight, especially with the soundproofing. And it must've been just loud as hell for them in there, too, considering...I mean, we could hear it all the way outside, like I said, right through the front door. Once we got in, it was just—at what seemed like *assaultive* levels of volume, even with all our gear, the noise we were making ourselves: Flash-bangs on entry, yelling, what have you. Made you want to...

Staff Sergeant?

Excuse me.

(PAUSE)

It was my second-in-command who spotted the hinges, so we could open it up that way; if there was a lock on the outside, we never found it. We went in with halligan bars, tore up the plaster, knocked out the pins. It sprang open pretty quick, right at the same time the singing stopped...I *think* that's when it was. It was definitely over when we saw—what was in there.

Who. Was in there.

Ms. Groff?

Her, sure. Along with everybody else.

(PAUSE)

When we opened the door at last, pried it open, there was this... you know that kind of noise when you open a can of coffee? Vacuum sealed? It was like that. And then this rush of cold coming out, *intense*, like the dead of winter. Cold enough to crisp your ass-hairs. Plus this rush of...

Well, I know it sounds insane, but...air. Coming in past us. Almost strong enough to knock me off balance.

(PAUSE)

I don't think I ever told anybody that before.

Casualties?

Not by our hands, ma'am.

WINSTON JONAS, PARAMEDIC

Oh my God, man, you don't even know. I never saw anything like that, and I've seen a lot, like, a *lot*. Enough so's I can't sleep without medication, you get me? Yeah, it was bad.

Can you give me details?

I'd rather not. But that's what you came to me for, right? Yeah, you and everybody else.

(PAUSE)

So there was this secret room at the back, flush to the wall, no windows. They'd built it themselves. Had no lighting inside it. Just a triangular, black space—totally black, I mean like they'd painted it black themselves: The walls, the floor, the ceiling, all covered in this foam stuff with a layer of black paint slopped over it, for soundproofing. Thirteen adult human beings crammed in there, all standing with barely enough room to breathe, all staring upwards and singing, apparently, *real* loud. I don't know how they could bear it.

Why do you think they—?

Not my business. Not my job. I leave that to the experts.

Which ones?

Ones that specialize in *crazy,* lady. You feel me?

I do.

Uh huh. So—they were all dead when we got there, probably since ETF popped the door. I mean, they must've been, right? Because of the singing. Glad I didn't have to hear any of *that* shit, I can tell you.

They were so close-packed, we had to take them out one by one, lay them down on the body-bags and zip them up for transport. FIS Scenes of Crime needed to get in, take their samples. But we pretty much knew how they'd gone out, after the first few. Cyanosed lips, petechial haemorrhaging, orbital distension, second-degree burns over all the exposed skin—but not heat burns. *Cold* burns. Only thing came to mind at the time was, maybe if you drowned them all in liquid nitrogen, all at once, like they do to flash-freeze fancy snacks…

But that obviously couldn't have been feasible.

Yeah, no shit. I mean, later I did think of something else, but—

But?

. . . Hard vacuum. Decompression. Except even straight vacuum doesn't freeze you right away, you know? No air in space, so no, what's it called, convection. Whatever took the air out of that room took all the heat out of it as well, and out of everyone in it.

Still no fucking idea how.

MUSICOLOGIST KIKA RIOS

Tell me how you got involved.

I was brought in to analyze the Choir's…work, I guess. Their style.

By whom?

By Ada—Ms. Sagao, their neighbour. We've been friends for a couple of years; we met in a community choir ourselves, ironically, a downtown women's group. Stayed in touch over Zoom after rehearsals shut down. So one night I actually heard them over Ada's speakers, and I said, "What the hell is *that?*" and Ada told me the story. Well, I was fascinated, on a professional level.

"You tell me," Ada said. "Is that even music?"

"Oh, I think so," I told her.

I asked if I could hear more. "Come over," she said, "pretty much anytime, and just wait. You can't miss it."

So as soon as I'd got my latest booster and was clear to go into other homes again, I went over to Ada's place, ran some recordings, then took them home and tried to figure it out.

How would you summarize your findings?

Well, I—oh, can I ask? Am I going to get in trouble, for the recordings? Privileged communications, or something?

At this point, that seems...unlikely.

Okay. Good. Well, I recorded like three hours' worth over a couple of nights, then processed it through my editing suite. Have you listened to it yet?

No. I was hoping to.

I'll send you some files. It's...just *insanely* complicated. The base is done in the same atonal style you get in throat-singing, or death metal, where it's all about speed and force and the harmonics are accidental at best, all percussion and dissonance. Syncopation, speed riffs, ululation like you get in tribal music. But then they'd layer in some operatic tremolo, real Mozart's Queen of the Night aria stuff, combined with sounds like gongs and flutes and kanglings, and they'd punctuate it with roars and shrieks. Very...animalistic.

Were there lyrics?

Uh, yeah. In the beginning, most of what you heard were actually vocables, stuff that just sounds like language: you know, like "doo wah diddy, diddy dum diddy doo." But other stuff turned out to be real phrases in weird, archaic languages—I had to get a university colleague to identify some of it. He said he recognized Sanskrit, Aramaic, plus some other thing he thought might be actual Proto-Indo-European. And some he didn't recognize at all.

Could he translate any of it?
It wasn't clear enough, no matter how I cleaned it up. Or—that's what he said. Thinking about it now, maybe...I mean, it was just this look I caught on his face, but I wonder if, maybe—he understood more than he said. Just enough to, uh...know he didn't want to understand the rest?

I don't know. That could just be me.

One thing you have to understand, though, is...I'm making the Choir's work sound like just random chaotic noise? But it wasn't. It was very carefully structured. Like, Bach-level complexity. Deeper, even. At full volume in that tiny space, it must have sounded like a cross between a battlefield and a voodoo ritual. Those decibel levels, that close-quarters vibration, it's almost...well, it's the kind of thing they're trying to make directed-energy weapons out of. The kind of thing that induces religious ecstasies. Altered states. Hysteria.

If that woman, Zusann Groff, if she wrote and arranged that herself, then she was either the biggest musical genius I've ever run across, or she was completely psychotic. Or both.

"Both" sounds about right.
Yeah. I mean, given.

HAL KASHIGIAN, FORENSIC PSYCHOLOGIST

Tell me how you got involved.
I was contacted by Zusann Groff's mother, Akela Halloway. She wanted...to understand, I suppose. How this could have happened.

"This."
The Suicide Choir.

Hm. And how did it?
You want my report, basically? Well, it's true that privilege doesn't apply, not with Ms Halloway *or* Ms Groff—they were never my patients, nor did I ever sign any non-disclosure agreement. I always make it very clear to clients that in order to make an assessment after the fact, I have to be free to use whatever evidence I gather or conclusions I reach in my own work later on, and Ms Halloway had no problems with that. So...

(PAUSE)

...all right, then.

The Choir didn't leave any sort of testament, no bible, no diaries. Zusann Groff was their host, which probably made her their leader, but that "Mouth" epithet, in the initial hot-line call? Much like the implication there were children in danger inside the unit, this appears to have been fiction. Groff didn't re-name herself, or give herself a title; she was no Shoko Asahara waiting to happen, any more than the Choir was Aum Shinrikyo. The only people they ever seem to have threatened were themselves.

Though she trained as a lawyer, Groff had always been interested in music. She was what you'd call an auto-didact on the subject. In particular, she was fascinated by the idea that some vocal musical performers could produce not only emotional effects on their listeners but also physical effects on the world around them: opera singers hitting notes so high they shatter glass, for example, or the theory that certain vibrational frequencies can cause hallucinations—the "fear frequency," they call it. How a standing wave of 19 hertz in the infrasound decibel range, right below the bottom end of human hearing, can make people feel like they're either seeing ghosts, or about to see a ghost.

What do you mean?
Don't worry, we'll get there.

In or around November 2019, Zusann Groff first began advertising for participants in a "musical experiment." She auditioned over a hundred people, picking twelve: Lila Dabney, William Rhoads, Jenny

Birthwell, Myung-Jin Heo, Holt Werkheim, Sarai Goshen, Morgan Morrison, Alena Rostova, Tegan List, Geza Heliot, Michael Young, and Victoria Spurling.

Why those people? What did they have in common?
They could all sing? And they took Groff seriously, too, I can only assume—that would have been the real deal-sealer. They believed in what she was trying to do.

They wanted to see ghosts.
In the beginning, maybe. But later on…

Anyhow: the Choir members all met in a common space at Birthwell's condo, up until Toronto citizens were asked to socially distance themselves as of March 2020, and meeting publicly became impossible. As the government's plans to deal with the global COVID-19 pandemic became more and more restrictive, they were physically separated, yet drew emotionally closer. They rehearsed by Zoom, continuing to work on the music they'd been developing. Each became the subject of noise complaints from within their various buildings.

At some point, however, something happened. What, exactly? Again, hard to tell. We only know the results.

They started moving in with Groff.
Yes. They moved in, one by one; they committed to the next phase. And so, by degrees, they changed from a choir—a community—into a cult.

Is that what they were?
What else? A cult doesn't start out like a massive pyramid scheme, you know, or a super-church—a cult can be a family, an office…thirteen friends in a condo who build themselves a windowless room, pack themselves in like sardines, sing until they pass out. All that's required is that they believe something for which they have no immediate proof.

They didn't leave anything behind, though, like you said. So—how can we know what they believed?

We can't, not thinking normally. So the only way we can try and reproduce their train of thought is by thinking, um...*ab*normally, metaphorically, poetically. Magically.

Magical thinking?
Of course. Like any other religion. Doing the same thing over and over, absolutely believing you'll get a different result from the one that logic, science, the basic rules of physics say you will—I mean, that's *faith,* isn't it? That's the very definition.

Most religious conversions still need some kind of catalyzing experience, though.
Sure, absolutely. These were people whose image of the world had already been undermined by Groff, her ideas, the possibilities of impossibility. And then things start to change all around them, without warning—a pandemic, a plague, "alternative facts," Fake News. Panic, depression, zealotry on all sides, and they realize they have no power to affect any of it, no power over anything but themselves. So they did what they thought they had to, and believed whatever made those choices sound ... well, not *logical,* exactly, at least to anybody outside the magic circle. But inside...
  (PAUSE)
Tell me that doesn't sound at least a *little* familiar.

But it's...ridiculous, isn't it? To think that—
Think what? That horse de-wormer cures COVID? That pedophile Jewish vampires who secretly run the world keep stables full of kids they torture for their adrenochrome? That if you only stand in a closet and sing long enough, hard enough, a door will open in the ceiling—a door to somewhere else, *anywhere* else? Because given the current situation, "anywhere else"...no matter how unspecific...starts to look pretty fucking good.

All of that, yes.
Hey, don't tell my uncle. Without QAnon to fall back on, he'd probably drink himself to death inside of a week.

How does...something like this start, though?

How does anything? Someone got an idea—Groff, probably; she heard a voice, or she had a dream, or whatever. And she told two friends, and they told two friends, and so on...it spread like a meme, because everyone she told was equally afraid of the same things she was afraid of. Fear makes for fertile soil.

Look, these were lonely people, just like the rest of us. They wanted to get together and do something special—like church, like bowling, like a mosh pit. Remember going to clubs, how stacked it used to get? Swaying on the dance-floor, like a single huge, giant hug? Breathing in each other's breath as you sang along to whatever was playing?

Yeah, I'm old, I get it; I lived through AIDS, kid. When everything—everyone—you love is suddenly infectious, you have to choose your options, take your chances.

Not every kind of worship is summed up by a monk praying in a cell; not every kind *can* be. People need to touch, to share, even if all they share is the same delusion, even if it's something that could kill them. If staying alive means letting go of human contact entirely, then what's the fucking point?

They're dead now, though. That's the point.

Is it? Maybe. Maybe.

(PAUSE)

Do you know there was a deadman's catch on the inside of the hidden room's door, rigged to open if whoever was closest to it went slack? Heo was a contractor; she probably designed it. So I don't think they were looking to die, necessarily. Just...

Why didn't the door come open when what happened—happened, then?

Maybe it would have, if Naji's team hadn't broken in.

Oh, and one more thing. Did you know the Choir all had retinal damage that *pre-dated* their death injuries? The same kind of damage they all showed afterwards, but less of it—little dots just over the pupil, tiny sections of intense degradation, seared there by extreme cold. If you look at them close up, very close up indeed, they look like little galaxies.

Which means ... ?

No idea.

Listen, you're an adult—I'm sure you've already noticed none of this "means" much at all, in context. A lot of times, life...and death... seems utterly inexplicable, to the point of cruelty. Like: "This was just a thing that happened, make of it what you will." Whatever the Choir ended up with, is it any better than what we're left with, or worse? A dying earth and a plague in progress, melting ice-sheets, rising water-levels? Dead fish, bleached-out coral, garbage islands?

So I'll tell you what I told Ms Halloway, if a little more bluntly: I can tell *what* I think happened, but not why...never why. Because if any of us are looking for answers, one way or the other, I think we're going to end up disappointed.

So you don't know why they contacted the hot-line, then. Why NFT was brought in.

...My best guess? Witnesses.

Witnesses?

Even bible-less cults want to proselytize.

YOUR HEART IS A HOUSE ON FIRE

NADIA BULKIN

I met my first ghost when I was sixteen, at the Harper Hotel. When she was alive she'd been Francine Forrester, a banker's wife, but I never met Mrs. Forrester. I met the Blue Lady, and it was the Blue Lady who saved my life.

I'd come to the hotel with my so-called friends – Katrina, Bell, I don't remember the others – not because I wanted to go to the college party they'd heard about but because I was already in the car with them, speeding down Highway 9, and I was so numb that it was easier to let myself be dragged along by whatever current I happened to be in than try to figure out what I actually wanted to do. Where I wanted to go. Who I wanted to be. Mostly, I wanted to be dead.

I was agitated at the party. Where my heart should have been pumping with excitement, I only felt a slowly smoldering burn. I ground ice cubes between my teeth, thought about tearing the skin off my hands, until Katrina dragged me into the hallway and said I was being a huge bitch to some guy who was trying to talk to me. I didn't want to go back inside at all after that.

Down the sixth floor hallway was an open door exuding a soft light. It was the moon, I soon saw, hanging in the center of the balcony like an engorged firefly. Like an invitation.

It can take years for a smoldering fire to burn itself out. Centuries even. That's what I was thinking about as I crossed the padded carpet of room 616 and stepped onto the balcony: how long I would have to endure my existence. Ninety years? It sounded like hell.

I leaned over the railing, enough for vertigo to start pounding my head – and that was a relief, because at least I was feeling *something* – and then I felt something else. Something special. Presence. That's what the ghosthunting community calls the combination of sensations caused by being in the company of something that is not alive but projects a force as if it might be. The psychic itch when someone's got eyes on you, except these eyes aren't blinking anymore. A mix of barometric pressure and electric buzz. It was coming from behind me.

Most people think that the dead crave life, and that is why their presence makes you feel so exhausted. But the Blue Lady standing in the doorway didn't look hungry, exactly. She looked sad. At first her milky eyes seemed fixed on me, but as she floated forward, passing straight through the bed, I realized that she was looking past me, toward the moon and the night and the emptiness. She wanted the same relief I did. Except she actually went for it. Rushed toward the balcony and tumbled like an Olympic diver over the edge. I just happened to be in the way.

I'd later learn that the Blue Lady had a path that I was in, that she had jumped off the balcony of 616 to end her time as Francine Forrester and transform into something timeless. All I knew was that I saw color when she heaved herself through me. Not just the royal blue of her dress but the red of blood, the yellow of wheat – an entire rainbow burst in my throat. And I felt *life*. Imagine a wave that doesn't break around you but actually washes your bones. Imagine how light you'd feel. Imagine how ready you'd be, to float off the earth itself.

And I didn't want to be dead anymore. For about a week, anyway.

Bell found me sitting on the balcony of 616 after noticing that I wasn't at the party.

"Please don't tell anyone," I said, because I wasn't ready for everyone to know how unfixable I was. I even managed to cry a little – forced the turmoil up out of my smoldering chest cavity and into the open, so Bell would know it was real. She promised to keep it quiet.

But she did tell my mother, and my mother took me to a doctor. I didn't mind taking an antidepressant every night before bed – I could

pretend I was healing myself in my sleep – but I didn't like my therapist. She was a Very Nice Lady in the new part of town whose light oak
bookshelves and sporty little children seemed too far removed from my
reality to take seriously. Not that my attempts at recreating the relief I'd
gotten from the Blue Lady worked either. Because that was what it was,
really, *relief*, an absence of pain, the momentary lightness of not having
to carry a body in a constant state of ache. Neither the hypercoasters
at Cedar Point nor bungee jumping at the local gorge helped for more
than a fraction of a second.

"Have you ever seen a ghost?" I started asking, whenever I got
bored. I asked classmates, sales clerks, delivery guys. Only my aunt
– my mother's sister – ever said yes. "A little old man," she said, "who
lived in the attic. I don't think he was a *bad* man."

I still saw Katrina now and then, though only from a distance.
We exchanged fake smiles from across the hallway, wished each other
"good breaks" and "good lucks" until the world beyond our high school
swallowed us. But I never spoke to Bell again. Her betrayal saw to that.

I started doing paranormal investigations in college. My mother made
me promise I'd go to Club Day, and of course I gravitated to the only
table that had a big cartoon ghost on display. "Have you ever seen a
ghost?" the boy behind the table asked, offering me a smile and a little
BOO! pin. His name was Jonah, and that pin still pierces my favorite
jacket. Sometimes I'll run the sharp point against my skin, just to see
if it can put a dent in my state of dull sorrow, but it never does. There's
just nothing like a wailing ghost.

The college ghosthunting club had far more rules than I needed: a
buddy system, limitations on time spent in a haunt based on internet
anecdata. Jonah insisted I follow them at first, because ghosthunting is
dangerous for most people and it was the only way the school would
let them keep their accreditation. But when he saw how I reacted to the
child-ghosts of Honeycomb Park – quiet and contented and ready for
a good night's sleep while everyone else was vomiting and crying – he
acknowledged that maybe I was indeed different.

"What's up with that?" Jonah asked. "Why are your poles flipped?"

"Are we sure that ghosts drain energy? Maybe ghosts give energy, and everyone else just can't handle their vibes."

"Wow, that must mean you're real special then." It sounded harsh, but Jonah was laughing. It made me laugh, too, squirming in the grass.

"All I know is all I know," I said.

Jonah was a biology major, though, and he wanted us to be in the business of evidence – real evidence that would get us noticed by the greater ghosthunting industry. These were the early days of *Spectral* magazine, of GhostCon – the practice was fluid and growing fast, and everyone was trying to carve their name into the cement while it was still wet. In China, ghosthunters had started wearing body sensors to test the theory that ghosts drain energy from the living in order to manifest, and Jonah suggested we use this technique to prove that ghosts didn't affect everyone the same way. We decided to test it out at Shearwater House, a private home three states away whose website promised "never-before-seen psychic mindfucks."

Shearwater was managed, back then, by a man named Aaron Cork. He was one of those men who confuses a desire to visit his property with a desire to visit his pants – there's no shortage of them on the paranormal circuit – and I suspect he saw a desperation in me that he mistook for vulnerability. I was young, and too overawed by the layers of slippery presence in Shearwater House to notice his intentions until he was sidled up too close, whispering in my ear in the billiards room, where bioluminescent vines were crawling out of the wood-paneled walls.

"I just want to feel the presence," I whispered back, pulling his hand from between my thighs. His sigh curdled the air in that room before his oppressive energy shifted away.

Free of Aaron Cork, I wandered out of the room and up the stairs to the second story, where other ghosthunters had reported feelings of intense dizziness. It was indeed formidable, the presence at the beginning – or end? – of that hallway, like you'd shot up a hundred floors instead of one. But I didn't feel sick. For me the darkness had the lush, purplish texture of a softly-breathing night flower, and as I watched, what looked like petals peeled back to reveal a brilliant light.

A searching light. A star's light. The single most beautiful thing I would ever see.

We regrouped at dawn, outside. As expected, Jonah's numbers had plummeted through the night – he was wrapped in a blanket, sipping a water, looking pallid. But my numbers went up. All of them. Temperature, pulse rate, blood oxygen saturation level.

I had proof. Proof that the dead made me feel better, not worse. Proof that they lifted me out of a psychic tar pit of my own making. I could have cried, if I was the crying kind.

Shearwater House changed everything for me – but it really *changed* Jonah. While I had seen the starburst upstairs, Jonah had seen his childhood home in Shearwater's living room – the sofa his sister had spilled juice on, the kitchen cabinets that weren't installed right, the rug they inherited from his grandmother. All of these things had turned to ash in a long-ago fire. For the rest of the semester, Jonah took to wandering around campus, searching for secret passageways that would take him "home." Home to Shearwater. He said he couldn't wait to go back.

Except Aaron Cork banned us all from ever returning, claiming that my positive energy readings were "unverifiable" and "possibly fraudulent," and further that I was a "black hole of negativity." I willed myself to laugh about it over drinks at the Swan Dive. *What a creep,* everyone said. Except for Jonah, who was shooting cold bullets at me from across the bar. Shearwater had a hold on him. He blamed me for taking it away. It saddened me.

"Talk it out with him," our friends urged me. "He's messed up," they said. But my sadness hardened back into the wall I'd stood behind since childhood, and I didn't. Since Jonah was no longer interested, I resumed our project without him – strapped on my sensors and went back to all our local haunts, bringing a couple freshmen to document my vitals. My specialness. And they loved watching my numbers spike, like children drinking in a firework show.

A few months before graduation, around the two-year anniversary of our Shearwater trip, I woke up from a restless dream to panicky messages with subject lines like "Jonah" and "WTF." Jonah had broken into Shearwater House, and Aaron Cork had shot him in the leg – he had the right, since Shearwater was in a stand-your-ground state. Jonah was arrested from the hospital.

I decided not to go to graduation. Partly out of solidarity with Jonah, even though he never replied to any letters I sent to Cook County Penitentiary, and partly because *Spectral* had written a feature on me – "The Next Generation of Ultra Ghosthunters" – and that was more than I would get from my useless history degree.

TravelX agreed to sponsor my ghosthunting after the *Spectral* piece came out. They set me up with the best equipment, hired a television producer to manage my channel. My mother wasn't pleased about my decision to go pro, but I told her we had no idea how long this "trick" of mine was going to last and we'd better ride the wave as long as we could.

With TravelX's new equipment, I could register the impact each undead entity had on me in perfect digital clarity. Quantification steadies the heart, I think. Yes, big numbers fill you up, the way a shadow does when it fills the blank spaces in your soul, the way achievement does when you're being toasted with champagne – *absolutely amazing, the greatest ever* – but it's the act of measuring your life that keeps you calm. You are known, it says. You are seen. You place.

And I placed high, in those days. *Spectral* had come up with a composite metric to measure the energy transferred between ghosts and a human body, and for a while I was posting some of the highest numbers worldwide. 550 at the Tower of London. 580 at Gavarin Castle.

TravelX sent me to Tanamera in the hopes I'd break 600. A sea of ghosts comes crawling down its Membakar mountain every full moon, commemorating a nighttime volcanic eruption that had once stripped the countryside of its people and livestock and vegetation. The surge of presence when all those souls return is almost unbreathable within a kilometer of the mountain.

A few ordinary ghosthunters were also holed up in the Tanamera Dream Hostel – two American goths, an Aussie schoolteacher – as well as one boy named Fox who was wired wrong like me and hoping to land his own sweet sponsorship deal. Most ghosthunters, I must say, aren't very interesting. Self-absorbed, conceited, love the sound of their own tired philosophies. I tuned them all out and sat at the bar, looking at a map of Membakar. The woman running the hostel, Santi, asked if she could help answer any questions. "I'd just like to understand the dead," I said.

Santi gave me a hard look. "Don't you just want ghost pictures?"

As always, I tried to be a good ambassador of the practice. We weren't *hunting*, we were *chasing*. We weren't *sightseeing*, we were on a *pilgrimage*. Santi didn't buy any of it.

"If you want to understand the dead, then you should know what Tanamera means," she said. "Red soil. You know what *that* means, right?"

Yes, I thought; it means people died here. Just like people have died everywhere. I'd seen three-hundred-year-old ghosts of people who died at age twenty-seven. Life is the interlude, the extended layover in the world's worst airport. Death is the long stretch. Death is forever.

"It means this is a place where a *lot* of blood spills. Not just because of the volcano."

Santi tolerated me better than the other ghosthunters, but she didn't think any of us had any business being there. I asked her: if she was so upset by us, why would she operate a hostel catered directly to us? Santi made the universal sign of cash. "If I do something disrespectful, God will make sure I suffer the consequences. I'm ready for that. But you?" She snorted. "You probably don't even know what a consequence is."

She was wrong about that. I was familiar with the consequences of my success: the pressure to break my own records; the way other ghost-hunters clung to my shadow, eager to steal the presence from right under my nose. At least that boy Fox actually wanted to learn from me.

You had to make yourself as small as possible to attract ghosts, I told him as we dragged our equipment up the mountain. Squash your soul as flat as you can possibly get it to make the most room for them. They're looking for vessels.

"You don't think they're looking for life force?"

I snorted. "I don't know about you, but I don't have much of that."

"So why do you think we're, you know, the way we are?"

He had so many questions like that. "Who knows, kid," I almost always replied.

"My mother blames herself," he said quietly.

Ghosthunting follows the laws of nature: you must know when to give. When you're thrown into whitewater, don't try to stand; when a tornado's coming, get as low as you can. As soon as the living birds launched en masse from the living trees, I knew that none of us living ghosthunters could last very long. There's only so much pressure suits and oxygen packs can do when presence is generated by so many dead. The dead don't march like an army you can dodge, after all. They seep. They coat the mountain with their disembodied limbs, their peeled faces, their burned hides. Their chaos is so profound that the eye of their storm must be God, I think.

Again and again, that's what they said.

Within fifteen minutes, I lost sight of Fox. Informal protocol says to maintain visual or audio contact at all times, but I'd made it clear to Fox that we weren't a team. "Go get your record," he said. Somewhere in the howling dark I heard him laughing giddily, like a child, and I figured he was fine. He sounded fine. I was at 586 and he sounded fine.

Again and again, they said, *until it ends with us.*

The glory of their infinite return lifted me by the ribs like a fish on a hook, as if they meant to fold me in – but when I hit 601 and the alarm on my right glove went off, they released me. Spat me out, really. I knew it was time to run and so I did, downhill, in the dark, screaming with glee, tripping over my boots until I lost my footing and hit my head.

I woke up in my room at the Dream Hostel, tucked so tightly into bed that the sheets were practically a straitjacket. After struggling for longer than I care to share, I ripped myself free and staggered downstairs, where the atmosphere was filled with such silent tension that I earnestly thought the ghosts of Membakar had veered off path and invaded the hostel.

But they weren't ghosts, the people gathered there. Their wobbly faces bore all the soft confusion of the living – those frustrating, half-formed feelings that only boil down to the bone in death. All except for a silver-haired woman who stood statue-like in the center of the room, staring at me. She had already reached that point of ultimate clarity, I could see. "Who is that?" I asked, but everyone was stone-silent until Santi forced me back to my room.

"Fox's mother," she said, before I could ask again. "She has to take him home."

I didn't understand. "He needs a chaperone?"

"Shh!" Santi pointed at the ceiling. Another universal gesture, one that even a non-believer like me could understand: *monkey's gone to heaven.*

Officially, Fox died of a catastrophic cardiac event. It was the first time someone like us had been killed while ghosthunting. Local authorities shut down Membakar for the rest of the season pending an investigation that would never happen, but I still hung around the Dream Hostel, wondering if Fox had at least died happy. Wondering why I was too gutless to follow his lead. I ended up throwing my phone into the ocean along with my meds.

A TravelX representative showed up a few days later. I thought they were worried about the fancy phone they'd paid for, but no. "Without your medication, you're a liability," she said, holding out a trembling, sweaty palm. "Please, show me that you have them."

They saw me as a public safety hazard, I realized. A risk to the living. A rogue poltergeist. How disappointing to know that the creep Aaron Cork had turned out to be right. "They're at the bottom of the sea," I said, and I thought she was going to weep.

———◆———

In the end, I didn't lose my TravelX sponsorship because of what happened to Fox, or even because I went off my meds without authorization. I lost my sponsorship because I stopped being able to hit 500 anymore, even when I mined fresh haunts. They said we were "going in different directions." I said not to make me laugh.

So when I was invited back to Shearwater House, I didn't have much choice but to go. It had come under new ownership – a nicely-dressed couple with matching undercuts who wanted to "professionalize" the place. Commercialize the place more like, but at least that meant they could pay me an honorarium.

At the airport, I got picked up by a man I'll call Corporal X. He'd missed out on war by a generation and was very bitter about that fact. As he drove me to Shearwater, Corporal X told me it wasn't my fault that I wasn't hitting 500 anymore. "It's the material," he said. "They don't make people like they used to. What gets left behind is weak. Just blows away in the wind." I guessed, based on sheer statistics, that ghosts drained him the regular way. He confirmed. "Does that make it easier for you?" I asked, counting the palm trees along the road. "Make it easier to chase ghosts when it doesn't take so much out of you?" But then Corporal X went silent, and I realized that he *wanted* it taken out of him. He *wanted* to be drained to nothing.

They say these are the times we live in. I suspect some people – myself included – are simply born this way, with smoky little lumps of coal where their heart should be.

A visit to Shearwater House came with a tour guide and guardrails now. Protocols. Everyone wore a safety whistle. A safety rope was available. Normally I'd have laughed at this, but after what happened to Fox I didn't have the energy to argue. I went back to the second story hallway where I'd seen the light in the darkness, sensors on my vest and whistle around my neck. I also had a camera on a head strap, though my video recordings had never been very compelling. I thought that if I could just show others what I'd seen, it would outweigh all the bad I'd done.

But the dark was different that day. Emptier. Flatter. A pale light endured at the end of the hallway, bobbing to and fro like a jellyfish, but when I held my light up I saw only a blurry copy of myself. Its eyes stretched out and its mouth drawn shut like some lost homunculus.

Repulsed, I stopped recording. I never went back to Shearwater again.

Instead, I went home. My mother was dying of a cancer no one had caught, and she needed someone to help make sure her end of days were bearable. I told her I could use the break, and I meant that.

"Visitor," my mother said one day. For once she wasn't reading my sticker but looking past my head, at the corner of the hospital room. My heart seized with a familiar excitement that probably should have shamed me, but I'd never gotten the chance to chase ghosts in a still-functional hospital. I'd been to the ruins of St. Mary's, even the grounded old hospital ship the *SS Pilgrim,* but the dead don't stick around decommissioned institutions, I've found. More proof that they covet the living, except for the living that covet them.

But it wasn't a ghost standing in the doorway. It was Jonah. I'd forgotten that his sister had been in nursing school when we were in college. Turned out she'd specialized in oncology.

Jonah said he was doing well, though he was not the same kid who went into Cook County Penitentiary. He was calmer. Mellowed. There had been no shortage of ghosts in prison, he said, and he'd reached a sort of détente with them – he'd leave them alone, and they'd leave him alone. You couldn't afford to get psychic-sick in prison on top of everything else.

"It's wild that you're still getting off on ghosts," he said as we sat in the cafeteria, sipping from paper cups. Jonah drank his coffee black, now, though I still shoveled three packs of sugar into mine. "I guess you really are wired different."

I was momentarily tempted to let him believe the story he'd apparently chosen to believe about me, that I was a famous ghosthunter living the life we'd dreamed of at age nineteen. "My stats aren't as good as they used to be," I admitted, stirring my coffee. "And have you seen the new crop of kids coming out of Russia? They're hitting 600s every other week."

He gave me a twisted smile that hadn't changed since college. "And you're still one of only one percent of people who gets positive readings off a ghost. I'd say that's pretty special." *Special.* It touched me that he still called me that, though I'm sure the only sound I made was my typical derisive little grunt.

"I have a new theory," I told him, "Maybe they take away my bad energy. Remember what Aaron Cork said? Maybe they drain off my bad vibes. Let a little bit of light in."

Jonah winced; he apologized for letting Shearwater interfere with our friendship. There were times in the years that had passed that I had indeed been angry, furiously so – usually I'd need to be drunk and antsy from having gone months without a chase, when the passing touch of a human hand could send me into a thunderstorm of self-pity and regret – but that day, I wasn't angry. Shearwater was a dark mirror, and I told him so.

I was just glad to have Jonah back.

———◦•◦———

For a few months after my mother died, all I wanted was to travel back to a safer, smaller time. Jonah and I tried to relive our glory days – stalking the Swan Dive, dropping in on the old ghosthunting club and sitting in the back of the auditorium like the pair of washed-up creeps we were. The club had shrunk substantially since we ran it – it was just a few kids now, arguing about ancient, dried-up haunts. Was Amityville real? Was Poveglia? Jonah kept egging me on to jump up and announce myself, but I refused, saying it was gauche. The truth was I couldn't stand the thought of those strangers' eyes on me. I'd come to hate the feeling of being observed.

Maybe it was a lingering side-effect of Shearwater's bite. Maybe Shearwater had only laid bare a self-disgust I'd always carried. Either way, I stayed cocooned in my black sweatshirt with my sunglasses on.

Despite my disguise, one kid did recognize me. "You're a legend," this kid Val said, eyes wide and gleaming with as-of-yet undashed hope. God, I thought, how horrifying. I had the sudden thought of myself preserved, mounted, covered in a golden glaze.

Jonah and I took the club to the Harper Hotel, hoping to ease them into real ghosthunting. But they'd renovated the sixth floor, room 616 was gone, and the Blue Lady no longer had her balcony to jump from. The concierge claimed to have no idea who I was talking about, though a housekeeper vacuuming the space that should have been hers said she hadn't been seen in years. Once again I was hyperventilating on the sixth floor, only this time I was clawing at repainted walls, tripping on now-invisible knots of carpet. I heard Val asking Jonah, "Is this part of it, is she sensing something?" But it was just me. It had only ever been me, that burned-out popcorn kernel at the bottom of the bag.

I stayed short-of-breath the entire drive home, cowering in the backseat as other cars blew past us with their mufflers roaring and their horns blaring. It was the dying of the loudness that bothered me more, that fading wail into silence. I could barely hear Jonah telling me to calm down under that transient thrashing dying of the world; I might have been wailing myself. "Where the hell did she go?" I was saying. "Where the hell do they all go?"

And then the death-sound swallowed us. Jonah was looking at me when the world began to swerve and away when the world crumpled. They said he drifted into the wrong lane, then lost control when he overcorrected. I really hoped, while we lay crushed and waiting for the Jaws-of-Life, that we would both survive. Yes, I was still a gutless coward. But Jonah deserved to live.

"Finally," Jonah said, "We'll know."

I asked him what he meant by that, trying to keep him awake. But Jonah, my poor Jonah, never got the chance to explain.

I stopped looking for the dead after the accident. After the funeral. I gave "normal life" my last best shot: I got an office job in the laughably-named "historic downtown," I bought a little house. It was a new build with modern appliances on the edge of town, where the dying old trees had been rooted out and the young trees had yet to grow tall.

And I'd still get asked, while going about my business – why don't you chase anymore? Won't you visit this little haunt of mine, just enjoy the thrill of the chase? Because they knew, these askers, that I was washed up. That I didn't have it in me anymore, whatever that "it" had once been. Sometimes my ego would want to punch back. But then the adrenaline would wear off, and I'd go back to my little house, and I'd turn off all its lights, and I'd wait.

Wait for night to fall. Wait for the walls to creak. Wait for a damp cold and the smell of soil to spread through my little house, to lie heavy on my ribs. There's no need to chase ghosts when your own house is haunted.

"I'm sure you could still do it if you wanted," Val said during a grocery drop-off. I've stopped wanting to have much to do with the outside. Chai tea with Val on the back porch is about all my nerves can manage. They invite me to Halloween parades in the fall and Christmas ghost story readings in the winter, but I can't. I'm needed at home. "I saw an article saying it's genetic, how we respond to the dead. So you'll never lose it."

But I did lose it. In the morning my limbs are heavy and my head's in a fog. After all these years chasing an ecstatic high, I appreciate the deeper wounds that pain can satisfy. But it is ironic that it's happened now that I live with a ghost who won't leave me alone. Now that I'm tired all the time. Now that I have less to give: less bad energy, less good energy, less anything.

I don't mind, though. I've been selfish.

Over 100 billion human beings have lived and died on planet Earth, and almost all of them have faded into the wallpaper of the walls that remain, gotten swept out with the weekly garbage. Just dust mites, coughed out and dispersed. Not every little psychic imprint is a fully-realized ghost, just like not every ripple in the ocean is a wave. A ghost is a swell. A defined, discrete, unique entity with multiple documented sightings. A true ghost is a finding. A jewel.

Jonah. Turns out he was the special one.

I'm afraid he's angry with me, that that's why he stays in the shadows, hiding his face. I've tried apologizing, tried explaining that all I could do was care for myself – and he'd seen the poor job I did of that, didn't he? Sometimes I think I hear him sigh – a low, tortured rattle that spreads like mold through the walls. I'm afraid it means he's suffering, over there in the dark.

So take me, I say. Take what I have left to give, piece by burning piece.

ABOUT THE AUTHORS

MATTHEW M. BARTLETT is the author of *Gateways to Abomination* and other books of supernatural horror. His short stories have appeared in a variety of anthologies and journals, including F*orbidden Futures, Vastarien, Year's Best Weird Fiction Vol. 3,* and *Lost Signals.* He has recorded two albums for Cadabra Records, *Mr. White Noise* and *Call Me Corey,* both with backing music by Black Mountain Transmitter. Two of his stories, "Ginny Greenteeth" and "The Mill River Revenant," were also adapted for Cadabra, read by actor Laurence Harvey and Anthony D.P. Mann, respectively. He lives in Western Massachusetts with his wife Katie Saulnier and their cats Peachpie and Larry.

NADIA BULKIN is the author of the short story collection *She Said Destroy* (Word Horde, 2017). She has been nominated for the Shirley Jackson Award five times. She grew up in Jakarta, Indonesia with her Javanese father and American mother, before relocating to Lincoln, Nebraska. She has two political science degrees and lives in Washington, D.C.

BRIAN EVENSON has published over a dozen books of fiction, most recently the short story collection *The Glassy, Burning Floor of Hell.* His collection *Song for the Unraveling of the World* won a Shirley Jackson Award and a World Fantasy Award, and was a finalist for the Ray Bradbury Award. He teaches at CalArts and lives in Los Angeles.

KURT FAWVER is a writer of horror, weird fiction, and literature that oozes between the cracks of genre. His stories have won and been nominated for the Shirley Jackson Award and the Bram Stoker Award. He's had work published in venues such as *Nightmare, Lightspeed, The Magazine of Fantasy & Science Fiction,* and *Weird Tales.* He's the author three short story collections—*Forever, in Pieces, The Dissolution of Small Worlds,* and *We are Happy, We are Doomed*—as well as numerous chapbooks. Kurt also holds a PhD in literature and teaches writing classes at several colleges. He's glad to be a part of your literary world.

Formerly a film critic, journalist, screenwriter and teacher, GEMMA FILES has been an award-winning horror author since 1999. She has published two collections of short work, two chapbooks of speculative poetry, a Weird Western trilogy, a story-cycle and a stand-alone novel *(Experimental Film,* which won the 2016 Shirley Jackson Award for Best Novel and the 2016 Sunburst award for Best Adult Novel). She has two new story collections from Trepidatio *(Spectral Evidence* and *Drawn Up From Deep Places),* one upcoming from Cemetery Dance *(Dark Is Better),* and a new poetry collection from Aqueduct Press *(Invocabulary).*

RICHARD GAVIN's work explores the bond between horror and the numinous. He has authored six volumes of fiction, the most recent being *grotesquerie* (Undertow Publications, 2020), and several books of esotericism. He dwells in the North. His website is www.richardgavin.net.

CRAIG LAURANCE GIDNEY writes both contemporary and genre fiction. He is the author of the collections *Sea, Swallow Me & Other Stories* (Lethe Press, 2008), *Skin Deep Magic* (Rebel Satori Press, 2014), *Bereft* (Tiny Satchel Press, 2013) and *A Spectral Hue* (Word Horde, 2019). *The Nectar of Nightmares,* his third collection, was released by Underland Press in 2022. He lives in his native Washington, DC.

CODY GOODFELLOW has written nine novels and five collections of short stories, and edits the hyperpulp zine *Forbidden Futures.* His writing has been favored with three Wonderland Book Awards. His comics work has been featured in *Mystery Meat, Creepy, Slow Death Zero,* and *Skin Crawl.* As an actor, he has appeared in numerous short films, TV shows, music videos by Anthrax and Beck, and a Days Inn commercial. He also wrote, co-produced and scored the Lovecraftian hygiene films *Baby Got Bass* and *Stay At Home Dad*, which can be viewed on YouTube. He "lives" in San Diego, California.

MICHAEL GRIFFIN's latest collection *The Human Alchemy* (Word Horde) was a 2018 Shirley Jackson Award finalist. Other works include a novel, *Hieroglyphs of Blood and Bone* (JournalStone, 2017), and his debut collection *The Lure of Devouring Light* (Word Horde, 2016). His stories have appeared in *Black Static* and *Apex* magazines, and the anthologies *Looming Low Volume I* (Dim Shores, 2017), *The Children of Old Leech* (Word Horde, 2014), and the Shirley Jackson Award winner *The Grimscribe's Puppets* (Miskatonic River Press, 2013).

He's also an ambient musician and founder of Hypnos Recordings, a record label he operates with his wife in Portland, Oregon. His blog is at griffinwords.com.

MICHAEL KELLY is the former Series Editor for the *Year's Best Weird Fiction*. He's a Shirley Jackson Award and British Fantasy Award-winning editor, and a four-time World Fantasy Award nominee. His fiction has appeared in a number of journals and anthologies, including *Black Static*, *Nightmare Magazine*, *The Mammoth Book of Best New Horror 21 & 24*, *Postscripts*, *PseudoPod*, *Weird Fiction Review*, and has been previously collected in *Scratching the Surface*, *Undertow & Other Laments*, and *All the Things We Never See*. He is the owner and Editor-in-Chief of Undertow Publications, and editor of *Weird Horror* magazine.

GWENDOLYN KISTE is the Bram Stoker Award-winning author of *The Rust Maidens*, *Boneset & Feathers*, *And Her Smile Will Untether the Universe*, *Pretty Marys All in a Row*, and *The Invention of Ghosts*. Her short fiction and nonfiction have appeared in *Nightmare Magazine*, *Best American Science Fiction and Fantasy*, *Vastarien*, *Tor's Nightfire*, *Black Static*, *The Dark*, *Daily Science Fiction*, *Interzone*, and *LampLight*, among others. Originally from Ohio, she now resides on an abandoned horse farm outside of Pittsburgh with her husband, two cats, and not nearly enough ghosts. Find her online at gwendolynkiste.com

ANYA MARTIN was weaned on Friday Night Frights, has always rooted for the monster, and regrets abandoning her earliest career aspiration—digging for dinosaurs. Her debut collection, the critically acclaimed Weird spec-lit collection, *Sleeping with the Monster,* was published by Lethe Press. Her novella *Grass,* originally a Dim Shores limited edition chapbook, has achieved praise internationally as a pivotal tale of the Weird Renaissance both in Spanish translation by Dilatando Mentes Editorial (as *Hierba*) and in Czech translation by Medusa Press (as *Tráva*). Her fiction has appeared in many anthologies and magazines. She blogs at ATLRetro.com and co-produces/co-hosts The Outer Dark symposium and podcast, spotlighting a diverse spectrum of contemporary Weird/spec-lit creators, with Scott Nicolay for This Is Horror. She has a husky named Curv, is half-Finnish, has an anthropology degree from Smith College and a master's in communication from Georgia State University, and also works as a freelance journalist and editor. Her author Website can be found at www.anyamartin.com, her Twitter handle is @anya99, and her Instagram is @AnyaMartin99.

S.P. MISKOWSKI has received two National Endowment for the Arts Fellowships. Her second novel, *I Wish I Was Like You,* was named This Is Horror Novel of the Year. Her books have been finalists for a Bram Stoker Award twice, and for a Shirley Jackson Award four times. Her stories have been published in *Supernatural Tales, Black Static, Identity Theory, Nightmare Magazine,* and in numerous anthologies including *Looming Low, The Best Horror of the Year Volume Ten, Haunted Nights, The Madness of Dr. Caligari, There Is No Death There Are No Dead,* and *Darker Companions: Celebrating 50 Years of Ramsey Campbell.* Author site: https://spmiskowski.wordpress.com

DAVID PEAK's most recent book is The World Below (Apocalypse Party). His other books include Eyes in the Dust and Other Stories (Trepidatio Publishing), Corpsepaint (Word Horde), and The Spectacle of the Void (Schism). He lives in Baltimore.

ERICA RUPPERT, HWA. lives in northern New Jersey with her husband and too many cats. She writes weird horror and dark fantasy, and her work has appeared in magazines including *Unnerving, Lamplight,* and *Nightmare,* on podcasts including *PodCastle,* and in multiple anthologies. When she is not writing, she runs, bakes, and gardens with more enthusiasm than skill. Her novella *Sisters in Arms* was released by Trepidatio Publishing in July 2021.

CLINT SMITH is the author of the short story collections, *The Skeleton Melodies* (2020), *Ghouljaw and Other Stories* (2014), as well as the novella, *When It's Time For Dead Things to Die* (2019). Of late, his work has appeared in *Supernatural Tales, Nightscript,* and *Vastarien: A Literary Journal.* Clint lives in Indiana, along with his wife and children, just outside Deacon's Creek. Read more at www.clintsmithfiction.com.

SIMON STRANTZAS is the author of five collections of short fiction, including *Nothing is Everything* (Undertow Publications, 2018), and editor of a number of anthologies, including *Year's Best Weird Fiction, Vol. 3.* He is also co-founder and Associate Editor of the irregular non-fiction journal, *Thinking Horror,* and columnist for *Weird Horror* magazine. Combined, he's been a finalist for four Shirley Jackson Awards, two British Fantasy Awards, and the World Fantasy Award. His fiction has appeared in numerous annual best-of anthologies, and in venues such as *Nightmare, Postscripts,* and *Cemetery Dance.* He lives with his wife in Toronto, Canada.

JEFFREY THOMAS is the author of such novels as *Deadstock* (Solaris Books), *Blue War* (Solaris Books), and T*he American* (JournalStone), and his short story collections include *Punktown* (Prime Books), *The Unnamed Country* (Word Horde), and *Carrion Men* (Plutonian Press). His stories have been reprinted in *The Year's Best Horror Stories XXII* (editor, Karl Edward Wagner), *The Year's Best Fantasy and Horror #14* (editors, Ellen Datlow and Terri Windling), and *Year's Best Weird Fiction #1* (editors, Laird Barron and Michael Kelly). Thomas lives in Massachusetts.

BROOKE WARRA is the author of horror and weird fiction stories and the owner of The Naked Wytch, an artisan bath and body shop. Her story "I Feel Better Now" was nominated for the 2018 Pushcart Prize after appearing in *Vastarien: A Literary Journal.* Her novelette *Luminous Body* took home the 2019 Shirley Jackson Award for its category. Brooke lives and writes with her family in the Midwest.

Shirley Jackson award-winner **KAARON WARREN** published her first short story in 1993 and has had fiction in print every year since. She was recently given the Peter McNamara Lifetime Achievement Award and was Guest of Honour at World Fantasy 2018, Stokercon 2019 and Geysercon 2019. She has also been Guest of Honour at Conflux in Canberra and Genrecon in Brisbane.

She has published five multi-award winning novels (*Slights, Walking the Tree, Mistification, The Grief Hole,* and *Tide of Stone*) and seven short story collections, including the multi-award winning *Through Splintered Walls.* Her most recent short story collection is *A Primer to Kaaron Warren* from Dark Moon Books. Her most recent novella, *Into Bones Like Oil* (Meerkat Press), was shortlisted for a Shirley Jackson Award and the Bram Stoker Award, winning the Aurealis Award. Her stories have appeared in both Ellen Datlow's and Paula Guran's Year's Best anthologies.

Her most recent books include the re-release of her acclaimed novel, *Slights* (IFWG Australia), *Tool Tales,* a chapbook in collaboration with Ellen Datlow (also IFWG), and *Capturing Ghosts,* a writing advice chapbook from Brain Jar Press.

A.C. WISE is the author of the novels *Wendy, Darling* and *Hooked* (forthcoming) from Titan Books, along with three short fiction collections including *The Ghost Sequences,* recently published by Undertow Publications. Her work has won the Sunburst Award for Excellence in Canadian Literature of the Fantastic, and has been a finalist for the Sunburst, Nebula, Aurora, Lambda, and Ignyte Awards. In addition to her fiction, she contributes review columns to *Apex Magazine* and *The Book Smugglers.* Find her online at www.acwise.net and on twitter as @ac_wise.

ALVARO ZINOS-AMARO is a Hugo and Locus finalist with some fifty stories published in numerous magazines and anthologies, including

Lackington's, The Journal of Unlikely Entomology, Analog, Lightspeed, Beneath Ceaseless Skies, Galaxy's Edge, Nature, and volumes such as *The Year's Best Science Fiction & Fantasy, The Mammoth Book of Jack the Ripper Stories, This Way to the End Times, Shades Within Us: Tales of Migrations and Fractured Borders, Blood Business, The Unquiet Dreamer: A Tribute to Harlan Ellison, Nox Pareidolia, It Came from the Multiplex,* and *Shadow Atlas: Dark Landscapes of the Americas.*

ABOUT THE ARTIST

YVES TOURIGNY is a greying biped who resides in Ottawa, Ontario, with a dog and some very patient humans. He is currently involved in some interest or another, or possibly trapped under a fallen bookcase. Send help.

ABOUT THE EDITORS

SAM COWAN is a micropress publisher (and occasional editor) who lives in dystopian California with his wife and two special-needs cats. He continues to stoically endure this cut-rate reality.

JUSTIN STEELE is school counselor by day and a Shirley Jackson Award nominated fiction editor by night (and weekends). His anthologies include *Children of Old Leech* from Word Horde, and *Looming Low Volume I* from Dim Shores. He currently resides in Delaware, but can often be found at weird fiction cons all over the country.

DIME SHORES

weird horror
strange science fiction
dark fantasy

limited-edition chapbooks and anthologies

dimshores.com